WINTER'S STING

WINTER'S STING

IRON AND EARTH
BOOK TWO

SARA T. BOND

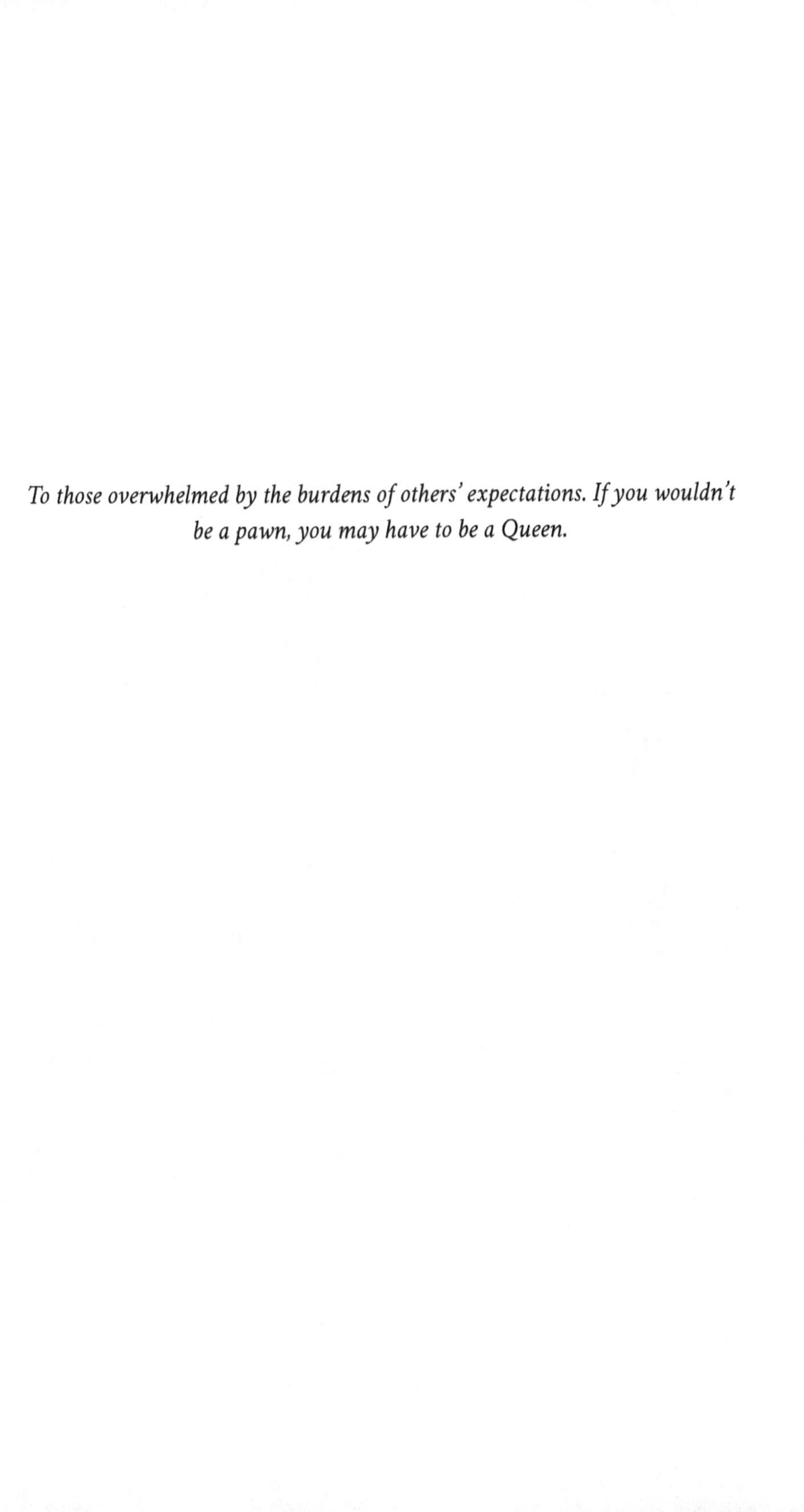

To those overwhelmed by the burdens of others' expectations. If you wouldn't be a pawn, you may have to be a Queen.

CHAPTER ONE

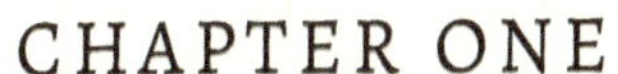

The Greenwood Knoll had a distinct taste of bubbly prosecco with notes of pear, green apples, and something floral I thought might be jasmine. I licked my lips and breathed deep of the effervescent excitement, letting it dance over my tongue and set me to squirming with anticipation.

I closed my eyes to revel in it—this overwhelming sense of potential and hope. Over the past several months, an air of solemnity had hung around the Knoll. The losses we'd suffered, the deaths. This was different.

Despite crackdowns from the Fairy Courts around the Gates, the solitary fae community was optimistic. We had the chance to start anew, with new beginnings, a new life.

We had a new baby!

The Atlanta troupe of maenads was currently flitting about, pulling tables together, setting up floral arrangements, and hanging honest-to-Mab bunting to celebrate a child of their own. Their sister Semele would be introducing her little one to the whole troupe today. The hope, the excitement, and the heady feeling of seduction that had me reeling were theirs, not mine.

But I could feel it. Taste it. Swirl their magic around my tongue and let it go straight to my head. If I chose, I could lean up against that potential, cozy up to it and harness that hope and energy toward something substantial. Something powerful.

Opening my eyes, I reminded myself that the feelings I bathed in were only borrowed. Where once I could only taste at the edges of the magic of other fae creatures, these days, my magic opened their emotions and power to me, allowing me to sample them like a flight of wine, savoring each one and getting tipsy on their borrowed power. If I liked the taste, I could claim it. Wield it.

But this magic wasn't mine. I couldn't just take it for myself and my whims.

Still. What I could *do*! Hope, excitement, lust: they were all power in the right hands. And I could inspire it, encourage it, whip it into a frenzy.

"Nachos up," Meara called from the kitchen, pulling me away from the urge to burrow into that magic and see exactly what might happen.

I swallowed down the bubbling thrill and turned to the kitchen.

"I got it." Varon intercepted me, reaching a hand out to pat the bar as he moved from his bouncer's post at the front door back to the kitchen faster than I could rouse myself from the twisted tangle of my borrowed emotions.

He disappeared through the swinging kitchen door and emerged almost immediately with two trays of nachos piled high with black beans, tomatoes, cheese, and melt-in-your-mouth barbecued pork brisket. As he passed through the group of maenads, he fumbled when they clutched at his sleeves, stole chips, and flirted shamelessly.

"Girls, girls," I called, safe behind my bar. "Leave my moody bouncer alone. He's not the babe you are looking for."

"He's the babe I'd like to take home," Payal laughed as she kissed his cheek, which turned a mottled red. "He can call me Mommy."

Varon stiffened and shot me a look of panic.

"Release the drake before you get burned," I said, my stern words weakened by the fact that I was holding back laughter.

The girls obliged, falling away from him in giggling coos and affectionate nothings. Their emotions released yet another wave of excited flavor into the air.

For once, the maenads were all in agreement: there was only one male they were really interested in today. And at his age, he could barely crawl, let alone deliver nachos.

"When does the guest of honor arrive?" Mikka asked as she slipped onto a barstool across from me and gestured for a beer. Mikka Balaur was Varon's fraternal twin and the other bouncer for the Knoll. They were quite the pair: tall and pale but with thick black hair and large, heavy features. While Varon looked like a Romanian count, with his hooked nose and deep-set eyes, Mikka softened those same features with thick red lips, hooded brown eyes, and her long black hair currently tied back in a thick braid.

"We've got a while," I replied as I dutifully pulled the tap handle and began filling a pint glass with Kolsch for my best friend. "Semele says Callum naps until two every afternoon, so we can expect them any time after. Seeing as it's still a quarter 'til, I think we have plenty of time for the girls to work themselves up for a proper baby debut." I placed the full drink in front of her.

"Joy," my best friend mumbled as she took a healthy swig of the beer. "More pastel decorations."

Mikka might not have been impressed by the party preparations, but I was relieved to see she was still carefully watching Brynn and Carissa tease each other with bunting. Honey brunette Brynn had wrapped black-haired Carissa up in a length of tulle fabric and was dancing and pulling her closer and closer until they eliminated the gap between them and locked lips. Carissa, entangled in the fabric and unable to reach her arms up past her elbows, instead reached around and grabbed Brynn by the ass, pulling her closer. Mikka's eyes got wider, and she licked her lips as she watched the maenads kiss ardently.

The taste of cedar smoke and pepper twisted through the prosecco flavor in the air, and I homed in on it immediately. It had been a long time since my friend had shown interest in, well, anything, and the signature taste of her fire magic heating up to meet the maenads' power encouraged me. Ever since last summer, she'd been mired in a stagnant depression.

Typically, fiery and loud and confident, all fall and winter, Mikka had been withdrawn, sullen, and almost cold. But if watching the maenads flirt lit a fire in her and encouraged her to chase some tail of her own? Well, a little push against her stirring power wouldn't hurt.

I took a steadying breath and on the exhale expanded my awareness, feeling first the air as it left my lungs, then the edges of my body, then the perimeter of the Knoll. Finally, as I stilled myself and reached the edge of my consciousness, I felt the warm pulse of the Greenwood Gate.

The portal between the worlds stood silent and sleeping on the banks of the Chattahoochee River at the edge of our property, but as I reached for it, the Gate woke. The concentration of power and energy that could open a path between the Iron Realm and the Eternal Realm beyond recognized my questing touch. The latent magic stirred as I turned my mind and intentions toward it. It seemed to preen, almost like a cat leaning into a pet, and I knew that I could direct that vast reserve of power at will.

I took another breath and pulled it into me, opening the way, tasting its green, verdant flavor.

My back rolled for a second as I adjusted to the intense but pleasant feel of it. The Gate's magic felt like touching a live wire, but instead of burning me from the inside, it soothed and caressed me like silk through my veins.

As that power brushed against and through me, I brought Mikka's taste of peppery whiskey smoke to the forefront of my tongue. I licked at my lower lip and let the feel of her magic coat my mouth and warm my blood. My fingers tickled with potential flames lurking just under the surface, and I itched to wield Mikka's fire.

Instead, I nudged it toward the fruity bubbles of the maenads. I let the tastes mingle, giving spice to the prosecco and giving it a hint of honey and lemon to ease the mix. The result was a complex but almost perfectly balanced blend of sweet, strong, and delicious.

A cocktail of my own design.

Mikka straightened, pulled her shoulders back, and stretched her neck. A spark of life seemed to have ignited in her as the corners of her thick lips quirked upward. "Maybe I'll help them. Hang some bunting or something." She dropped from the stool and strolled over to Carissa and Brynn, offering to untangle the former from her tulle bindings. The girls grinned wickedly as they both turned their attention and intentions on Mikka.

Job well done.

I let out a breath and released as much of the taste of their magic as I could. Letting it wash through and away from me. My head felt vaguely like it was floating as the power slowly faded away. I kept the Gate open, though, letting its magic flow freely into and through the area surrounding the Knoll.

A low thunder of voice rumbled behind me. "Be careful with that. It's getting easier for you."

"How did you know?" I said, embarrassed as I turned to face Argus.

At nearly seven feet tall, my dragon boss and owner of the Greenwood Knoll towered over me, his arms crossed over his broad chest. He chuckled as a small hint of smoke escaped his otherwise human-looking nostrils.

"You think you can hide something like that from me? I've watched over you for almost a century. I know when you're up to something." His eyes sparkled with amusement. "Plus, you're glowing like someone just showed you a good time in the cellar."

I flushed with embarrassment. Never mind that I *had* actually been caught having a good time in the cellar just last night. And it had been a *very* good time. This felt like something I should feel shamed for.

"I wasn't trying to hide anything," I insisted weakly. I'd only been accessing power that was my birthright. Same as any fae.

So why did I feel like I'd been caught doing something wrong?

"Did you have Mikka's permission to help her with your magic?" The amusement in Argus's eyes shadowed, as he considered me gravely.

And there it was.

"I only gave her a nudge," I insisted.

"Siobhan," Argus began. "I know having an active power is new to you."

"I know, I know." I turned away from him and opened the under-counter dishwasher that was releasing steam behind the bar. I stepped back and waved away the cloud of vapor that billowed out.

I had already heard the lecture that was going to follow. Using your magic on others without their consent was not something done in polite society. Even if you thought you were doing something good and benevolent, like giving away luck or even easing pain, you could never know the consequences of your actions. You could give someone false confidence that led to them taking dangerous risks. You could rob someone of the grief they need to heal and leave them open to worse hurt in the future.

Our unspoken—okay, sometimes spoken—law in the solitary community was to only use active powers to affect ourselves or with permission on others. Not every fae community followed these rules, but the solitary fae knew we had a responsibility to others. We never used active magic on others without consent.

Before this past summer, though, such rules hadn't applied to me. I'd never had an active power, never been able to affect other people with my magic. This part of fairy magic was new to me, and I was still learning how to navigate my abilities.

Argus stepped around me and into the still billowing cloud of steam from the dishwasher. Without waiting for the glasses to cool, he began pulling them out and reshelving them. "Mikka hates being pushed."

"I know," I sighed. But it had been so easy. I had barely even thought about it before reaching out to the Gate, wrapping its power around Mikka and the maenads, and pulling them together. Mikka had always loved flirting with the maenads before she'd fallen into this recent funk, and they were more than willing to welcome her back into their attentions. It was so easy to exert my will onto the world and make everything right.

Argus passed me a martini glass to put along the hanging shelf behind me, and I accepted it without thinking. The blisteringly hot glass burned my fingers and I yelped, nearly dropping it. But the pipe-weed and brine taste of Argus's power was right there. I focused some hind part of my mind on him and imagined forging my fingers in a furnace, as immune to flame and heat as any dragon, and the burn retreated immediately.

I placed the glass in its place and turned to find Argus staring at me again.

"Siobhan," he said, sadness in his tone. He'd obviously felt me borrowing his magic. Instantly, I felt like an adolescent, disappointing my adopted father once again.

"I didn't use it on you," I protested.

"That's not the point, and you know it."

A flush of guilt flooded me, and a rush of anger spilled over to squash it. I knew in a moment that I could have pulled harder on his magic, called forth the full force of the flame he kept so well controlled. The tobacco-salt taste of his power called to me, begging me to sip, to gulp it down, and seize what should be mine. In an instant, I could have burned everyone in the bar with barely a thought.

That power tempted me.

And from the resolve that suddenly smoldered in Argus's eyes, he knew it. He had felt me tasting at the edges of him, he had recognized it, and he had responded. He was prepared to meet whatever magic I called with his own. The man who loved me like a daughter had steeled himself against me. As if I were a threat.

The fiery anger in me suffocated under a deluge of shame and fear.

Without turning to face him, I grabbed a shot glass off the barback, pulled down a bottle of middling whiskey, poured, and threw the liquid down my throat. The burn of peat chased away the shame and anger, and I turned back to Argus, an apology on my lips.

My boss hadn't moved, but his brows furrowed, and a small growl came from his throat. "I don't like it, Siobhan."

There were so many ways I could take that statement. I could assume he was judging me for using my magic recklessly and react again with defensive anger. Or he could be upset that I hadn't taken time to seek consent for how I was using other fae's magic. Or was he criticizing the fact that a half human who'd never had power before could suddenly wield the magic of the strongest fae around her?

Then the corner of his mouth turned down and his eyes softened, and I realized Argus Ladones, full-blooded dragon fae and Keeper of the Greenwood Knoll, wasn't mad or disappointed. He was scared.

Not of me. For me.

I squashed down my angry reactions. "I'm fine," I said automatically, both deflecting his concern and insisting on its truth to myself. "I'm sorry for not being more careful. Everything's fine."

Neither of us believed that, but I resolved to make it so in the future. For Argus's sake, if not for mine.

In the meantime, though, we had a bar to run.

"What do they still need?" he asked, noticing another half dozen maenads flowing into the bar. "And how many baby showers does one child need? This is, what, the fifth?"

"Technically, it's not a shower. It's a sprinkle," I said.

"What in Mab's name is a sprinkle?"

"Well, Baby Callum was born a little over three months ago, around Samhain." I explained as I extended the bottle of whiskey to him and began to pile a tray with delicately cut rocks glasses. "Baby showers happen before the baby comes to prepare the mom for the baby's arrival. We've done that already. Today, we're just celebrating his debut to the public. So, we just sprinkle Semele and the baby with presents and merriment."

Argus didn't try to keep his opinion from his face as he sneered at our largest table already piled high with gifts for the baby boy. "Sprinkle, shower? Any more of this nonsense, and I'll declare a flood warning in here."

I laughed and passed him the tray of glasses. "You're not wrong, boss. Everyone is excited about the little guy."

Who could blame us? It was the first solitary fae baby born in

Atlanta in nearly a decade. As annoyed and gruff as Argus pretended to be, we both knew how significant this birth was for our community.

He hoisted the tray and moved around the edge of the bar. "Well, don't get too excited. If you get overwhelmed by anything, if the energy in the room becomes too much for you, I want you to pass off the bar and step outside."

"Gus," I drawled his name in the way that ground his teeth. "I handle karaoke night every week, and just last week put down a fist-fight between the valkyries and ogres on Varon's night off. Without getting overwhelmed." I made sure to add in that last point, still smarting from his criticism.

"I know," he said begrudgingly, but we both knew what had just almost happened between us. "Just, be careful, baby girl." His eyes softened at the corners again, and I was suddenly willing to promise anything to reassure him.

"Thanks, boss. I will be."

He had already turned, though, and was yelling across the room. "Jocelyn!"

Our blond maenad waitress giggled and tore herself away from the throng of her sisters that had enveloped her as she arrived. "Yeah, boss?"

"I know you're off for the night, but you still answer to me. Remind your sisters this is not a bacchanal. Your crew needs to keep things under wraps as much as possible. And if Siobhan needs to step out for any reason, you step in to pour drinks."

She pouted for a second but quickly huffed and accepted the tray of drinks he passed off to her. "Fine. But it is technically a bacchanal, because Callum is a boy and as the son of a maenad he's a bacchan by birth—" Argus's glare was enough to stop her. "Yes, sir. No nudity, sex, or shenanigans at the bar. We know the rules." She turned her attention to me. "And I always have Shiv's back."

She winked at me, and I blew her a kiss. Despite a rocky start to our hiring Jocelyn at the bar, she and I had developed a decent friendship over the past eight months. She was flighty and flirty and prone to dating our customers, leaving a trail of broken hearts, but she was also loyal, a hard worker, and all of her discarded conquests ended up drowning their sorrows on her nights off. I'd made an entire mortgage payment off of tips from her scorned lovers.

She said she had my back, and I trusted her word.

Not that I would need it.

"Everything's fine," I repeated. "Kaia's on her way, and Mikka and Varon will help run drinks so I can man the bar. And I've always got you." I batted my eyelashes at my gruff boss.

He had no time to growl at me, because the door slammed open again, and ten more maenads and sylphs, assorted sidhe and elemental fae of all kinds began to arrive, laden with gifts, flowers, and more power than I was ready for.

The tastes and energy of their magic surged over me as their enthusiasm bubbled forth, so I turned to that part of my mind still connected to the Gate. My thoughts still twined about with that silken feel of power that called to me, leaving me heady with potential energy. I had to cut it off, but denying the high it gave me was hard, like pulling myself out of a good dream or climbing out of a warm hot tub into cold winter air. I had to steel myself for the drop of leaving the buoyant cloud of that magic, pull my feet under me, and step out into the real world.

As the first of the new arrivals stepped up to order drinks, I finally severed my connection with the Gate, pulling myself away and building walls around my mind. I imagined a fortress of stone around my consciousness, surrounded by a moat. I drew mentally into myself, retreated into my castle, lowered the portcullis, and raised the drawbridge.

It was a crude mental image, but it appealed to the part of me brought up on stories full of dragons and princesses and fairies that looked nothing like the dragons and princesses and fairies I had actually known all my life.

Whatever, it worked.

I told Argus I wouldn't get overwhelmed, and I meant it. I could handle this.

My connection with the Greenwood Gate faded, and I felt the barrier between our worlds go back to sleep. I would reawaken it in a few hours at dusk, but for a time, it would rest.

And I would serve.

CHAPTER TWO

What can I get y'all?" I asked again and again as the guests swarmed the bar over the next hour.

Champagne, wine, and vodka sodas were the dominant orders, but I was happy to mix up martinis, cosmos, and other easy cocktails for the group. I loved that they all knew better than to order labor-intensive drinks like mojitos or frozen margaritas. My customers knew how to behave in a bar: they kept their orders simple, kept their tabs open, and always tipped well at the end of the night.

Nearly everyone arrived with gifts, though I couldn't imagine Mellie still needing anything for the child's next five years. As Argus had pointed out, this was at least the fifth party celebrating little baby Callum. We'd hosted three of them here at the Greenwood Knoll.

Still, it wasn't often the solitary fae got to celebrate something like this. Mellie's was the first pregnancy outside the Courts I'd been able to follow all the way to birth. And I'd left the Summer Court of Atlanta over fifty years ago.

Even with all of their interventions and breeding programs, I could only recall a few dozen Court fae that had given birth successfully in the past half century. Maybe five or six births each year across the entire Atlanta metro area, and most had been trying for decades: Shaylah, Rin, Portia with her twins.

I guess a little excessive enthusiasm could be excused with my patrons.

The fact they decided time and again to celebrate such a momentous occasion with us at our little pub meant the world to me. The Knoll was a safe place for all of the fae in Atlanta, no matter their allegiance. Summer, Winter, or solitary, all fae were welcome, and I was going to do everything I could to make sure it stayed that way.

Our vila waitress Kaia arrived only fifteen minutes late, blowing in on a wind of her own making, full of quick excuses that faded as easily as steam. She grabbed her apron, tied it on, and immediately began clearing empty glasses into the dishwasher. Kaia had been with the Knoll for almost five years and was one of the most reliable waitresses we'd ever had. She kept her personal drama to herself, ran drinks with a speed that rivaled the North Wind, and could quell a rising storm with a few well-chosen words. She was always a breath of fresh air.

"Sorry I'm late," she said as she breezed in and gave me a brief kiss on the cheek before picking up a tray of red wine. "The three lilin at table four are arguing about a shared boyfriend, but if you can get them a round of ciders before Mellie finishes packing the baby into his adorable pram out front, I bet I can distract them with the fact that their beau is going to start receiving AARP letters in the next five years."

I snorted and grabbed a six pack of local peach cider cans. "Get 'em, girl."

With the wines balanced in one hand and the ciders in the other, she winked then blew right back out into the room, white-blond hair dancing down her back. I loved that girl.

As Kaia took over running drinks to the tables, Argus made excuses to get off the floor and disappeared up into his office over the bar. I couldn't blame him. There was a lot of feminine energy in the bar, and we'd barely gotten started.

Within minutes, the fae of the hour arrived with his mother. Even high up on a step stool, grabbing a 20-year bottle of bourbon from the top shelf, I knew the moment Semele Tyne walked in. She pushed open the door, and a blast of cold winter air came rushing in, reaching me all the way back at the bar.

Cooing gasps and shrieks of delight filled the air, but they were nothing compared to the taste overwhelming my senses. It was like little I'd experienced before: a symphony of flavors as the combined magic of all the fae in my bar flooded my senses. Strong floral and fruity notes undulated with earthy spices and verdant plants. I could taste sea salt, smoked tobacco, and rich loam that quickly morphed into bright citrus, green grass, and sweet caramel. It was ever-changing, ever-evolving, but no less assertive and powerful for its flux.

What's more, over it all, I could taste the honeyed apple flavor of Semele's own magic. As with all the maenads, the taste of her danced on my tongue, effervescent and bubbling with optimism and potential. Her particular power was crisp and honeyed, sweet and bright, like a hint of autumn in the depths of winter, with a bite of cinnamon spice underneath it all. Her magic rose as she fed on the outpouring of love, and everything took on a slight veneer of that gingery kick she brought with her.

The bar tasted so alive, I nearly lost my footing on the stool.

"I got you," Varon said, a hand to my lower back and another on my hip as I swooned and then stumbled down the two steps. He helped me down to a sitting position, taking the expensive bourbon and setting it aside until I collected myself.

He stayed looking at me with concern as I took deep breaths to get a hold on all the magic I could taste. Something in me wanted to reach out and seize that power, claim it as my own, and direct it as I chose. I could make this entire bar dance to my whims, and my head spun with unrealized potential.

I closed my eyes and pushed it away. No. My magic didn't work like that. It never had. It wasn't supposed to. I didn't need power like that.

Slowly, the mouth-watering draw of all that magic faded to the background of my mind. I became aware of Varon's hand on my shoulder, rubbing lightly as he spoke softly. "You're here. You're okay. Come on back."

Opening my eyes, I could see that only a few seconds had passed. Mellie was still in the doorway, lifting baby Callum out of his stroller and looking every inch the proud mother as she cooed to him and then turned him to face the room.

No one had noticed my episode on the stool. Other than Varon, that is.

"Thank you," I said as I patted his hand, still on my shoulder.

"Yeah, well. Argus asked me to keep an eye on you," Varon said, shrugging. He gave me a small squeeze and smile before going to help Semele relocate the stroller off to the side of the room.

I gave myself a moment or two more to gather myself, bring myself back into my body. The taste of the magic still danced through me, tempting me, but I did my best to ignore it. I bit down on my tongue until the coppery tang of blood overshadowed everything else.

My stubborn half-fae body immediately wanted to heal itself from the self-inflicted hurt, but I concentrated on the sharp pain in my mouth and clung to it. I needed this wound. I pushed away the tingle of cells wanting to stitch themselves back together and swallowed the blood that pooled in my mouth.

I could get through this. The party would only last an hour or so.

Grabbing a glass, I poured myself a quick shot of tequila and washed the red away from my teeth. It wouldn't do to present as a frenzied redcap at a baby shower. Sprinkle. Whatever.

Pressing my tongue to the roof of my mouth, I reached under the bar and pulled out one of the several cases of champagne I had chilled. Kaia and Jocelyn were ready to start handing out the glasses as I poured, and the maenad clan reached a frenzy of coos over the cuteness of their newest member.

I had to admit, the kid was pretty adorable. He took after his mother with hair the color of winter wheat, an almost silvered honey color. He was peering around with wide cerulean eyes as he was passed from hand to hand, far more alert and aware than the average human would be at nearly three months old.

Whether that precociousness was typical of fae babies or bacchans in particular, I wouldn't know. I don't know that many of us in the bar would. It didn't stop all the girls marveling over his eye contact, his smiles, his ability to turn his head as champagne corks popped, or kick his abundance of wraps and blankets aside.

It was decided: little baby Callum was the most perfect child ever born.

Mellie soaked up the admiration and appreciation for the creature she'd brought us. She practically held court as she moved from group to group, hugging and kissing every one of her sisters, graciously accepting gifts, and enjoying the endless train of champagne and compliments. She looked amazing, with a new softness to her figure.

When I'd first met her, she'd been a slight and willowy thing, resembling more a dryad than a maenad. Her long blond hair swirled in gentle waves and only emphasized her ethereality. Pregnancy had brought a fullness to her face and a roundness to her figure that was beautiful and sacred. When she had visited the Knoll over the fall, she had turned heads with her growing belly and maternal glow. Everyone wanted to be near her, to be close to the miracle happening in her.

Now with the child born, she was the model mother figure, curved and soft and magical in a way that most fae only dream of.

As the girls downed their drinks and destroyed plates of nachos and mac and cheese balls, mini tacos and sliders, their magic slowly settled and faded into the background. I was able to move about freely, shaking up cocktails, pouring wine, and directing my crew about the festive space.

I had few chances to talk to anyone beyond comments about Mellie and the baby, and after a while, my responses became automatic. "Yes, she looks amazing." "Callum really is a miracle." "Maeve's blessings on them both." "No, you're right. He's definitely cuter than any of the Summer Court babies."

"I don't know about that," a haughty voice said from the edge of the bar. "I was a damn cute kid."

I was surprised to see who was there. For the first time in four months, one of my oldest friends, Shiro Harada, stood leaning against the bar. He was tall and lean, clothed in tailored black slacks, a well-fitted white shirt with French cuffs, and a set of diamond cufflinks. There was also the distinctive silver fern frond pin on his left breast pocket, signifying his loyalty to the Summer Court of Atlanta.

"Oh yeah, you were a real fox," I said dryly. Considering he was a descendant of Reynard the Fox on his father's side and a kitsune on his mother's, it was a cheap joke.

He didn't miss the edge in my tone, but he still offered a light chuckle before taking a stool at the end of the bar. "This little shindig seems to be in full swing." He took in the gaggle of Mellie's sister maenads holding up small shirts and pants and cooing, as a group of sylphs sampled the food trays and marveled over the new collection of soft books and colorful teething toys. Nearly every other eye in the place was directed toward the baby who had been passed back to his mother and was now enthusiastically nursing. "I can almost imagine that kid will do all right. Even without Court nurses, he will never want for babysitters with all these aunties around, will he?"

"We take care of our own," I said, less able to keep the sharpness out of my reply. "We may be solitary, but we're not exactly alone."

Ignoring the fact that I wasn't being entirely fair to him, I started to walk away. I knew it wasn't his fault he'd been so absent from my life lately. I knew things were not great with his Court and my pub, and that Summer fae had been warned to stay away from me and mine. But I was still allowed to be upset that of all people, Shiro had followed orders.

Last summer, Shiro had been one of the only ones who stood beside me when the Court refused to help. A pair of killers had threatened the solitary community, picking off patrons of this very bar, and the Summer Court turned its back on us. As I had searched for answers to keep my people safe, I'd found a Queen powerless to do anything, and a princess regent all too willing to let the disloyal solitary fae fend for ourselves.

Never mind that Queen Illythia was my mother and the ruling princess, my sister Bryony. According to them, I had rejected my obligations to them long ago, so it was only fitting that they leave me and my entire community defenseless. Family justice is no justice at all.

Despite his allegiances to the Summer Queen and her regent, Shiro had helped defend me, even going so far as to offer himself as my second in a royal duel against a Winter Queen. Though Mikka had ultimately been the one to fight and suffer for me, Shiro had been willing to put himself on the line. It could have been the end of his career with the Court, but he'd stood by me when I needed him most.

Then he'd gone and accepted a promotion as primary scribe to my sister, and I'd hardly seen him since. I knew it wasn't as simple as him choosing his career with the Court over our decades-long friendship, but it certainly felt like it as weeks went by without a word from him.

I kept my back to him and pretended it took my entire concentration to uncork a bottle of cabernet. I twisted and pulled and grit my teeth against the frustration and hurt I felt that things were so weird between us. I couldn't think of what to say to erase the tension that simmered.

Thankfully, Shiro broke first. "Don't be like that," he said eventually. "I'm sorry. I wasn't trying to pick a fight."

Sighing, I turned to face him. "I know."

"And I'm sorry I haven't been here."

"I know," I repeated. "You're not allowed to fraternize with the enemy."

He winced. "You're not the enemy."

"I know that. You know that. But does Bryony still know that?"

He gestured helplessly, his palms up and empty. "What she knows and what she reveals are always at odds. But this is uncomfortable. Let me change the subject. I brought a gift." He gestured to a stuffed giraffe that stood near the entrance. It was over six feet tall, and Mikka couldn't help giving it the side-eye as she sat her post on the stool by the door.

"Mother, I'm guessing," I said, smirking. There was no way Bryony would send something so ridiculous. There was no way she would send a gift in the first place, honestly. "Tell her that next time, a gift certificate is a lot easier to take home."

Shiro shuddered. "Second guess your mother? No. I value my life still."

"Fair enough," I laughed, as I grabbed a shaker and the cognac to mix Shiro his favorite drink. One French Connection to restore our connection.

Shiro shook his head, though. "No drink for me. I'm afraid I'm not staying."

The look on his face let me know it wasn't his choice to drop the gift and dash away like he'd dropped a Molotov cocktail through the window. He was just following orders.

"Time to scurry back to your mistress," I said bitterly, as I slammed the shaker back down.

"Shiv," he started, but I cut him off.

"No, it's fine," I said, doing my best to tamp down the heat of anger building in me. "It's not your fault my sister is paranoid and doesn't want you anywhere near me."

"Maybe she wouldn't be so paranoid if you exercised a little more discretion," he began.

I gaped at him. "What?"

He met my gaze directly. "I mean, you're opening the Gate regularly, way more than is standard and for far longer than anyone would dare."

"There's no law that determines how often I open the ways," I protested. Not that the laws of the Summer Court would apply to me anyway.

"And it's letting in far more ambient magic than normal," Shiro continued. "That alone would have the Court on edge."

"Oh, Mab forbid the solitary fae have access to an ounce more magic than the Courts would prefer!"

"But on top of that," Shiro ignored my sarcasm. "You've got known members of the Fair Folk passing through here regularly."

"We're a way station. A pub! Everyone is welcome here. You know that."

"And that's not a problem with most people. But the Fair Folk were the ones behind all the trouble last summer."

"Talisa and Hannah were the only ones who killed people," I insisted, having been the one who finally faced them down and stopped the rogue members of the political group. "It had nothing to do with the Fair Folk."

"Oh, come on, Siobhan. You can't be that naive."

"What does that even mean?"

"I'm just saying…" Shiro let his voice trail off.

I wasn't about to let him off the hook, though. "What are you saying? Exactly?"

He took a deep breath and looked me directly in the eye. "I'm saying that if I didn't know you better, I could maybe be convinced that you actually were in league with the Fair Folk."

I couldn't believe what I was hearing. Shiro was suggesting exactly what my sister had believed of me when she'd ordered me to Court to defend myself. That I was power hungry and willing to do whatever it took to put myself on a throne. Whether that be killing innocent fae and stealing their powers through their blood or throwing in with an ambitious political group that hated everything the Courts stood for, she had believed me capable of it.

And Shiro was here acting like that was a reasonable thing to think. "But you do," I said softly, blinking away tears.

"Do what?"

"Know better. You know better than to believe that. Right?"

Shiro opened his mouth but then quickly closed it. He squeezed his eyes shut and shook his head as he stood from his stool. "I know you wouldn't do anything to hurt your friends. Not on purpose, anyway."

A hand clapped down on his shoulder. "Time to go, Courtier," Mikka said. She was tall, dark, and radiated a drake's angry heat. "You made my friend cry. I'll escort you out."

"No need." Shiro stood and without another glance at either of us, he pushed past her and out of the bar, back to the palace that owned him.

Mikka watched me as I wiped at my face. "You okay?"

"Fine," I said, trying to ignore the feelings of hurt and bewilderment. How could Shiro think that of me? That I was exactly as treacherous as Bryony had always thought?

I didn't want any trouble. I just wanted to serve drinks, take care of my people, and steer clear of the messy politics of my family and the Fairy Courts. Was it so much to ask that people believe that?

Mikka didn't seem to be paying me much heed, though. She had a distant look on her face as she turned and watched the maenads laughing and carrying on around baby Callum. Clearly, the brief flirtation with Brynn and Carissa hadn't cut through her melancholy.

"What about you?" I asked. "Are you okay?"

"Fine," she echoed automatically.

I should have known a little bit of flirting wouldn't fix what was wrong with Mikka.

I still didn't know all of what happened to her when she entered the Summer Court's dueling ring on my behalf. I knew that Lada, the Winter Queen she faced, had poisoned her mind with something so terrible that Mikka had been willing to kill herself rather than continue to fight. I knew the fierce, fearless drake that had entered the dueling circle was not the one who came out. Whether it was the lies the Ice Queen fed her, or the fact that I had then used stolen magic to wrestle her back from death, whatever changed her still had its grips in her.

What a pair we made.

"Well, come on, then," I said as brightly as I could. "This is a party, right?"

Mikka blinked at me. "Yay for the crotch goblin," she said as dryly as if she were celebrating an empty keg.

Somehow that cut through my fake cheer and pulled out a genuine laugh. "That's the spirit!"

And though Mikka shook her head as she walked back to her stool, but I could see the edges of a smile on her lips. It was enough for now.

CHAPTER THREE

By the time a million presents had been opened, several cases of prosecco had been drunk, and a metric ton of brisket nachos and southern eggrolls had been consumed, I thought the party would finally wind down. The guests were in the highest spirits, the guest of honor had gone down for his second nap of the event, and I worried Mellie's face would get stuck in a permanent grin.

But no one showed any signs of slowing down. People were actually still arriving. I was about to have to go down to the cellar to get another case of wine. These fae were drinking like someone else was paying. Mostly because he was. The whole shindig was once again being sponsored by the maenads' favorite billionaire benefactor Thierry Kellan.

He'd footed the bill for several events at the Knoll over the past year, and despite making his home base in New York, I heard he was now a regular at the Atlanta Court. I did my best to steer clear of the royal palace as much as possible, though, and since the elusive fae never came into the Knoll himself, I'd yet to meet him. I didn't much mind, so long as he continued to spend freely and tip generously.

I'd keep pulling out crates of bubbles if the girls kept drinking and Kellan kept paying.

Though I did hope the party would die down soon. My head was swimming with the bubbly prosecco taste of the party-goers' manic energy. I'd either need to take a break to catch my breath soon or risk another magic overload. Varon was preoccupied with clearing the tables and dodging roaming maenad hands, so he might not be able to catch me falling off another ladder.

That boy was about to be snatched up by someone hungry for a good time. Or more likely, a couple someones.

I shook my head laughing. There were worse ways to go.

Mikka, meanwhile, was still perched by the back door, barely listening to a human man talking her ear off. Someone should have warned him that Mikka almost exclusively dated women, and femme-presenting ones at that. Poor guy was wasting his time.

Surprisingly, I noted a sizable contingent of humans celebrating today. They mingled with the assorted crowd, only occasionally raising an eyebrow at silver eyes, scaled complexions, fur, and talons on some of my regulars. Each of the humans seemed well-adjusted to fae without glamours and were polite and respectful as they sipped at their cocktails. I noticed one or two with small vials of blood on chains around their necks or wrists, a sure sign that they were partnered with one of my patrons.

Blood sharing had once been a condemned practice amongst our kind, only practiced by the uncivilized underclasses of fae. Lately though, it wasn't just the redcaps and hinkies trading magic.

What I didn't see was any evidence of the usual Summer Court monitors. Bryony probably thought I hadn't noticed her lackies coming in and lurking by the doors, listening to private conversations, and drinking only soda waters and juices.

They were more than welcome to come and enjoy themselves, but it was obvious to anyone paying attention that most of the regally dressed sidhe and elemental fae in my very laid-back pub were there only on orders. They certainly weren't having fun whenever they hovered over the table of clurichaun listening for any whispers of sedition. The Court should really train their stooges in subtlety.

It's good they missed the memo on this particular party. It was private.

I scrambled down into the cellar to find one last case of prosecco to add to Thierry Kellan's tab and emerged to find Argus stepping up on to the stage on the far wall of the bar. At seven feet tall, he already dwarfed anyone else in the bar, but up on the raised platform, he towered over all and drew every eye to him.

His booming voice rose. "I would like to propose a toast!"

Every voice echoed in unison. "A toast!" Raised glasses glinted in the artificial lights of the large wrought-iron chandeliers that hung down from our high ceilings.

"Mellie, we are so happy for you," Argus continued in a lower tone. "Over the past few months, we have gotten to know you better, and I consider you a vital part of the Greenwood Knoll family. You have blossomed into a beautiful mother, and we could not be happier to finally meet our newest and most promising young nephew."

Semele beamed and blinked away tears, while her sister Brynn wrapped an arm around her and squeezed.

"Of course, the introduction of young Callum here today means more than just another cause for celebration. Though, no one would deny you as many parties as you want to throw here." He signaled to me, and I popped the cork on yet another bottle.

As if on cue, the bar cheered with one voice. Argus might be gruff and antisocial on most days, but the man could work a crowd like no one else.

"No, Callum is more than just a welcome addition to our extended family. He is more than a comfort to his mother and more than a miracle to her sisters. He is a gift from the gods, because Callum is a symbol."

The bar had gone quiet as Argus spoke. Semele's beatific smile sharpened, as she hung on every word. Her maenad sisters clutched at one another as they nodded, and even the humans developed a hungry light in their eyes.

"This boy is a symbol that life is possible. The birth of such a child to a solitary fae, a healthy, hale child to someone outside the Courts is rare. The Summer Court would like us to believe such a birth impossible. That we need their fertility measures, their breeding programs, to bring new life into this Iron Realm. They want us to believe that to survive as a people, we must rely on them and their measured magic for everything. That we must give up our freedoms to live, and love, and fuck as we wish. But Callum is proof that they are wrong."

A cheer rang out, as the girls whooped in agreement. Their enthusiasm urged Argus louder, and the prosecco taste in the air became peppered with notes of lemon and sharp green apple.

"Callum and his precious mother remind us that something greater is within reach. The solitary fae of this realm are capable of so much more than we even dreamed. When we are free to determine our own paths, we will not just survive. We will thrive! We don't need Queens and their protections to grant us permission to be everything we can be. We don't need them to dictate the circumstances by which we further our lines. And we don't need to wait on those Queens to dribble out the magic that is our birthright."

He turned then to look at me, and a taste of pipeweed and salty brine brushed over my tongue. The room warmed, and I felt my breath catch as my world expanded. For a moment, I could see myself through his eyes, standing behind the bar, wild black coils shaking as I trembled with the power that flowed through the room. My deep topaz skin shone, and my citrine eyes flashed with barely contained magic.

I struggled to separate myself from his perception, to pull myself back into my own body. But his presence was too powerful. He controlled the room, and I was filled with the strength of his magic. I couldn't even stop to consider how it was possible, that I was able to access his magic without connecting to the Gate first. It was out of my control. *I* was out of my control.

Unaware or unconcerned, Argus surged forward with his speech, pulling the entire bar along with his conviction.

"Through the Gates, we have the means of accessing our own

power. That power has been bounded in the past, locked and controlled by the capricious whims of our Queens who control our access to Fairy. We as a solitary people have had to slowly accumulate power over weeks of patience, rationing our strength and hoping that what we held in our veins was enough to get us through the next trickle of magic we could get. We have been limited by the willingness of others to weaken themselves that others might thrive."

Argus spoke of the sacred duty of Gate Keepers to open the ways twice a day. We bled ourselves, giving up our own personal power and magic to hold the Gate open and allow magic to trickle freely into this realm from Fairy. It was a duty he, and I, and all those here at the Knoll took seriously.

It was a duty that had been sullied last year when Talisa, my one-time lover, and her human accomplice Hannah had taken it upon themselves to sacrifice others to gain more magic for themselves. They'd drained other fae, people they called friends, held the Gate open longer to give them more access to their power, all in an attempt to further their political aims.

Argus continued. "We know that any one of us would be willing to take those sacrifices on. That we would bleed if it would strengthen our community, our family." I saw some of the humans subconsciously reach for their vials of borrowed magic. Someone had bled to give them a measure of power. "But there is another way. We are no longer bound by the rule of Queens. We can open the ways any time we want, without waiting for approval by those that don't rule us. If they're willing to take a stand, we have our own leaders and those who can bring us together as a people, a truly equitable and fair folk. We have strength in our unity if we can follow it. Our own people will be our liberation."

He stared me down long enough, that others picked up on what he was talking about. The maenads, sylphs, dryads, and even the humans of the party turned to smile at me. They knew. They knew that I could open the Gate without a blood sacrifice. That I could open the Ways between the realms with only a thought. That I was the reason they had enjoyed more ambient magic throughout Atlanta for the past several months.

Maybe Shiro had a point after all.

Still, I struggled to meet their eyes, as their own mania increased. They were riding an emotional high, and the unique gift of maenads was to amplify feelings. They were feeding off of Argus's energy, pouring that power into one another, and all of it was filtering through me as I stood there paralyzed. I could feel them all, taste their unique magical signatures. Pear and honey, lemongrass and peach, wisteria and citrus and honeydew and lime and chamomile and and and...

Argus didn't stop. "The time of Queens is nearing its end, my friends. Soon, no Queen will be able to deny us our right to magic. No Queen will stand between us and the fair exercise of power. No one will deny us freedom. My friends, the old ways are dying. Now is the time for a new path forward. It is the time of the Fair Folk!"

Another cheer rose up, and in a moment the Knoll disappeared as the wave of their energy seized control of me. I could do nothing but ride it as the tide surged, drowning out all perception. All sight, sound, smell, was overwhelmed by knowledge and the taste of each of their desires.

Carissa's hopes had a sweet softness to them, a peach-fuzz newness to the prosecco hope of her dreams. She had recently bought a house in the suburbs and was excited to start a family of her own. Semele's success with Callum gave her hope that it was possible, and she was hard on the hunt for not just a night's pleasure, but a stable father for her children. Varon would do nicely. Or maybe one of the young hobgoblin busboys. Milo had a youthful charm about him.

Milo was eying Elea, one of the youngest of the maenads who had recently shed her braids for an array of bantu knots that showed off her delicate bone structure. She looked like a bird with hollow bones, perched for flight as her bright eyes darted around the room, but Milo knew from experience that she was strong enough to pin him up against the stairs when she was in the mood. His hunger for her was tinged with hops and grounded with a maltiness that bordered on sweet.

Tasting of saffron, cardamom, rhubarb, and chamomile, Meara, who was lurking in the doorway of the kitchen was contemplating planting some specialty herbs off the back of the Knoll. She'd heard that if enough ambient magic was coming through the Gate, that it might be possible to maintain a usable garden. If what Argus said was true, she could save herself the weary trip back to Fairy and avoid having to beg for some of her favorite spices.

At his post by the door, tasting of smoke, toffee, and a salty finish, Varon had nothing in his mind but Argus's words. He was filled with hate and anger, with hunger. After what happened to his sister, he hated the Fairy Courts more than ever. They'd robbed Mikka of her vitality, of her spirit. She was barely hanging on, and it was all because of the evil Queens at the heart of the whole system. Lada, Bryony, weak Illythia who faded away into her carnal blamelessness, they were all at fault for Mikka's pain. He would gladly watch them and their Courts burn if it would bring his sister's fire back.

Kaia, Jocelyn, Tobin, and the small group of clurichaun that had gathered in the front room. All of them were laid bare to me, until I couldn't keep their thoughts separate. I didn't know who was friend or foe, worried or elated. The voices and thoughts swirled through me.

Above it all was the fact that Shiro was right.

No one present could deny that Argus was in open rebellion against the Queens of Fairy. And that the majority of my customers were in league with him. The Fair Folk saw me as the one who would lead them to this new future they envisioned, and that made me a threat to my mother the Queen.

Argus's voice just penetrated my dissociated state. "So, again, I would like to propose a toast."

"A toast!" The roar of the crowd rocked me as my vision danced with a haze of purple tinged green light. Thoughts flowed without ceasing, eddying around each other in a turbulent maelstrom of magic and identity.

"To Callum and Semele, and all they represent for the future!"

"To the future!" The voices screamed out in jubilation, their power surged, and the world disappeared.

CHAPTER FOUR

I swooned as it all overtook me, crying out in an ecstatic moan. I could have exploded into a million stars or melted into a sticky puddle of ice cream or burst into an inferno and consumed the entire bar. I was there, and then I was everywhere and nowhere. Everything and nothing at once.

Until a voice and a touch brought me back.

"Siobhan, I'm here. Hang on," the voice said.

I had the sensation of movement. Of a body. It jolted me from the nothingness. Reminded me I was something. Someone. Somewhere.

Then the world returned. And the voices that filled it. And I felt them all tumbling out through my lips, desperate to be spoken, to be brought to life with my voice. I had to speak them. They were more real than I was.

"He's right you know? I know. We could do so much. We're more than they ever bargained for."

"I think I had too much to drink. I should ask for a ride."

"Is that report due tomorrow or Friday?"

"She could change it all for us, if she wanted to. Did you feel what she did? What that means?"

"We'll find where they hurt. They'll never know what hit them."

"I don't care. I need him licking where I'm slicking, if you know what I'm saying."

"There, right there." Yes. That voice. Gasping in pleasure as skilled fingers found their target. That voice was mine. And it was out loud.

An intake of breath as something broke through the cacophony inside of me. Warm tingling centered deep inside me, responding to something physical, carnal. Real.

I focused on that feeling in my core and chased it. Let it grow and chased toward its climax.

"They should really get more fans in here. It's stifling."

"His blood makes me sing."

"She's not our salvation. She can barely get through a shift."

"But she's channeling the Gate. You felt it."

"It's already paid for. I don't know why I can't take a bottle or two with me."

"Yes! Rhys, yes. There. Right there." Me again. I recognized the taste of them finally. The feel of their forked tongue as it darted around my sensitive earlobe, and their fingers as they found my center and coaxed me back into my body.

"Right here, Siobhan," their voice echoed in a low voice. I clung to the smooth tone that had become so familiar to me. The assured feel of their hands, strong, firm, and comforting. They always knew exactly where to touch me, to inspire pleasure, to inflict pain. Over months, their fingers had learned the planes of me.

Or rather relearned.

We'd first taken each other in the mid-sixties. We were both still young. Mere children. But we found each other. Rhys as a new palace guard. Me as heir to the Atlanta throne. But we found each other. A basilisk and a princess. Discovering each other in empty rooms throughout the palace. Finding out who we were to each other. To ourselves. Tasting and tempting.

I'd been a little bit in love with them even back then. They were my protector and my friend. They'd seen me as something more than a charge to protect. I'd been someone special. And they had such an eager desire to chase pleasure with me.

Now that we'd found our way back to each other, they put their expert knowledge of me to work after I lost myself again at the Knoll. Deftly they found the rhythm, the intensity of the climax needed for me to find my way back to my body. Rhys used our intimate connection forged and reforged over decades to guide me away from the vast nothingness of everything and back to something specific. Specifically, an explosive orgasm.

I cried out and clung to my lover, gasping as the waves of sensation surpassed the draw of the magic. The moment I crested over the precipice, the voices ceased.

Fully in my own mind and my own body again, I rolled over on top of them and returned the favor with vigor. Rhys had such a delightful body, after all.

I'm not sure how long we stayed tangled up in each other, enjoying the feel of claiming the moment, chasing our own and each other's pleasure. At some point, though, I did let go of pure sensation and take stock of where I was, of what had happened.

We were upstairs in Argus's office above the bar. I was lying on the huge, overstuffed couch with Rhys breathing evenly as they draped over my naked body. Their head nestled in the crook of my neck, just above my breasts, our skin lightly sheened with well-earned sweat. Their breath was slightly cooler than mine, causing my nipples to pebble. I squirmed a little, feeling the vaguely rough upholstery of the couch scratch my back.

Rhys let out a low chuckle and blew out a more intentional breath, as they traced the goosebumps emerging along my skin, stirring me to thoughts of round two. I trailed my hands down their spine, enjoying the feel of the scales. By sight, their skin looked as smooth as my own, but with such intimate touches, I could feel the subtle differences of basilisk scale from mammalian skin.

I could flip them underneath me and run my tongue the wrong way, up toward their neck. They would resist minimally, as I held them down and worked them up again.

But I knew now was not the time for that. We'd been up here long enough. And I had to ask.

I laid some extra kisses along their forehead before I sighed. "How bad was it? Really?"

Rhys sat up and scooted back on the couch, giving me space to sit up myself. "It wasn't great. I think these episodes are getting worse, Shiv."

I nodded. It's not like I could deny it after losing it in front of such a big crowd. My magic was getting stronger, and the consequences were becoming more apparent.

"Were you pulling on the Gate when it happened?" Rhys stood to go fetch their shirt and picked up my jeans and underwear from the floor.

"I don't think so." I wasn't even sure anymore. There was so much magic and emotion from the concentration of maenads and Argus's speech, that I couldn't even be sure where it all had come from. Had I subconsciously reached out to the Gate to channel the overwhelming power in the room? Or had that all been me?

I admitted as much out loud. "I was so caught up in everything, I don't know how it all happened. With the energy of the party, all those psychic amplifiers, and everything that Argus was saying in his toast, about me and the Gate and what it could mean for the Fair Folk, maybe I did it accidentally?"

Rhys frowned the second I mentioned the Fair Folk. "We're going to come back to that, babe."

My lips pursed. It wasn't like I was keeping secrets from Rhys. But they were still a Knight of the Atlanta Court. I should probably be more circumspect about what I discussed with them, given my boss was now openly admitting to rebellion against the Summer Court.

Though if Shiro was doubting my intentions, and Rhys had arrived in time to hear any of Argus's speech, they would be well within reason to question whether I was as involved as it seemed I was.

What a mess.

"Did I say anything?" I asked, carefully. "When it was happening, I mean?"

Rhys sighed again. "You said a lot, actually. You channeled. Some recognized their own thoughts. And some of their closely guarded secrets."

I squeezed my eyes shut. "Mab's breath. I sounded like a Queen in full madness, didn't I?"

Tasting and accessing other faes' magic, channeling their inner thoughts, losing track of the outside world as I succumbed to the thoughts and powers that flowed through me. It was exactly like the madness that consumed Fairy Queens, and there wasn't a fae that wouldn't recognize it for what it was.

"Not entirely that bad," Rhys said gently as they passed me the black t-shirt that had been tossed over a chair. They were being kind. "But it was familiar enough that there are going to be some more rumors to combat."

Irritated, I tugged my shirt back on over my head. The last thing I needed was for the entire solitary community to be wondering whether my episodes meant I had a Queen's powers.

Rhys winced. "You know I'm going to have to report this to the palace."

Correction. *That* was the last thing I needed.

"I know," I said standing up and beginning to pace the room. No matter the relationship Rhys and I had, they couldn't act against my mother the Queen, or my sister Bryony, her heir. Even though we tried to pretend it wasn't happening, I was almost certain that my lover had to regularly make reports to Bry about my activities, the company I kept, and whether I was likely to make an attempt on reclaiming the throne that was originally supposed to pass to me.

Never mind that I had no intention of ever becoming Queen of Atlanta. If I was displaying new magical abilities, channeling others' power, and generally exhibiting the more unfortunate side effects of wielding a Queen's abilities, my sister would have a conniption.

"I don't suppose you can let this one get to her by the usual gossip channels? Give me a day or so to prepare for her response?"

Rhys chuckled. "It's adorable that you don't think people left the party and immediately went to report to her. Not everyone who informs the Court is a paid spy, you know."

"I know," I said again.

"It doesn't have to be a bad thing, you know." Rhys sat down on the couch and pulled me back down to sit beside them, wrapping a leanly muscled arm around my shoulders. "If what you're going through is related to the Queen's Curse, there are ways to control it. Maybe you can even go talk to your sister, get some advice? You missed out on a lot when you left Court so young, but she has been presumptive heir ever since. She might have some ways to help control the worst aspects of what you're going through."

I hated to admit it, but Rhys was right. On Mother's retirement, Bryony would take over as conduit, and for decades, she had been receiving training on controlling the madness that followed. Every heir to a Summer throne was taught how to carefully partition her thoughts, separating them from the influx of voices, powers, and personalities that would stream through her when she took over as Queen for her region.

That is, after all, the primary duty of a Fairy Queen. They are not mere royal figureheads, nor are they political leaders and legislators, though they certainly fulfill both of those roles. No, the main job of a Fairy Queen is to serve as the magical conduit for their region.

All of the magic the fae wield comes from our home world of Fairy, and we all carry some small measure of it within our blood. But the amount most of us can contain within ourselves is small and finite. If we use it up, it's gone until our bodies slowly regenerate it, or we return to Fairy and take in as much as we can. My dryad friends described it as fairy photosynthesis, in a way; we take the air and essence of Fairy and convert it into magic.

There are other ways of accessing our magic, though, without ever leaving the human world. One is through proximity to the Gates. The Greenwood Gate is Atlanta's portal to Fairy, and whenever it opens, ambient magic from the Eternal Realm drifts through into the Iron Realm. Any fae close enough essentially breathes in the magic of our home world. Proximity matters, as does the length of exposure.

Relying on the Gates can limit the amount of magic most fae can carry. Time and proximity are scarce and considering it requires a blood and magic sacrifice to breach the Gate, holding it open exacts a toll on its Keepers.

That's why most fae access their magic through their Queen. The Queen acts as her own Gate, bridging the worlds, allowing magic from Fairy to flow through her. Any fae pledged to her Court, loyal to her, can access as much magic as they want at any time, pulling it through the continuously open conduit of their Queen. Unlimited magic passes through her without obstruction and flowing out to all of her subjects.

As you can imagine, this greatly affects the Queen. If she is not careful to protect herself from the unceasing amount of magic, and, conversely, to build walls against the hundreds of fae she is constantly linked to, she can find herself pulled under the tide of all the power, connection, and knowledge she holds within her.

But none of that was related to what I was doing. I wasn't a conduit between the Gate and the solitary fae. I might tap the Gate from time to time, but I wasn't funneling magic to anyone. I was merely tasting it, connecting to them, occasionally, apparently, accessing their magic.

It was completely unrelated.

The way Rhys was looking at me with concern, though, I knew I couldn't ignore the similarities.

"I'll talk to Bryony," I agreed. "Just not yet."

Rhys nodded, understanding my reluctance. "It's going to be sooner rather than later, babe. Because I didn't just come here to coax you back from the edge with my oh-so-skilled tongue play."

They raised my hand to their lips and flicked their forked tongue over my knuckles in a snaky kiss. I giggled as expected, but it wasn't enough to distract me from what they said.

"Yeah, hey. Why are you here?" I pulled my hand away and narrowed my eyes. "You knew I was busy all weekend. And we don't have a date until Monday. You better not be here to cancel on me. We agreed you would finally watch the Brendan Fraser classic *The Mummy*."

Ignoring my deflections, Rhys took a deep steeling breath. "Lada's in town."

I felt my blood freeze, which was appropriate given that Lada was the Winter Queen who last summer had tried to kill me, had given Mikka PTSD, and was now apparently my sister's best friend in the whole world. Any time she came to town, I could be sure she was whispering sweet nothings and fratricidal thoughts into my sister's ear masquerading it as friendly political advice.

I almost wished I could just deal with the bitch face-to-face and get this all over with.

"She's going to summon you to Court tomorrow."

Fuck, I immediately wanted to take my thought back. (And if Mab could stop answering my dread directly, that would be great, thanks.)

"She's going to summon me, or Bryony is going to call me? Or is the actual Queen of that Court going to be the one to call me? Is Mother even a part of the Court anymore?" I asked pointedly. I stood and towered over Rhys. "Or, Mab forbid, are any of them going to realize that I'm not a member of any of their Courts? I'm not their subject to order around. I'm solitary. I'm a Keeper of the Greenwood Gate with my own sovereignty. And I don't have to answer any summons they want to issue."

Gaze steady and patient, Rhys waited for me to finish my indignant tirade. "Brunch is at eleven."

I deflated. They knew I wasn't going to defy a call to Court. I sank back down to the couch once again, dropping my head into my hands. "There better be some fucking mimosas."

Rhys put an arm around and pulled me in close, dropping a kiss on the back of my hair. "Your sister knows better than to try and have a civil conversation without some social lubrication. But you should be prepared. It looked like bad news, given Lada's mood when she arrived."

A dismayed moan was my only response. I couldn't be sure if my summons was because of my emerging powers and unsanctioned openings of the Gate, or because of the Fair Folk and the Knoll's role with the group. Or if it was just to offer a gift for Semele's baby's debut. For all I knew, it could be all three.

I wasn't even a century old, and I was already too old to keep playing these games.

CHAPTER FIVE

R hys left after a short attempt to cheer me back up with their aforementioned skilled tongue play, but with the news about my inevitable meeting with my sister and Lada, I was not in much of a mood for sex of any kind. Graciously they understood and left me to finish out the night at work, as they, no doubt, had to now go and report back to the palace.

I let them depart quickly while I picked up pillows and straightened the room, avoiding going downstairs to clean up whatever mess my latest episode had left in the bar. The volume was way down after the mania of the party, and the taste of sparkling wine and botanicals had notably faded.

Only a few straggling maenads remained, picking decorations off of chairs, packing up leftover snacks and gift wrap, and mingling with the regulars that were slowly filling the dining room. My usual group of clurichaun were at their table over by the large fireplace opposite the bar, and they already had a round of beers half consumed. Some earth elementals were at the far end of the bar with a pair of dwarves I didn't recognize. I assumed they were recent arrivals from Fairy from their decidedly retro appearances in woolen cloaks and wooden toggles in their beards.

Carissa and Brynn were among the maenads still present, and as Carissa stepped up on a chair to grab a swag of bunting off of the wrought-iron chandelier, Brynn reached up and pulled her down.

"Not in your condition, young lady!"

Carissa stepped back down gracefully giggling and put a hand over her belly protectively.

"You're pregnant?" I gasped as I approached them.

They both stared at me strangely, then exchanged a look between themselves. Carissa cleared her throat. "Yeah, Siobhan. I didn't really want to step on Mellie and Callum's big moment today, but you kind of spoiled that."

"I—" I stopped myself. That must have been what Rhys meant by me spilling people's secrets. I felt the whisper of peach bellini trace over my tongue. "I'm sorry. I didn't realize."

Carissa grinned then, over her annoyance already. "Oh, it's fine. Apparently, Adara is only about a week or so later than me, so we can go through our pregnancies together like sisters should. And Mellie is beyond excited to guide us through the experience."

Adara was another of the maenads, one who didn't frequent the Greenwood Knoll as much, but it seemed I'd shared her secret as well.

Three maenads. Solitary fae. All pregnant within a year of each other. Suddenly Argus's predictions about a changing world weren't so far-fetched.

I offered a weak smile as I struggled to keep up with everything that had happened without my awareness. It was like piecing together memories after a night of drinking. "I'm truly sorry I shared your news without permission. I wasn't quite myself."

"Yeah, girl, we noticed," Brynn said. She pursed her lips. "Are you feeling okay?"

I nodded. "I am now, thanks."

"I'm sure!" She laughed. "When that sexy Queen's Guard came and swept you off your feet and carried you upstairs, I'm not going to lie, I was a little jealous. He's gorgeous."

"They," I corrected. "And yes, Rhys is pretty incredible."

"Are they your consort?"

I flinched. The question wasn't totally off base, or even rude, considering that Rhys was my lover and doing their level best to ground me in my body whenever I had these episodes. But only Queens had consorts. And I wasn't ready to say that what I was experiencing was equivalent to a Queen's madness. There was too much bound up in the idea.

"Rhys is a wonderful partner, and I'm lucky they were there. I'm not used to active magic, yet. They're just helping me through it."

They both nodded, knowingly. The former powerlessness of Illythia's oldest half-human daughter was well known throughout the Knoll. Throughout Atlanta, truth be told. And if I had ever hoped to keep my new abilities secret, that time was embarrassingly past. I was shit at keeping secrets these days, even my own.

They spoke excitedly at the same time.

"Can you really access the Gate any time you want?"

"Are you connected to Fairy magic all the time now?"

I forced a smile and started backing away. "I think Meara's calling me in the kitchen. I'm glad y'all had a great time at the party. And sorry again." And then as awkwardly as possible, I fled the floor of the Knoll and ducked down the hall to the kitchen.

Passing through the swinging door, I almost barreled right into our busboys, Milo and Tobin, who were on their way out with extra bus tubs.

"Whoa, Shiv!" Tobin barked. Then his gaze softened as he took in my panicked look. "Hey, are you okay?"

"Yeah, I'm fine. Just a little overwhelmed."

"We got you," Milo said. "Anyone we need to toss?" He popped his neck while Tobin cracked his knuckles, raring for a fight.

Milo and Tobin, both hobgoblins of only about thirty years, were all of five and a half feet each, and possessed only minor telekinesis and the ability to pass through rooms unnoticed should they choose. The idea of them tossing out any of the more powerful fae currently in the dining room in my defense endeared them so much to me.

"No, no one is giving me grief. Thank you, though," I said sincerely. "I'll be okay. I just needed a moment to regroup."

"Regroup?" Tobin's thick eyebrows shot up and waggled lasciviously. "Isn't that what your lover was here for earlier?"

Milo slapped his friend upside the head. "You redcap. You're not supposed to draw attention to it."

"I was being subtle!" Tobin whined, rubbing the back of his bushy brown hair.

"You miscreants! Out of kitchen." The thick Slavic accent of Meara boomed from the back. The boys disappeared, and I took a breath.

"Thanks for that."

Meara appeared from behind a rack of jarred herbs and loosely stacked produce. She pressed a mug of something steaming into my hands. "Drink." Then she turned and disappeared back into the depths of her domain.

"What is it?" I didn't wait for an answer as I trusted to her ministrations. The tea she'd given me was thick and spicy. It had notes of turmeric, cardamom, and ginger, but there was something foreign and spicy whispering through it, almost like anise or licorice but also mustardy with a strong kick. Meara was constantly sourcing exotic ingredients through the Gate, so I had no doubt this was something from Fairy, and more powerful and expensive than I warranted in this moment.

Still, I knew better than to protest the gift, for that is what it was. I simply sipped at the spicy drink and let it ease the tension I was holding at the finial of my neck. I let go of the anxiety of everyone knowing what was happening to me, or at least of guessing at it. What had happened was past. It was public, and it was past. I could only move forward and face what was to come.

Blinking rapidly, I realized those were the healthiest thoughts I'd had about my situation in weeks. "Meara, can I have some more of this tea to take home?"

She poked her head over a head of leafy greens. "Only if limit to six ounces twice a day." Her eyes narrowed at me, as if she doubted whether I could hold to her instructions.

"Why? What happens if I have more?"

"Your grounding increases until you sprout roots, and you can't break with earth until you counter effects with vapor-dew, which does not grow here, or you draw blood. A lot."

I blanched. "Okay, how about I just have a glass when I come into work each day?"

"Good thinking." Her face disappeared again.

"Thanks, Meara," I said as I took my mug and went back out into the dining room again, head full of healthy, helpful thoughts.

The maenads had cleared out, and all evidence of the baby sprinkle had been removed. The table of clurichaun were hunched over their beers and conversing intently, while the dwarves and earth elementals were laughing loudly over a shared joke over by the bar.

I could have gone back behind the bar and hid some more while I prepped garnishes and glassware for the evening rush; but feeling more grounded and secure than I had all day, I moved my way over to the table of clurichaun.

A trouping fae, the clurichaun were related to leprechauns, but instead of traipsing around rainbows and dispensing gold coins, these brothers liked to drink and share good times. Wine, beer, whiskey, they loved it all, and they could dispense or dismiss drunkenness and euphoria or depression in equal measure. They also had incredible luck and could share that with those they liked best. For instance, bartenders who kept them several rounds deep whenever they wanted.

I had been avoiding them too much lately, my guilt over their losses weighing heavily on me. Two of their brothers had been caught up when Talisa and Hannah had embarked on their murderous spree to wrest more power from Fairy. Baerd's girlfriend Kari had been one of the earliest victims, and when he'd confronted Hannah, he'd likewise been attacked. Gair was the final victim before I stopped them.

I may not have been the one who killed the clurichaun brother, but I should have been able to save him. I'd been there when he died. I'd almost harnessed the ability to save him. If I'd recognized my potential a little sooner. If I'd focused on him instead of stopping Talisa and Hannah.

His death was my fault as much as anyone's, and not even Meara's miraculous tea could erase the guilt I felt.

His clan welcomed me warmly despite this.

"Siobhan!"

Leland, the youngest of the clan, stood up and embraced me. "Can you sit? It's not busy. Come have a beer with us."

Without waiting for a response, Alden pulled out a chair, and Cormac began pouring a fresh glass for me from the pitcher. Leland ushered me in, and before I knew it, I had a glass in hand as the boys of the local cluri clan checked in with me.

"We heard what happened at the baby party earlier," Cormac said. He was one of the older members of the group, pushing upward of one hundred fifty years, with a dull streak of Pinot Gris blond hair through his oak barrel brown. His face was soft and fatherly, rounded with years of heavy drinking, but still strong and alert. "We worry 'bout ye, girl."

"I'm fine," I began, ready to protest, but several of the men in the group were nodding their heads. I wanted to shrink away at the thought that my worst moments were again the topic of public conversation, so I took another sip of my tea instead of the beer in front of me. It helped settle my anxiety, and I reminded myself that these men had stood beside me and defended when they had every reason to hate me. They'd lost a brother, and they still came to the Knoll constantly to support and defend me and my chosen family. "Thank you for your concern," I started anew. "I'm okay now, though."

"Course ye are," Alden said, lifting his glass in a toast. "Never met someone stronger." His eyes twinkled, and his black hair fell about his eyes. Alden was one of the younger members of the group, but I'd noticed him stepping forward as a bit of a leader of the group after Gair's death and Baerd's disappearance.

It was an intimate and loyal group. Young Leland, Alden and Cormac, Holden and Lachlan and Thane, all of them with skin of oak and pine mottled with splashes of white and red wines, their hair in shades of cedar and sequoia and birch.

"Aye," Alden said, watching my gaze around the group. "We are missing them, too."

I finished my tea and took the courage it offered to ask the question at the forefront of my mind. "Have you heard from Baerd at all?"

Alden and Cormac exchanged a look, with Cormac shaking his head slightly. "Aye," Alden said, as Cormac sighed with a low grumble. "We have."

Pushing my tea mug away, I took hold of the pint glass and leaned back in my chair waiting for Alden to continue. Cormac continued to shoot daggers at his younger brother, but Alden ignored him. "Last time we saw him, Baerd was in a bit of a state. He's been more dedicated to the idea that there is a way to get the Summer Court out of the Iron Realm. Said he was on a mission."

"A mission?"

"He came here to the Knoll, about a month ago to talk to you about it," Leland said excitedly. "He thinks you could be the key to it all."

Cormac groaned and grabbed his own glass. He nearly tipped the pitcher over to empty it into his drink and clunked the empty container to the table. "I'll be outside." Then he stomped his way to the back door between the bar and the hall to the kitchen and bathrooms and disappeared out the back door.

The *thunk* of the heavy oak seemed to shake the room, but that might have only been the effect of it on his fellows. The clurichaun clan was one of the closest-knit groups in Atlanta, and seeing any tension between them rubbed against me like sandpaper on silk.

"I didn't mean to—"

"No, lass, 'tisn't you," Alden said. He always leaned further into his Gaelic brogue when stressed. Just as Gair had done.

I tasted the ghost of stone fruit, red wine, and pine as I remembered Gair, and I couldn't fight the prickle of tears at the edge of my eyes.

"Baerd lives, still," Alden said, reaching across the table to grab my hand as it rested beside my pint of beer. "That alone is thanks to you. Semele lives. As does her son. You live. And the Knoll still stands. Lass, if ye can't take comfort in what you saved over what we've lost, then ye aren't as strong as I give you credit for." Then he squeezed my hand until I looked up at him and met his eyes.

"Thank you," I said. And I should have left it there. Alden had shut down the opening for conversation. But I couldn't leave it alone. Of course, I couldn't. "But what is it Baerd is hoping for? Why is he going to Fairy? And what does it have to do with me?"

Alden pulled his hand back at that. He pursed his lips and then took a slow sip of his beer. He seemed almost reluctant to speak any further on the subject.

Leland had no compunctions about staying quiet around me, though. "Whatever happened, Baerd never gave up on the ideals of the Folk. He still believes our people can rise against the Courts. Be powerful and free."

"He's not the only one," I said under my breath, thinking of Argus.

"Say that again," Alden agreed, also under his breath, and smiled at me.

Ignoring our commentary, Leland continued. "And since Hannah still insists it was Talisa who killed Kari, not her, the two of them been talking. They're trying to figure out a way they can fight Summer without hurting anyone. Baerd insists Kari's death won't be in vain. He thinks they can find a way to send all the Courts packing back to the Eternal Realm for good. And that you might be able to give them the power to do it."

My stomach in knots, I finally reached for the beer they offered and took a sip. Leland had just said that Baerd had been in regular contact with Hannah, who was supposed to be securely locked up away from any members of the Fair Folk. And that they were working together, still, on behalf of the Fair Folk.

I was going to have to have serious words with Mikka and Varon about their houseguest. But if Varon was as enthusiastic about the Fair Folk as his thoughts had betrayed, that might be a losing battle.

Varon. Argus. Leland. How many of those here in my bar were doing exactly what the Summer Court feared they were? Were they all hoping that there was some way to empower themselves against the Fairy Courts, and that I would be the one to help lead them?

Clearly, not everyone agreed, even amongst this close family of brothers. Holden and Thane's eyes glittered with excitement at all Leland was saying, while Lachlan looked uncomfortable and refused to meet my eyes, while Alden squirmed. And Cormac had stomped off rather than talk further about Baerd and his mission.

"I don't know whether I can help Baerd in Fairy," I said carefully. "But I hope he finds his way home soon."

"He knows the way," Alden said sadly. "But he might not recognize it when he arrives."

The table went silent with tension.

"A toast," I said as I lifted my beer to the group. "To family. May your brotherhood be whole again soon." They echoed my toast as one, tapped their glasses against mine, and all took a gulp of their drinks.

I clinked and retreated, taking my half empty glass back to the bar before throwing out what I hadn't drunk in the sink.

"You know that'll be waiting for you in the next world," Varon said in a low voice as he slipped in next to the well.

I knew the legend. That for every drink that you wasted, every sip of spirit that slipped down the drain or was spilled on the floor, that you would have to drink it when you passed in order to cross over into the next life. As a bartender, it was literally one of my least favorite myths. "Var, I throw out a hundred times that amount of beer every night."

"Yeah," he said. "But that one was a drink for you, in honor of something. That is one that weighs on your soul."

I couldn't stop the groan and eye roll. "If I succumbed to every superstition of our people based on beer, wine, and liquor, I'd never be sober."

"I think that's the point."

"Obviously, we need better mythologies. Fine. How about, I've literally visited the place between worlds, and there was nothing to drink there?"

"That sounds bleaker than I'm used to from you," Varon admitted as he moved around the edge of the bar and took my glass to put it in the dishwasher under the bar.

I laughed. "You're right. That's your role in our family. What's up, short stuff?" I asked, tilting my head back to look up at him as he stepped close to me. The nickname made me laugh because though I was over five foot nine inches, Varon and Mikka were both six foot something and always towered over me. I was still older, so I could call the twins munchkins if I wanted.

Varon obligingly stepped over and placed a kiss on the top of my head. "Hey, sis."

I folded myself into his arms and let myself be enveloped. "Hey, bro."

He wrapped his arms around me and squeezed me tight. "You doing okay?"

"If anyone else asks me that, I'm going to do my best to channel the whole of the Gate's energy, steal your fire, and burn this entire city to the ground."

He loosened his grip around my shoulders. "Fair enough. I'm sure we all deserve to die in your flaming tower of righteousness." His words were bleak and monotone, but I could see his eyes dancing as he teased me. He held up his hands in surrender and took a step back.

"I'm fine." Sweeping a handful of cut limes into a large glass jar. "Though, I suppose I should go take care of opening the Gate for the evening."

I had been lax with my Gate duties over the past few weeks. Knowing that I could access it any time had me forgetting that it was still my responsibility as a Keeper to hold the Way open at least twice a day.

"I'll do it," Mikka said from the door. And before I knew it, she had slipped from her stool, made her way across the bar, and out the back.

Varon and I traded a look as the door slammed behind her.

"I should probably go check on her," I said, wiping the juice from my hands onto a towel. "Varon, would you mind keeping an eye on the bar for a few minutes?"

He waved a hand and continued to slice up the fruit on the bar. "Better you than me."

With that optimistic dismissal, I dashed out the back after Mikka.

CHAPTER SIX

Aburst of cold greeted me as I pushed out the back door. January in Atlanta might not get as cold as it does in some places further north, but we definitely flirted with freezing temperatures at times. This seemed to be one of the colder weeks of the year, as the biting air nipped around me.

I immediately ducked back into the warm bar and snagged one of the many coats and jackets left hanging on the hooks along the back wall. Customers constantly forgot their things after a night of drinking, and instead of getting rid of them, we left a collection hanging for anyone who might need something warm when they ventured out onto our extensive back deck. People were always thankful when they could bundle up and make their way down to one of the many firepits along the river.

The black coat I grabbed was puffy and modern and smelled lightly of cardamom and ginger. I zipped it up as I made my way down the steps of the upper and lower decks and down to the clear back expanse of our property.

The Chattahoochee River glittered ahead of me, and I rushed to the path that disappeared in the trees running alongside the water. The Gate was just downriver of the Knoll, and the woodchip-covered path cut through towering pines, oaks, and sycamore trees, hiding the Gate from view, even in the dead of winter.

Within a few hundred yards, though, the bare path gave way to an empty expanse that was familiar and welcoming. A little under fifty yards, the clearing extended from the edge of the trees down to the river, and despite the cold, the moss here was lush and green. I wasn't entirely sure whether the verdant ground here was a testament to mild Georgia winters, or it was a factor of proximity to the Gate and exposure to magic year-round.

The Gate Between Worlds connected the Iron Realm, Atlanta specifically, directly to Fairy, the Eternal Realm. It was a portal that allowed for the fae to cross between the human world and our home world as easily as walking between rooms.

Well, maybe not quite as easily as that. After all, it took a blood sacrifice to activate the Gate. No one had to die, but blood did have to be offered up to open the Gate. Blood and magic, preferably willingly given, to wake the magic and bridge the divide between worlds.

Mikka was offering up her own magic. She had a knife pressed to her forearm and was just drawing the blade across her olive skin, watching as the crimson blood welled up. She stared at it for a moment, her face in repose. Then she dragged the tip of the knife back through the flow, coating it, before she stepped up to the Gate itself.

The Gate wasn't overly large or ostentatious. It wasn't carved of marble or adorned with jewels. It stood simply, a crude arch made of well-worn riverstones that seemed to stand without mortar or cement. Three people could walk through it side-by-side comfortably, four if they were friendly. Nothing indicated the monument as anything important.

But as Mikka pressed her blood-laden knife and offered up the magic it contained, her drake magic, the Gate came to life. Sigils carved along the inside of the arch glowed as they drank in Mikka's offering and began to open the way.

As she stepped back, the space inside the arch shimmered with a glow that reminded me of an opal's fire. It was prismatic, reflecting and refracting light, and it had a purple tinge, flowing down from the transverse of the arch over the empty space between, until it was clear that something wholly other stretched there now.

The taste of it consumed me for a moment, and I lost touch with where and who I was. It was verdant and lively, herbaceous and slightly piney, like a floral gin with a shot of wheat grass and adrenaline. Just the taste of it made me feel like I had been sleeping up until this moment, and now, now I was alive.

And so was she. The Gate whispered to me in a thousand voices at once. There was a constant flow of voices, of flavors, of feelings as she connected to me, embraced me, welcomed me. I couldn't parse it all as so much flowed into me. The unfiltered, unceasing magic, the unrelenting affection, the unwavering recognition. Here, now, I was seen. Really seen.

"Hello," I whispered to her.

"Hey, Shiv," Mikka replied, not realizing I had not been speaking to her.

It took me several moments to blink away the whispers of the Gate and find my way back to the real world. Mikka was watching me carefully when I did, and I wasn't sure if she'd been waiting five seconds or five minutes.

"You didn't have to come check on me." She wiped her knife clean with a black bar towel she'd brought with her and slipped it into its sheath clipped onto her jeans. "I'm still just as much a Gate Keeper, even if I have to do things the old-fashioned way." She then took the towel and held it just below the shallow cut she'd made, to catch the blood that still actively flowed from her arm. It would likely be healed within the day, without intervention.

Or I could do something to speed things along.

"May I?" I said, as I reached for Mikka's arm and waited. She looked at me strangely, then slowly lifted her arm up, exposing the cut toward me.

I placed my hand over it and reached out to taste the verdant green flavor of the Gate. The taste danced over my tongue playfully, filling me with that alive feeling again. I closed my eyes to focus, and reached out for Mikka's magic, the peppery whiskey I knew so well.

Once I could hold both tastes in my mouth, I let my own magic bubble forth. The effervescent, citrus-sweet taste that reminded me of a French 75 came to the fore, and I chased after it as I opened my eyes to focus on Mikka's arm.

The cut was bare before me, and before I could question how I was doing what I was doing, I felt deep down what it would take to repair that wound. How the skin would stitch itself back together, how the cells would replenish, and the cut walls of the vein would mend. I'd done it a million times on myself, and I knew I could do it for Mikka.

She stared down in wonder as her wound seemed to disappear from her skin. No doubt, she would feel a prickle or light itch as her skin rapidly restitched and the blood beneath the surface rushed to provide white cells to replenish the oxygen it took. In seconds, it was like she'd never cut herself.

Mikka reclaimed her hand and flexed it, twisting her arm back and forth before looking at me with one eyebrow raised. "Another new trick?"

"Old trick," I clarified. "Just newly applied." I flexed my own hand as the tingle of Mikka's magic faded when I released my hold on her. The pulse of the Gate, though stayed present in my mouth and my chest.

"Why, though?" She said as she turned away and walked over to the stone bench that was set up a few feet away from the Gate's archway.

"Why not? I'm just trying to help." I followed and sat down beside her.

She pursed her lips and avoided looking at me. "The Gate stays open so long as the blood flows. With you cutting off my free blood flow, healing me, you just ensured that it's not my magic or my sacrifice that holds the Gate open. It's you and your new magic doing all the work."

I did know that. I had been a Keeper for thirty years. Of course, I knew that.

I just hadn't been thinking about that when I healed her.

At once, I realized then how arrogant what I'd done appeared. Here I'd been hoping to help my friend, to do something nice for her. And instead, I'd robbed her of her purpose out here, erased her sacrifice, and jumped in as the solution to a problem I'd created.

"I'm sorry," I said, genuinely contrite.

Mikka sighed. "I know you meant well, Siobhan. But you can't just swoop in and fix people. Sometimes you have to let them heal on their own time."

Whatever I was going to say in response—which let's be honest, would have been emotionally driven and too defensive—was cut off by a pair stepping through the Gate from the other side.

As Mikka had pointed out, it was my power holding open the Gate, and I could taste their magic before I saw them. One had a mix of light and airy cranberry, lemon, and oranges, a slight bite of ginger, and a hint of thyme. The other had a predominant note of cinnamon, and it spoke to me of strong spice. Cardamom, ginger, turmeric, and star anise all weaved together with a hint of vanilla.

I recognized that second flavor profile and was unsurprised to see Kiral, the monogamous consort of Lada, the Winter Queen of Romania walk through the Gate. He and I had met for the first time last summer, when Lada had arrived in Atlanta to seek out answers about her murdered subject.

Since our initial meeting, I had only encountered him a handful of times when he and Lada were present at Court with Bryony and I had to appear for interrogations about Talisa and Hannah's activities.

Kiral had always been in the background of those interrogations, just behind Lada, ready to offer support should Lada overtax herself and lose her grounding with her body in this realm. Other Queens I knew of would rely on an entire team of consorts and lovers to help when they suffered episodes of madness, but Lada only had Kiral. Her monogamy was a novelty in our culture.

If Lada was in town, as Rhys had warned me, it didn't surprise me that Kiral was close at hand.

He led a very tall, very handsome male sylph through the Gate, but they both stopped when they saw Mikka and I seated there to greet them.

Kiral narrowed his eyes at me. He obviously harbored just as much love for me as did his mistress. "Halfbreed."

And apparently, he harbored the exact same bigotry, so I returned his greeting in kind. "Fuckboy." I never was much one for deference.

The man behind Kiral stiffened, and he darted a glance at the Queen's consort, sure that I was about to be struck down for my belligerence. But Kiral merely snarled and turned his attention back to his colleague. "The Keepers here are solitary drones only. Pay them no mind."

With that, the pair swept past us. No doubt they would not be stopping in for a drink at the Knoll with the other solitary peasants. Kiral would likely have a car waiting to take them both to the palace where his Queen lodged with my Queen-wannabe sister.

"See you soon, sweetie," I called after them and was rewarded by a stumbled step, a stiffened shoulder, and hopefully a few ruffled figurative feathers. I didn't think Kiral had any actual plumage. Though with the sidhe, you never could tell. All sorts of fun races ran through our bloodlines.

Mikka laughed. "You don't have to always pick a fight with the Court fae."

"Says the reigning champ of punching up," I said as I poked her in the ribs. "I've had to step up my game lately, because someone has been falling down on the job. If you keep brooding, I might even have to start hitting on the maenads and lillin just to keep them coming around."

"Coming around? You did that on purpose."

"I would never." I laughed, and she joined me. It felt good to hear, even though it only lasted a few seconds before we fell into companionable silence again. "I've missed you," I said softly. "I'm really trying to not push you to talk or anything before you're ready, but I've really missed my best friend."

She sighed. "I know. I'm sorry." But she didn't elaborate, and I didn't push her to open up any further. As she had said, she needed to heal at her own pace.

Still, that didn't mean we had to sit in silence.

"There is something I need to ask about," I said after a respectful few moments had passed.

"Hmm," she said, not looking up from the nails she had taken to cleaning with the tip of her knife.

"Leland said something about Baerd."

Mikka stiffened beside me, and she slowly lowered the knife. "Yeah." She knew already what I was about to say.

"About talking to Hannah recently."

"Yeah," she said, more slowly.

I faced her directly. "Meeks, Hannah is being held prisoner at your place. She is supposed to be isolated, for her safety and for everyone else's. You promised Argus and myself that you and Varon would hold her in solitude until we could be assured of her fair treatment by the Courts when we turn her over."

"Yes."

"But you're letting her entertain visitors? Not just any visitors, either. Fair Folk? Baerd? You do remember she tried to kill him."

She finally looked me in the eye. "And you."

"And me!" I was getting frustrated by her utter lack of emotion. "Why aren't you taking this seriously, Mikka? She is a killer. She sacrificed friends of ours, members of the Court, and you're right. She would have killed me, all in a quest to gain magic of her own. And you're just letting her have playdates?"

She was silent for a moment. "You could have killed her. Why didn't you?"

"Because I'm not a killer."

"And I'm not a jailer." She stood then and peered down at me, anger simmering just behind her fiery eyes. "I didn't ask to be the one responsible for her, but I did what was required of me. I wasn't asked to be cruel to her, nor was I asked to punish her for what she did. That's not up to me."

"It's not up to me either," I protested.

"Perhaps. Things have changed now, though, haven't they?"

"What are you saying?"

"I'm saying that you've put me in an awful position. You've got all this new power. People are looking to you for answers, and you're refusing to do anything with it, while pushing off the real work to everyone else." Her shoulders lifted and fell in frustration. "I know you didn't ask for any of this, but neither did I."

"All we've asked is for you to keep her at your house."

"Exactly. That's all you've asked, Siobhan. Whatever she did, she's still a person, and she's living in my home. I'm not going to refuse to talk to her when I deliver her meals, and I'm not going to turn away anyone who wants to offer her a little companionship when she wants it. I'm not a monster."

"I know you're not—" I started to stand, but she put out a hand to stop me.

"I'm not finished. I know you said you want to stay out of the politics of what happened. That you want to be neutral when it comes to the Courts, the solitary, and the Fair Folk. But Hannah has said some things that have made me think. She isn't all wrong. Yes, she was wrong about what she did, how she went about what she did. I don't excuse what happened. But she's not as bad as you think."

"I know—"

"And maybe if you got over this delusion that you can be this island of calm in the middle of the tempest brewing around you, maybe you might actually do some good for this community you insist is yours to serve. Maybe if you opened your ears and listened to more of the people who are willing to risk their own peace, you might learn how to stop a war."

With that, she turned on her heel and walked away, leaving me alone with the Gate and entirely too much to think about.

CHAPTER SEVEN

Getting to Court was only mildly painful at eleven on a Thursday morning after a night of very little sleep. The ghillie dhu that cursed I-285 to perpetual traffic were diurnal and were usually taking their midmorning nap around noon. So, I only hit two major slowdowns on the twelve-lane highway and was able to exit off Riverside Drive with only one close call as a truck driver on his cellphone narrowly missed merging into me.

As Atlanta driving went, it was positively uneventful.

I took my time easing down the residential street full of multi-million-dollar mansions. Towering Greek Revival homes were set far back on sprawling lawns, along with some Neoclassical, French Provincials, and even a cottage style house that no one would ever describe as cozy or homey. I continued until I came to a particularly garish Mediterranean-style home with imported Italian stone, a red tile roof, and more arches, balconies, and heavy wooden shutters than any one house could need.

The Gothic wrought-iron fence loomed over my eight-year-old Honda Civic as I pulled up to the electronic security box. I tapped in the code and waited for security to confirm my identity.

The gate almost immediately began to creak open, splitting down the middle with a heavy rumble. I coaxed my car along the polished stone path past the main house with its ostentatious fountain. I avoided looking at that monstrosity directly. It's a rare person who enjoys seeing their mother's nude form immortalized in marble and spouting water from her breasts and hungry, upturned mouth, and I was not the exception. I kept my eyes forward and navigated around the drive, past the two-story carriage house, and angled toward the back corner of the property.

The same Chattahoochee River that wound along the edge of the Greenwood Knoll's banks skirted the castle grounds, flowing downstream to the royal palace. As I navigated the vast acreage, the polished stone gave way to small pebbles. I passed a series of manicured gardens full of boxwoods and plants that were not native to the South, before the drive ended in a bank of pines and oaks with a narrow path between them. Branches reached out, almost scratching along my car as I squeezed between and headed straight for a thick line of oaks ahead of me.

Instead of slowing down, I pressed down on my gas pedal and flung myself and car toward the wall of trees. The moment my front bumper met the trunks, the glamour disappeared, and I passed easily through the back entrance to the Atlanta Summer palace.

The drive was once again smooth and open as I navigated over an immense expanse of lawn to circle the back half of the hidden property. It was just as immense as you would imagine for a Queen's home, with red brick and pristine white trim, looking like Kensington palace had been transported to the edge of Atlanta. Large decks and balconies spanned the length of the building on multiple levels down to the oasis of the pool. At night, the grotto was lit up like a stage show, and it was where most social events happened.

In the morning light, the sun glinted along the roof of the detached solarium off the west wing, and the gardens sprawled all the way down to the river. Though the landscaping was mostly dormant for the winter, there was still plenty of greenery. Come spring, this place would be covered in lilac, honeysuckle, daffodils, and hyacinths, but for in the winter cold, it held a sleepy potential. Ferns, grasses, and native plants curled around the paths and pools as Mother's many private lagoons steamed with their artificial heat.

I pulled up to a detached building on the east side of the palace, which I refused to call the garage. It was practically a warehouse with room for over two dozen cars, including my mother's Lamborghinis, a handful of electric vehicles, and my sister's growing collection of vintage Corvettes. I made sure to park my battered Honda directly out front, showing off the missing hubcap on the rear driver's side.

Climbing out, I saw Magdalene herself already making her way from the main house toward me. That was unusual. Mags was Mother's personal valet, and while she did personally welcome most important guests and family who came to visit, she didn't often come down to the driveway to do it.

She didn't rush, just walked steadily toward me as I approached the back of the palace. As soon as she was close enough, she bobbed a small curtsy with her head pointed down. "Siobhan, welcome back, Your Highness."

"Hi, Mags," I ignored her courtesies and opened my arms for a hug.

She smiled and accepted, hugging me warmly. Magdalene was a small blond woman who appeared only twenty-something but was over four hundred, and had raised my grandmother, mother, and me and my siblings. I might have a good six inches of height on her, but being in her arms made me feel like a child, protected and secure.

I held on to her for several beats before releasing and looking past her up at the palace. "I'm guessing you're supposed to stop me out here and prevent me from breaching the house's new and enhanced wards?"

"Her Highness and Her Majesty are expecting you in the solarium for a light brunch," Mags said smoothly, tacitly agreeing to my assessment but refusing to cast negative light on her employers. Her smile did quirk toward wry, though, so I knew that no matter how exactly she would follow the wishes and whims of my sister, she might not personally approve of every choice made.

"Thank you, Mags." I reached out and took her hand to give it a squeeze. I appreciated that she was put in a tight situation where my family was concerned. But given the fact that she had served over four generations of Queens in my line, I also knew that it was nothing new and nothing she couldn't handle.

"I'll escort you there," she said, beginning to walk and expecting me to fall in step beside her.

Naturally, I did so, not wanting to give her any grief, and knowing full well that none of this was her fault. But that didn't mean I would keep my mouth shut.

"I'm not even allowed up at the house now? Is that spearheaded by the frost queen or does it come from Bry?"

Mags didn't slow her gait. I knew she couldn't answer my questions, so I just kept talking.

"I wonder, is it really warded against me, or is everyone just on notice to deny me access? If I rushed the house, would I be tackled or zapped into the river? Or just trapped as the gardens seize me and turn me into the latest topiary? I've seen nymphs do that at the Knoll. It was really impressive. And since I've no interest in being a permanent fixture at the Court, I'd love to know what would happen. Would you have to stop me if I just ran toward the back door?"

She sighed as I paused my rambling and spoke patiently. "If you cross the threshold, your feet will freeze in place, until someone can come remove you from the grounds."

"Freeze, huh? So it is Lada's doing. I had a feeling. The Ice Queen is becoming quite the fixture around here, isn't she? Are she and Bryony officially an item, or is that still just hearsay?"

Mags returned to ignoring me, as she and I walked the long way, skirting the far end of the grotto. Most of the water was hidden by the oversized leaves of lush hostas, elephant ears, banana plants, and monsteras. Still, steam rose from the heated waters, giving the place the air of a transplanted rainforest. It took only a small amount of magical energy to warm the water but given Mother's erratic disposition of the past few years, new technology had been brought in to heat the pools more reliably.

Beyond the alfresco sauna, we stepped onto a path of flat gray stones bordered by dormant lavender and rosemary plants. The way was mutedly fragrant, but the scents did nothing to calm me as the solarium loomed up ahead.

The building was just off the west wing of the house and made entirely of glass and delicate green iron crafted in an art deco style. Filled with rare plants gifted to our family over the years, it was part greenhouse and part entertainment space. The solarium was large and open enough to host a mid-sized banquet or wedding but was often used for more intimate gatherings. On more than one occasion, Mother filled the place with couches and beds and cushions while silks hung from the ceiling, creating a maze of shifting alcoves and secret chambers for not-so-quiet and not-so-intimate encounters.

Thankfully, there were no silks in sight as Magdalene opened the door. The space was mostly empty aside from a white-clothed round table set for three, beside which stood two regal women.

Bryony Aislin Illythia was tall, toned, and lithe. She had honey fair skin and shining wheat blond hair swept back from her face with golden combs and then left to fall about her shoulders in carefully sculpted waves. She wore a flowing cotton dress of goldenrod with long sleeves and tiny printed purple flowers that fell just above her ankles. The ruffles and gathers gave it a prairie feel, but the way she held herself showed the casual clothing was just a costume.

The other woman wasn't even attempting to be anything other than what she was. Lada Casimira was much smaller than my sister but had the presence of someone ten feet tall. Her hair was thick chestnut brown, tied back at the nape and falling down her back. Her skin was pale as new snow, but her cheeks dewy, her lips soft pink, and eyes as black as death. She looked for all the world like a porcelain doll, delicate and precious and fragile. She had eschewed the casual dress code, opting instead for a charcoal pantsuit with some sort of metallic thread that made her glimmer like a threat.

Standing together they were gold and silver, the two rich tones of my demise.

Mags closed the door behind me, and with the snick as it pulled shut, I was alone with the two most dangerous people I'd ever known.

"Siobhan," Bryony said brightly, as if my arrival was a pleasant surprise and not the result of her summons and the underlying threat that denying her carried. "I've missed you."

She moved to me with grace, sweeping me into a hug that felt practiced and fake. As I raised my arms to awkwardly return her embrace, I wondered briefly who she was performing for. There was no one else in the room, and I was sure Lada was aware of my strained relationship with my baby sister.

"Did you miss me, too?" I said over her shoulder, watching as Lada lifted a glass of champagne from a side table and rolled her eyes. Oh, yeah. Lada knew very well what an act this was.

"Please, have a seat. You're going to love brunch. Fokes in the kitchen has started poaching the eggs in red wine and foie gras and serves it with this fontina mushroom toast. It's amazing."

She pulled out her chair and gestured for me to take my own, without acknowledging Lada. The table was round, and the chairs were equidistant apart, so it didn't matter where we sat; there was no head of the table. "How Arthurian," I muttered as I pulled my chair out.

To her credit, Lada chuckled as she took her seat.

The moment each of us sank down, a trio of fae entered the solarium from three different doors. Each had her own bottle of champagne and carafe of orange juice, and they came up behind the left elbow of each of us at the table, pouring first a sampling of OJ into delicate stemware, then following with a generous pour of bubbles. As the foam from the champagne settled in our glasses, the servers stepped back a few steps and stood at attention, ready to refresh our glasses at the slightest signal.

I knew we were supposed to pretend they were invisible, but the awkward placement of only three of us at the table with our own personal attendants made it utterly impossible. As my brunch companions each took a sip of their drinks, all I could see was the servants. I struggled not to turn around and dismiss my attendant so I could enjoy breakfast and the inevitably awkward confrontation without witnesses.

I was entirely too out of practice with this royalty thing.

No sooner had our stemware touched the silk tablecloth, than the doors opened and three more servers entered with our food. Our empty chargers were removed and replaced with plates full of gorgeous poached eggs on wilted greens, punctuated with golden toast points. Small plates of sausage links, and bowls of raspberries and pomegranate arils were placed opposite our golden mimosas, and I had to lean back as my server shook a napkin loose and draped it into my lap.

The food servers left the solarium, but the drink servers remained.

"As much as I'm probably going to regret this," I began. "Can we dismiss the witnesses?"

Bryony's gaze narrowed, but Lada suppressed a grin. We all knew that the servers were there to keep us from killing each other, and it was beyond gauche for me to point that out. But having chaperones wasn't really helping us. If anything was to come out of this meeting, we couldn't have limitations on what was said or done.

And frankly, if Lada wanted to kill me, we all knew that witnesses wouldn't stop her.

"Yes, please," Lada said.

It was Bryony's turn to roll her eyes. "Leave the bottles on the table," she said, addressing the staff around the table. "And if we've not departed in half an hour or called for blood clean-up, bring us another round."

A bottle of bubbles for each of us, every thirty minutes? If that didn't set the tone for how badly my sister saw this going, I don't know what would. I gulped back half my glass and let my server replenish me before she made a hasty and welcome retreat.

Suddenly, there was nothing but delicious gourmet brunch, insanely expensive cocktails, and enough tension in the air to strangle any one of us like a garrote if it turned its attention our way.

Lada carefully cut a piece of her poached egg, spooned it onto her toast, and took a bite while Bryony and I watched each other warily.

"So, I guess I should ask," I began, before Lada made a sudden gesture and sharp noise.

She chewed and swallowed, before raising her gaze to us both. "We are not starting that yet. I'm not going to let good food go to waste while we sour each other's stomachs with talk of our differences." Her eastern European accent was strong as she lectured us. "If you cannot find a civilized and neutral topic to discuss before we finish our foods, then I am content to eat in silence. I encourage you to do the same."

She returned her attention to her food.

I bit my lip as I looked to my sister, who stared back at me. Then I shrugged and began to dig into the food. It really was delicious. The eggs had a rich creaminess that was balanced by the earthiness of the mushroom toast. An involuntary moan escaped my lips as the flavors melted on my tongue.

"Told you," Bryony teased, as she took a bite of her own. "Fokes is a genius."

"Can I send Meara by to learn this recipe?" I asked. "She has been thinking of building a brunch menu at the Knoll, and she would love this."

"I'll ask. Fokes is territorial, you know."

"I understand why." I took another few bites and the sausage links on the side added just the right amount of umami salty complement to the dish. "He really understands food. I'm not saying I'm up for coming over for brunch every week—"

"Oh, Mab forbid," Bryony interrupted.

"Because Meara would kill me for disloyalty," I continued. "But if I get a craving for this, I might just have to show up on your doorstep once in a while…" I punctuated my thought with another forkful of toast and egg that engulfed my tongue with flavor.

"That sounds like a threat," Lada said, not looking up from her food.

"Only because you don't like me," I said with my brightest smile.

"Only," she replied forcefully, "because I do not trust you."

"And that's only because you are a bigot. You didn't trust me from the moment you met me, because I'm half human."

"Of course," she said, reaching for her mimosa. "The word of a half breed is half broken already."

"Hey, hey, easy." Bryony spoke before I could throw my drink in her face. Which was probably ideal, because I'm pretty sure Lada could freeze the blood in my veins before my drink had a chance to soil her pretty silk pantsuit. "What happened to spoiling brunch?"

Lada gestured to her empty plate. "I have finished. Shall we get to business?"

As much as it pained me, I pushed aside the last three bites of my own breakfast. Game on.

CHAPTER EIGHT

Alas, Lada and I could only sit there and watch as Bryony ignored our attempts to get things started. The would-be Queen carefully focused on her mushroom toast. She cut a small piece of bread, scooped up the exact amount of mushrooms and deliberately avoided our gazes as she brought the food to her mouth, clearly enjoying the bite. The next bite involved the last of the foie gras, painstakingly scooped up with the tip of her knife and spread over the last remaining crust of bread.

Finally, when her point was made abundantly clear, Bryony settled her silverware over the last remnants of her food and reached for a sip of her drink with one hand and rang a bell beside her plate with the other.

In an instant, the three table attendants came to claim our plates, remove any extra food, top off our drinks, and immediately retreat. I couldn't blame them for their haste; the tension in the room was explosive. From Bryony's hot anger and Lada's cold resentment, I was half convinced a tornado would begin swirling in a few moments.

"So what happens when you two have a lover's spat? Does a thunderstorm break out?"

Lada frowned and looked at Bryony, who shook her head in confusion.

"Oh come on," I said, unable to contain myself. I'd already pissed off both queens this morning. Surely a little extra needling wouldn't hurt me, right?

Yeah, yeah. I know.

Still, I barreled forward. "Everyone in the Court is talking about it. Lada has spent more time here than in her home court in Romania, lately. If y'all aren't keeping each other warm through the winter, what are you even doing with each other?"

Exasperated, Bryony groaned as Lada started to turn pink.

"I have a consort," Lada protested and stood up, her hands on the table as she glared down at me.

"As do many Queens," I said, leaning back in my chair and sipping at my mimosa. "Many consorts for many queens. That's how you get new queens. I know biology. Do you?"

Bryony pursed her lips and let out a noise that could have been interpreted as a warning growl if one were feeling generous. I wasn't.

"My sister can't help you get an heir, but she can certainly thaw relations between our Courts. It's a great diplomatic move, really, romancing a future Summer Queen. But honestly, it's overkill, Lada. It's been done before. Winter already claimed our brother."

Apparently mentioning Dariel was one step too far. "That's enough, Siobhan." Bryony snapped.

"It's funny," I continued, fully ignoring her. "You two are the most prudish royals I've ever known. No public displays. No spats. No nudity. Might it actually be love between you two?"

"Or maybe some of us are mature enough to foster friendships and alliances across Courts without fucking each other." Bryony said. "Now will you stop acting like a child and stop trying to start a fight?" She turned to Lada. "And will you stop cracking my foundation and remember that my sister is likely to be defensive when called to Court?"

I looked below the table to find that the stone floor beneath Lada's feet had frosted over and was showing signs of hairline cracks.

"She is not defensive," Lada said matter-of-factly as she shrugged off the freeze that had settled around her. "She is in open defiance. As she has been from the beginning."

"You can't defy someone who has no authority over you," I said smoothly eying the tiny brunette. "This Court has no claim on me and hasn't for many decades. Any time I come here, it's out of the goodness of my heart. Even if you do try to hide my visit in the solarium like some dirty secret."

"Nothing you do is secret, *sister*," Bryony said, tipping champagne into my glass. Apparently, we'd done away with watering down our drinks with orange juice. "That's why you're here."

"Is Rhys reporting on me, after all?" I huffed but accepted the bubbly. It was dry and sparkling, and way too expensive to turn down.

"Actually, your lover is quite tight-lipped when it comes to you. It's caused some tensions with their sentry partners who keep asking for gossip. But no. Your basilisk is quite loyal."

That warmed me. I suppose that Bryony could have been lying in order to keep Rhys in my bed and close enough to keep an eye on me, but it didn't feel that way. Rhys had every opportunity to learn everything about me and inform on me to their employer and the Court. But they never asked for more than I volunteered, never expected more of me than I was willing to give, and apparently, never betrayed me to those who might mean me harm. After decades in the Atlanta Summer Court, followed by some of the worst possible romantic relationships, it was comforting to think I might have finally taken up with someone worth a damn.

"You're here," Bryony continued, "because of your new connection to the Greenwood Gate. You have been consistently breaching it outside of normal times, opening the path in a way some might think excessive."

"'Breaching' is quite the word choice. It's my duty to open the Gate every day. And there's no law that dictates when a Keeper can access the Ways. Dawn and dusk openings are customary, but we can open it any time we have someone who needs to make a crossing. Or just because."

Lada glared. "You have been going at it far more than that. All day you are opening the ways, letting in Fairy. You are playing with something you do not understand."

I snorted into my drink. "I've kept the Gate for nearly fifty years. I'm pretty comfortable with the process."

"Yet the process has changed. *You* changed it. Or do you deny that you do not sacrifice blood or magic to the Gate? That you open it carelessly without thought to what effects your new ability might have."

I bit my tongue on an angry retort as Lada barreled forward. "And there is question of why? Do you derive more power this way? Do you siphon from the Gate's magic as you siphon from other fae? Or are you channeling magic to them?"

"What are you talking about?"

Bryony held a hand up to her friend but kept her eyes trained on me. She lifted her glass of champagne halfway to her mouth but didn't bring it any closer. "Answer the question, Siobhan. Are you able to serve as a conduit for your people?"

I gaped at her for a moment, back straight, lips pursed, then back to Lada who clutched her champagne flute with white knuckles. They didn't take their eyes off me, watching my every movement. It wasn't just about getting answers, I realized. They were *scared* of me. Of what they thought I could do.

It made sense. The only time they had seen my magic up close was in the dueling ring, when I'd nearly killed Lada. But that had been an accident. Mostly.

Lada had challenged me to a duel when she believed that I was connected to the murders that rocked our community. I had refused, because at the time I had no active magic with which to fight her, and Mikka had stepped in to fight as my proxy. When Lada nearly killed my best friend in the dueling circle, I had tapped into a power I didn't know I possessed, broke through the ancient magic that protected the circle, and nearly stripped Lada of her own magic to save Mikka.

At the time, I hadn't known what I was doing, and since I was even now just learning how to wield my newfound powers, I wasn't sure I could offer Lada many assurances that I would never accidentally almost kill her again.

Granted, if I had full control of my powers, I might still use them against her. The bitch rubbed me the wrong way.

But it was sobering to know that much of her current hostility was due to fear. Of me.

"No, sis. I don't channel any extra magic to anyone. If I open the Gate, they can access the magic themselves. That's true no matter how or how many times I open it. But they're not getting it through me. I'm not a conduit."

"Lies," Lada screeched as she shot to her feet, her chair falling behind her. "It has been seen. You are a conduit. You speak with others' voices. You access their minds. Their secrets."

"Speak with their—" I stopped. "You heard about the baby shower."

"Of course, we heard about the baby shower, Siobhan," Bryony said. "And the speeches made."

I gritted my teeth, thinking of who in my bar had been a guest for the shower and who had been a spy for the Summer Court.

"This is about the Fair Folk. I have nothing to do with any of that," I said quickly. "I want nothing to do with your political spats. My loyalty is to this city and its people alone. Even if there are plenty of people in this town who would be happy to stand up against your overbearing Court, I'm not a part of it. Every person that comes into the Knoll and asks about joining the Fair Folk, I tell them the same thing. I'm not a part of that, and they won't find it in my pub. I just want to live in peace, away from all your political nonsense."

"Cut out her lying tongue," Lada spat, standing to lean over the table as much as her tiny size would allow. The air chilled as her anger rose, and her breath froze in the air. "Or I will do it. She supports the Fair Folk. There is blood on her hands."

"What blood?" I yelled back, unable to hold back anymore as I took to my feet. It was satisfying that I towered over the tiny queen, and she had to lift her head to look at me. "There's no threat from them anymore. Talisa is dead. Hannah is locked away."

"Where?!" Lada slammed her hands on the table, knocking her

glass over on the table, champagne spreading over the white table-cloth. "You have harbored your traitor human all this time. Protected her from justice. And now your people have killed again."

I stilled at that. "What?"

Bryony closed her eyes and pinched the bridge of her nose. "Sit down. Both of you."

She waited patiently while we glared, unwilling to be the first who sat.

"Now." She didn't have to raise her voice. Even without a Queen's power, Bryony was still full of authority, and we felt the thrum of her power through our veins. This was her Court, her home.

We took our seats, refusing to take our eyes off each other.

"What did she mean about blood, Bry?" I asked. "What happened?"

Bryony held out an open palm to Lada, who reached into her blazer's inside pocket to pull out a collection of folded papers. Lada's jaw clenched as she passed the papers to Bryony, who slowly unfolded and shifted them until she found the ones she wanted. She smoothed the crease on the first and laid it on the table in front of me.

It was a printed photograph. Of a body.

There was too much familiar about the body. Eyes open and devoid of magic, throat slit. She was beautiful even in death. Slight and delicate, she looked like a strong breeze might pick her up and spin her through the air. A sylph would be my guess. Her hair, long and white, lay lifeless around her pale face; pale blue eyes that should swirl with a tempest of clouds and mist and dew were dead stones of lapis.

"Oriana was royal," Bryony said. "A sidhe of Mab's line, like us. She was the second daughter of the Queen Adrona, a Winter Queen and a cousin of Lada's. She was found dumped at the foot of the Greenwood Gate. Not here in Atlanta, but on the Fairy side, so technically the Whitewood side. And there was a note."

Bryony unfolded the other piece of paper, with presumably a copy of the note that was left at Oriana's body.

With Iron resolve and Eternal fidelity
The Fair Folk pledge solidarity

Freedom for all, Power to the least

The copy of the note Bryony handed me was in black and white, but I could see that it was crudely painted by hand with a thick liquid. Given the body with a slit throat, I assumed it was written in her blood.

Bryony continued to explain. "This is not the only royal who has turned up this way, either. As far as we can tell this is the third fae of the Winter Court who has been killed. Each royal has been discovered in Fairy, near the Whitewood Gate, drained of blood, and with credit taken by the Fair Folk with an identical note."

"That's awful," I said sincerely. After everything that happened last summer, the dead fae and the fear that seized our community, I couldn't imagine anyone wanting to recreate that. But if it was taking part across the Gate in Fairy, I wasn't sure what they wanted me to do about it. "I am sure the Winter Court is doing all they can to get to the bottom of this."

Beside me, Lada pursed her lips with a sour expression on her face.

Bryony patted her friend's hand. "The other Court is not moving as swiftly as some would like." My sister was ever diplomatic.

"They are Mab-cursed cowards." Lada was very much less so. "Winter lock themselves down, hide away, and insist nothing is happening. They will not investigate, and they have forbidden action from each of their Queens, even though it has touched three different Courts." Deflated and discouraged, Lada looked younger and more helpless than any time I have seen her.

Bryony reached out a hand and placed it over Lada's on the table. She gave it a squeeze and offered an encouraging smile. "We'll get to the bottom of it. You'll be safe."

Looking between them, at the desperate hope in Lada's eyes and the calm assurance in Bryony's, I saw a connection that was stronger and more certain than any that I've ever had with my sister.

A twinge tugged in my chest, but I dismissed it. Bryony and I might be sisters, but we had never been family in that way.

"So," I interrupted their moment. "You two are taking care of this yourselves. Without the larger Courts."

"In so many words," Bryony admitted.

That was risky. A Summer heir and a Winter Queen working together was rare enough. Working to address a problem the Winter Court had already forbidden action on was worse. As far as I knew, the Winter Court had a much stricter hierarchy than the loose-reined Summer Court. Any action that undermined their tight grip of control was dealt with swiftly and surely.

"And you came to me, why? I barely know anyone in the Winter Court."

"We are demanding you turn over your criminal friends in the Fair Folk so we can stop these monsters and end their campaign of terror," Lada said. "You can start by handing over the human Hannah."

"I'm not giving you someone just so you can kill them." I spat back at her.

Bryony held up her hand to stop Lada from reacting. I could tell her patience was wearing thin. "We are asking for your help, Siobhan. Oriana was just the latest victim, but by all indications, she will not be the last. I understand the solitary and the Fair Folk have grievances at our Court, but there are better ways to address their concerns than murder. This isn't even a grab for power. They're acting as terrorists, and that will not be tolerated."

"If they're even the ones responsible," I said. "All you seem to be going on is a note that could be written by anyone. It could just as easily be a copycat using the Fair Folk as a convenient scapegoat."

Bryony nodded grimly, pouring herself another small measure of champagne. She offered it to Lada who shook her head. "That is something we have considered," she admitted. "But at this point, we have no other leads."

She sipped her drink slowly and watched me steadily, searching my eyes. Then she sighed. Clearly, she had not found what she was seeking. "You're our only avenue of hope, Siobhan. You know enough people that we suspect are connected with the Fair Folk. You and Argus." She took a deep breath. "I understand your desire to stay out of politics, but you literally work at the crossroads. You see and speak to almost everyone that comes into and out of Atlanta. You can be the key to ending threats to our city before they start."

My stomach dropped away. I knew what Bryony was trying to do. She wasn't trying to be cruel, but she was asking me to inform on the people who came to my bar to escape the pressures of her Court. They came there to be free, to be part of a community that owned themselves and controlled their own futures. She was trying to protect her people by asking me to betray mine.

My sister continued. "If you will not turn Hannah over to us for questioning," she paused and waited for me to shake my head no. "Then we have to rely on you to get answers. Please, sister. I do not want a repeat of last summer, and I worry things will get worse before they get better. We need answers, and we need them soon."

As much as it pained me to admit, I knew she was right. Even if the Fair Folk ultimately disavowed their actions, no one could deny their radicalization in the group. The movement had inspired their crimes. Pretending that the Fair Folk had nothing to do with this murder would be foolish. They were connected, even if not directly culpable.

And I couldn't ignore that a considerable number of people at the Knoll were members of the rebel group. They weren't even hiding it, and unless I wanted to cover my eyes and stick my fingers in my ears until a war broke out around me, I had to face that.

Besides, if there was another threat to the fae, even if it originated across the realms, there was every chance it could spill over into my backyard. That made it my responsibility. I might not serve the Courts, but I had a duty to protect my own people.

If that meant helping Bryony and her psychotic BFF, so be it.

"We are willing to compensate you quite generously, if that helps," Bryony added, unnecessarily at this point. But I wasn't about to let her know that.

I passed Bryony my glass and waved for her to fill it up. Let the would-be-Queen grovel a bit more. She could afford it.

"Let's talk terms."

CHAPTER NINE

Over the next hour, Bryony and I hashed out the details of our arrangement.

Lada at one point lost her temper and began screaming that I should be locked up until I could prove that I wasn't directly involved with the killings, despite my not having crossed through the Gate in months.

She murdered quite a few plants with her frostbite and had begun speaking of dead babies and shriveled wombs as she paced back and forth around the perimeter of the solarium, channeling her subjects and speaking in new voices before Kiral, Lada's consort, came in to collect her.

When the door opened and Kiral came in, there was no one in the world for him but his Queen. I don't know if he saw Bryony or myself at all. He went straight to his queen and knelt beside her, taking her hand in his.

At that point, I'm not sure Lada was even aware of him. Her eyes were distant, and her voice low, speaking in a language or maybe even several languages I didn't understand. The temperature in the solarium had dropped dangerously low, and Bryony was doing all she could to keep us warm with a bubble of summer weather around the table.

Heedless of frostbite, Kiral reached for her hand. The moment he made contact, she seemed to collapse in on herself. One moment she was everywhere, unable to stay in one place or find her body. The next, she was laser-focused on her partner. She was present and there. With him.

"Forgive us," Kiral said, while Lada refused to take her eyes off her consort or break contact with his skin. "She has been too long in this wretched realm, and it wears on her. We will take our leave and return to Fairy, if granted."

Bryony nodded, and Kiral guided his Queen away.

With Lada removed, Bryony and I came to terms.

First, I agreed to stop opening the Gate indiscriminately throughout the day and recommit to the twice daily schedule. Bryony insisted that it had nothing to do with the fact that more magic was flowing to solitary fae, and everything to do with sticking to a consistent crossing schedule for inter-realm travel. I doubted her explanation but agreed that I would honor the dawn and dusk openings more consistently, instead of waking the Gate whenever she called to me. Given its effects on me, limiting my access to the Gate and her magic was probably a good choice in general.

Second, without informing on members of the organization directly, I would find out what I could about the Fair Folk's involvement with the recent deaths in Fairy. I would speak to Argus, who, while he was obviously part of the Fair Folk, also had a great deal of affection for my family. He and I would do what we could to get to the bottom of things and, if we could, prove the innocence of the Fair Folk in these matters. If we found any indication of involvement or knowledge about the murders, though, I would turn over the perpetrators to the Court's justice.

There would be no protecting those responsible, considering the high-profile nature of these killings. The victims were royal. The murders would face royal justice.

On that note, I would be able to keep Hannah safe for the time being. I assured Bryony that Hannah could not be involved as she was very much under house arrest in Mikka and Varon's basement apartment, and despite her visitors, was not able to leave. She had been warded in by the Grey Meranti, and there wasn't a fae alive who could break her enchantments.

However, if there was any indication Hannah was connected to this newest set of murders, she would be turned over immediately and without question. If anyone was connected or was able to provide information about the killings, I was to turn them over immediately.

And because there could be no good reason for killing someone, I agreed.

Granted, it was hard to say no, when she told me what she offered in return. For any information I could provide, Bryony would pay handsomely. She would not only help redirect a year's worth of Fairy wine and spirits to the Greenwood Knoll to fill out our cellar; she would also pay off ten years of the mortgage on my house in Marietta.

Further, Bryony would release Rhys from the demands that they report back to her on my changes in mood. I reminded Bry how poorly she'd reacted when she had discovered our mother had a similar arrangement with one of my sister's lovers back in the seventies. Bryony had delivered the snitch back to Mother Dearest in pieces over the course of several weeks. Through no fault of that poor man, who had after all only been following the edicts of his queen and enjoying the attentions of a very eager young princess, he had lost several fingers, toes, and other, er, appendages, before Bryony released him to regrow his precious parts. Thankfully, he had kappa lineage, and regeneration was a welcome—but long and painful—option.

I was not about to turn on Rhys like that, but I didn't like the uncomfortable position our situation placed them in. I wanted to enjoy my time with them without worrying about what I said in moments of vulnerability. Or in my less lucid moments. Though, if I wasn't accessing the Gate as much, it theoretically wouldn't be a problem in the future anyway.

Then there was the final term of our agreement. I took a deep breath and had to be honest with my sister. "I need some help that only you can give."

The tension in her jaw was evident as she pursed her lips and ground her teeth together. She nodded stiffly. She already knew what I was talking about.

I continued. "I don't think it's full madness, but it is getting worse. And it doesn't make any sense, but I'm dissociating more often these days."

She nodded again. "And it's only after accessing the Gate? Your new magic?"

My new magic. The magic that was my birthright as the daughter of a Queen. The power I had given up when I left the Court, dropped my allegiance to Summer and disconnected my magic from our mother. Magic I had no right to and could not fully explain.

"It shouldn't be happening at all," I said. "I'm not a Queen."

"And you won't be," she said, her face flushing slightly as she stared me down until I averted my eyes. "Mother's legacy passes to me. As you insisted."

"I'm sorry." My voice was as weak as my apology. "I don't want this either."

Bryony shook her head. "It's never mattered what you wanted. Or what I want." She took a deep breath, her shoulders rising and then settling, her chin held a little higher. "You're accessing the Gate's magic and experiencing the Queen's Madness."

I swallowed over the knot of fear that settled directly in the middle of my throat. I was hearing voices that belonged in other fae's heads. I was speaking with voices that weren't mine. I was separating from myself and unable to find my way back. "I don't know if it's the Madness," I started, but Bryony broke in.

"The symptoms are the same, though. Whether you're channeling magic to anyone or not doesn't seem to matter." She frowned. "It is strange. Typically, it is the channeling, the connection to the other fae that we've credited with causing the madness. Half of my training is in learning to quiet the voices of those who draw their magic through the conduit."

"But I'm not—"

She stopped me. "I know. You're not a conduit. You channel nothing to them. But you connect, right?"

I thought about what happened when I tasted other fae's magic. I could identify them each by their unique flavor signature. I could sometimes feel what they felt, use their magic, breach their innermost thoughts. I might not be able to push magic to them, but I was connected in a most intimate way. I nodded.

"Yes," my little sister nodded. "We should be able to help you."

"We?" I repeated.

"Mother and I," she said as if it were a matter of fact. She stood then, our meeting at an apparent end. "You will come back Saturday morning. At nine."

I cringed. "Can we make it later? Friday nights we don't close the Knoll until after three."

"Nine," she repeated as she stood up. She gestured to the door. I was being dismissed. "I trust you can find your way back to your car." Then without waiting for a response, she turned and left through the solarium door that led back to the house, and I was alone.

No guards, no Magdalene to escort me out. I briefly considered testing the wards on the house and trying to sneak in to check on Mother. If I was going to show up at practically the crack of dawn on a Saturday, maybe I should make sure she was in good enough shape to actually offer help.

On second thought, though, given Bryony's caginess, if I was going to be back here in a few days, I could always press my luck then. It was barely noon today, and I had already had my share of the stress of the Court. However Mother was, she would hold until the weekend.

I grabbed the last opened bottle of champagne and sipped from it as I navigated the cold grounds alone, crunching through the gardens and around the steaming pool with its many private lagoons. It was so quiet, I could hear water lapping at the smooth stone edges. The palace was typically more reserved in the winter, but seeing the place completely empty like this was disorienting. There was almost always some small gathering happening. Lower royals and courtiers would lounge by the pool, socialize on the patio, strategize and scheme on the balconies.

But I didn't see a soul as I made my way to the car.

Except one.

My shoulders fell away from my ears and a grin spread across my face as I saw Rhys leaning casually against my old Honda. They always had that effect on me, calming and exciting me at the same time. It helped that they were just so pretty to look at: a strong angular face with cheekbones that could cut you down to size and full lips that could point toward pouty if they weren't always pulled into knowing smirks and smiles. Their long dark hair was tied back at the nape of their neck, showing off a tight undercut, and I got a shiver imagining releasing that silky hair and running my fingers through it, before knotting it around my hand and directing those pouty lips exactly where I wanted them.

Naturally, they read all of that lust in my gaze from a distance and greeted me with a knowing chuckle. "Glad to see you in one piece." They opened their arms, and I slipped between them, lifting my chin to welcome a deep kiss. They darted the merest hint of their forked tongue against my lips and chuckled again as I moaned a little in appreciation.

"I'm guessing you're working," I said, knowing the answer. As much as Rhys loved their job as a Knight of the Atlanta Court, they only came onto the grounds of the palace when they were paid to be there. "Lucky you, I'm not even a security threat today." I preened a little at that, only to earn a swat on the ass.

"You and your sister together are always a security threat. Whenever you two have a meeting, Captain Lyris keeps her best water elementals around in case of fire."

I squeaked in indignation. "What? I couldn't call a single flame to my name until recently!"

"And that didn't stop you from lighting an entire suite on fire two years ago when Bryony accused you of stealing her leshy gardener away."

"Oh, yeah," I said guiltily. To be fair, that had been an accident. I had come as summoned to answer to my sister's belief that her favorite landscaper had defected from the Summer Court thanks to me. I had had nothing to do with the fact that Jaromir had become a regular at the Knoll, taken up with one of our local dryads, and decided the solitary life appealed to him.

Bryony had been furious, because it was at least the third member of the palace staff that had defected in the past five years. She accused me of putting something in their drinks and attempting a coup on her Court.

Then, instead of reminding her that I had no aims on her precious Summer Court, would never sit on the throne, and didn't want the responsibility, I may have pointed out that it wasn't even her Court yet. And I may have called her a wanna-be Oona with the abilities of an adolescent sprite on a sugar bender and the mentality of a mogwai during a rainstorm. At which point she screamed at me that I wouldn't be happy until I saw the entire fae monarchy toppled and as miserable as me and stormed off.

She'd slammed the door behind her so hard that she'd knocked over a bottle of firewhiskey that she'd presented as a peace offering at the beginning of our meeting. It had shattered on the floor and spilled the contents all over the floor, leaving only the single glass she'd poured resting on the table beside me. I'd done what any reasonable person would do and downed the contents of my glass so the whole thing wouldn't be a waste. Firewhiskey takes twenty years to distill, after all.

But I didn't finish every drop, and when I threw the glass to the hardwood in disgust and fled the palace, I'd apparently infused what was left with my anger. The moment I closed the door to the suite, every drop of firewhiskey on the floor ignited. The room had smoldered for fifteen minutes before anyone arrived to clean up the mess Bryony and I had left, and they'd had to replace the entirety of the room, the subfloors, and the plumbing and electricity in the walls.

"You've never needed magic to ignite the world, gorgeous," Rhys said, honeyed tongue ever at the ready.

"Ha ha," I said, snuggling into their embrace for a moment. Rhys only had a few inches on me, but with their broader frame, constant combat training, and lean muscles, I felt small and sheltered in their arms. As I was nearly 5'10" myself, I took full advantage of the feeling. "I don't know. Apparently, I'm a threat to queens of Summer and Winter alike."

Rhys's second chuckle was lower and more strained. "Unpredictable magic is understandably frightening. Though, I would be lying if I said I didn't appreciate how nervous you make her Winter majesty." They gave me a little squeeze before they put their hands on my shoulder and pushed me enough away to look me in the eyes. "She's demanded I make sure you are fully centered and grounded in your body before you leave."

"That's cute, after she's the one who fell apart in our meeting and had to be escorted out. Well, then," I waggled my eyebrows suggestively. "Unless the Court is assigning you as my official consort?" Their eyes went wide, and they pulled back enough that I knew the thought terrified them. Fair. Being an official consort entailed a lot more than just dating. Rhys would have to be on call to me any time I had a power imbalance. They'd be my permanent booty call.

It was a lot to ask.

Before Rhys could protest, I snuggled back into their arms. "Never mind, babe. Consider me grounded enough to leave under my own power." I then attempted to pull away.

They didn't let me get away with the dismissal, grabbing me by the elbow and stepping back again to consider me fully. "How did your meeting go? For real? You didn't taste either Bryony or Lada's powers during your meeting? No sampling? No connecting with them?"

I thought back to the meeting. Despite everything that happened, I didn't reach for my magic at all. Both my sister and the Winter Queen had used their powers during our meeting, and it had barely registered with me. I hadn't tasted the cloying vanilla of Bryony's magic or the caramel apple taste of Lada.

"Huh," I said, surprised I was realizing it for the first time. "I didn't. Do you think that's because of the wards they've set up? Or did I restrain myself?"

Rhys shrugged. "You're getting better about how you access your power. A lot of it is still unconscious, though. And given what happened at Mellie's party…" They let the thought trail off.

"Thank you, again." I reached up to grab their hand off my shoulder to squeeze their palm. "I don't know what would have happened if you hadn't been there."

They took a deep breath before returning my squeeze. "I wasn't sure it would work for a minute. You were pretty far gone." Their thick lips pursed into a line. "I hadn't seen it happen like that before." They swallowed but continued to avoid my gaze. "I've seen Queens in the throes before, but it's always been different with you."

My body flooded with a cold flush. After everything of this morning, I didn't want to hear any more about it, but I needed to know. If I was going to get any of this under control, I needed to know what happened when I lost track of my senses, when the magic seized me. Nothing would get better from ignoring this problem. "How so?" I asked, my voice barely a whisper.

Rhys grew thoughtful. "Well, Queens seem to turn inward." Rhys looked up at the castle. "When Illythia detaches, she appears to be listening to something inside of her. She doesn't see anything that's around her and channels the fae she's connected to. She speaks in their voices, one after another, and it all bottlenecks until she's not making sense or one of her consorts brings her back. Lada does the same." They stopped and frowned at me. "Their mind is loosed from their body, but it's still contained within."

"And that's not what happened with me?" I asked. I was impressed at how steady my voice sounded.

"No. It's not," they stopped and considered their words. "Siobhan, you were not contained. You were everywhere. I walked into that bar, and it was like you were everywhere. Instead of others coming through you, you were coming through them. I could see flashes of you through everyone's eyes, like they were still home, but you were popping in to peer out their windows. Then you would speak, and it would be their voice, stolen and pushed through your mouth."

I couldn't repress the shiver that passed through me. I had no memory of any of what they described. Whatever secrets I had unveiled, I didn't know them if I spoke them. I had consciously experienced everything to the end of Argus's speech. Then I had only known Rhys and their intimate touches in the upstairs office. Everything between those moments was a haze.

"What then?" I asked.

Rhys let a low rumbled grunt escape their mouth. "Well, people seemed to recognize what was happening. They were getting ready to flee before you turned your attention to them, and I had to do something. I had to trust to our agreement."

Our agreement. A few weeks ago, at the beginning of the new year Rhys and I had a sit down. I'd been dissociating more and more lately, losing track of time when I connected too deeply to the Gate or simply brushed against another fae's magic. I would get a taste of someone and would follow it, only to find myself several minutes later having no idea what happened.

My coworkers had noticed and had attempted to break me out of my dissociated state with little success. Mikka and Varon attempting not to burn me as they reminded me that I had a body and to return to it. During one Saturday night karaoke Varon had nearly introduced second-degree burns to my right arm before realizing that flame was not going to bring me back to myself.

It hadn't worked. Apparently, I seemed to retreat even further, hiding from the pain.

That was when Mikka remembered that consorts had been used to ground fairy queens in the throes of madness and kissed me in an attempt to bring me back before the next song.

I learned of all of this after. As far as I knew, I had been serving margaritas to a group of sylphs getting ready to sing Careless Whisper at the peak of karaoke before I woke up, an hour later, and the bar was getting ready to close.

That was when Argus suggested I ask Rhys to be on standby for future episodes. He calmly pointed out that Queens had been suffering dissociative episodes for centuries when they accessed their magic. As they had proved time and again, nothing was as effectual for bringing a girl back to her body as intimate contact. I needed something safe and consensual that connected me physically, emotionally, and intimately with my body. Something that made me want to come back to it, rather than retreat further.

Given we had been dating for several months by that point, Rhys was happy to take our casual and occasional hookups to a more serious place. And I was, too.

"I'm glad you were there," I said, pulling them close into a hug. "I don't know what I'd do without you right now."

They leaned into me and kissed the top of my head again, but there was something hesitant in the way they held me.

"What is it? Do I need to leave?"

"No," they started. "I mean, yes. You are supposed to, and I quote the good captain, 'vacate expeditiously.' But that's not it."

"Lyris can give me five more minutes with you, I'm sure." I said as I nestled in closer, wrapping my arms around their broad, strong torso and inhaled their unique sandalwood and cedar scent, with a faint undertone of cucumber. Their smell sometimes lingered on my sheets after they stayed the night, which happened far too infrequently.

"You can tell me," I said when Rhys remained quiet. "I promise I won't get upset."

They made a noise that was a cross both amused and skeptical. "Don't make promises." They gave me another soft kiss before they released me and took a step away. "I think you need to take another lover."

Of all the things I expected them to say, that wasn't it. "I what?"

"It was luck that I was there yesterday, Siobhan. Luck alone. I have responsibilities here at Court, and I can't always be there when you need help grounding. And your needs are becoming more frequent, not less. I know you have been trying to get a hold on your magic, but until you start actually getting trained to process what's happening—"

"I am," I interrupted. "Bryony agreed to help me. Along with Mother. This Saturday morning."

"Wonderful," they said. "I'll ask leave to be there to help. And I'm not going anywhere. I truly care about you, and I plan on sticking around for as long as you'll keep tolerating my presence. But mastering on your powers is going to take time. You're going to have more episodes like that. At work, or at home. If I'm not able to help you back to yourself when those happen, you need to have someone who is more present, or who can be called on in an emergency."

"Mikka and Varon—"

"Nearly burnt you to the bone trying to get you back last time."

I looked down at my right forearm where Varon had held me. When I had come to, I could smell the burnt flesh, see the skin that had flaked away, and not felt a thing. Even as I had regained my consciousness, my body had already been healing itself, protecting me from the pain, and nullifying any chance that shock or pain would work in the future.

But taking another lover?

As much as I teased Lada for her monogamy, I also wasn't keen on taking on a string of random lovers. Promiscuity and polyamorous relationships were common among my people. My mother's sexual proclivities were well known, and even if Bryony had resisted settling down with anyone, she kept things casual and fun with a number of members of Court.

But I'd always been a one partner at a time kind of girl.

I wasn't opposed to it ethically or even emotionally. I didn't have any hangups about multiple lovers or the idea that being with someone else would change the way I felt about Rhys. But I liked where things were now, with one person.

Plus, I had no idea who else I would take back to my bed.

I suppose if it was a matter of practicality, I could ask one of the regulars at the Knoll. I'm sure if they knew the reason for my request, they would gladly help. Some of them would even do so enthusiastically.

But the idea of asking someone just for utilitarian reasons? Divorcing the physical act entirely from emotional or even platonic connection? Mab's voice, sex was wonderful for so much: intimacy, release, even just fun.

Using it as a crutch for my inability to keep my sanity when my magic became too much for me felt cheap. It felt wrong.

"I'll think about it," I said.

Rhys inclined their head. "I just think it's a good idea. Just in case."

I couldn't keep the hurt from my voice. "Has anything changed? Between us, I mean."

"Between us, no." Rhys swept me back up in their arms and gave me a squeeze. "I still think you're incredible, and I love being around you and with you. And if you cancel our Mummy Date, I might cry."

"You can't call something a Mummy date. You've met my mother." I laughed but did a poor job of hiding the small sob that escaped with the noise. "Then it's not you rejecting me. It's something else."

"It's everything else, babe. You are amazing, and I'm not going anywhere." They gave me one last squeeze and released me a final time. "But you are. Go back to the Knoll. I'll do my best to hold things down here with the Court. At least at the moment, I'm pretty sure you and your sister share a single enemy."

"The Fair Folk?" I was getting tired of this same refrain.

"No. The Winter Court." Rhys's eyes glittered dangerously. "Be wary of Lada and her consort. And any who come in their wake. This realm doesn't seem to matter to them. Nor any of us in it."

With that dire warning, Rhys turned on their heel and made their way back to the palace.

CHAPTER TEN

Thursday night might not seem like a busy one for a local bar. Everyone thinks the weekends are our busiest times. And mostly, you would be correct. If it wasn't for the fact that karaoke happens twice a week at the Greenwood Knoll. Saturday karaoke nights were our busiest night, with a waitlist that began over an hour before anyone sang a note, and lasting well into the wee hours of the night. That was the night when all the stars of Atlanta came out to show off. Whether they were solitary fae or belonged to the Courts, they would come and take the mic to show off impressive range, great song choice, or just enough bravado and star power to bring the house down.

But Thursday was our night for the die-hard karaoke fans. It was for the ones who wanted to try new songs in front of an enthusiastic audience. For the ones who were new to the game. And for the ones who were just there to have a good time.

The bar was full of the latter that Thursday. Everyone was ordering shots and multiple rounds of beer. Some were signing up to sing, but most people just seemed to be interested in being around good people. The mood was soaring, and I couldn't dwell on any of my concerns when there was such a positive flavor to the night.

Okay, I could dwell on one concern in particular. Rhys's suggestion. With every attractive lilin or siren that took the stage, I wondered if they'd be interested in an indecent proposal. Not that I'd offer them a million dollars. Or that I thought sleeping with me was worth a million dollars. You know, suddenly this analogy was falling apart around me.

Essentially, I approached the entire night with an eye to who might be my next potential lover in an emergency. Was the next singer someone I would consider a lifeline to a world I had abandoned for a few minutes? Was I attracted enough to the person ordering a local IPA to rely on them to tether my consciousness to this world? Was I willing to take a chance on anyone to put my body and my emotions on the line? And what did either of those really matter when it came to the safety of my community?

Kaia and Jocelyn both suggested I just hook up with the first maenad who licked her lips at me. I had only to point out that my last go with a maenad had ended with me on the wrong end of her knife before her partner shot me. They both backed off at that.

I longed for the days when all I had to worry about was who needed refills and who was likely to skip out without paying. You know, like Monday.

I reached behind the bar and grabbed a bottle of mezcal, poured myself a shot, and knocked it back before turning around to face the next thirsty patron.

A microphone thrust forward and Izolda my resident karaoke jockey smiled at me. "You're up."

My brain short-circuited, and I merely blinked for a few seconds at the vila who stood before me. Her white-blond hair glinted in the lights that she directed over toward us at the bar. "I didn't sign up to sing."

"In weeks," she said, and I realized our voices had been amplified to the rest of the bar. Izolda didn't need a microphone to project our voices. The fact that she offered me a mic at all was a testament to her respect for me. I could control whether I would share my voice with the rest of the bar. All I had to say was no.

"I, uh, I didn't prepare a song," I said weakly as I accepted the mic. After we'd done over a decade of karaoke together, Izolda knew every single song I knew and how to put it into my optimal range. She was an artist, and her performers were merely paintbrushes to the mural she painted each night.

"I got you," Izolda said with a wicked grin. "In honor of your newest romantic quandary."

I had a bad feeling about this. But with the lights trained on me and my voice amplified for all, I could do nothing but accept. Thanks to Izolda's magic, I didn't even need to step up to the stage between the fireplace and the back wall with the balcony. Every eye could see me just fine behind the bar. I could sing from there whatever song was chosen for me.

I waited with anticipation, as the beat started. "Yoooo, I'll tell you what I want!"

"NO" I screamed immediately, only to have Izolda and about half the bar break down into hysterical laughter.

Spice Girls. Of all the choices, Izolda had thrown Spice Girls as the gauntlet.

Apparently, my situation of needing a new lover was no secret. I looked around to glare at Kaia or Jocelyn or even Mikka or Varon but could find no one to focus my ire on. It probably didn't even matter. Izolda could measure the heart of her singers and her audience to a precise point. She must have clocked the fact that I was sizing up everyone who so much as brushed my hand tonight.

That song's particular message wasn't one that I wanted to support though. "If you wanna be my lover" might cut to the point, but it wasn't exactly subtle. True that with this crowd, subtlety wasn't really on the menu, but I could use a little more nuance if I was sending out a public booty call.

"Okay, okay!" I protested, much to the delight of the bar of regulars that I knew embraced and loved me. They all cheered as the music ceased and the spotlights focused on me, waiting for an explanation. "Fine! You all know my situation, I gather. Given my recent, uh, change, in magic, I've been struggling to explore my powers safely. And I'm needing some help grounding."

A low grumble responded as the majority of the bar nodded and smiled and traded knowing glances. Some of them lifted their drinks up in solidarity or sympathy. From somewhere in the back of the bar some femme voice shouted, "I offer myself as tribute!" The laughter that came afterward told me everything I needed to know.

"Mab's tongue, I swear, it seems like y'all understand my life better than I do." I was exasperated, but strangely comforted. "Okay, fine. I'll sing something about it. But not Spice Girls."

A few groans popped up, but for the most part there were cheers to support my decision. I leaned over to whisper my song choice in Izolda's ear. She smiled and nodded, agreeing to my suggestion, and within seconds my song choice started.

Ella Fitzgerald's "Someone to Watch Over Me" started up. I made some changes to the lyrics, of course. "A certain lad" became an "unknown one" I had in mind. All the "he" and "him" lyrics became "they" and "them," but the message was clear. I was out here and looking for a lover. And I'd never felt so vulnerable.

I poured myself into the song, feeling every lyric, embracing the longing of the song and feeling profoundly the loneliness at the heart of the story. I opened myself up and let the bar see how vulnerable I was in this matter. To their credit, they listened, they responded, and they embraced me.

That doesn't mean I was comfortable with it.

At the close of the last note, I practically threw the mic at Izolda so she could pass it off to the next singer, but it seemed to take her forever to accept it from my hand, remember who was up next, and locate them in the bar.

In the gap that followed, I had plenty of volunteers who were willing to watch over me, and absolutely none of those offers was innocent of the innuendo involved. Any one of them would be happy to jump into my bed, or closest booth or bathroom stall, should it come to that. Knowing smiles, subtle flirtations, and outright passes all followed me.

None of that did anything to ease my trepidation about taking a lover from my patrons.

Over the next hour, I had more than my share of offers to get to know many of them better. Several asked when I got off work, whether I had a break to explore if we were compatible, and a few if I was interested in attending their own private parties later. I was sorely tempted with the dryads who asked me to join their weekly spa trip to try them all out in turn. But if I was questioning my ability to take a single lover, I knew I wasn't ready to take up with an entire troop just yet. Certainly not all at once.

"Hey, Siobhan." I looked up to see a handsome vodnik smiling at me. His long green hair was pulled back from his face to show watery green eyes and thick pouty lips. A line of black fish scales lined his hair line and set off his face with an iridescent sheen.

"Hey Palmer. What can I get you?"

"Can I get a lager? And maybe a date?"

"A date?" I smiled as I turned away to pour him a beer. "You sure you don't want to just find an empty booth like everyone else?"

He only gave me a half smile in response. "It's not really my style. And I don't think it's yours from what I've seen of you over the years. But if you're interested in getting to know someone better, I'd love to get to take you out somewhere that isn't where you work."

His genuine and unassuming approach warmed me. "That sounds nice. Thank you, Palmer. I'm a little overwhelmed tonight, but if you want to hit me up later this week?"

Passing him the beer he ordered, I was thanked with another smile, this one bigger and more genuine. "Deal."

Turns out there were some decent offers amidst the thirsty ones. It was a comfort, albeit a small one.

I was halfway through shaking up a round of kamikaze shots for a pair of gremlins when the heavy oak front door slammed open with a gust of wind that was so powerful it blew out the fire in the giant hearth opposite the bar. Several screams followed as a tall figure walked into the bar, white-blond hair streaming in a wind of his own making.

It was the tall male sylph that had arrived through the Gate with Kiral. I got a full look at him as he stalked through the crowd directly toward me. Though he was narrow and willowy, he was solid and tall, not quite the seven feet of Argus, but well over my five foot ten inches. He was dressed smartly in loose-fitting navy trousers, and a flowing shirt of ice blue with long sleeves that swirled in the wind he carried with him. In one hand was a dark sack, but he appeared unarmed. His hair was long and silky, skin pale as winter snow, and his eyes a dark blue that reminded me of a frozen lake.

The expression on his face, though, was the coldest of all. Everyone in his path shrank away, and I glanced around for Mikka or Varon. One of them should have been at the front door, but no one was on the stool inside, and I couldn't see anyone through the dark of the open doorway.

I'd have to take charge.

"This is a place of sanctuary," I said in my steadiest voice, as I reached out with my magic. He tasted of winter citrus and ginger, cranberry and smoked thyme leaves, but the feel of it left my tongue frostbitten. He was pouring magic off himself, but none of it was directed toward violence or any sort of threat to anyone here, so the protective wards of the Knoll had not been activated. At least not yet. "You can do no harm to those here or you will invoke the old magics."

"And what of the harm done to my sister?" The man spoke with a similar Eastern European accent to Lada's Romanian. "Will the old magics recognize her murder? Will they hold Siobhan Illythia accountable for that?"

As any child knows, it's never good when someone invokes more than one of your names. "I don't know about your sister, sir," I said carefully. "But I have hurt no one."

He finally stopped his slow march across the room as he arrived at the bar. Only the long wooden partition stood between us as he towered over me, his eyes full of hate.

"But you harbor her murderers here. You use your name and your power to keep them safe." He looked around the room at my assorted solitary fae patrons. Their faces were by turns confused, worried, and angry. Many were defiant as they stared down this single Winter Court fae who had ruined their good time. "Is it not true that the group known as the Fair Folk gather in the Greenwood Knoll? And that they oppose the rule of Queens and their Courts?"

At that, a number of the expressions slid to scared and confused while others steeled, ready for a fight. Not everyone here was associated with the rebel group, but I had little doubt that everyone knew something of their politics. The Fair Folk who were in attendance wouldn't go down without a fight, no matter what magic prohibited it.

"What quarrel do you have with the Fair Folk?" A single voice came from the middle of the room. Every head turned to find Leland, the youngest clurichaun, standing defiantly at his clan's usual table.

The tall sylph threw a malevolent grin my way before focusing on the clurichaun. He walked through the crowd, parting them like chaffs of dead wheat. "My sister, Oriana Adrona, princess of Winter, was murdered in the Eternal Realm. The Fair Folk claim her death with a promise of more to come. In her name, I bring retribution."

Then he lifted the sack he carried, opened it, and pulled out a large round object, which he plunked into the middle of the table of clurichaun. It was the head of Baerd, the missing clurichaun brother. His brown hair was so thick with blood it looked as red as Gair's had once been. The expression on his face was one of terror, eyes wide and mouth open.

Screams filled the air, and people began pushing each other to get away from the Winter fae. Several fled the bar altogether, but most simply cowered behind tables or along the walls as they continued to watch, to pay witness to what would happen next.

The clurichaun at the table gaped at their brother's face returned to them, and Leland openly wept.

The Winter sylph turned his attention back to me as he stalked toward me again. "If the Fair Folk would have a war, then I am happy to bring it into their home. Siobhan Cambry Illythia, you harbor the Fair Folk in this public house. They have killed my twin, and you grant them sanctuary. I, Orion Cato Adronus abjure you in the name of Mab the Mother, in the names of Oona and Beira, Summer and Winter, and the cursed Nour who divided them. You will find her killer, or you will turn over the leaders of the Fair Folk to answer for this crime. You have one turn of the moon, or you will pay for her death with your own. Then my Court will rain retribution down on this realm."

He reached into his loose-fitting sleeves and pulled out a knife, which he quickly sliced across his palm. He let the blood well up for a moment before he flicked his wrist in my direction, the blood slinging through the air to spatter across my face.

As it touched me, my magic rose to meet his in a rush. For a brief moment, I could taste our individual flavors, mine lemon and gin, his ginger, cranberry, and orange. Then the overwhelming taste of the curse overwhelmed it. Cinnamon, anise, and lemon bound with the lightning copper taste of electricity as the curse seized hold of us both.

Our magic inextricably bound us together now, until the curse was complete. I had a moon cycle to meet the terms of his curse, or my connection to Fairy, my magic and my power would be ripped from my body and soul. I would not survive it.

Only the one who invoked the curse could rescind it, and with the hate that filled Orion's eyes, I did not believe that would happen.

Orion Adronus. Oriana Adrona. Daughter of Adrona I remembered the look of the dead fae from Lada's photograph and saw the resemblance clearly on the face that glared at me now.

There would be no rescinding of this curse.

I had twenty-eight days to find Oriana's killer or turn over the leaders of the Fair Folk, many of whom I suspected were friends and colleagues of mine. Or else I would suffer a fate worse than the one poor Baerd did.

I was truly and irrevocably fucked.

CHAPTER ELEVEN

If ever there was a time to disassociate and check out for a little while, it would have been in the aftermath of Orion's curse. But I couldn't access my magic at all in the shock that seized me.

I was numb and the world without flavor as the Winter sylph stormed out, knocking my bewildered and scared patrons aside. When the heavy oak door slammed shut once again, heads turned to me for answers. I could only stare blankly back.

"Siobhan," Izolda said, suddenly at my elbow, her voice not amplified for once. "What do you want me to tell them?"

What did I want to tell them? I wanted to scream and rage. What did they want me to do? All I had ever done is serve my people, serve this community to the best of my abilities. I wasn't even a princess anymore, and I'd stayed here to serve as a Keeper, a bartender, a confidante for everyone who walked through those doors. I'd held open the Gate with my own power for decades, giving them access to Fairy magic without any sacrifice on their own part. I'd given them sanctuary in the Knoll, I'd protected them from the worst the Summer Court had to offer, and I'd done it all while staying neutral to their worst rebellious tendencies.

I'd maintained the safety of this sanctuary by staying neutral.

And yet, here I was again being dragged into the politics of the Court and the idiots in my community who couldn't stop picking fights.

The solitary fae of Atlanta had become too bold. They thought they were safe only because of the great sacrifices of those who protected them. Now, for the first time in decades they were witnessing a small fraction what the Courts were capable of.

The head of Baerd was just the start. I knew what the Courts would do to maintain power. To crush the Fair Folk's rebellion before it even got started.

It didn't even matter if anyone in the Fair Folk actually was responsible for Orion's sister's death. The Courts wouldn't risk losing more control to uncertainty and terror. They'd wipe them all out just to erase the question of who was responsible.

And it all had earned me a blood curse in the meantime.

So, what did I want to say to my scared and concerned patrons?

I wanted to scream and never stop.

Before I could open my mouth to release the rage and fear and desperation that warred inside of me, the door slammed open once again. Argus stormed in, an unconscious and bleeding Mikka in his arms and a furious and terrified Varon on his heels.

The need to help cut through my shock, the numbness faded, and the world came flooding into my senses.

"Get everyone out," I said, seizing the control I absolutely did not want. "We'll resolve tabs later. If there are any healers who are available to help with Mikka, they can stay." I waved to Tobin who was standing wide-eyed by the kitchen door. "Send Meara!"

Then I sprang into action, vaulting over the bar and going to the first big table. With a sweep, I cleared away plates and glasses, letting them crash and shatter. Argus followed and laid Mikka out on the surface, cradling her bloody head with a stack of bar towels that Milo offered.

Varon took her hand and looked to me. "Can you help her?"

"Yes," I snapped, already pushing away the edge of Orion's frost-bite and searching for the heat of Mikka's magic. More than harnessing other fae's magic, healing was something that came naturally to me.

I reached out to Mikka's head wound first and was greeted by the taste of stifled smoke and pepper, covered with a freezer burn. Questing with my thoughts, I could feel the edges of the wound above her right temple. The cut was long but shallow, and as was the way with head wounds; though it bled profusely, didn't seem to be serious.

I let my power creep through our connection, and slowly stitched together the layers of skin, restoring blood flow. Then I reached a little deeper to see if there was damage below it. Sure enough, there was a small amount of swelling around two places in her brain at the front of her skull and then at the back. She'd probably been hit from the front and slammed into something. There was also a fair amount of frostbite settling in along her hairline that I quickly warmed and banished.

A few seconds of focusing on her bruising, and I was able to take the swelling down enough that I could check the rest of her body for damage. Finding nothing else, I wondered briefly at the power of the blow that had managed to render her unconscious but leave only the barest hint of a concussion. It had to have been incredibly deliberate and precise, showing me that whoever had done it had been in complete control of themself.

The question was how Orion had been able to attack Mikka at all.

With her stabilized, I could afford to ask the hard questions. I wheeled on Varon. "Where were you? How did this happen?" I didn't wait for his response, reaching for one of the towels under Mikka's head and beginning to wipe away the blood that had made her entrance so gruesome. Then I glared up at Argus. "And where in Mab's name were you? Why is it that every time things go completely sideways, I'm the only one left holding a curse on her head?"

A thick stream of smoke escaped from Argus's nostrils as he struggled to hold his temper with a deep exhale. "Is Mikka stable?"

I threw up my hands. How hapless did he think I was? "I wouldn't be screaming at you if she wasn't!" I didn't mean to, but having accessed my power already, I snatched at my boss's pipeweed and whiskey taste and let out my own stream of smoke in a huff.

"Watch it, Siobhan," Argus growled. He looked around the bar, at the few stragglers that remained after the mass exodus.

A few solitary lilin stood around, likely willing to offer their ability to transfer psychic energy, and a single Summer Daione Sidhe stood awkwardly in a corner. I vaguely recognized her as a distant cousin of mine, but I knew she was very much still loyal to my mother's Court.

Argus gestured to her. "Maylie, can you come restore some warmth for Mikka and soothe her mind until she wakes up?" She nodded and moved over to cradle Mikka's head and share some of the power she controlled through the Summer Court. "The rest of you, thank you for staying to help. We'll be open later in the afternoon tomorrow, or we'll see you all for karaoke on Saturday."

He turned and gestured to Varon who held open the front door, indicating everyone else should get out. Quickly.

The lilin and final witnesses took their things and fled into the cold winter night outside until the only ones who remained were those of us who worked there, the clurichaun clan, and Maylie.

"There's nothing I can do," she said with a look to me. "Everything is healed. Mikka's mind is at peace, and she only sleeps to restore her strength." She lifted her chin and peered at me down her nose. "My little cousin's got a talent for healing."

My hackles were still raised, and my lip curled up in an involuntary snarl. "Not the moment to curry favor, May," I said. "But thank you for your help."

As her eyes darted between me glaring at her, Varon as he stood sentry at the door, and Argus looming near Mikka, Maylie blushed and made her retreat. With a protective fury, Varon followed after her and slammed the door. I had the distinct feeling he would have lit her on fire if he could have.

Like that, the interlopers were gone, and it was just family left in the Knoll.

Argus turned with a roar, and the hearth blazed to life with the fire of his frustration. The flames subsided as Argus ducked behind the bar, grabbed a bottle from one of the upper locked shelves, and walked over to the big table where the remnants of the cluri clan cowered.

He clunked a large thick glass jug on the table on the opposite end of the table from Baerd's head, which still sat staring out at the room.

"Can we find a more respectful place for our friend?" Argus's voice was thick with emotion but left no room for refusal. Cormac stepped up and swept Baerd's head from the table and stormed out the back door with it. I wasn't sure what he was going to do, but I had no doubt that everyone trusted that it would be proper.

The rest of us, myself and Varon, Kaia and Jocelyn, Milo and Tobin, and even Izolda took chairs around the large table. This was family business.

Taking his time, Argus set out rocks glasses for each of us and poured at least a finger of the walnut-colored liquor into our glasses. Each of us took our glasses and waited.

After a moment of consideration, Argus lifted his glass and spoke in a subdued tone, his eyes focused on the table in front of him. "A toast."

"A toast," we echoed somberly.

"To fallen friends, and the justice that will be carried out in their names."

"To fallen friends," we all repeated.

"And to justice," echoed the clurichaun brothers as well as Kaia and Varon.

"To justice," Meara said loudly from the kitchen. I turned to find her lifting her own private flask, taking a swig, and disappearing back into her domain. Well, at least we knew where Meara stood.

I let the honeyed liquid burn down my throat before I spoke. "Do you want to start the debrief, or should I?"

Argus didn't look up, keeping his eyes down. I couldn't tell if he was furious, sad, or just tired. "I can surmise enough myself," he said finally. "The Winter sidhe cursed you in the name of his dead sister."

"Yes. But she's not the only murdered fae. There are others. Several

Winter royals. I either find their killer, or I turn over the Fair Folk to answer in full for their deaths."

"Or you suffer the consequence of the curse," Jocelyn pointed oh so helpfully. Kaia jabbed an elbow in her side. "Ow, I'm just saying."

"That's not happening," Varon growled. "Siobhan is blameless, and I'll be thrice-cursed before we let her go down for this." He clenched a fist that was beginning to smoke.

Argus lifted his gaze and held Varon still with it. The younger drake swallowed and lowered his eyes.

Argus took a breath before speaking in a low tense tone. "Mikka had an anonymous request for a crossing this evening and was holding the Gate. It seems it was a trap to lure all of us away. Varon felt when the sylph attacked his sister, and he grabbed me to come help. When we arrived, Orion was holding her by the throat, demanding answers about the Fair Folk and the Knoll. And about you, Siobhan."

Angry tears pricked at my eyes. Orion had arrived with Kiral just two days ago. I had little doubt that Lada and her consort had been filling his head with tales of the evil half-human bartender and her rebellion at the Knoll. I had a lot of doubt that my sister had said a single word in my defense.

"When I demanded he let Mikka go, he slammed her into the side of the Gate and came at me. I moved to defend myself but before I could lay a finger on him, the coward spun himself into the wind and fled here. Mab-cursed sylphs."

He growled and a whiff of smoke escaped his nostrils.

"We scooped up Mikka and brought her right back here, only to watch him breeze off from the parking lot." He gulped his drink and slammed the heavy glass down so hard I was surprised it didn't shatter. "Likely hiding at the palace where we can't touch him."

"But he brought harm to a Keeper," Leland said weakly. "Will the old laws not hold him accountable?"

"He attacked Mikka at the Gate," I said. "Sanctuary laws cannot be invoked in a place made possible by discord. It's why we have Keepers to protect the crossings and guide people to sanctuary if they need it.

The wards only work on the Knoll itself, though. We could make a complaint against him with his Court or with the Atlanta Court if you think it would make a difference."

No one did.

"So, what now?" I asked, shooting a glance back at Mikka. She was breathing evenly but hadn't moved. "How do we fix this? How do I avoid a grisly end? Because I just got magic and would not like to feel it ripped from my soul just as I start figuring it out."

Argus turned his big brown eyes to mine, fire smoldering just behind his pupils. "That's not going to happen, *louloudi mou*. Baby girl, if the Fair Folk exist for anything, it's to protect people like you and Mikka. To take up for those the Courts would rather forget exist entirely."

"Oh good, at least we're over denying that you're all a part of the group."

"Um," Kaia raised her hand. "I'm not a member. And I don't think Milo and Tobin are super political either."

"Oh, we joined the Fair Folk a month ago," Milo said, clinking his glass with Tobin.

"Fuck yeah," Tobin agreed as he downed his drink. "Anyone who wants to piss in the pools of the Summer palace and keep the sidhe checking under their beds for hobs? They forget we have teeth. 'Bout time we remind them pretty fae that we're menaces."

Jocelyn smacked the busboy closest to her upside the head. "That's not why most of us joined, you pix-brained inbred."

"Hey," Milo said coming to his brother's rescue. "You want to talk inbred? Sticking it to the Queens and their sister-fucked cousins is a more than acceptable reason to bomb a few—"

"Enough," Argus boomed. My coworkers sobered up. "I don't care why you joined. And I don't care if you want to join," he said meeting my eyes. "I don't need a pledge of loyalty to know you have my back, Shiv, just as you know we have yours." He considered the people assembled at our table and beyond to Mikka and Meara. "We're family. And that's enough."

Everyone nodded and agreed.

"I don't want to join, though," I said. "I'm sorry. I'm not turning my back on you, on any of you. And I'm not saying I won't do all I can to protect each of you as I have always done. I'm a Keeper of the Knoll, and I will continue to serve this community as is my duty. But I don't want to be involved in these squabbles. I can't be. Not with my family being what it is."

"Begging pardon, Siobhan." A voice came from the otherwise quiet clurichaun. It was Alden, his wine deep eyes, watery but focused. "But ye are involved. Even without Orion's curse, ye have been a part of this movement ever since ye left your mother's Court."

"I have been no such—"

Argus lifted a hand to stop my protests before I could even get started, and I shut my mouth. He gestured for Alden to continue.

"Whether ye want it or not, Siobhan, ye have been the face and voice of anyone not aligned with the Courts since you declared yourself solitary fifty years ago. I know ye want nothing to do with leading this movement. Gair told us and told us to keep ye out of our mess. And none of us will push you to do anything ye aren't comfortable doing. But pretending ye are neutral when the Courts only see ye as the enemy and the people see ye as a leader? Ye become an empty symbol. Ye become what they want you to be. If ye won't speak for yourself, plenty will speak for ye."

I wanted to fight against what he was saying. I wanted to say that he was wrong, that they were all wrong. No one spoke for me but me. I shaped my own destiny. That was the whole reason I left the Court, left my family, my legacy.

"Fine. Great." My voice dripped with sarcasm, and as my stress mounted, I could feel the edge of my power beginning to creep along the table, tasting for magic. Kaia's soft molasses faded into the malt of the hobs, the deep red wine taste of the clurichaun twined about the prosecco of Joscelin, with Argus and Varon holding things down with smoky whiskey. I pushed it all away as hard as I could. "Thank you all so very *very* much. I try and do the right thing and stay out of your mess, and I'm screwed over anyway."

"You're not the only one paying the price," a quiet voice said from the other end of the table. It was Leland, and he was looking to the back door. "But at least you have a chance to do something about it."

"Like what?" I said, my anger just barely abated. I tasted his power. He was rich tannins and stone fruit, currants and apricots. "Do I turn you all over to my sister and her crazy best friend to be strung up on the palace walls? Because that is how this ends."

"No. You find the killer," Leland said simply.

"And we will help you," Argus said firmly. "Tomorrow, you and I are going to take the afternoon."

"Track down a killer in an afternoon?" I said dryly.

Argus wasn't cowed by my anger. "To meet with someone with more resources who might."

Right. Because what this story needed was more characters on the page.

He stood up. "Everyone go home. I may be calling on each of you in the next few days. Milo and Tobin, help Varon get Mikka home. Kaia and Jocelyn, can you make sure each other get home safely?" They lived just a few blocks away from each other near downtown Marietta. "Alden, I will be in touch regarding services for Baerd. Get Cormac home, and we can discuss how we can help your clan. Your losses have been greater than most, and we may ask your boys to take a step back." He raised a hand to forestall any protest. "We will talk about this further later."

With that, we were dismissed. Everyone took to their feet and gathered their things. Milo, Tobin, and Varon discussed the best way to move Mikka without disturbing her too much, while the clurichaun departed out the back, ostensibly to find Cormac as he mourned and cared for Baerd's head.

"Wait, that's it?" I said. "We just leave?"

"Tonight? Yes," he said, taking my empty drink and beginning to assemble the glassware on a tray. "I'll clean up here. You show up here tomorrow at noon. You and I are headed to meet someone."

I put my glass on his tray and looked up at him. At all seven feet of dragon. At the man who had cared for me, protected me, and sheltered me for fifty years when I had nowhere else to go. Who stepped in as a father when I'd desperately needed guidance. Who gave me a job and a purpose beyond what I'd been trained for.

And then hid an entire secret life of political rebellion and outright defiance of my mother's Court for at least a year. "And what? What do we do then, Argus?"

"You trust me, baby girl." He swept forward then and enfolded me in his great embrace. My head found its comfortable spot, along the right side of his chest, while my shoulder nestled under his arm. His lips found the crown of my head. "I've always got you. Always."

A shaky sigh escaped my lips. As scared as I was, my family still held me in its embrace. My true family: Argus, Mikka and Varon. Meara and the boys. They'd been there for me when the entire world turned its back on me. When I walked away from the Court, they'd been the ones to catch me, to remind me that I was worth love and respect. They were my people.

The Knoll was full of my people. I'd chosen this community and served them. I loved them and they loved me. I could trust them with my safety, with my city.

I took another breath. I wanted to trust this. Everything in me told me that I could trust the family I'd chosen. They wouldn't sacrifice all the stability we'd built, the life we'd pieced together from the scraps given us by the Fairy Courts. "Can you promise me that your people aren't responsible for these deaths? That the Fair Folk don't actually claim these dead Winter fae?"

He held me closer. "I understand why you would doubt us. Given all that happened." He stopped. There was no open-ended statement. We both knew he meant Talisa and Hannah's murders. "But everything the Fair Folk has given themselves to this year is to counteract those past crimes. We want to bring power to our people and remind them that they are more than the Courts say they are. We have power of our own." He squeezed me tighter. "And you reminded us of that."

My stomach dropped. "Because I've been opening the Gate more."

"Because you've reminded us that all of our magic comes from the same place." He pulled away to look me in the eye. "Baby girl. If you stopped opening the Gate by yourself, any one of us can take on the sacrifice. We've been weakened because we assumed a lifestyle of individuals. The Court has always benefited because we solitary fae have operated as if we exist in this world alone. But we are stronger together. You, and I'll admit, Talisa and Hannah, reminded us that even if we don't bow to a Court, we are not truly solitary."

I couldn't say anything, but he echoed only what I had always believed. We were a community. We were united not by pledges or promises to a controlling power. We were united by our shared identity. By our shared experiences in the world.

It should be enough.

"The Fair Folk are more than motivated to get to the source of these claims, even without your looming curse. But with you on the line? I'll burn it all down to get to the bottom of things."

I pulled away to look up at him. "Really?"

"With my baby girl on the line? Nothing will stop me from eliminating this threat. If you trust nothing less, trust that."

I did.

CHAPTER TWELVE

I never arrived early to anything, but I was at the Knoll at a quarter 'til noon Friday morning.

The hour was blasphemous to my own personal sacred clock, which preferred never to see dawn. I worked in a bar for Mab's sake. But between early morning brunches, super rebellious political meetings, and my training with my sister and mother tomorrow, I was spending entirely too much time out of my bed before noon.

Let's just say it didn't put me in the most positive mood.

I sat in my old Honda angrily nursing my quad espresso mocha until Argus came out the front of the building. He went straight for his own car, a GMC Yukon SUV and gestured for me to join him. I clambered up into the cab and handed Argus his coffee, dark roast with no cream, but twelve, yes, twelve sugars.

He nodded a thanks, gulped about half the steaming drink down, and threw us into gear.

"All right, so a small head's up. I had to pull a formal favor to get this meeting today."

A formal favor amongst the fae operated in much the same way as a curse. It used old blood magics to bind two people together and secure a promise for a future act, to be called in by the favor holder. If the favor was not granted as asked, the one who failed to honor the favor would have their connection to Fairy severed, cutting them off from their magic entirely.

It was a pretty big deal.

"Wow," I said, sarcasm dripping from my voice. "This guy must really be excited to see me."

Argus rolled his eyes. "I think his exact words were 'I have no interest in bedding Atlanta's local ciguapa, thank you Argus.'"

I almost choked on my mocha. That was a new insult. Ciguapas had a reputation for being cruel, deceitful, and literally consuming their sex partners during the act. Having never met a ciguapa before, I couldn't speak to the truth of these rumors, but it sounded like something started by a man who didn't get what he wanted from a woman.

"Don't worry," Argus continued. "I told him the odds of you sleeping with him were lower than the odds of him denouncing the Fair Folk and committing to the role of consort for some Queen. And seeing as this whole group was his idea in the first place…"

"Great. So we're not only going to meet with the very person I've been cursed to turn over to the Court's justice, he's also a raging misogynist."

A huge shoulder shrugged beside me. "He's not a fan of our matriarchal royal system. But he's a regular at many Summer Courts, and you're literally the only person he has consistently gone out of his way to avoid."

"Again, not the best compliment I've ever received. Who is this asshole?"

"You'll see," he said and kept quiet for the rest of the drive to downtown Decatur.

We pulled up right in front of the Stone Pub at 12:30.

"Now, keep an open mind," he cautioned as I followed him.

I didn't want to think about what that might mean, coming from Argus.

He tugged on the polished wood handle shaped like a stag's horn, and the heavy oak door gave way to reveal a dark but open space. There were scattered tables of diners enjoying a leisurely lunch, and a few people sat up at the bar, but the place felt empty with the two-story vaulted ceiling.

A smiling brunette human broke from a conversation she was having with a waiter leaning up against the wall and greeted me. "Two for lunch?"

"We're meeting someone upstairs."

The hostess's eyes grew wide. "Absolutely, Mr. Ladones. The Belgian Bar upstairs is reserved for your party. I'll send someone up to get your orders shortly."

We took the stairs along the left side of the wall up to a loft area. Past a pair of intimate two-seater tables that overlooked the main bar, we took a left into a low and secluded area. The Belgian Bar was against the closest wall, large coolers full of cans and bottles and growlers of Belgian beers: saisons, wheat, dubbels, trippels, and Flemish sours.

Argus's eyes sparkled. I knew he would kill to get at the Stone Pub's supplier, even though they were a human-run establishment. To the sides and above the polished wood bar were intricately etched pint glasses, goblets, and steins of various shapes and sizes, all lit from behind to showcase the artistry of the vessels.

While Argus surveyed the offerings, I turned to consider the rest of the space. Everywhere was dark wood and hidden nooks and corners. A few tall tables stood sentinel around the bar with backless stools, but the eaves of this loft were carved out with cloistered booths.

It was to those that I headed and tucked into the very last corner of the last booth, I found him.

Of course. I should have known.

Thierry Kellan.

Wealthy eccentric, infamous solitary fae, mysterious benefactor of maenad baby showers and frequent guest of the Summer Court.

And easily the most gorgeous man I'd ever seen. He had flawless caramel-colored skin, fair and just barely sun-kissed, with tousled black hair that was artfully styled to look both polished and unkempt.

His storm-gray eyes were deep set beneath dark and heavy brows, and they were trained intensely on me.

His lip curled with distaste, but that was quickly replaced by a genuine smile as Argus came up behind me. "Argus," he said, pulling himself out of the booth and extending a hand to my boss. They grasped forearms and pulled each other into a hug. Like they were old friends.

"Kellan, thank you again for meeting with us."

"There's not a lot I wouldn't do for you," he said, eying me again.

"Siobhan," Argus said. "Allow me to introduce Thierry Kellan, founder of the Fair Folk."

Because, of course.

Kellan did not extend a hand to me but instead swept it out palm upward indicating the opposite side of the table. "Won't you both join me?"

I slid in, with Argus after me, trapping me in the low, deep booth. We took a few minutes to consider each other.

So, Thierry Kellan was the leader of the Fair Folk. The most powerful solitary fae in the United States, if not the world, was also the rebellious mastermind of the first successful movement of unaffiliated fae in millennia.

In the human world, Kellan was known as a young entrepreneur with preternatural good luck. He'd first surfaced in their media in the late 2000s, with a real estate portfolio that shamed even the most ambitious New York speculators. He owned entire blocks of Atlanta, New Orleans, and Charlotte, and I had no doubt he controlled more land across the country.

He'd since invested in countless markets and businesses, dipping his toes into tech speculation, AI development, and even occasionally nonprofit management. He'd helped design and build independent and self-contained communities in Arizona, Oklahoma, and Washington State with outreach to the most marginalized groups, including veterans, immigrants, and homeless youth.

He was also the most notorious solitary fae in the country, and yet, no one knew much about him. He'd made a name for himself in human circles a decade ago, and despite few public appearances had quite the reputation for influence, though he rarely seemed to get directly involved in any power struggles, human or fae. No one quite knew what to make of him. Rumors were that he was over six hundred years old or younger than even myself, that he'd been born in the Iron Realm or was a long-lost royal from the Eternal, and, lately, that he was human with stolen fairy powers. No one knew his exact lineage, what his magic was, or even his race.

Even sitting across from him, questing at a taste of his magic, I couldn't get a lock on him. One moment, he was a rye Manhattan with surprise notes of elderflower, then the next he tasted of smoky Mezcal and Aperol, an unusual combination that created a surprisingly refreshing cocktail on my tongue. Whatever he tasted of, it was strong. The power of him was overwhelming in a way that I only felt around Queens and the Gate itself.

Who was this man who Argus trusted with our lives?

As I considered him, he watched me in turn. He and Argus made small talk, but he barely took his eyes off me. I felt stripped bare and more seen than I think I'd ever been in my life. The feeling prickled against my comfort, and I squirmed in my seat.

Instead of easing into the conversation he and Argus had established, per usual, I went on the offense. "All this time, it's been you? You're the Court's big bogeyman?"

He blinked once before his eyes crinkled in pure delight, and he laughed. "Bryony warned me you would come in swinging."

My blood ran cold immediately. "My sister knows we're meeting? But—"

"But what?" his eyes sparkled with mischief. "Are you worried what your sister will think about you meeting with her enemy? Or are you more worried I'm a spy for her?"

I gaped at him for a moment before I realized he was teasing me. Surely Bryony didn't know we were meeting today. Or who he was. She would never allow him at her many social gatherings if she knew he was the leader of the Fair Folk.

Or would she?

I didn't even have time to work through complications of that before a waiter appeared to take our orders.

Before I could even ask about their draft list, Kellan spoke. "Three Vichtenaar ales and two orders of the pierogies," he said. The waiter disappeared as quickly as he had appeared. "A Flemish sour ale," he explained to us. "One of my favorites."

"Very good," Argus said, with a quiet smile. "Now, are you going to make nice, or are you going to continue playing games with my girl?"

Kellan sighed before offering a forced smile to me. "Hello, Siobhan. I am Thierry Kellan. Our circles have long overlapped, but I haven't been forced to meet you until now. It was not an oversight, and I will not apologize for it. But circumstances require our meeting, and with my hand forced, I suppose I will not put it off any longer."

I didn't expect him to be so blunt. He kept his easy smile, but nothing about him warmed to me. "Why would you avoid me?"

"You are politically toxic, my dear, and I have made it my business to be as amenable and useful to as many people as possible."

"Wow," I said. "And here I had heard you were charming."

"Normally, he is," Argus chuckled. "But he's not often this honest. I rather appreciate it. Though," he said and raised an eyebrow across the table. "I'm not sure any of this fulfills his end of our bargain."

The air around us turned to stone, as Kellan dropped his forced amiability. Argus had said he'd been forced to offer a favor for this meeting, and that even then Kellan had been hesitant. I wondered again at the exact nature of Kellan's magical gifts and held my breath as an unspoken conversation passed between the two men.

After what seemed an eternity, Kellan nodded.

"Very well. Argus has asked me to help you meet your obligation to Orion and your sister and track down Oriana's killer. Considering the other option to end the curse was to turn me and Gus here over to the Courts, it was quite self-serving to agree to the proposition."

"And yet you still fought me tooth and nail to get you there," Argus growled, though there was little menace in it.

"Nothing comes for free, friend."

They shared another moment, secret smiles on their faces.

"All right, that's enough of that," I said, fed up with the dynamic at the table. There was no way I was going to be able to speak freely with Kellan, so long as the men at the table kept leaning into their apparently long shared history and excluding me through meaningful glances. "Argus, can you take a walk?"

He snorted but already started scooting out off the bench. "I can. Kellan, good luck. Siobhan, at least listen and remember that this is someone I trust."

The waiter arrived then with our food and drinks. Argus snagged a glass and his beer.

"I'll be downstairs when you finish here." He raised his eyebrows in a challenge. "Play nice."

And with that he left me alone with the enigma that was Thierry Kellan.

CHAPTER THIRTEEN

Confused but professional, the waiter poured a pint each for Kellan and myself and put a plate of pierogies in front of each of us before making a hasty retreat.

Without taking my eyes off Kellan, I sipped at my beer. It was tart and complex, with a sour cherry and woodiness on first taste, and a slight vinegar and brown sugar back end. Its bite clipped at my tongue and soothed my first instincts for sharp retorts.

Kellan ignored me as he speared a brown-butter-covered pierogi. He flipped it over a time or two as if it held the answers to some great question. Then he cut it in half and considered the sweet onions and pecans inside. Then he finally skewered a piece and brought it to his mouth.

"So, you're just here to cover your own ass?" I said.

"Shh." He held up a finger. "You're so aggressive. We just met. Give me a second." He continued chewing, savoring every second of his snack. "They brown the butter in sage and something else I can't quite put my finger on, but it's absolute magic." He swallowed and then opened and trained his stormcloud eyes on me. They seemed almost to churn with his thoughts as he considered what to say to me.

"I'm here because Argus asked it of me. Argus Ladones is one of the most decent beings in either realm. He is loyal, honest, and always does the right thing. If he told me my own death was necessary to protect the fae of this realm, well, I might not jump at the suggestion, but I would certainly consider it."

The fact that I agreed with him and felt the same way about Argus didn't soften my reaction to the man sitting across from me. "And you're going to claim that's your goal then? The goal of the Fair Folk? To protect the fae of this realm?"

He sat back with his beer and considered me. The line of his jaw was sharp, and I appreciated the way his white button-up shirt pulled against his lean, but well-muscled, body. He was almost distractingly good-looking until he opened his mouth. Then he smirked, and his smug tone assaulted me again. "What exactly did you think the goal of the Fair Folk was?"

I glared. "I don't know. Cause trouble for the Queens and Courts? Grab at some power for the solitary fae? Moan and complain in local watering holes about how the little people could do so much better if they were in charge of things?"

Kellan frowned as he sipped his drink. "And you think the people you know and respect who are members of this group would be willing to risk their freedom just to grouse about politics in your bar?"

I squirmed in my chair. "Well, no."

"After all they have done to build a safe place for the solitary in Atlanta, do you truly think Argus and Varon and Mikka would undermine all of that just to annoy your royal family?"

"No, I—"

He worried a hand along the edge of the table and stared me down. "And do you think Gair and Baerd would put their lives on the line for petty squabbling?" The image of Baerd's head on a table at the Knoll turned my stomach. Of Gair, kneeling by the Gate, offering the last of his blood so I could possibly stop his murderers as they ripped a hole between the worlds.

"What about Talisa?" I lashed back. "And Hannah? Are you going to claim they were acting selflessly as they killed their way to greater magic? As they stole their way to more power? Under your guidance?"

His cheekbones seem to sharpen as his gray eyes darkened, and a taste of bergamot and vanilla danced over my tongue. "They were not mine. They betrayed the organization just as surely as they betrayed you and the entire solitary community. I will not excuse their actions, though I will defend their motivations. They recognized as many of us do that power in this realm is ruthlessly rationed to benefit only those at the top. They saw a way to seize some of that power back, and they took it. They lost their way when they got even a taste of what the Summer Court withholds from us all. I only wish they had come to me when they learned that they could share magic through bloodletting. We could have worked together to leverage that knowledge. I could have guided them."

"And what would you have told them?"

I watched as he grew still. His speech had been impressive, but it felt like a politician deflecting blame. I could see why people followed him when he talked about ideas and principles. But did he offer real solutions, or was he just another fae who rested on power and charm?

"What," I continued, "does the Fair Folk offer that the fae can't get on their own or by pledging with the Courts? Argus threw his lot in with you. Half the people I know and love apparently agree with your goals. So, tell me. Why should I do the same when you have straight up said you don't trust me? Why should I protect the Fair Folk from Summer when so far they've done nothing but cause trouble for Atlanta and inspire radicals to kill people?"

He took another sip and looked at me squarely. "The Fair Folk believe that the power of Fairy should not be controlled solely by the Queens of this realm. We should not have to pledge our loyalty to an outdated and dangerous sham of a government ruled by the whims of tyrannical matriarchs that quite literally lose their minds as they throttle the power that could pass freely through the Gates. Magic should be accessible to any and all who possess the ability to wield it. And yes," he says, anticipating my interruption, "that includes humans."

My chest felt tight as I realized he was giving voice to many of my own views on my mother's Court. Access to power should not be limited to those who bowed and scraped and bent themselves to the mandates of a system that gave them no voice. Magic was a part of the fae. It lived in our very blood and was our heritage, whether we lived in Fairy or here. It belonged to all of us. Or it should.

It was part of the reason I had become a Keeper, willing to open the Gate as needed, to sacrifice my blood and magic to allow the power that was our birthright to pass to all who could use it. If there was a way to bypass the Gates altogether and allow magic to flow freely, I would take it. I *was* taking it. I was opening the ways remotely as often as possible for just that reason.

"But what does that look like?" I pushed, refusing to allow him to wiggle out of an explanation. "How do you democratize power without bleeding people dry to keep the Gate open constantly?"

"Apparently, some of us don't have to offer any sacrifice to open the Gate."

"I don't believe that I'm your solution. I only came into this ability recently, and your organization has been around long enough to have another plan. So what? You undermine the Queens and the Court system. Then what? Do we set up a rotating blood sacrifice to keep the Gates open constantly, draining one or more of us at a time so that others can have a little more power? How do you even decide who weakens so that others have more? Are you going to make that decision as the organizer of the 'Fair' Folk?" I put strong finger quotations around the idea that anyone should be deciding who should be sacrificed for others to benefit. "At least Queens are willing to offer up themselves and their sanity for their people. Are you willing to make that sort of sacrifice?"

"I am. Any number of us are." A look of pity crossed his face. "You don't have to be raised as a royal martyr to dedicate yourself to the betterment of others."

I started to protest. "I never said—"

"Once upon a time, there were no Gates. There was no rationing of magic, no artificial scarcity to keep the Queens in power. Anyone of Fairy kind could create a passage between the realms. They could cast a circle, open a portal, and draw down magic or cross over. Magic was free. Perhaps, if we worked together, we could find our way back to that."

"Worked together with who?" I pressed him, annoyed by his moralizing. "You've lied to everyone, but you've been playing both sides beautifully. I've heard that you meet with the Summer Court several times a month. You are the darling of my sister's Court, and I've heard you're one of the few solitary fae Lada Casimira can tolerate. And yet, you're bankrolling and employing the most rebellious maenads, paying for monstrous clurichaun bar tabs, and apparently inspiring acts of murder? Again."

Kellan's hand that had been flat on the table suddenly pulled into a fist that he knocked on the wood, his knuckles white with a barely contained anger. A metallic taste crossed over my tongue, like the charge that fills the air before lightning strikes. I wondered again at what kind of fae he was, what power he contained to change taste so rapidly.

When he spoke, his tone was tight but controlled. "If you believed that I was truly responsible for those dead Winter fae, you wouldn't have agreed to this meeting. And Argus would have never left you alone with me."

He wasn't wrong. I might not trust him, but I knew Argus wouldn't knowingly put me in danger.

Still.

"If you and the Fair Folk aren't responsible for these latest deaths, then how are you supposed to help me find their killers? Why wouldn't it be better to just turn you in and save myself?"

Kellan's gaze dropped town to the table, and he shook his head. Then his shoulders started to shake, and I realized he was chuckling. "You do not disappoint."

The sour mash of the beer wasn't the only bitter taste in my mouth at that moment. "What does that even mean?"

His lips pursed together, which made the line of his jaw sharp enough to cut glass. "It means that Argus was right to bring us together. Because no matter how lofty you pretend to be, no matter how many masks you wear at Court and in your bar, you are just like me. You're willing to do what it takes, *whatever* it takes, to do what you think is necessary."

"I do what is right."

The look he gave me made me feel stripped of my glamour. Suddenly I felt like I was exposed in my pure otherness. Gone was my human-looking light brown skin and curly black hair. Gone were my safe honey-brown eyes and soft rosy glow on my rounded cheeks.

I was myself in his eyes: feral and wild. Topaz shining skin and citrine eyes. Obsidian curls, knife-sharp features, and a tiger's graceful menace. Under Kellan's gaze, I felt seen for exactly what I was and could be: a tightly coiled mass of desire, want, and need that in the right hands was a honed and dangerous weapon.

"That you believe that makes you useful." His voice was low and inviting, tightening something deep in me.

"Useful?" I swallowed against how I responded to him and tried to steel myself. "Are you going to use me, then?"

"I am." His gray eyes lit up.

"And my friends? My family?"

"Whatever it takes."

"Then why should I trust you?"

"You shouldn't. Argus is a fool to trust me the way he does. But he needs me. You need me. And loathe as I am to say it, I need you. At the moment."

"For what?"

"For this next step." He looked away, breaking the spell between us as he speared another pierogi and made quick work of it. "You need to release this curse by finding the killer of the Winter Fae. I need to know who's implicating my group. What's more, we both need Lada gone, from Atlanta, if not the Iron Realm altogether."

"Lada? What does she have to do with this?"

He snorted. "Do not tell me you are about to come to her defense."

"Absolutely not. I would be happy to never see her kewpie doll face again. But do you think she is connected to the murders?"

He lifted his beer glass and tilted it back and forth, considering the remaining contents. "She is certainly the one who convinced Orion you are responsible for his sister's death." He raised an eyebrow. "She's not your biggest fan."

"I've noticed," I said.

"And while I wouldn't put it past her to sacrifice a few distant family members to turn sentiment against my people here, I do not think she is the one to blame for the Winter deaths. It's not her style." He sipped his beer. "I worry more about her influence over your sister and the impact her particular biases are having on policy here in the city. Just like the Atlanta airport, the Greenwood Gate is one of the more well-traveled gates between our realms. Believe it or not, the Queen who controls that gate affects what happens throughout the country. I'd rather keep that Queen free of the grasp of someone who would happily see this realm burn, taking all of its human-tainted fae with it."

He summed Lada's views up well. "So how do you propose to get rid of her? And how will that help me with my curse?"

A wide smile spread across his gorgeous smug face. He then drained his glass and pushed himself out of the booth. "You and I are headed to Fairy."

"Wait, what?"

He grabbed his navy wool coat from the hook on the end of the booth and slipped it on. "Siobhan Illythia, it has been, well, I won't say it's been a pleasure. But it's been productive. I will see you Sunday for our crossing."

"I didn't agree to working with you, and I am definitely not going into Fairy."

He paused in buttoning his jacket. "You are. There have been three murders, all of royal Winter fae who rarely venture here to the Iron Realm. Oriana of Adrona's Court was much beloved, and I have several contacts in the Naboskova Court that may be able to help us figure out why she was the one targeted. So far, the Summer Courts have no information they can offer, and I have contacts in almost all of them. If anyone in the solitary community has any idea of what happened, neither Argus nor I have been able to parse it out. And we are far more connected than you can imagine. So, to save you from your own unfortunate death and to clear the name of my people, we must go to the scene of the crime and determine why Oriana was killed."

"B-but," I stammered, as I pushed myself out of the booth to stand before him. The ground had shifted under me, and I was trying to find my balance as Kellan had already moved on. "I have to work."

"Argus will let you miss a day of tending bar and keeping the Gate if it means saving your life. I will speak to him if you're so worried."

"I can speak to him myself, thank you," I said indignantly. I didn't need this arrogant man acting as an intermediary between me and the man who had adopted me fifty years ago.

"Excellent. It's agreed then. I shall meet you at the Gate Sunday morning. Nine o'clock."

"Nine? In the morning?" Why did everyone in my life insist on early mornings? "Could it wait until after noon?"

"Nine," he repeated, his eyes dancing with merriment over my misery. "And," he said, looking me over. I suddenly became aware that I was wearing a simple cotton t-shirt over jeans, while he was dressed in nice blue slacks, a pressed white button-up shirt, and now a very luxurious tailored navy jacket. "Consider dressing for Court. Fairy Court. There is an event we will be attending, and there are those who may take offense to your more, um, casual fashion sense."

I opened my mouth to give him another indignant response, but he was gone before I could say anything.

That's not to say he walked away. I blinked, and he disappeared.

In a world with magical beings, you might assume that I was used to people vanishing on me like that. You would be wrong. I had never once seen a being disappear into thin air.

Blinking at the empty space where he had stood, I wracked my brain trying to think of a fae power that would enable him to do that. Even fae with invisibility powers didn't just vanish. They could wrap shadows around themselves, fade into the background, and cast glamours that caused people to look past them. But if you had been looking at someone directly, they could not simply disappear.

What kind of fae was he?

What was Argus thinking trusting him?

And what was I going to do walking into Fairy with him?

CHAPTER FOURTEEN

After fetching Argus from the downstairs bar where he'd struck up a lively debate on cans versus kegs for beer storage, he'd taken me back to the Knoll and tried to convince me that a trip to Fairy with Thierry Kellan wasn't the trap it sounded like. He was still trying to convince me as we prepped for the Friday night dinner rush.

"You can trust him," Argus assured me as he chopped potatoes in the kitchen of the Greenwood Knoll.

"Smaller pieces," Meara scolded him without looking up as she passed me a mug of her special tea. "It is late. Smaller pieces cook through faster, and I don't want to boil the outsides to mush for the stew."

"Yes, ma'am," Argus mumbled. He might own the Knoll, but in the kitchen, Meara was Goddess. He took more care, cutting the peeled potatoes into half-inch pieces as instructed.

"Even he said you were a fool to trust him!" I said. "Argus, he straight up said he would do anything to achieve his goals. And I think that means using you and me and anyone any way he can."

He shrugged. "He talks a big game, but the lad's heart is in the right place. He is a lot like you."

I bristled because that was almost exactly what Kellan had said. "What do you even know about this guy, Argus?" I paced in front of the empty expo line where finished dishes would be lined up to go out to our guests. "No one can seem to tell me anything about his powers, his allegiances, where he came from, or even how old he is. Do you know? Do you know anything about him?"

"I do," Argus said. "But his secrets are not mine to share." He indicated the forgotten mug in my hands. "Drink your tea."

I stopped moving and groaned before sipping my grounding tea. As Kellan had emphasized, Argus was loyal, honest, and always did the right thing. If he was guarding his friend's secrets, I wouldn't get anything out of him. "At least tell me this. If he takes me into Fairy, am I going to be safe?"

Argus paused with his knife poised over a raw potato half. His brow softened, and he nodded to me. "He will protect you."

The knot of tension I held at the small of my back eased only a fraction. We both knew there was no way to be safe going into the Eternal Realm.

"He's really taking you into Fairy, is he?"

"That's apparently the big plan. Or at least as much of it as he's shared with me."

I began pacing again. I hadn't crossed through the Gate since I'd nearly died trapped between the realms, and until Kellan had insisted we were going, I had absolutely no plans to cross that barrier any time soon. It wasn't just the near-death experience of limbo inside the Gate as I bled out from a gunshot wound and emerged unscathed with magical powers I couldn't control or explain. It wasn't just that I could feel the Gate reaching out to me any time I approached or that I wasn't sure what crossing through her arch would mean. Whether I would become trapped between the realms again. Whether I'd have my powers stripped away, or worse, enhanced. It wasn't the crossing at all that I hesitated over.

It was that going into Fairy in any circumstances was fucking terrifying.

There was a reason so many of the fae had relocated to the Iron

Realm. Fairy is a wild and uncontrolled place, a realm of pure magic. Magic is the substance of Fairy. It is more than just in the air or infused in the earth; it is in the space between the particles of air, in the ether, the very fabric of reality of the realm. It's not just like you breathe in the magic; it envelopes you, infuses you, changes the essence of what you are the longer you exist within it.

Fairy magic is eternal, and it affects all it touches, granting near-immortality even to mortal beings as it changes the very blood of those who dwell within it. Time stands still in the Eternal Realm.

That might make it seem like a gift, and in some ways that is true. It empowers all indiscriminately, charging the natural magic of fae creatures the longer we spend in Fairy. But that sort of magic changes you. It twists and feeds on your essence, expanding what you are, what you could be.

And there are plenty of beings in Fairy who are more than happy to feast on all that magic.

The fae I knew in this realm were distant descendants of the creatures of fairy. Dragons that breathed fire, basilisks with forked tongues, krakens with curious wandering appendages, they all were still vaguely person-like. They walked upright, with a head, two arms and legs each, and generally compatible with fae and human partners alike.

The fae creatures of Fairy were not so compatible with humanity. Animalistic, feral, and savage, it seemed impossible that so many wild species had ever met somewhere in the middle to create our existing races.

In Fairy, basilisks were full snake creatures, stretching fifty feet long and as wide around as a sequoia. Dragons had scales and wings and claws and were much larger than Argus's seven feet tall. Trolls that walked stooped and hefted boulders as easily as pebbles regularly attacked travelers on the paths and dragged them home for breakfast.

The cryptids that roamed the wilds of Fairy would as soon eat anything person shaped as mate with it.

And those were just the regular monsters.

There were also the political ones. The Winter Court was the ruling entity in Fairy, just as the Summer Court was predominant here in the Iron Realm. Though they were outright antagonistic to incursions into their world from solitary fae, they also jealously guarded against Summer. After all, they blamed the Summer Courts for weakening the fae race in the first place.

Moving to the mortal realm and interbreeding with humans had weakened the purity of fae lines. It had rendered us susceptible to shorter lives and death and was the primary reason fertility amongst our kind had dwindled. The fae had lost their distinct sense of identity by pretending to be human and breeding with them. Mongrels, half-breeds, mutts, and hybrids, the half fae were less than human in the eyes of Winter. I'd heard it all leveled at me personally, even though most royal lines had some intermarriage in their history.

According to the Winter fae, Summer fae and the solitary who had splintered from them were why our people were on the brink of extinction, and if our people were ever to thrive again, we must all be brought back to our homeland, and the purity of our race restored.

It was no wonder I dreaded traveling to Fairy.

"Do I have to go with him?" I whined to Argus.

"No," Argus said. "I won't make you do anything, *louloudi mou*, you know that." He scooped a handful of small potato pieces into the big pot that Meara had set aside and began to fill it with water from the tap.

I sighed. It was always a bad sign when Argus called me his little flower. It either meant he was worried, or he was extra focused on easing my worries. "But?" I prompted him to continue.

"But Kellan has the best connections in both realms and is more likely to get answers fast. I can do what I can from here, and I have some suspicions I will follow up on. We'll have Varon and Mikka interrogate Hannah, and we can use a few of our connections at the Summer Court, but they're limited. With your curse, we are operating on a short timetable. The murders took place in Fairy, and answers are most likely to come from there. Kellan is able to move in circles there that are completely closed to me and my people. If he's offering his help to investigate, it would be foolish to turn him down."

I knew he was right. I didn't have to be happy about it. "Fine, fine, I'll go."

Argus came around the edge of the expo line holding the heavy pot and bent over to kiss the top of my head. "That's my baby girl." He left to deliver the soup to Meara, and I skulked out of the kitchen.

Fretting about Fairy was a problem for later. I still had to survive tonight's Friday rush, training with Mother and Bryony in the morning, and another round of karaoke tomorrow night. Maybe I could get some sirens to start a riot over a power ballad, get trampled, and be too injured to travel.

A girl can dream.

The bar was mostly empty as it was still just late afternoon, but I knew as the daytime fae got off work and the more nocturnal creatures began waking, we'd fill up in no time. Mikka and Varon were bringing up cases of liquor from the cellar below the Knoll, while Kaia and Jocelyn stocked them in their proper places behind the bar.

Whiskeys, bourbons, ryes, and Scotches made up one part of the bar, with vodkas, rums, gins, and tequilas on the opposite side. In between were the liqueurs, amaros, vermouths, appertifs, and other specialty liquors. There were also the drinks we imported from Fairy. These usually went in a locked cabinet below the main shelves, but we kept a few on display.

My favorites included a creamy dark liquor that tasted like bitter chocolate and orange that eased melancholy and a caramel-colored mixer that tasted of sweet citrus and a hint of coconut. It had a very low alcohol content but loosened the tongue of those who were anxious to talk. It wasn't a truth serum, per se, because the drinker had to actually want to speak what was on their mind but was nervous or ashamed for one reason or another. All our bartenders were under strict orders to only use that mixer when requested by the person imbibing. Consent was key at the Knoll.

I kept out of the way of the liquor restocking and grabbed a crate of glassware to put away. Friday nights were always busy, and it was best to get as much as possible organized early. Argus had amassed quite the collection of specialty glasses for various kinds of beer, wine, and cocktails. Pints, pilsners, some glass boots for beers, coupes, martinis, and cordials for cocktails, stemmed and unstemmed wine glasses.

There were even some personalized mugs for our most loyal regulars; each of the clurichaun clan had their own copper mugs that hung right above our ale taps. The maenads had once had their own collection of etched glass champagne glasses, but almost all of them had been shattered one exciting night when one of their members went through a rough breakup and threw her full glass of vodka into the lit fireplace. The dramatic bursts of fire inspired the rest of the troupe to toss their drinks in as well, and it had taken Mikka and Varon's combined powers to keep the resulting flames from burning the celebrating troupe as they danced about and demanded an effigy of the unfortunate ex.

Mikka sidled up to me and knelt down to the cooler below the bar. She lifted a hand, and I automatically began passing her martini glasses to chill. We slipped into an easy, quiet rhythm, having done this dance for many years. I handed her a glass, she slid it to the back of the cooler, repeat until full. We could do this with our eyes closed.

Though Mikka did look up at me. "I hear you met the big man. Kellan?" She held my gaze for a beat, long enough for me to realize she cared what my reaction was to meeting the leader of the Fair Folk. It meant she held him in some regard. As did Varon. As did Argus.

So, what did I think of Thierry Kellan?

I lifted one eyebrow and shrugged a shoulder casually. "Honestly, for such a big reputation, Kellan was shorter than I thought he'd be."

A snort escaped her as she accepted the glass I offered. She saw right through me. "Please. That man swallows any room he walks into."

"Only because he's got such a big mouth."

She stopped and stood to consider me. Then, her persistent melancholy melted away as a familiar fire lit beneath a mischievous grin. The old Mikka beamed at me as something wicked kindled just beneath the surface. "Oh no!" She laughed. "Oh, no, Siobhan. You're attracted to him."

"Absolutely not," I snapped. "He's easily the most arrogant person I've ever met. And I grew up with Queens. And my sister." Thinking of him, my stomach churned. His smug assurance that he was right. That I was exactly who he thought I was. That people would follow him, and he could challenge a system that had been in place for millennia. "He's not my type."

"Nonsense," Mikka said patiently. "He's everyone's type."

I laughed then. It was an empty platitude. "I seem to recall you saying that about me once."

She sucked her teeth at me and let her dark eyes rove up and down my body. "Exactly my point."

Then she sauntered away, passing the rest of the staff as they suddenly found themselves busy and pretended not to be listening in on what we had been saying. Varon waggled his eyebrows at me and thrust his chin in his twin sister's direction. He had apparently noticed the improvement in her mood as well.

I shrugged but grinned at him. Even if it was at my expense and a delusional idea, a scheming Mikka was always better than a depressed one.

CHAPTER FIFTEEN

The bar was well stocked by the time the regulars came trickling in around four, and things were in full weekend swing by five-thirty.

The atmosphere was generally somber, thanks to the events of the previous night. Whispered conversations about seeing Baerd's head on the table and exactly what my curse entailed haunted every table. It felt like every time I opened my mouth I was chasing away the ghost of a new rumor about my own demise or the inevitable horrific death of the next member of the Fair Folk.

Of which there was an inordinate amount present. Not only were the usual maenads and clurichaun present, there were entire groves of dryads, and the children of lillin were milling about. As sex fae, the magic of the lillin usually lent a flirtatious and lusty atmosphere, but that was in short supply that night. All of them expressed sympathies to Baerd's brothers, and many asked after my state of mind. I wasn't sure sometimes if they were asking about my search for a new lover or the curse, and mostly just brushed off their inquiries.

Palmer, the cute vodnik who'd asked me on a date earlier was present, and he gave me an extra big smile when he ordered beers for him and his friends. I thought he might make another pass at me, but he merely thanked me for the drinks, tipped generously, and returned to his group.

There was a group of fire elementals showing off near the flaming hearth against the far wall. The fireplace and mantle were wide enough to fit a good six people standing side by side, and it quickly became the site of a fun new game.

The fire fae were sculpting galloping centaurs, salamanders, and albers out of the smoke and flames and sending them in races around the ashes. A group of kobolds and gremlins placed bets and groaned as kappas lobbed shots of water in front of the fire creatures to skew the results. One alber, a fish-like creature that swam through flames, exploded into a ball of steam when hit directly by a jet of water, and I thought for a moment I'd have to step in to stop the alber's ifrit creator from boiling the responsible kappa alive. Before I could get out from behind the bar, though, Mikka inserted herself between them and had them both shaking hands and laughing over the fact that the steam had been so thick, no one could see who won the race anyway.

A squeal of laughter from the far end of the bar stole my attention away from the commotion at the fireplace. Naturally, it was the maenads welcoming in the weekend. Kaia had already supplied them with their usual bottles of champagne and wine, and they were passing around small plates of pimento cheese on rye toast points, mini caprese skewers, and okra fries.

At the center of the group was a beaming Semele Tyne, without her baby.

"Mom's night out?" I teased as I made my way over to the group.

"Siobhan!" Mellie cried out. "I didn't get to talk to you at the party."

"Yeah," I said. "Sorry about ruining that."

"Ruin?" Mellie's face fell. "Oh honey, no. It was a wonderful party. I'm so sorry we overstimulated you."

"Over—what?" I'd lost control of my powers in the middle of her celebration, crossed boundaries by accessing the powers of her guests without consent, and exposed the most privately held secrets of her friends, and she was apologizing to me? "No, no, sweet Mell. I should have a better grasp on things by now. I shouldn't be losing it like that."

"Nonsense," she reassured me, as she accepted a fresh glass of champagne from one of her sisters. "Girl, if anyone understands losing it, it's a maenad. When I get turned on? When a mania gets a hold of me? Any of us?" She gestured around to her sisters. "Well, it's hard to stop an avalanche when things start collapsing. How do you think I ended up pregnant?"

She laughed, and the group laughed with her. Maenads were known for their sexual appetites and their episodes of mania, hence the name. They had powers of psychic enhancement, the ability to concentrate and intensify emotions and urges, especially those of a sexual nature. The problem for maenads was that their power went both ways; if they used their powers to increase attraction or jealousy, it affected them in equal measure. This frequently caused them to be victims of their own magic as they amplified their feelings and those around them.

A maenad's mania could be dangerous.

Or beneficial, I suppose.

"I am so happy for you and your sisters," I said, catching a glimpse of Adara and Carissa both in the group, sipping at cranberry sodas. "Two more babies?"

"Three," Mellie said in a stage whisper. "There must be something in the water, because Yvette just found out today."

"Three?" How was that even possible? Including Semele, that made four maenads of the same clan pregnant in one year, when I couldn't remember more than four or five simultaneous pregnancies across the entire Atlanta Court ever. The fae didn't reproduce at such a rate. They hadn't since the time before the worlds divided, before the fae came to the Iron Realm and erected the Gates.

Now there were going to be four maenad babies inside a year. Four solitary babies.

And I could see no explanation for it.

It was good news, though. Surely.

"That's incredible, Mellie," I said, allowing her excitement to infect me. "Does that mean more parties to celebrate? Because I could use a pick me up."

"Yes!" She lifted her champagne glass to her sisters. "I would like to propose a toast!"

"A toast!" The entire bar echoed her call and raised their glasses, dropping their conversations instantly. If the Knoll had any recognized ritual, it was their mutual respect for a toast.

"Tonight, we may have much to mourn, but we also have much to celebrate. For every life lost, may there be more created. To the expansion of the solitary fae! May we ever be free, ever be fae, and ever be fair!"

Voices echoed select phrases. "To freedom!" "To Baerd!" But the loudest toast I heard across many of my patrons was the implied one Semele toasted. "To the Fair Folk!"

I pressed my lips into an uncomfortable smile. The secret group was no longer interested in being secret. Their clandestine group was coming into the light, confident in their power, their righteousness.

My desire to remain neutral wouldn't stand for much longer.

I pressed my lips. "I guess that means more Thierry Kellan sponsored events. Can't wait."

Semele raised an eyebrow at the serrated edge of my question. "Uh oh. Siobhan? What's going on?"

Everything had grown loud and boisterous. People were celebrating, drinking heavily, and forcing merriment as if in deliberate rejection of a pull of reflection that such a moment would otherwise require.

All I could think about was the cost of it all. By his own admission, Kellan was willing to sacrifice others to get what he wanted. Baerd, Talisa, me.

And I still didn't know exactly what he wanted.

"I just want you all to be careful. The Fair Folk seem very driven. And I don't want to see any more of you put in danger."

"Mells, come on!" One of Semele's sisters tugged at her arm, asking her to leave the mopey bartender alone and come party.

"Just a sec," she replied, shrugging her sister off. She leaned over the bar and motioned me closer. "Hey, Siobhan." She held her peace until I gave her my full attention.

"I'm not Talisa. I know I've kind of taken on the role of big sister to my troupe, or maenad mom, as it were. But I'm not like her. I'm not willing to sacrifice anything or anyone for ideals. The troupe comes first. My family comes first. My kid. Comes first." All softness was gone from Mellie's face as her protective ferocity seized her. I had no doubt that she could rip someone to pieces with her teeth if Callum or any of her family was threatened. "I will not let anything threaten them. And that includes anyone from the Fair Folk. But it also includes the Courts."

"I know," I said.

"I know you do. Because from all I know of you, you are the same as me." She reached across and squeezed my hand, and a sweet mix of honeyed apple and ginger flooded my senses. "Everyone tells me that you have been fighting for this community for decades. Keeping us safe from the Court and your family. The things you have sacrificed to keep us free."

I blinked away sharp emotions that pricked at my eyes. I hadn't realized most people even knew how much I had intervened on their behalf. The petitions I took to Court. The deals I had made with Bryony and my mother to keep individual fae free from their whims and rules and punishments.

"Just consider," Semele continued. "The best way to keep us safe might not be trying to remain a neutral wall between the Court and the solitary. At some point, you might have to pick a side." She gave me another squeeze and then turned back to her troupe.

The maenads gave a cheer as Mellie threw her hands up and declared that she wanted to dance. They gathered around, grabbed each other's hands, and scrambled up to the stage area and started dancing with each other and anyone they could coax up with them.

I half wanted to throw my concerns to the wind and join them, stop thinking about all that kept me stuck and grounded, and just let go for a bit. What a relief it would be to indulge in the freedom they all valued so much. To let go, let loose, just be in the moment and be exactly what Semele suggested: free, fae, and fair.

But I couldn't. I had only had a taste of what happened when I dropped my control, and it had terrified me. Unleashed magic, curses, and death followed in my wake. No, I had to keep my feet on the ground, keep my magic to myself, and keep my politics as neutral as possible.

The cost of my freedom, from my family, my responsibilities, might be more than this world could pay.

CHAPTER SIXTEEN

I had known Saturday morning would come too early. Argus had insisted that I leave the Knoll by one in the morning, but the bar still hadn't come close to shutting down. In fact, the maenads were on their third wind, having convinced the fire elementals to craft them each their own flaming halo for an impromptu Beyonce medley. Despite my best attempts to remind them that karaoke wasn't until the next night, they'd insisted on their own personal concert, complete with choreography. When I'd finally walked out the door, they'd been coordinating with a brownie to commission costumes for a full performance next week.

Argus comforted me saying I would probably be in Fairy with Kellan and wouldn't have to suffer through that particular show.

It wasn't the reassurance he thought it was.

Still, I couldn't spare any thoughts for that at the unfair hour of nine on a Saturday morning. The sun was entirely too bright, the air too cold, and my nerves too tight for me to think of anything but staying calm as I climbed all twenty-seven front steps of the Atlanta palace.

I wished I had a thermos of Meara's tea to stabilize me, but I hadn't thought to ask for a traveler cup before I left the bar the night before.

It was probably for the best, though. I didn't know what this training session with Mother and Bryony would entail, and there was every chance that a tea that suppressed my tendency to dissociate would interfere with what we were trying to accomplish.

Then again, I wasn't sure what today was supposed to accomplish or what I was hoping for.

I'd asked for help managing my magic and dissociations, and Bryony had agreed. Both of those actions were novel enough that I was going to move forward carefully.

At the top of the grand staircase, I approached the twin twelve-foot-tall doors which simultaneously opened inward, silently and majestically. My feet didn't freeze in place immediately as I crossed the threshold, so I assumed they'd lifted the wards temporarily.

Or maybe Lada was dead and her evil had left with her.

A girl could hope.

Magdalene greeted me in the foyer with a formal half bow as she inclined her head and bent at the waist. "Good morning, Your Highness."

As always, I ignored the tiny blonde's formality and gave her a hug. "Morning, Mags."

"Your mother is waiting in the East Ballroom."

I pulled away. "No Bryony?"

Magdalene's cupid bow mouth pursed tighter. "She is attending to another matter and will join you shortly."

Briefly, I considered pushing Magdalene for details, but I knew that would result in very little information, would make Mags uncomfortable, and wasn't something I really needed to know. "Is there—"

"Ianna already has a full carafe of double espresso mocha lattes for you and will be checking in an hour if you need more."

"I can feel my soul buzzing already."

"Excellent," Magdalene said. "Then, may you have the luck of the Morrigan, this morning."

She turned and walked away, leaving me to question what she meant.

Morrigan was a daughter of Mab, youngest sister to Diana, Morgana, and Nour. Whereas Morgana and Diana were known as the twin goddesses of death, and Nour was the divider of worlds, Morrigan had been born after the separation of the realms and was known as the lucky one. She'd been born into a time of peace as the wars of her sisters had ended.

Granted, there was peace only because her sisters were tending to their dead and trying to rebuild their shattered worlds.

The luck of the Morrigan was a mixed blessing to say the least.

Dutifully, I made my way to the East Ballroom where my mother waited.

The lower levels of the palace were dedicated to all of the Atlanta Court's public-facing purposes. Off the West Wing were the official spaces like meeting rooms, offices, and at the far end the Court audience chamber.

The grand chamber was where the whole Court could convene for the most serious matters, like hearings, trials, and duels. When the Summer Court needed as many witnesses as possible, they went to the one space that extended beyond the physical bounds of the palace building. The space of the audience chamber could expand and change to suit the needs of the matter. It could be as intimate as a bedroom or as sprawling as a coliseum, ready for gladiators and fights to the death.

I did my best to avoid being called to the west wing.

The east wing was for the palace's more social purposes. Ballrooms, libraries, salons, and game rooms were interspersed with more intimate spaces. There was a movie theater, a full gym and basketball court, and several bars and pubs opened to the Court-pledged fae of the city. Most bedrooms and overnight lodgings were on the upper levels of the palace, but there were still special rooms that attended to the unique needs of visiting fae throughout their time in Atlanta.

If you think I'm being vague and cryptic, that is on purpose. I could no more easily lay out the many unique proclivities of visiting fae than I could describe the individual feathers on the head of a harpy. Whether it was a kelpie who needed a quick hot humidifier for a few hours after a dry Georgia winter night, or a shadowman who needed zero light exposure to prepare for a few hours under the Atlanta sun, there were spaces in the east wing that could adapt to each individual fae's needs in an assortment of discrete situations.

And apparently the large East Ballroom had been prepared for training me how to master my new powers.

I made my way down the extensive hall and entered the ballroom. In this iteration, it was large and open, appearing like a gymnasium with polished wood floors and an assortment of mats in the middle. There were two lush green wingback chairs with baskets of assorted pillows in various shapes beside them, and a large chaise lounge, upon which my mother was reclined, an arm thrown over her eyes.

My mother. Queen Illythia.

Her beauty still stole my breath away. She was classical perfection, a goddess among mortals. Her alabaster skin was dewy and rose-tinged at all her pulse points. Warm chestnut curls tumbled down around her shoulders and her décolletage swelled just above a sapphire blue gown that hugged slim frame and generous curves. It was evident she was not wearing a bra.

She was petite where I was tall, slim where I was full, fair where I was dark.

My mother was the standard to which I was continuously found wanting, and it hurt sometimes just to look at her. She was a goddess, the image of fae perfection, and my little sister Bryony took after her.

I wasn't like them. I wasn't poised and polished, light and dewy. I was unrestrained and a little rough around the edges. Where they were the dawn, I was dusk. Where they were fair, I was dark. And where they were pure fae, I was something else.

Seeing my mother on display on her fainting couch didn't make me amenable to her charms. It put me on the defensive.

"You are gorgeous as always, Mother," I said. "Shall we take tea and get started?"

"By tea," she said, not opening her eyes from her recumbent position. "You obviously mean coffee." Her thick southern accent reminded me of a cross between Dolly Parton and Dixie Carter.

"Well, yes," I agreed. "Bean water is superior to leaf water."

My mother finally moved her arms and opened her eyes a slit. "What are you talking about?"

"Nothing," I said, recognizing the table up against the far window with two teapots, several pots of sugar, and not a carafe, but a full tankard that I assumed held my coffee.

I breezed past my mother, reached past the delicate teacups, and grabbed a large mug. Opening the spigot on the tankard and filling my cup, I discovered that, yes, it was a perfectly blended mix of espresso, milk, and chocolate.

"Ianna is a goddess," I murmured as I sipped at my mocha.

"You're different," a low voice said directly in my ear, startling me so much I nearly dropped my mug.

"What?"

Mother had crept up behind me and was examining me carefully. Her voice had dropped into a curious whisper as she skulked around me. As she circled around to face me, she reached out and brushed a curl out of my eyes.

"Ah," she said, her smile growing wild and predatory. "Is she in there?"

I put my mug down. "Mother, is everythi—"

She suddenly reached up and grabbed either side of my face, pulling me down to her. I held as still as possible. She might be six inches smaller than me and as big around as a weeping willow branch, but she was easily one of the most powerful and terrifying beings this side of the Gate. At her best, Illythia Elora Arietta could turn the Winter baby queen Lada Casimira inside out with a snap. At her worst? She could do it to me by accident.

So, I held perfectly still while my mother searched me for whatever she was looking for. In an instant, her teeth bared, and she snarled deep in her throat. Then just as suddenly her face softened. "Siobhan, sweetheart, how good to see you!"

Without releasing my face, she bestowed kisses on each of my cheeks and forced me to bend over further so she could kiss my forehead.

"What has kept you away for so long?" She breezily dropped her hands from my face to pour herself a cup of oolong.

I let go of the breath I'd been holding and forced a smile as I took a careful step back and away. "Oh, you know, things are always busy at work. And I haven't really been welcomed at the palace whenever Lada is in town."

She waved away my concerns. "That girl is just territorial. I think she has a thing for your sister."

I laughed. "Yeah, I had that thought, too."

"Maybe Bry will finally take on a consort role when you take the throne? I'd be proud to have two consorts in the family."

It was a lucky thing that Mother voiced that particular thought when my sister was not in the room. She seemed to have forgotten again that I was no longer in line for her throne, that Bryony was her heir, and that my little sister would rather throw herself into a pit of venomous cockatrices than be anyone's consort. The role was fine for our brother Dariel, but Bryony had always aimed higher.

"I didn't think it advisable for two conduits to serve that role for each other," I said diplomatically. "But maybe that could work."

"Bryony? A conduit?" She cocked her head to the side, looking for all the world like a concerned golden doodle. Her honey-brown hair hung around her face artfully. Then something caught her attention over my shoulder.

I whirled to see what she was staring at, but there was nothing. Too late, I turned back to find Mother directly in front of me again. An iron grip encircled my throat, and though she was too small to lift me off my feet, she yanked me forward enough to throw me off balance before launching me backward across the room.

I was airbound just long enough to be thankful for the mats scattered around the room and crashed hard enough to lament they weren't more of a cushion. The wind whooshed out of my lungs, but my mother was on top of me before I could take another breath in.

She snarled in my face, her blue dress bunched up around her knees as she squatted over me and pulled me up. "She's not yours. Not yet. I'm still here."

"Mom," I gasped. "It's me. It's Siobhan."

Her teeth bared. "I know that. I got you, baby. I'll take care of this."

A sharp taste of juniper and rosemary entered my mouth as I could feel my mother gathering magic. I was too scared to spend thought on the fact that it was one of the few times I had ever tasted her unique flavor, unmasked by all the other magic she channeled.

"Mom, no." I struggled against her grip on my hooded sweatshirt, fingers digging into her arms and hands, my legs scrabbling underneath her, but it was like fighting against a mountain.

"It's okay," she said soothingly, her skin beginning to spark with electricity. "I'll burn her out."

"Mother!" I shouted. "Please. Don't do this!"

I tried to kick her off me, unconcerned at injuring her. Thrashing and screaming did nothing as she stood and lifted me with her.

Then soft hands reached around her back, cupping her breasts gently, and I felt her grip on me falter. A dark face appeared over her shoulder as one of the hands moved to smooth the hair away from her neck. Kanha began to kiss her neck gently.

"Lythy. Lythia. Come back to me." His hands kneaded her chest, fingers pinching at her, and she moaned, eyes closing. Her grip on me loosened further.

I took the chance and ripped myself away as she turned to meet her consort's mouth with her lips. I crashed to the ground as another of Mother's consorts came rushing in.

"Sorry, Siobhan," Dulcea said breathily. "We shouldn't have left you alone with her."

The willowy blond dryad didn't stop to check on me, though, moving instead to administer more attention on the immediate danger in the room. As Kanha kissed the mad queen passionately, Dulcea reached around and began guiding them back to the fainting couch, her hands twined in my mother's hair as she whispered in her ear.

Mother let out a moan as Dulcea guided her back and down onto the couch, where Kanha draped himself over her, his hands exploring lower on her body as he pushed her dress aside.

I rubbed at my sore throat as Bryony breezed into the room and headed straight for the refreshments table. "You started training without me?" Bryony was apparently unconcerned at my gasping and panting alone on the floor as Mother was attended to by her amorous consorts.

"I don't know if that counted as training," I said, my voice harsh and bruised.

Strong hands reached under my shoulders. "Are you all right?"

Rhys helped me to my feet and immediately began examining me for injury. Their fingers lightly brushed along my neck, no doubt noting red handprints, and possibly light electricity burns.

Then they peered deep into my eyes.

"I'm fine," I said, knowing they were searching for signs of madness in me to match my mother's. "I didn't even reach for my magic."

"Good girl," they said, and they brushed their lips gently over mine. "Good girl, Siobhan."

"Why not, though?" Bryony said, taking a seat in one of the wing-back chairs with a saucer and steaming cup of tea in her hands. "Isn't that what you're here to learn to control? What if that was part of your training?"

"I'm sorry," I said, brushing Rhys aside to glare at her. "I didn't think trying to match power with Mother was the way to go about things if I want to live."

Undisturbed, Bryony took a sip of tea while Rhys guided me to the other chair. I sat gingerly, and Rhys ran over to fetch my coffee.

"Well," she said, glancing at the activities taking place on the chaise. "I don't think Mother is much use to us at the moment. It's a shame you had to trigger her and show yourself as a threat before she was able to teach you how to channel your magic."

I nearly choked on my mocha. "I did no—"

"Anyway, I don't think I can hold your hand through this either." She avoided looking at me, as she crossed her legs, drawing attention to the fact that she was in a smart knee-length black dress. Hardly what one would wear to a training session of any kind.

"What's going on, Bry?"

"Given news I have recently received, I don't think I'm going to be able to help you with your little problem."

"Little problem?" I was confused. Mother let out an ecstatic moan from her couch, and I used that as the opportunity it was. "Does that look like a little problem? Our mother just threw me about and tried to fry me alive with lightning because of my *little problem*, and you seemed to understand that a few days ago. Now you want to pretend like it's no big deal. What's changed?"

She uncrossed her legs and leaned forward, her cup of tea held steadily with one hand. "I'm sorry, Siobhan. You said yourself you are not channeling magic to anyone and are therefore not acting as a conduit. That is where a queen's madness comes from. A queen is experiencing so much magic and touching so many people's consciousnesses that she has a hard time separating her internal reality from the external. Lada explained that what you are experiencing is quite different."

"Mab's twat, of course this is because of Lada."

"Watch your tongue," Mother said lucidly as she extricated her own from Dulcea's mouth. Her consorts were well trained and instantly pulled back from their ministrations to help Mother smooth her blue dress back down over her thighs and up over her exposed breasts.

I squeezed my eyes shut and balanced my coffee mug on the arm of my wingback. It never got any more comfortable seeing my mother in such exposed circumstances.

Mother only smirked. "Oh, Siobhan, if you can reference your forebear's personal anatomy so cavalierly, maybe the sight of a real one shouldn't make you so squeamish."

"Very much not relevant here, Mother," I said, unwilling to open my eyes yet. "This is not about you."

"She's right," Bryony agreed. "It's about Siobhan leaving. Given she is actively lying to me about her actions and the source of her new power, I am afraid I am left with no other choice. Say goodbye to your eldest, Mother. She's no longer welcome at Court."

"Nonsense," Illythia said, pulling herself up to her feet, her mussed hair the only sign that she had just been in the throes of pleasure just moments ago. Dulcea was already behind her Queen, sweeping tendrils of hair back into an artfully messy updo.

"Mother, through blood magic, your daughter is illicitly accessing the Gate to channel more of her own magic and funnel it to unauthorized solitary fae in your Queendom, undermining your power in the region. What's more, under suspicion of murder, Siobhan has been cursed by a member of the Winter Delegation of Albania who is a guest of our Court. She has protected and harbored enemies of this Court, and according to my guest this evening, she has plans to go to Fairy and meet with leaders of the Fair Folk in an attempt to foment a rebellion against your authority."

"I'm doing what now?" I stood, forgetting the coffee mug that I had balanced and sending it crashing to the ground.

Bryony stood more gracefully, handing off her cup to my lover in an obvious display of control. The expression on her face was caught between anger and grief. "I defended you. For months. I told Lada that she was wrong. That there was no way you would turn on your family. Or, barring that, that you would never sacrifice your people for your own gain." She raised her hand toward the door and gestured for someone to come in. "I'm sorry I was wrong. But not near as sorry as your people will be."

Rhys was left holding Bryony's teacup as two other members of the Queen's Guard approached me and stood ready to grab me by the arms.

"Rhys, I am sorry. You may escort Siobhan out, but I will ask you to return to your duties as soon as she is gone."

They nodded, accepting the terms as they went to set her cup on the table. I was not so agreeable.

"Wait just a minute. I'm not going anywhere."

"Siobhan, you are lucky I am not locking you in a cell beneath the palace. It is only because you are my sister, a royal of this Court, and I am not quite the tyrant that your Fair Folk believe me to be. To be honest, it's against my better judgment to let you go free, back to your rebel friends. And I am sure I will live to regret this. But I am letting you go today in the hopes that you choose to do the right thing and turn over the leaders of the terrorist group to rid yourself of your curse. You will find no further help here." She signaled to the guards. "Remove her and see that she does not return."

The guards moved closer, but Rhys stepped in between them and me. "I've got this." The guards stopped as Rhys stepped closer and lowered their voice. "Siobhan, it's for the best that you go back to the Knoll. And if you can, stay out of Fairy. Whatever you planned to go there for is not worth it."

Straightening, they nodded down at me. It was clear that we couldn't have a conversation here. They stood beside me and motioned a hand to toward the door.

With a single backward glance to my sister, who avoided my gaze, I accepted the guidance out of the room, down the halls, and out of the front door.

Blinking in frustration, I tried for a stoic face equal to Rhys's. I failed. By the time we passed through the front doors, I had tears pooling in the corners of my eyes and threatening to fall down my face. I turned to my lover in the hopes of finding some comfort but knowing better than to find any. They were still on duty to the very Court that was ejecting me. "Hey, I hope we're still on for our Monday date?"

Rhys's hand clenched at their side as they fought the need to reach out and comfort me. Their lips formed a quick "I wouldn't miss it," before they walked back into the palace. The pair of guards that accompanied us turned and followed them, and Magdalene was there to pull the door shut.

As she did so, though she looked from me, back into the building. Thankfully she was closing the door slowly enough that I could see who had her attention.

There, in the middle of the grand foyer was Thierry Kellan, watching me with a smug and satisfied look on his face.

CHAPTER SEVENTEEN

H e betrayed me," I said for the fifth time, my voice echoing in the deep and cavernous underground cellar of the Knoll. "He sold me out!"

Argus merely motioned with his chin for me to step aside as he hefted a huge keg of beer over his shoulder from the loading elevator and carried it toward the tap hookups directly underneath the bar.

The cellar extended the full length of the bar and beyond, dug deep and set with stone floors and heavy wooden shelves that stored hundreds of different liquors, elixirs, and beers. From cheap plastic bottles of vodka that were used to mix up limoncello and infused mixers, to the imported tinctures and tonics and potions from Fairy, everything remotely drinkable could be found in the Knoll's cellar.

Leading into karaoke night, though, we were mostly focused on prepping the beers, wines, and easy mixed drinks our regular clientele would be ordering. Argus had already cleared the tap lines and was able to screw the long hose directly to the new keg of our latest local dark lager. "You don't know that he actually betrayed you," he said again. "Thierry is smart and knows how to play the game when you and I don't even know the rules."

"Maybe he's good at it because he sets up his allies before selling them out. Bryony specifically said he told her that I was going to Fairy to build a rebellion. Why would he do that? I'm not even a part of the Fair Folk. He is! You are! I just want to live my life!"

"And the only way to live it is to trust those of us who are trying to help you," Argus said, still appearing unmoved by my outbursts. "Think about it, baby girl. Your sister was going to find out you were traveling into Fairy. Illythia knows all who pass through the Gate, and their spies would report back immediately. They already believe you to be in league with the Fair Folk. What Kellan has done is throw suspicion on you to make sure that as many eyes as possible are on you."

"I'm the bait? How does that help us track down the killer? If I'm going to be watched so carefully, and they already think I'm the one responsible for the deaths, I won't be able to do a thing to actually investigate."

He chucked my chin. "But he will. His contacts will. Everyone will be focused on you, as they would be anyway. It's your first trip to Fairy in decades. And the first since you manifested magic. Everyone is going to be watching you no matter what. You are the misdirection, baby girl."

"So he's using me. I don't trust him!" I was ready to throw up my hands.

"You don't have to. I'll trust him for the both of us," he said. "Go to Fairy. Be a distraction. Show off your new magic and let Kellan track down the killer. Then you can both come back, clear your name, and you can go back to being neutral. You don't have to muddy your paws at all in the political mess the rest of us muck around in."

"That's not fair." I had never asked for him or anyone else to protect me from the world. I'd left my mother's Court with eyes wide open. Or at least I had assumed. Was I really so naive about the world?

Argus sighed and stood up. Opening his arms wide, he beckoned me forward. I accepted his embrace, leaning into his chest, and letting him hold me against him. It was like being hugged by a sequoia, but his even breathing and furnace heat calmed me. "I'm sorry, baby girl. I know it's not fair. This world never has been, but I've shielded you from the heavier parts of being on the wrong side of the Courts for too long."

"Thank you," I said, my voice muffled as I buried it further in his chest, wrapping my arms as wide around him as I could. "I just don't know how I can go into Fairy if I can't trust the person who is guiding me through it. But I don't have any better ideas. I can't do any of this alone, and I have to hope that the people I trust are also trusting the right people. I hate it, but I don't know what else to do."

I groaned and pulled away to look up at the man who swore to protect me whatever came our way.

He'd been the one to catch me when I fell out of the lofty tower of the Summer Court, away from the safety of my mother's power. He'd protected me from every threat, from all those who had thought to sleep with me to get a leg into Court politics, from the predators who saw a lone woman and thought to have a good time. From everyone who just wanted to use me for their own purposes. Argus had been my safe harbor for almost fifty years, and he was asking me to trust his judgment in this. But it was hard.

"How do I go into the wilds of Fairy with someone who talks out of both sides of his mouth?"

"You take a friend like your partner suggested," Argus said.

"Who? Who would willingly go into Fairy for an undetermined amount of time to chase down a lead that might or might not actually exist?"

"I'll go," a voice called out from the top of the stairs above us.

"See?" Argus said, releasing me. "Mikka will go."

I glared up the steps opposite the edge of the kitchen unable to see over the racks how many of the rest of the staff was up there listening in on our conversation. Privacy had never been a part of my life. I don't know why I sometimes expected it anyway.

"Fine," I shouted up the stairs at my friend. "You can come, if you sing tonight and convince me through song."

Argus chuckled and pushed past me to grab the next big keg. From the top of the stairs, only silence answered my challenge, as I knew it would. In almost thirty years of karaoke nights at the Knoll, Mikka had only stepped up to the mic four times that I knew of.

Once had been when she joined the maenad troupe for a disastrous rendition of "You Don't Own Me" by Lesley Gore in the nineties. They'd gone through two cases of champagne after one of their girls had a grisly breakup, and they'd been feeling the First Wives Club wave. They'd fallen back to allow Mikka the lead on the chorus, and she'd choked, barely making it through a single line.

The other three attempts had been duets where she took the supportive role to some diva she'd been dating at the time. The girlfriend would croon and sing her heart out, while Mikka echoed key phrases and whoo-whoo-ed through the song.

As fierce a tiger as my friend could be in a fight, she was a kitten on the stage. Challenging her to sing was the easiest but not the kindest way to shut her offer down.

"Maybe Varon will go with you instead?" Argus suggested when no further response came from upstairs.

I shook my head and lifted a case of cabernet up from the ground. "Can you even spare two of us at the same time? Kellan didn't specify how long we'd be there." Granted, I added silently, if he was planning to simply hand me over to the Winter Court as I feared, he'd be back in a matter of hours, and I'd simply disappear.

"I can spare you both for a night or two. If things go sideways, I'll come after you myself and close the bar on Monday."

How he'd know to come was a mystery, though. It wasn't like it was easy to pass messages across the realms. There was no email or carrier pigeons. The only consistent communication through the Gates was through the Queen's connections to their subjects. Because they were able to channel magic through their people, they could connect to their minds to observe what was happening on the other side or to pass messages back and forth.

The main problem with that was the psychic burden it placed on the Queen and the garbled messages that resulted. You could never be sure that the message sent from one side was the one that was received.

Though I guess if my mother received an SOS from one of her own about her daughter, that might cut through her madness. Then again, I reached up to the bruises still around my windpipe from this morning. Maybe not.

"If things go sideways badly enough," I replied, "I hope you will name a drink in my honor, price it obscenely high, and charge every order of it to the Court in my sister's name."

He laughed. "Deal."

I trudged up the stairs with a case of wine, and though no one was waiting at the door, I still felt everyone's awareness on me as I stepped into the dining room. Kaia and Jocelyn were cutting lemons and limes while darting glances my way; Milo and Tobin pretended to wipe down tables that were obviously already clean. Varon had a broom in hand, sweeping in front of the bar, while Mikka brooded on the barstool by the front door.

"Thinking of a song?" I teased and hefted the wooden wine case onto the bar.

Mikka only scowled, but I could see Varon grinning at me as he ducked his head. He wouldn't risk upsetting his twin, but he clearly appreciated the ribbing I was giving her. The tiptoeing around each other was so unnatural. It was nice to go back to our teasing, sibling dynamic.

Things soon picked up and customers began flowing in as the afternoon progressed, I thought that would be the end of it. Mikka would forget about her offer, I'd grit my teeth and get through what I needed to, and somehow things would work out. Kellan and I would go into Fairy, find the villain red-handed, get some piece of information that would blow the case wide open, or we'd come back, and Argus would have already collared them. And things would get back to normal.

Normal like the crowded sign-up list, the constant requests for beers and vodka sodas, and reports on what was happening in my community.

"Shiv, did you hear about Santino? He caught his ex with a

Summer courtier, and Tino forced him to announce his biggest shames down Peachtree at rush hour."

Santino was a luduan who could detect truth and lies in another's speech and make them confess to them when called.

"Oh, no. Which Peachtree?" I asked. Considering Atlanta had something like 73 different Peachtree streets, roads, avenues and boulevards, this was not an unreasonable clarification.

"Street. Right through Midtown."

I laughed. At rush hour, Peachtree Street would be at a standstill, so all the drivers would be forced to hear whatever recitation of sins Tino decided was a worthy penance for cheating on him. And Tino was a petty bitch, so I had no doubt those confessions were juicy and detailed.

"Let's hope he comes in and dedicates a song or two," I said. Tino loved to sing and dedicate call-out songs and let people guess what they meant. For instance, last month over three weeks, he'd sung a different song from Taylor Swift's Red album to a different person. Turns out they had all been cheating on the same vila.

Funny thing was, they each disappeared soon after Tino's performances. They should have known better than to mess with a trooping fae; any fae with family is a dangerous fae.

It made me excited to see what song he came up with to sing tonight.

Even before the songs started, though, there was drama. Though Izolda managed the karaoke signups, fielding requests like a champ, she still had the unenviable task of negotiating expectations. There was the group of iele celebrating a birthday singing several Amy Winehouse and Adele songs in a row, as well as the kobold and gremlin fighting over who was more appropriate to sing "Iron Man."

I just hated that the conversation was happening at all. "Iron Man" was not a karaoke appropriate song. Someone should remind the boys that just because they had an affiliation with metals, that did not mean they had to announce that with their karaoke song choices. At the very least the entire genres of rock and metal would work just as well if they felt the need to label themselves. For example, "We Will Rock You" was a perfectly valid choice and was a crowd pleaser.

I was pouring a rare round of Manhattans when a familiar but unexpected voice cleared her throat in the mic.

Mikka stood on the stage shifting from foot to foot, holding the microphone in front of her like it was a rabid raccoon she'd picked up off the street.

"I'm going to dedicate this to Siobhan," she said.

A suggestive cheer went up from the crowd, no doubt playing off the previous public karaoke confirmation that I was looking for a lover.

"Mikka can get it!" A strong voice shouted.

"Ew, no. She's my sister," Mikka said, and the bar erupted with laughter.

They knew. They knew the stories of all of us who ran the Greenwood Knoll.

I wasn't the only stray Argus had adopted.

He came from a distinguished line of solitary dragons. He'd spent lifetimes exploring the realms, making friends and enemies in both Courts. Then, two centuries ago, he'd taken on the mantle of Gate Keeper in Atlanta and built the Knoll to act as its sanctuary. He'd been adopting wayward fae and providing them a safe place to call home ever since.

Meara had joined him after years of solitary living on the outskirts of Louisiana. She was cagey about where she'd come from originally, but her eastern European accent spoke to a background in one of the Winter Courts. In the late 1800s, she'd apparently spent some time with the New Orleans Court as their cook where she'd learned all manner of delicious recipes. She'd thankfully remembered them and brought them with her when she decided the bayous were too lonely.

Mikka and Varon had taken up with Argus when their parents in the Winter Court of Moscow had insisted they breed with the optimal fae families of their region. They'd renounced their royal lineage and joined a distant uncle who ran a reputable sanctuary on the other side of the iron realm. Argus had been more than happy to receive them.

And my relocation to the Knoll from the Atlanta Palace was entirely too well known.

We'd all chosen this life. It made us family, which mostly meant hands off of each other.

"Anyway, here's 'Wonderwall,'" she said.

The crowd chuckled appropriately.

The music that started was not by Oasis.

It was a song I wasn't familiar with, but the lyrics were appropriate and spoke directly to me. With a strong rock ballad, Mikka told me that no matter what happened, she was on my side. She would follow me and walk beside me even when things got hard. Her voice was strong, assured, and unquestioning.

The final notes of the song fell around me like thick snowflakes, dropping softly but assertively, accumulating around my heart.

Though she'd kept her eyes closed through most of the song, Mikka turned and leveled me with a direct gaze, her look a challenge to my denying her right to accompany me to Fairy. For decades, she had stood by my side. She'd been my champion in duels, my girl in breakups, my berserker in bar fights. We were a pair, without ever having to define what we were to each other.

I'd known Mikka was dealing with emotions too big for her to voice, lately, and yet, I'd never really thought to give her an avenue to express them. By asking for her to sing to justify her right to protect me in Fairy, to be my friend, in front of everyone, I'd forced her hand. And I'd used our friendship to do it. I'd manipulated her.

Did that make me any better than Kellan?

Mikka handed off her microphone to Izolda and walked away from the stage.

Despite her extreme stage fright, my best friend had stood up there in front of everyone to make her case. There was nothing I could deny Mikka at this moment.

I continued to serve drinks, pouring beers from the tap, cracking open cans and bottles, and pouring wines and cocktails to anyone.

It only took two songs more for Mikka to come up to the front of the bar and confront me. "We good?" She left no room for discussion.

I nodded, and she nodded, and everyone at the bar noted our exchange.

Wanting to say something to allay their concerns or distract them, I laughed. "I guess we're going into Fairy. Heh. Nothing like a midwinter vacation in the tundra."

Mikka didn't smile, standing stalwart as a totem before sacred lands. She was a pillar of strength, of power, of invulnerability.

She simply said, "Tomorrow." And walked away.

Standing there like a simpleton, it took a nudge from Jocelyn to get me to respond to the patrons at my bar. "Shots? Anyone?" I squeaked out offering the biggest grin I was capable of. "Tequila means you think we'll make it back by Monday. Vodka means you don't."

I sold at least 30 tequila shots, and only a handful of vodka shots in the next few minutes. It didn't do much to ease my concerns about Kellan, but it was a comfort to know my people believed in me.

I tried hard not to make note of those who ordered vodka. After all, not everyone appreciated tequila. It didn't mean they were voting against me.

CHAPTER EIGHTEEN

The next morning, Mikka was waiting for me on the front steps of the Knoll. She was dressed for battle in leather pants, a cropped t-shirt, and a men's leather jacket—all black, all attitude. A slash of red lipstick and a fierce grin completed her costume.

"Ready to storm the castle?"

I couldn't help but return her grin. This was the Mikka I had been missing. "Absolutely."

She dropped down the steps and swept me into a hug. The taste of cedar smoke and pepper made me aware she was using a small amount of her power to warm herself and me, and maybe to strengthen herself for what was to come.

Pushing me away, she held an arm up and spun me around. "Let me look at you. What is all of this?"

I considered my outfit. "Too much?" It had felt weird to trade my normal jeans and t-shirt for proper fae clothing, but I had done my best to take Kellan's clothing suggestions seriously. I needed something in which I could move in and run through Fairy, but that was also ostentatious enough to remind everyone that I was still a Queen's daughter.

My leggings were made of a thick but soft deer hide, treated with protective magic. My top was a green fitted cotton stitched with shining runes of strength and power, and over that a vicuna wool cloak embroidered with vines and leaves native to Georgia. It was a simple, practical traveling outfit rendered luxurious with exquisite materials, superb craftsmanship, and indulgent embellishments.

The statement pieces, though, were the necklace and coronet holding my thick black coils out of my face. My mother had gifted me the two pieces when I'd reached my majority at Summer Court at the ripe age of twenty-five. They were made of an assortment of cut stones, some common like white sapphire and lapis lazuli, some rare like black opal and tanzanite, as well as some I had no names for. A single teardrop of alexandrite dropped in the middle of my forehead, and depending on the light, it changed color, shifting from purple and blue to green. It was jewelry fit for a Queen, or a disgraced princess turned supposed revolutionary who might or might not be a murderer with undiscovered or unannounced magical powers.

"It's better than jeans, at least," a voice said from behind me.

Thierry Kellan walked up, dressed impeccably in perfectly cut slim navy trousers and one of the most gorgeous coats I'd ever seen. The under layer was an elaborate golden brocade that seemed to twist and twine across his chest with living vines. It crept up his neck, exposing only a sharp V of the hollow of his throat. Sharp lines of his navy jacket cut straight down from his collar, tracing the length of him and falling into heavy tails. His cuffs were embroidered with the same elaborate living gold, and his shoulders extended straight out in sharp points that looked to be edged with golden scales.

He was as sleek as a kelpie in a midnight sea and as seductive as raw power. He was dangerous, desirable, and damning.

It only made me hate him more. "You." I nearly spat the word. "You sold me out to my sister. My sister!"

He ignored me entirely. "Mikka, good to see you again. I assume you will be joining us on our sojourn." He inclined his head toward her.

"Better believe it, buster," she grinned wider. "Someone's got to keep Siobhan from killing you."

Looking between them, I realized they had already established a level of familiarity and comfort and wondered briefly how much time they had spent together. How long had Mikka been involved with his group? And what more did I not know about the people around me?

I opened my mouth to give Kellan another piece of my mind but was interrupted by a low voice behind me.

"Hold up." Argus was standing at the top of the steps of the Knoll. His large frame took up most of the wooden doorway. Arms crossed over his broad chest, he frowned down at us. "Kellan, you've got both of my girls in your care. If anything happens to either of them in Fairy, there is no power in this world or the next that will protect you from me."

He nodded, but his grin never faltered, and a mischievous gleam shone in his eyes. "You're the boss."

Argus's eyes narrowed. "Get your answers and get out. You told me you can put things right. I'll take you at your word, but things are moving that are not in your control. If we need to go topside to protect our people, if we need to pull the masks down and come into the light, then I will make that call."

It was Kellan's turn to glower. "That is something we will discuss when I return."

"When *we* return," I added.

His jaw hardened at me. "We. Of course." He looked back up at Argus. "Was there anything else?"

In response, Argus motioned for me. I didn't hesitate, running up the stairs, ready for any advice or warning or information he might want to share with me. I felt wholly unprepared for this trip. I didn't know anything about this man who Argus trusted with my life. I didn't know what he had planned, how he might protect me, how he might undoubtedly betray me.

Surely not for the last time this trip, I wondered why I had ever agreed to this journey.

I voiced none of this, as I pulled myself up to my full five foot ten inches in front of my nearly seven-foot-tall boss. I probably seemed a toddler to him, anyway, but I stood like a queen.

"Don't let him speak over you, *louloudi mou*." He cupped my cheek with his large hand, forcing my chin up, making me meet his eyes. I squared my shoulders and answered his challenge. "You had authority long before you had magic. You had power before any of them looked your way. Remember that. With Kellan, and with the others you will face over there. Remember that your voice is as strong and as right as any they possess."

I felt the flame of his passion in the warmth of his fingers along my jawline. It was familiar and safe like a hearth. "I will," I promised. "Anything else, Yoda?"

He snorted, a small puff of smoke escaping his left nostril. "Impertinent you have always been."

"Why do you think I washed out of Summer Court?"

He gave me exactly the withering glance my sass deserved. "None of this attitude will fly across the Realm."

My throat went dry at his fatherly tone. "I know." I did. I knew that I would have to be on my best behavior in the Winter Court where hierarchy was very much the law of the land. "How do I do this? How do I walk through the Gate into that world with someone I don't trust?"

Gently, his hot lips pressed against my forehead. "You trust that I wouldn't put you in his hands if I didn't think he'd keep you safe." He then rested his chin on the top of my hair as he watched Mikka and Kellan conversing quietly. "Else, you trust that Mikka has your back and would gleefully disembowel anyone who threatened your well-being?"

I studied Mikka a moment, who sensed her name being invoked and bared her full teeth at us. "That I believe."

"Good," Argus said. "Then trust also that you can take care of yourself." He grabbed my hands, pulled them together and brought them up to his lips and kissed them. "You are more than they ever reckoned for, my love. And if I trust anyone to bring you back safe, it's not him or her. It's you."

My hands gripped in his, I couldn't hold him tighter, couldn't squeeze him to let him know I understood. Instead, I reached out with my magic. I pressed outward with my awareness, reaching beyond the surface of my skin to where it contacted his hands, where it brushed against the air he displaced. The warmth of him was tinged with a mesquite flavor, a smokiness and green tobacco taste that lingered around us. It smelled of brine, saltwater, and home.

I breathed it in and let it wash around me like a second skin. This was home. This was safety. This salt and smoke was where I belonged.

Why did I have to leave it?

Swallowing away my fear, I gave Argus a last look. "Sure you won't come with us?"

I studied my father figure. Argus didn't have a distinguished dad look to him, resembling more a retired wrestler or a tiny giant. His face was wide, with a short-bearded chin and full lips. His golden-brown hair was close cut, so he didn't have to worry about its length, and under heavy brows were his eyes.

Turbulent seas, limpid pools, aqua lagoons. Every analogy felt empty. Argus's eyes were a briny moor set aflame. They were a dark murky green that sparkled with flecks of amber fire. Sharp and attentive, those eyes saw everything as they watched after me.

His mouth quirked. "No, I can't come with you. A target is the worst bodyguard you can have." He laughed and hugged me into his chest. "There are few fae who are less hated in certain Winter Courts than myself, my love." He said it without chagrin, but still there was a slight catch in his voice. I had never gotten the full story of how he'd burned so many bridges in Fairy. I guess it was yet another thing to ask him about when I got home.

I took a breath to say something inspiring or reassuring or confident, but nothing came out.

Instead, he stepped into the space I couldn't fill. As always.

"Just live through this, baby girl. That alone is enough of a rebuke to everyone who doubts us."

I couldn't help but grin back at that. He didn't always give me answers to what I needed, but I knew that no matter what happened, he was going to be there.

"I'll do my best," I said.

Without another word he went back into the bar, leaving me alone with Kellan and Mikka.

"Let's do this," Mikka said bouncing back and forth on the balls of her feet, full of excited energy that she'd been lacking. If I had known all it would take was a dangerous trip through Fairy to break her out of her slump, I would have suggested this months ago.

Okay, maybe that's not entirely true.

I glared at Kellan as I rejoined him at the bottom of the stairs. "So how does this work? Are you really going to walk through the Gate with me after you declared me enemy number one to my sister? Wouldn't that blow your cover?"

Kellan sighed and brushed some invisible lint away from his gold-embroidered cuffs. "Are we not over that yet?"

Mikka held a hand in front of me to stop the lunge that was coiling up inside of me. I wanted my fingers around his perfect little throat.

"Enough," Mikka said, a hint of amusement lurking in the corner of her mouth. "Siobhan, you and I will go ahead through the Gate. You're right. We can't be crossing over with Kellan if he's supposed to be keeping an eye on you over there. He'll cross over in another hour, and we'll conveniently stumble across him on the way to Adrona's palace."

"And I'll deliver you to Lada's cousin with a pretty little bow around your neck." Kellan smugly watched me grow redder. "The better to hang you with."

Mikka continued as if he hadn't said a thing. "Coincidentally, Kellan will join us before the night is out. Adrona will be forced to throw an event to welcome us, especially with two prominent visitors."

"Then what?" I interrupted. "What kind of investigation can any of us do in the middle of a proper Fairy Fete?"

Giving me a look that was both pitying and disdainful, Kellan sighed. "The same kind of investigation you would do in your bar. Or your mother's Court. Seduce. Cajole. Listen." He crossed his arms over his chest. "I understand this is not how you planned things, but you're too smart to act this obtuse."

I'm proud to say I didn't stamp my foot or throttle him or attempt to access Mikka's fire and flambé him from the inside out. Instead, I turned on my heel and began stalking toward the path to the Gate.

"And don't worry," Kellan called as he settled into an Adirondack chair to wait at the Knoll until after we'd crossed. "I'm sure Queen Adrona has plenty of lovely dresses for you to borrow for the ball." He chuckled, and I could just hear him tell Mikka, "I did tell her to dress for the occasion, but maybe I should have been more specific."

Morgana save me, it would take every ounce of my control not to kill this smug bastard.

CHAPTER NINETEEN

I didn't even wait to get to the Gate before reaching out to her. Halfway down the wooded path I opened my awareness and searched for the wild growing taste of Greenwood. As always, she was there, eager to open to my request.

She opened easily, as though she had been waiting. Usually, first thing in the morning like this, she took a few moments to stretch, to sleepily bridge the gap between the worlds. That day, though, she was anxious to begin, streaming magic into the area around us for all local fae to access.

As I made my way through the Georgia pines and oaks that surrounded the Gate's clearing, I discovered why.

I was not the first person to arrive there that morning.

Two armed guards of the Summer Palace were standing sentinel on either side of the Gate, clutching tall pikes with sharpened spear points. They appeared concerned but unsurprised that the Gate had been opened before anyone arrived to shed blood. Bryony must have warned them of my new ability.

"Siobhan Cambry Illythia," the one on the left said. He was someone I was unfamiliar with, tall and muscled with a brow that threatened to collapse over his eyes at any moment. The other was slimmer and good-looking, but a sense of power radiated from him, causing the hair on the back of my neck to stand on end. They both were strangers, which concerned me since I thought I knew most of the knights and guards in the Court's employ.

I slowed my pace but did not stop my approach to the Gate. Tradition alone should keep them from attacking a Gatekeeper at the Gate. Still, after Mikka had been attacked by a member of a royal Court, I could not assume that tradition would keep us safe.

"That's me," I said. Mikka came up behind me, immediately falling into a protective stance at my left shoulder. "Are you needing assistance crossing the Ways? Or are you seeking sanctuary? You wouldn't be the first Summer guards to defect."

They traded glances before shifting their grips on their pikes, anchoring the bottoms on the ground but clearly pointing their tips in my general direction.

"You would do best to return to your place of business and remove yourself from this area," the slender guard said. "Under orders of Her Royal Highness Bryony and Her Majesty Queen Illythia, access to the Gate is restricted for the foreseeable future."

"I'm sorry?" I goggled at their words.

"We are under orders to keep anyone from accessing the Gate, opening it for unsanctioned reasons, and most importantly, to keep you in the Iron Realm."

"Are you?" I said carefully. I could already feel the heat growing at my back as Mikka spoiled for a fight. The cedar smoke and pepper taste of her power tickled my tongue, and I could feel the hint of her flames at my own fingertips. This close to the Gate, it would be nothing for me to borrow her flavor of magic, and it seemed my instinct was to reach for it. This could be fun. Or disastrous.

They must have noticed the small smile that emerged unbidden on my lips. Or maybe it was the fiery grin on Mikka's that caused them to move into firm and ready stances, their pikes lowering further toward us. "Go back to the Knoll, Siobhan," the muscled thug sneered. "You don't want to make us stop you."

I pursed my lips. "Now, you don't know me like that, Muscles. You don't get to tell me what I do or don't want." I reached out for his power and tasted bitter pine resin and hops. "Even if you had authority to prevent me crossing through that Gate, a mere heraclid like yourself might have a hard time stopping me."

His ready stance faltered for a moment as I identified his fae race accurately.

I flexed my fist, relishing the strength I borrowed from him with just a sample of his magic. His race was named for their herculean strength and durability. The merest taste of his magic, and I could feel a power that extended beyond my muscles.

"And you," I said, reaching out for the other guard. I got an overwhelming sense of sugar and mint and lime. "A liderc? Are you going to seduce me into staying here?"

He shifted then, transforming from a slender, attractive man into something much larger, much hairier, and much more terrifying. He loomed over me, new fangs glistening with venom and eyes flashing with threat. "I have other ways to stop you."

"Lidercs are shapeshifters," Mikka reminded me in a loud whisper over my shoulder.

"Got that part." It seemed they really were going to physically stop us from accessing the passage to Fairy.

Or at least they were going to try. I already had a hold on their magic, and this close to the Gate, I had to work to control myself from seizing more.

Mikka took a confident step forward in front of me. "Boys, boys, let's not push things out of control here. We understand you're under orders, but you must know that your rules are mere suggestions to us. We're solitary and don't pledge to your Court. And as strong and strapping as you both seem," she took her time looking up at all eight feet of the hulking, hunched liderc, "you're not a match for the two of us." She flicked her wrist back and open-palmed a ball of fire that rolled around threateningly.

The liderc licked his lips, and the heraclid popped his neck. They were spoiling for a fight.

"So we're doing this?" I asked, even as I pulled at the mojito and

IPA taste of the two of them. The flavors did not meld well at all and made me almost gag. Rethinking my plan, I immediately dropped the power of the heraclid and concentrated on the big guy. Syrupy mojito filled my senses, and I gulped it down.

I had no interest in borrowing his shapeshifting ability for myself, so instead, I throttled his power at the source, cutting him off from his connection to the Gate and his Queen. Like turning a spigot, I stopped the flow of his magic and watched as the liderc stumbled, shrinking back down to a form that was scrawnier and more pathetic even than he'd first appeared. His hair dropped away as his muscles withered, leaving a weak-limbed, pale-faced boy in his place.

He fell to his knees, confused and dazed, swooning to the mossy ground. I continued to gulp down his magic, reveling in the sweet minty power. I felt strong, giddy, seductive. I knew every aspect of his essence, his desires, his fears, his power.

Stepping up to the pathetic figure he'd become, I was his Madonna, a succubus, a siren. I could be his entire world if I wished.

I whispered his name. "Imre."

Longing suffused his body, wrenching him toward me. He was my plaything, my doll, my penitent worshiper, and he would do anything I asked in this moment.

"Imre," I said again. "Stop your friend." My words were slick as sex, wet and undeniable as pleasure freely given.

Slack-jawed and glassy-eyed, he nodded and turned to find the heraclid attempting to grapple with Mikka.

Mikka needed no help in fighting that brute. She danced away, flickering like a flame, singeing him with handfuls of fire each time he got close. She was playing with him, enjoying herself as he employed only brute strength to her whirling fighting style. She was easily as strong as he but chose only to use that strength when he surprised her and grabbed her from behind. She struggled only a moment before grabbing the wrists of the hands he'd wrapped around her and bending them backward, pulling a squeal of pain from the muscled man.

Neither saw little Imre creeping up to them. As Mikka burst from out of the heraclid's grasp, Imre lunged forward and laid a hand in the middle of his partner's back.

"Stop," I felt him whisper with the same flavor of power I had stolen. Imre was using the reserves of his magic after I'd cut him off from his Queen and the Gate, but he held nothing back. He used the full force of his seductive voice, and the heraclid's knees buckled. He dropped, landing with a thump, as he looked longingly at Imre.

Imre circled around the fallen man, who watched enraptured. Gently, Imre reached delicate, tapered fingers out and cupped the heraclid's cheek. The strong man wilted under the touch, leaning into the palm, his mouth open with desire.

I could taste the surge of Imre's power again, sweet and citrusy as he leaned down. "Stop," he said again. Then, hardly having to lean over given the size disparity of the pair, Imre brought his mouth down on the brute's.

My awareness was flooded as Imre used the last of his power reserves to rip at the soul energy of his friend. Bitter hops warred with mint and syrup that swirled with juniper and herbs and floral greenery. Images and voices assaulted me: lovers, family, blood and pain, pleasure and delight.

The argument and wasted words that ended years of tender moments and stolen joys. A healing hug that eased months of isolation and loneliness. Spoken words that brought instant understanding and the shouted curses that broke a heart. Laughter and tears, screams of pain and screams of ecstasy.

All of it, every moment of decades of life well and poorly lived, flooded into me until I thought I would explode.

Laughter.

Loss.

Love.

Life.

Then it popped.

A chasm opened in the world. A hole. A nothing where there had been something.

Two somethings. Imre. Hoyt. For that was his name. Had been his name.

And the green rushed in.

Like the forest that reclaims the abandoned field. Like the grass that overtakes the garden. Like the moss that creeps over neglected stone. Like shoots that sprout from forgotten potatoes and weeds that creep through the cracks and mold attacks leftover food.

The green taste of life was everywhere. Fairy, the eternal magic, flooded out of the Gate, pouring into the gap that was left, cascading over everything in its path. Endless torrents of potential energy ready to be wielded by any who could catch it.

The Gate surged with the sacrifices I'd given her, and I was overcome. She filled me with more than I could hold. My entire self resonated, shook apart with the chaos of pure life energy. I thought I screamed, but I had no mouth, no body, no self. I was nowhere and everywhere. I burned and froze, was shattered and remade between moments.

There was no sense, for I was nothing but sensation. No thinking, but I was pure thought.

It was as if I was stuck between the realms again inside the Greenwood Gate. Torn between Earth and Fairy, the Iron and Eternal Realms. As I had once before, I stopped fighting and opened myself to this power. I tried to find my connection between them, hidden in my half human and half fae sides, but I found nothing. There was no tether inside me connecting me to both worlds while I was trapped in the liminal space between them both.

I wasn't inside the Gate. I was in one place.

I wasn't. I was everywhere. But I was nothing. And nowhere.

There was no I.

There was only the magic.

And I was gone.

CHAPTER TWENTY

Coming back from nothing should be more jarring, but it felt like waking up slowly. There was a haziness as the void faded, and the world came into soft focus. There were small sensations I became aware of, light pressure along the back of my neck, wet persistence against my lips and tongue.

The taste of earth and spice and something I'd never encountered before. I chased after it, hungry for more. I wanted to bathe in it, to soak and luxuriate and make it a part of me. It was something like the darkest cherries or smoked cedar or the soil after rain. It was temporary, fleeting, and I wanted to know it before it left. It kept shifting, and I followed.

It led me back to myself; my hands twined in short black hair that was soft and silky wrapped around my fingers. My lips and tongue tangled with his, curious and hungry, exploring this taste that had me so enraptured.

I sighed as I caught my breath. "Sweet Mab, more."

In the space that opened between our mouths, he chuckled. "Not the first time someone's said that to me."

Already insinuated back into my body, my heated blood instantly chilled, and it felt like being dropped into a frozen pond, breaking through the sheet of ice. Shock, pain, and absolutely nothing hot remained in me.

I groaned in a completely different way, a disgusted and annoyed sound as I pushed myself away from Thierry Kellan. "You."

Of all the people to ground me and bring me back from my dissociated state, why did it have to be him?

With a delicate finger he wiped at his wet mouth and cocked an eyebrow. "You're welcome." He straightened his fancy embroidered coat, pulling his cuffs down. "I think she's back," he said to Mikka who was standing behind me.

Mikka was disheveled, her jacket torn and burned along one arm, her skin faintly smoking and smudges of ash on her face. "Thank, Mab," she said, reaching out to grab my arms and pull me to her. She wrapped me in a tight hug and squeezed. "Will you stop doing shit like that?"

I wriggled out of her grasp. "Like what?"

"Disappearing on me." Her voice had a fragility to it, like she was on the verge of breaking. She stared at me so intently, it felt like she was trying to hold me here with the force of her gaze. "Stop going where I can't follow. Please."

Recognizing her panic, I pulled her back to me and held her this time, gently stroking her back. "Hey, Meeks. I'm sorry. I'm not going anywhere."

"I wouldn't say that," Kellan said from behind me. "We've already come quite a way."

Wheeling to give him a piece of my mind, I realized that he was right. We had come a very long way.

We weren't in Atlanta anymore.

The sky was twilit, hovering between day and night and an unexpected iridescent lavender color that wavered and rippled, like a sea with no discernible shore. Around us were rolling hills of periwinkle blue, paths of green stones, and large-leafed trees dotting the landscape. Behind Mikka stood a quiet stone arch, a doorway that was currently sleeping, satiated, closed.

They'd managed to make the crossing into Fairy with me

unawares. And now we were all completely exposed just a few feet from the wrong side of Greenwood.

I reached out to the Gate, known as the Whitewood Gate on this side. She was sleeping now that we'd passed through, but I could feel something beneath the surface. There was a difference to her in this realm. I could feel a thrumming power beneath the surface, a barely contained presence that I couldn't determine as benevolent or menacing. She slept for the moment, satisfied by the sacrifices made to cross her boundaries and straight into danger.

The immediate surroundings told nothing about what awaited us even a hundred feet down the paths in any direction. If we started walking, we could find ourselves in the middle of a forest of thirty-foot-tall dandelions, complete with claws and teeth. One wrong step off the path, and we could be knee deep in a bog with shrieking eels or eternal stench or a quicksand of sadness.

Clear and beautiful was just what the realm chose to be around the Gate. Everything around us was open, inviting, and serene. There was nothing but potential and freedom and complete exposure to whatever threat might want to approach.

"We should get moving." I couldn't hide the tremor in my voice as I scanned the horizon, looking for threats.

Kellan was less than concerned as he crossed his arms, his upper lip curled and his gray eyes flashing with annoyance. "Or you could take a moment to thank me for kissing you so incredibly that you had no choice to come back to consciousness. Your mother would be disappointed in your appalling lack of manners, Your Highness."

"Don't call me highness," I said through my teeth. "But thank you." I licked at my lips, the enticing taste of him lingering. Still, I had the urge to swipe the back of my hand across my mouth or chug mouthwash. "I'm not entirely sure why you felt the need to assault my lips with yours considering I'd already eliminated the threats, but I'm sure you felt it necessary."

I expected another dry retort from him, a dismissal or criticism. Instead, his eyes darted to Mikka. "It was."

Mikka for her part was standing awkwardly, her hands jammed

into the back pockets of her jeans. "It's fine," she said. "Shiv's right. We have a ways to go."

"Wait," I said, realizing there was something I had missed. "What's going on?"

Mikka avoided my gaze and just started walking away from the silently menacing Gate and down the path. "It's fine."

I rushed to catch up with her and grabbed at her arm, turning her to face me. "What's going on, Meeks? What happened?"

"It's not a big deal," she insisted, pulling her sleeve out of my grasp. It was then I realized the smoking burns along her jacket weren't from her lingering fire power. There were distinct handprints on each of her biceps. Prints the size of my hands.

My mouth went dry, and my gut clenched. "Did I do that?"

She shrugged again and chewed at her bottom lip. "You weren't yourself."

"Don't," I whispered, nausea threatening to disgorge my stomach's contents. "Don't dismiss this." I surveyed the damage I'd apparently inflicted on my best friend, my protector, my sister. Burn marks on her arms. Scorch marks, not ash along her cheeks. Bags of exhaustion and pain that hadn't been under her eyes before our crossing. "I stole your power. And I used it against you."

I had no memory of it. The world had disappeared when Imre killed his friend and perished with the effort. When I had murdered them both. I had done that. And I hadn't been able to stop myself. I'd felt right. Righteous even. It had been necessary. To protect myself and my friend. And because the Gate needed blood to open.

The thought that I'd sacrificed them both without a single pang of conscience should terrify me. But that wasn't what had Mikka and Kellan treating me with care.

It was what happened after the Gate opened, and I'd lost myself. Whatever happened, whatever I had done had been enough to convince Kellan to throw out his plans and to get over his personal dislike of me as he attempted to ground me in my body with his tongue.

Apparently, attacking Mikka with her own magic was enough of a motivation.

"I'm so sorry, Mikka," I said.

She shook her head. "It wasn't you," she said, but she still wouldn't look at me.

She gave me a beat to say something more, but I had nothing I could say to make this right. I'd been where she was, excusing the atrocious behavior of someone I loved, explaining away the ways that she had hurt me. So many times my mother had crossed lines, had attacked me in one of her states and had no memory of it afterward.

I'd forgiven her, because it wasn't her fault. Everyone knew what the power that surged through Queens did to their minds. It was corrosive, chipping away at their control and rendering them a danger to all around them.

And now I was just like her. Attacking those closest to me, blind to the danger I posed just by accessing my magic. It didn't matter whether I was conscious of my actions. I was hurting the people around me.

Until I got this power managed, I had to tread carefully and keep my distance from anyone I didn't want to get hurt.

"I don't have any excuses," I said, wishing I had any way to explain what had happened, any way to apologize. "But I will get this under control. I won't let something like that happen again."

Mikka shook her head. "It's fine," she said again. "We should get to the Winter Queen's Palace. Even the roads aren't safe."

As she continued walking up the path, I noticed she kept a certain amount of distance between us, moving ahead just far enough that I couldn't talk with her or reach out for her easily. I couldn't blame her for not trusting me. I didn't trust me, either.

Kellan, however, was not afraid to approach me. As Mikka tromped off ahead of us, leading us on the path to the palace, he fell into step right beside me.

We picked our way gingerly as the way was pocked with holes and unexpected bumps. I wondered briefly what the road was made of; it wasn't quite paved, but it was also not packed dirt. It felt more organic, almost like wood, pliant and yielding, yet given to breakage and crumbling like stone or concrete. Each step must be deliberate, else we risked stepping into a sudden hole and turning an ankle.

Interrupting my thoughts, Kellan spoke. "I must say it's awfully arrogant to acquire the curse of a Queen's Madness without actually taking on the responsibilities of a conduit. Have you always had a martyr complex, or is that something you've adopted recently?"

I looked off in the distance hoping to see one of the wild cryptids of Fairy that could swoop in and eat this arrogant ass of a man. Maybe a troll or ogre could come from over that hill and make a quick meal of him to put us all out of our misery.

When no such creature emerged, I sighed. "I'm not in the mood, Kellan. What do you want?"

"I want to make sure you're ready," he said, dropping his irreverence for the moment. "What happened at the Gate was unfortunate, but it doesn't have to ruin my plans here. I have little doubt that Adrona will know about you killing the two Summer guards before the night is up, but I think we can use that to our advantage. It distances you further from your mother and sister's Court and the appearance of their influence over your trip here."

"If anybody thinks my family has anything to say with regards to my actions has not been paying attention for the past fifty years."

"And yet, you have never taken a stand against them."

"I have! I—" I stopped myself. He might be right. I had left the Court and renounced my claim as Mother's heir. I had refused to stand with the Summer Court on their policies many times. But as a Gate Keeper, I had always attempted to be neutral. I had never voiced opposition to the royal Courts of Fairy in a public setting, and I had always followed the rules and demands they placed on me and my community, even as I insisted on my solitary status. "It's complicated," I finally said.

"That is neither an excuse nor an explanation. It is a vapid and empty truth. And it's beneath you."

I wheeled on him. "What is your problem?"

To his credit, he didn't so much as flinch as I screamed at him.

I wished he had. Still, I pressed further. "You've done nothing but insult me, dismiss me, betray me, and straight up bother me since we've met. If you hate me so much, what are you even doing here? And don't you tell me it's just because Argus asked you to. We both know that's not the reason you're here."

He closed the mouth he had opened, no doubt to give me that exact response. The straight line of his jaw hardened as he grit his teeth, his gray eyes full of frustration. I wasn't playing his games the way he clearly wanted me to.

Good. An honest reaction. Let him get angry. I was angry.

Then, a hint of elderflower and rye crept into my awareness as his unique flavor of magic shifted again. I licked my lips, remembering the different earth and spice taste of his kiss and couldn't help but fixate on his lips in turn.

Kellan, naturally, saw the desire that flickered across my face, and he laughed. "I see. Craving more already?"

A blinding fury seized me and had me pulling from the magic that was all around me. I'd never attempted something like it before, but somehow, I knew how to attack. I didn't even need to access the Gate. Here in Fairy, magic was everywhere, ready for the taking. I didn't stop to think, just took a step back and lashed out with a scream of pique. I sent a burst of raw power at him, something blunt force to put him on his ass and remind him who he was messing with.

He barely blinked as he threw up a magical shield that caught and absorbed the brunt of my rage. The ball of energy I lobbed at him splattered and misted away a mere foot from his face, while he watched me impassively.

I gasped as my anger faded as quickly as it rose. "Ugh," I grunted. It would have felt so good to see him knocked flat, his smug look wiped from his stupid gorgeous face.

"That was interesting," he said, raising a single eyebrow. "Sloppy. But interesting." He took a step toward me, and I instinctively moved an equal step back to his amusement. "I'm not going to retaliate. I'm just curious what you thought that was going to accomplish."

"Forget it," I said, turning away from him and trying my hardest not to race after Mikka's retreating back. Deliberately walking slowly and holding my head high, I concentrated on breathing through everything I was feeling. The frustration, the fury, the fears.

"I will admit I'm taking a risk being here with you." The steady voice came from directly behind me, but I didn't flinch or react. I simply slowed down so Kellan could fall into step with me. "As you just evidenced perfectly, you are volatile, uncontrolled, and untrained in your magic. I don't trust you because of your connection with your mother's Court and your obvious desire to maintain a positive relationship with your sister. I can't rely on you, because you also wish to remain neutral in a city quickly drawing lines of allegiance. I can't even count on you being a consistent ally to our cause despite your entire social circle belonging to the Fair Folk, because you frequently substitute your own judgment over theirs. You are arrogant and think yourself humble. You are emotional and erratic but think yourself reasonable and consistent. You are as likely to lash out and attack as you are to protect and defend."

My fists clenched at my sides as I tried desperately not to prove him right by attacking him again.

He noticed. "And yet," he said with a note of amusement. "If we can get you under control, you could be an incredible asset for the Fair Folk."

"Get me under control? How exactly should I interpret that?"

He made a noise, a cross between a chuckle and a hum, that had me craving his taste again. "You have a unique ability to access the magic of other fae, but you have no idea how to wield it. Your connection to the Gate makes you almost as powerful as a Queen, but you appear to be even more at its mercy. You aren't even aware of what you are doing until you have done it, and that makes you incredibly dangerous. Until you master your magic and learn how to limit the power you channel, you are at risk of burning yourself out and taking half the city down into the flames with you."

There was nothing untrue of what he said. He was actually giving voice to every one of my fears. I wondered again at the nature of his magic; was he able to read my thoughts? Did he wield intuitive magic, or was he just good at reading people?

"Besides," he continued, "your erratic mood shifts lately are not your fault but are another symptom of your affliction. Argus called me in, in part, to try and help you with that."

"He wh—"

I didn't even finish the word when something huge crashed into us and threw Kellan and me from the path.

My head slammed against the ground, robbing me of vision and breath for several vital seconds. I only came to when hot air blew my dark hair out of my face and a rotten meat smell assaulted me.

I wanted to gag, but fear stopped the impulse as I gazed up into an open maw of fanged mandibles and plasma green magic.

The locals had found us.

CHAPTER TWENTY-ONE

Don't move, Siobhan," Kellan said from somewhere off to my left side.

I didn't deign to answer as the open mouth above me clicked its side mandibles, dripping saliva and sparking green magic. The air was filled with the taste of rotten meat, musk, and cucumber. Its long sinuous body wrapped around me, all thick muscle and scale. Two short legs perched on either side of me as the snake-like trunk reached up and curved down, and I could see the edge of its tail twitching beside me, as it curled up and back with irritation.

The large creature perched over me was as familiar as it was horrifying. It was a true basilisk, a wild fae that was distantly related to Rhys. This creature was pure animal, a race that had bathed in the magic of Fairy and refused none of its baser instincts. This was a monster that for centuries had devoured whatever fae it came across, absorbed the power in their blood, and grew stronger and more immortal.

And the way its tongue darted out to taste the skin of my cheek, I knew it was considering if I was the next easy meal in its diet.

I wondered how it would do it. Would it rip into me with its mandibles? It had two sets, offset from its main top-bottom jaws.

They allowed the basilisk to grasp wriggling and fighting prey. Would it use its magic on me? I couldn't see the basilisk's eyes, but it could petrify me if it caught my gaze. Those fangs that dangled from its main jaws were also poisoned, so a single bite could paralyze me and eventually cause my insides to putrefy and turn to mush. That could take days to kill me, though.

I guess it all depended on how hungry this basilisk was. And whether it considered either me or Kellan to be a worthy meal or quick snack.

Granted, it didn't have to eat me, either. It could just decide to roll over and squash us both under its immense side. How long was this thing? Twenty feet? Thirty? It had to weigh several tons given how its trunk was all thick muscle and metallic scale.

I squirmed, trying to pull away from the sharp claws of its short legs, and the creature growled. The sound was both sibilant and low-pitched, reminding me of a crocodile protecting its nest. Instantly, I stopped moving and let the basilisk test me again with its tongue.

"What do I do?" I said, trying to move as little as possible. Basilisks of Fairy were both deaf and blind, but their sensitive scales and tongues ensured that this one would know if I yelled for help or attempted to rescue myself. Aside from a pair of daggers in my belt, I was physically unarmed and given what had happened the last few times I'd accessed any sort of magic, I was hesitant to attempt anything along those lines. Still, I called out to Kellan. "If I try and do something stupid, will you promise not to use tongue when you call me back from the brink?"

"What? No. Do not pull on the Gate's power," he called back, somewhere further behind the basilisk. "I'm not kissing you again. I'll take care of this."

"We'll take care of it," Mikka called from somewhere else, her voice slightly out of breath.

This creature was so big, I couldn't see anything but the way its gray-green scales reflected the twilight glow of Fairy's sky and the iridescent roil of magic that peeked between its two rows of sharp serrated teeth and the fangs along with its four mandibles. Provocatively those various hinged jaws folded into each other, tucking teeth past and over each other and avoiding the tongue that quested out and in the direction where Kellan and Mikka circled the beast.

"It knows you're there," I told them, as the snake-creature's tongue licked out the right side of its mouth, then the left. It was feeling for them, tasting the air and finding how far away they were.

"Of course, it knows we're here," Kellan said. "But basilisks feed on strong emotions like fear. And lust. We're just not providing it easy meals at the moment."

"Does that make me the easy meal?" I tried not to let panic creep into my voice, but the way the basilisk shrunk toward me let me know that it could absolutely taste my terror.

I also tried not to draw parallels between this beast and my lover, but the similar taste of its magic was starting to mess with me. The way this tremendous creature tasted of Rhys twisted things inside of me. It was familiar and unsettling in equal measures as it scented me, squirmed in anticipation of tasting me, and almost purred in a low, savage way.

So many nights, Rhys had anticipated devouring me with the same hunger. I doubted the results would be as enjoyable with this distant cryptid cousin.

The taste of the basilisk filled my mouth stronger than before, and the hunger of my own magic rose to meet it.

"If you're going to do something," I said, to my friends my voice thick with denied power, "it should be sooner than later." I didn't know if it was fear or force that would drive my action, but an energy was building in me that threatened to explode at any moment.

"Mab's fist," Mikka cursed as the claws of the basilisk ground into the earth beside my body, and it leaned forward to me.

"Don't," Kellan warned on the other side as a flicker of flame sprang to life.

"I have to do something," she shouted back as a mesquite taste filled the air.

"I can take care of this," he insisted, and he too began pulling on his magic.

As everything around me was spinning out of control, I realized I had to act or risk losing myself again. I stilled my body, shut out my awareness of Mikka and Kellan. The cucumber and sandalwood taste of her—I just now realized the basilisk perched over me was female and thick with eggs. No wonder she was hungry. I focused on her flavor, sampling her strength and power.

It was raw, fluctuating, roiling with ancient instinct and the collected power of every fae she had eaten in the past several centuries of her life.

Reaching down to my sides, I palmed my daggers from their sheaths. The blades were shorter than six inches. They were all but useless. At best, I could wedge them just below the outside serrated edge of the basilisk's scales around her limbs, where the gaps were largest. Even still, there was no way I would ever find flesh. Not without help.

The untamed power of the basilisk coursed through me, and I pulsed it into the blades in my hands. Using the daggers as force directors, I slashed at the creature's wrist and pushed as much of the basilisk's own magic at her.

Whether it was because the power was familiar or I was lucky in my aim, it connected right beneath her thick plated scales and sliced through the tender meat just above her talons. Blood gushed out, and she reared back in pain.

The furious roar she let out clutched me low in my stomach as it resonated around us. I clapped hands over my ears and rolled away from the injured leg that she swiped at the place where I had just been lying.

I scurried back as fast as I could, letting Kellan and Mikka attack at will.

To my surprise, the amount of firepower flew at her was more than the two of them could summon. The basilisk reared back, flung away with an extraordinary amount of swirling energy.

I turned to find half a dozen fae in white uniforms and blue capes unleashing a stream of raw magic at the basilisk. She screamed as they pummeled her.

"Stop!" I shouted. "Don't kill her." The sound of her pain ripped into me, and I could feel my connection with her power wavering as she writhed. She could do nothing to fight back as the offensive magic rolled over her, tearing at her reason, her senses overcome with agony.

I pushed up onto my knees and faced the white uniforms before lashing out at them with her pain. "I said, stop!"

A concussive burst that came from the basilisk and me slammed into them. It wasn't enough to hurt them, but it severed their concentration and stopped the wave of magic long enough for the basilisk to gather her uninjured limbs under her and flee into the wilds of a forest that I could swear hadn't been there earlier.

I breathed a sigh of relief. I might not want to be eaten, but I didn't want the basilisk killed either. Especially given that she was pregnant.

My relief didn't last as the uniforms recovered and encircled me. Mikka and Kellan were already being held at swordpoint by the other half of the dozen or so soldiers.

They were an assortment of some of the most beautiful and terrifying fae I'd ever seen. Unlike the Summer fae who often maintained glamours and endeavored to look as close to human as possible, the fae who pledged the Winter Court and spent much of their time in Fairy rejected the idea that they should blend into any society that wasn't their own. Though each of these soldiers walked on two legs and held weapons with one of two hands, they embraced every difference from plain, vanilla humanity.

One guard had no discernible features across their flat white face aside from two small holes that I assumed were for breathing. Another had horns that sprouted from her head and spiraled back like a ram's, curling around into two impressive weapons. Still another had eyes that were the size of saucers and segmented like a spider's, reflecting light in all directions and constantly moving to take in the world. One had a snout like a wolf's, another a proboscis and a frilled head that extended straight back into waving tendrils of black fleshy fronds. There were fingers that had too many segments, legs that bent in the wrong direction, backs that bowed, and a fair number of wings, vined tendrils, and fingers of flame that were more appendages than decoration.

Each of the Winter fae was different, and yet they held themselves in a well-trained formation as they encircled my companions and myself. Dressed in uniforms of navy blue and gold insignia, they were all intimidating, but one stepped forward, commanding our attention.

"Siobhan Cambry Illythia," he began. He was not tall, but he exuded power. His skin was thick with bark and heavy with moss and vines that hung like hair. Branches adorned his head like hair, and he was built broad as an oak, but he was anything but wooden, moving with a controlled grace that spoke to training and physical mastery. "Thierry Kellan. Mikka Balaur. On behalf of Her Majesty Queen Adrona, I would like to welcome you to the Naboskova region. I am Captain Dusan. If you would allow us to escort you to the palace."

It was not a request, but given royal protocol, I did my best to respond as if it were. I wiped some stray moss or grass or whatever living plant it was that covered the ground here off the knees of my leggings and arranged my coronet so that the alexandrite teardrop fell directly center over my forehead. "Thank you, Captain. We would appreciate the escort. It is a shame you were not at the Gate to welcome us, or we might not have endured this unpleasantness."

Mikka chuckled behind me as my inner fae royal emerged.

"I beg your pardons, Highness. Your visit was not expected or arranged beforehand. And since the location of the Whitewood Gate fluctuates too frequently, we cannot safely maintain facilities permanently at the site without endangering my forces."

"A shame," Kellan joined in with a tone befitting any sidhe royal. "If your Queen invested in security on her side of the Gate, we might not have had to venture here for answers."

The captain bristled and his guard behind him shifted subtly. "My Queen's orders are not mine to question."

"But her security is yours to enforce?" I pressed, following Kellan's lead.

"Her security has never been more of a priority," Dusan said, shifting his hand subtly toward his sword at his side.

"Again, a shame it does not extend to all of her people." Kellan's words were a challenge, and I wondered what his goal was in antagonizing our escort.

"Enough," I said, calling on my authority again. "If you would be so kind, Captain. I believe we are all anxious to be off the Fairy Road and safely behind castle walls."

Truthfully, I could think of no place more dangerous than in a Winter Queen's hold. And entering with Kellan at my back, uncertain whether he was protecting it or looking for weak spots to stab? I'd take the basilisk again in a heartbeat. But that wouldn't accomplish what I needed to do here.

If we were going to get answers in Adrona's Court, I had to trust him just enough to get us through. He inclined his head and acknowledged my acceptance of our escort.

"Yes, by all means, Captain. Lead the way," Kellan said, and he held out an arm for me to take, cementing our alliance for this trip.

There was no turning back now.

CHAPTER TWENTY-TWO

With so many of us on the move, Fairy seemed to bend the road to our need. It should have taken Mikka, Kellan, and myself an hour or more to reach the Naboskova Castle as the region twisted in on itself, yielding to the desires of its residents over mere tourists like us. With the escort of a dozen Winter fae intent on a single location, the way was opened, and we arrived in a quarter of the time.

I almost regretted how little time I had to prepare myself mentally before the castle's outer walls stood before us. The stone rose up at least a hundred feet, extending at least six times as far in both directions before curving around to protect the inner city of the Naboskova Winter Court. Along the far edge of what I could see, orchards spread out, in the full bloom of spring, despite the winter season we'd left behind in the Summer territory of Atlanta. It was near impossible to keep track of the differences between political seasons and the actual climate seasons when traveling through Fairy, and I gave up trying to make sense of it.

We passed through an open set of gates that could admit everything from a family of trolls to a mated pair of basilisks to find a sprawling city. Dozens of two- and three-story buildings lined the inner walls of the fortress. We saw lodging houses, pubs, and many market stalls filled with fruits and vegetables, or fabrics and other goods for sale. We made our way past two avenues that stretched in either direction before the space opened up into a large inner courtyard.

All but four of our guard peeled off to the right, heading for buildings that I imagined were barracks or training buildings, given the considerable number of people in uniforms milling about. Like our escort, they were as varied in race and description as I'd ever seen, but they were all outfitted in the same sharp navy blue.

Only the good captain and an escort for each of us followed as we approached the castle itself. It was something out of a fairy tale, which was fitting. Grand and gothic with turrets and towers of white stone, crenellated parapets and balconies, gargoyles and carved statues, it was hard to know where to look. Both medieval and ancient, yet clean and crisp, it could have been built within the past few years.

Captain Dusan took the lead and directed us across another courtyard toward a low staircase and huge doorway. He nodded to the armed guards on duty there who waved their hands and opened the large wooden door with magic. It was a casual, but still impressive display. Here in Fairy even the doormen didn't need to worry about rationing magic or pulling their power through a Queen. Defaulting to magic means for even the simplest acts was easy and thoughtless.

Feeling ill at ease, I leaned on Kellan's arm as we ascended the handful of steps to a huge entrance hall. It was long and wide. To the right, I saw a staircase winding up to a landing and then branching out in both directions, no doubt to the living quarters of the castle's residents. There was also a wide passage beyond, the walls adorned with portraits and tapestries and leading to another grander staircase.

To our left was a staircase leading down on one side of the hall, while across from it the room opened to a wide space with ceilings so high I couldn't see. People were scampering from the stairs and into the open space, carrying flowers, fabrics, and food. They were obviously setting up for something.

"Told you to bring a nice dress," Kellan whispered to me, gesturing to the flurry of activity. "There's going to be dancing tonight."

That must have been the ballroom then. He was right that Adrona would throw a fête in our honor.

I glared at him, slightly angry that he was proven right, but also glad to know he had a feel for how things worked.

Captain Dusan ignored both left and right paths and led us straight to an intimidatingly long, tall wall of six paired, golden doors. He reached the middle set and stopped dead center. Ceremoniously, he raised a fist and knocked twice, the sound booming through with a metallic, yet musical tone, a low chord that conjured feelings both joyous and militaristic.

Dusan stepped back as the doors folded outward, and a light shone from the open space beyond, sharp and bright enough we couldn't see within.

"Dramatic," Mikka whispered.

It had the desired effect, though, as I felt my spine stiffen, my chin lift, and my stomach drop. Kellan strode forward with me on his arm and Mikka fell in behind us.

The light enveloped us and left us blinking as we crossed the threshold into a large throne room filled with people. Colorful insignia-decked banners and flowering green vines hung down, fluttering from unseen anchor points. A lush blue carpet extended before us, cutting the room in half lengthwise as fae in royal dress stood and watched our little procession.

It felt as familiar as any official event back home. There were mostly the familiar daoine sidhe that filled all the Courts: tall, lithe, elegant, and resembling the humans we lived among. There were also willowy dryads and leshies, languid loreleis and kappas that looked like they had just emerged from their ponds, and earthy oreads from the mountains.

But here and there were fae races I never saw in the Iron Realm. A feathered stratim with a hawk's beak and eyes in a woman's face held the arm of a tall man with facial gills and webbed hands. A gray-skinned gremlin only came up to the shoulder of his partner, who, if I wasn't mistaken, was a baku, a dream devourer. The baku had no discernible face, his visage obscured by shifting smoke and mist; even still, I could sense he was frowning at us.

They all were. Not a single fae watching us seemed happy or even curious about the interlopers crossing their path.

Too late, I realized we may have made a fatal mistake coming here.

The woman at the center of the dais smiled and beckoned us closer with her full arm like she was nothing more than a grandmother calling us in for fresh cookies after school. She was matronly, gentle and soft, a berehynia, a hearth mother with full cheeks and smile-crinkled eyes over a pointed nose and stretched lips. She was clothed in a thick blue velvet gown that was modest and simple.

Despite her unassuming appearance, she radiated power.

Being solitary, we did not kneel as we reached the dais, but Kellan and I both inclined our heads, acknowledging the Queen who sat above us.

"Welcome to Naboskova," she said. "I am Adrona, and while I am most curious why you chose to make the journey to our corner of the realm, I am happy you made it to our palace safely."

"Thank you, Your Majesty," I said. "I am—"

"Illythia's eldest. Siobhan. Yes," she said warmly, but I could sense steel under her words. "I was told you were coming. And with the man who would be king."

Kellan stiffened beside me, but he spoke evenly. "We are honored to be received by you, Majesty. I wish we were here under happier circumstances. We are here to mourn the loss of your daughter and offer our assistance in seeking justice for what was done to you and your Court."

Her thin lips pinched together for just a moment, but she was quickly smiling beatifically again. "Naturally, we regret the circumstance as well." She looked out over her Court. "The loss of any of our Court is an injury we feel personally. This one, though, I believe ripped a piece out of everyone in this Court. It is an offense that will not go unpunished."

"We grieve with you, Your Majesty," Kellan said. "And we are here to offer our support and aid in seeking out the ones responsible. Your daughter will not be forgotten. May Diana receive her."

"And Morgana mourn her," the Court responded in unison, their magic rising as they invoked the twin goddesses of death.

Adrona closed her eyes and accepted the offering they gave her. She was their Queen and was bound tight to their magic. Even here in Fairy, where she didn't have to operate as a conduit to funnel magic to her subjects, her power fed into theirs, and theirs into her.

Sworn subjects of the Winter Courts pledged their magic to their Queen in exchange for her protection in this realm and the next. Here in Fairy, they could count on protection from the threats of bestial fae, they could pull on greater magical strength than they naturally possessed, and they could pool powers with their fellow Court fae. Even when they crossed into the Iron Realm, they could access almost the full strength of their powers because of their connection through the Gate with their Queen on the other side.

Bridging that gap between the realms took its toll on Winter Queens, but spending most of their time in the Eternal Realm, they suffered fewer of the effects of serving as conduits as compared to their Summer counterparts. In fact, they thrived when they spent most of their time in Fairy.

Adrona certainly benefited, as she seemed almost to age backward before us, accepting the power offered by her subjects. Smile lines smoothed, and the gray in her hair saturated into rich mahogany brown. When she opened her eyes, I thought I saw a fraction of the pain she felt at losing her daughter, but it was gone almost before it could register.

"You are here to tell me the names of her killers?" Her voice had hardened with icy steel. She lifted a hand and gestured for someone behind her to join her on the dais.

My heart dropped as I recognized Orion, the twin of Oriana, and Adrona's son. He towered over his mother's shoulder and glared down at us. He looked nothing like his mother. Where she was soft and round and motherly, as warm as a home's hearth, he was tall, solid, and white as the winter frost. His glacier blue eyes bored into me, challenging and accusatory.

"She has brought herself and the leader of the Fair Folk to us, Mother. I believe that is answer enough."

I glanced at Kellan. Adrona had referred to him as the would-be king, and Orion called him out in front of the entire Court. If he had ever thought his role secret, it was clear that was not the case here. What game was he playing?

"Your Royal Highness," he said carefully. "Despite your accusations and beliefs about us, we both mourn your loss. To lose not only your sister, but your twin. We cannot imagine what you have gone through." He stepped forward though, setting himself just ahead of me. "But we are not your enemies here. As I have communicated to Her Majesty, we are here to help, to pool our resources and information, and to get to the true cause of our suffering."

Adrona smiled warmly at Kellan. "Yes, we have goals in common," she said before turning a dispassionate look at me. "But I do not quite understand the place Illythia's spawn plays here." She reached a hand up and placed it over the one her son had draped over the back of her throne. "I do not need her, beloved. You may play as you wish."

Orion grinned widely and before I realized what was coming a column of ice-cold air enveloped me, stripping my breath away and freezing me through. I would have screamed if I could find breath, but there was nothing but the frozen wind and the searing pain of my lungs crystallizing. If it weren't for my rapid healing, I don't know if I would have survived more than a few seconds. And it took a few seconds to remember to pull on the power of the Gate and my new magic to protect me.

I reached for the green taste I had come to know so well and found nothing. No grass or herb taste. I probed further, seeking for anything, and realized I had no sense of taste at all. It was like I had been rendered blind or deaf all at once. An entire sense had been cut off, and I could not find my magic at all.

I was trapped as the cold consumed me. I would die, frozen in a Winter Court, just as my mother had always feared.

"Stop," the gentle voice of the Queen cut through the roar of the wind, as all at once, the cold disappeared.

I fell to my knees, gasping, the cold stone of the floor biting into my knees as my body shivered so hard my teeth rattled. My fingers and toes tingled with the sting of frostbite, and my heart pounded as it tried to pump warm blood outward to repair the damage of Orion's magic.

Slowly, as I warmed, the world came back to me. Behind me, I could hear Mikka shouting as she was restrained, but before me, Kellan was kneeling by the Queen's feet, her hand in both of his as she looked down on him beatifically. Over her shoulder her son was glaring down at me, no doubt furious he wasn't allowed to keep torturing me.

"Very well," Adrona said sweetly, lifting her hand to Kellan's mouth so he could bestow a kiss on it. She waved her other hand, and in an instant, Mikka was at my side supporting me as I gained my feet.

"You may be correct," Adrona continued. She stood then, allowing Kellan to escort her up as she smoothed down her blue velvet gown. "Come, Little King. Let us talk more on this." She tucked her hand into the crook of his elbow as innocently as any young coquette and blinked her eyes up at him.

"Thank you, Your Majesty," he said. "You won't regret your mercy."

"I am sure we will both benefit." She gestured to her son. "Escort our other two guests to their quarters. They are under my protection for the duration of their visit, unless I choose to revoke that. If you cannot be cordial, at least do not kill Illythia's eldest. You've already made enough of a mess for me politically." I could see the muscles in Orion's jaw grinding his teeth together, as he nodded and accepted the command of his Queen and mother.

She then finally deigned to acknowledge me. "Siobhan Illythia, I am sure you have discovered, you are cut off from your magic. The wards of my castle prevent all who are not sworn to my Court from accessing their active power. You are here at my pleasure and my mercy. I'm sure you understand." She sounded like a mother explaining why a child couldn't swim in alligator infested waters. She was patient and understanding, but firm. "Still," she continued, "we shall see you at our ball tonight. We honor my late daughter. Whether we do so with dancing and feasting or witnessed justice and pain has yet to be decided." She bestowed an adoring smile on Kellan. "Let us hope you threw your lot in with a cunning tongue."

If I didn't know better, I would have sworn that Kellan blushed. Regardless, he let Adrona lead him to a door set behind the dais. I kept hoping he would turn to look at me, but he had eyes only for the Queen at his side.

The Court bowed as their Queen departed, before they directed their whole attention to their prince who stood glaring down at me as though he would gladly execute me before his entire Court if his Queen had not forbidden it.

"Come with me," Orion finally spat. "Let us discover how iron your resolve actually is."

CHAPTER TWENTY-THREE

Orion swept down, and I had to step back as he pushed past me and Mikka. He cut through the room like an icy breeze, the dozens of royals pulling aside and allowing Mikka and me to trail in his wake.

I had no idea how I was supposed to follow him after he had just attempted to kill me. Yet Adrona had declared in front of her Court that Mikka and I were under her protection, so long as she wanted. It was as good a reassurance as I was likely to get as long as I was on the wrong side of the Gate.

Every eye in the hall was trained on us as we fell into step behind Orion. I had no doubt they would immediately begin speculating about all that had been said in the throne room. Every word, every glance, every shard of ice and burn on my skin would be analyzed and obsessed over until the ball tonight. By then, they would no doubt have come to their own conclusions about my motives, the relationship between Kellan and me, my status regarding the Summer Court, the Fair Folk. I cringed to think of all the mistakes I had already made in coming here, how much I had exposed myself and my people just by being so public in my actions.

If I lived through tonight, I had no doubt that I would regret ever having trusted Kellan to bring me into Fairy. What had I been thinking? He'd already abandoned me to the mercies of a crazed prince and his unhinged mother.

And for what? So he could get answers to help rid me of a curse? He probably never had any intention of helping me. Thierry Kellan was there for his own gain. I should have trusted my instincts and stayed far away from him and his ridiculous Fair Folk. All the jockeying for position, these political games, they only brought trouble.

Trouble like following after the man who just moments ago tried to kill me in the hopes that he might not try to do it again later tonight in front of more witnesses.

Orion moved swiftly out of the throne room and turned left. Thankfully, Captain Dusan fell into step behind us, matching pace as Orion plunged us down past the first stairway and into the entry hall. To the left was another set of doorways that led to a tremendous banquet hall bustling to get ready for the evening's events. The other side of the hall was hung with portraits of the royal family. Adrona's was the largest of them, a lovely painting of her seated on a settee in front of a roaring fire in a grand stone hearth.

Beside her portrait on either side were two young women who couldn't resemble each other any less. The one on the left was dark-haired like Adrona, her face delicately heart-shaped and kind with full, rosy lips and dark eyes that sparkled with mischief. She was curvy and soft, also posed lying on a settee almost seductively in front of a library of books.

On the other side of the Queen's portrait was a young woman with white-blond hair and icy blue eyes. She was ephemeral, long and slight, almost insubstantial. She was beautiful as a wisp of cloud, as temporary as beach foam.

Oriana.

Her brother stopped and studied his sister. His own portrait was beside hers, and the resemblance between the twins was undeniable. The same white-blond hair, the pale blue eyes, and the taut, dangerous lines of their mouths. Neither twin was smiling in their portrait, and both looked like they could step from their frames and murder any who crossed them.

It made it all the more intimidating to be standing beside the subject who had already tried.

"Tread carefully, half breed," he said. "If Mother had not forbidden it, I would strip the air from your lungs just for the joy of it. Your people killed my sister, and I would have your blood in retribution."

"Your Highness," Dusan said, taking a step forward, and I could feel Mikka behind me, coiled and ready to respond.

"Hold your peace, Captain," he snarled. "I won't kill the guest."

"I am sorry for your loss, Your Highness. Truly, I am," I said, fighting every one of my instincts that told me to cut and run. "But I am not to blame for your sister's death, nor do I have any connection or knowledge of those who did. I know plenty of people in the Fair Folk, and I can't believe they would have done this. They have their grievances against Summer, but they have avoided violence—"

Before I could register that he had moved, Orion had me thrown up against the wall, his hand around my throat. My head slammed between two huge frames, sending stars across my vision, and I struggled to breathe around his fingers as they clenched my windpipe, the precious stones of my necklace biting into my skin. I reached for my magic, but thanks to the wards, I found only emptiness in the space where my magic dwelt. I was at his mercy.

> *"With Iron resolve and Eternal fidelity*
> *The Fair Folk pledge solidarity*
> *Freedom for all, Power to the least."*

He recited the note clearly. No doubt he had read it over and over again, this one clue as to who had so brutally stolen his sister from him.

"Anyone could have written that," I choked out as his grip loosened just enough. "Plenty of people want to see the Fair Folk discredited."

He leaned into me. "You defend them so vociferously, yet you claim not to be one of them." His eyes flashed with hate and lightning. "Perhaps you blame them to deflect from yourself."

"Why would I come here if that was true? I don't want trouble. I just want peace."

At once, he dropped his hand letting me fall once again to my knees gasping.

Mikka rushed forward, and even Captain Dusan came around the prince to help me back to my feet.

"Peace for who? The Summer fae? The solitary traitors? Your Fair Folk? Do you have any loyalties at all or are you only here for yourself?"

I started to answer, but he cut me off with a wave of his hand and another stolen breath. I choked as he sneered down at me.

"I would believe nothing you say. You turned your back on your Court. You betrayed your people already. Mab save anyone you have promised to protect. They will suffer more for trusting you."

He stormed away then, releasing my breath and leaving me with Mikka and Dusan.

The captain sighed. "It seems our prince has been called away to other obligations. If I may, I will escort you to your quarters." He extended a hand down the hall toward the grand staircase.

Mikka snorted. "Thanks, Dussy." She pulled on my arm, and we followed the captain the rest of the way up to our rooms.

The living quarters of the palace were sumptuous if old-fashioned. Unlike my mother's palace that had modern accommodations with individually outfitted rooms for all kinds of fae, the Naboskova palace was straight out of the Middle Ages. Three stories of balconied halls extended around the open air of the banquet hall below us. It was the second of these balconies that we were led down.

Dusan stopped at a door all the way around the far side of the banquet hall and opened it to reveal a private suite. There was a receiving room with couches and chairs, a small shelf of bottles and a table laden with snacks. Off the main space were two separate bedrooms with a bathing chamber between them. The furniture was ornate in a medieval way: heavy carved woods, thick carpets, velvet cushions, and embroidered linens.

I noted that while the Summer Palace showed off its wealth with magic-imbued enhancements—rooms that adapted to their occupants, refreshments that could be summoned with a single spoken request—this Winter Palace demonstrated power with hand-crafted luxuries. Magic was abundant here, so rooms that magically transformed to guests' needs would be unimpressive. Things that took time, like hand-carved headboards and spooled wood tables, embroidered bed sheets and brushed velvets, spun silk and sculpted art, all told of a Queen that commanded loyalty, respect, and power.

"You will find a selection of attire for tonight's festivities in the closet of the bedroom to the right. If nothing is to your liking, you can ring the bell pull by the door and someone will come and assist. The ball will begin at sunset. I suggest you attend promptly. Any lateness may be interpreted … poorly."

"Noted. Thank you, Captain," Mikka said, as she held the door for Dusan to leave. She closed it firmly behind him and wheeled to face me. "This was a spectacularly bad idea, wasn't it?" She had a grin on her face, but it was clear that she was as near to panic as I was.

"The worst," I agreed, rubbing at my sore neck and moving toward the room on the right. I might as well take a look at what was in fashion at Fairy balls these days.

"Well, good luck," Mikka said as she opened the door back into the hallway.

"Wait, what?" I wheeled as she shot me a big grin and bounced on her feet. "Where are you going?"

"I'm not made for balls the same way you are," she said as she gestured to the jewels of my necklace and coronet. "And we need answers that are more likely to come from those who operate beneath the ballroom than those dancing in it. No one has even noticed I'm here. So, I'm going to talk to security, make friends with the kitchen staff and get to the truth of what's rotten in Naboskova. You can draw all the hate of the Court, Kellan can dazzle the royals as he sells you out, and they won't even notice I'm downstairs doing the real work.

We'll get some answers and get out of here and back to the Knoll as quick as we can. Easy."

She waved at me and disappeared before I could convince her not to abandon me.

At least this awful adventure had her acting more like her fiery self. And I couldn't blame her for wanting to avoid the ball. I didn't want to go myself.

But we needed answers, and at the moment all I had were more questions.

Like why was Orion so convinced that I was the one responsible for his sister's death? Why did he hate me so much that he was willing to attack me and risk consequences both from my mother's Court and his?

To that point, what was Adrona's interest in Kellan? It was clear that they had met each other before our visit here, and she had said they had mutual goals. What game was he playing with her? With me? Was he setting me up to take the fall for the Fair Folk? What if they really were to blame for the deaths?

I worried that I had trusted too easily. Argus had vouched for Kellan. Mikka and Varon and the clurichaun all believed in his cause. Mab's breath, half of the people I knew and loved were part of his group. But that didn't mean that he wasn't going to sell me out to the first Court that offered him what he wanted.

If only I knew exactly what it was he wanted.

Freedom? Equality? Or was it all about power?

Adrona had called him "Little king." She seemed to have some idea of his aspirations, and they were apparently loftier than merely helping his solitary community. Yet, somehow, I'd allowed myself to be talked into coming here with him, expecting him to have my best interests at heart.

And here I was, stuck in Fairy with no resources, no allies, and no clue as to what I was going to do.

It certainly felt like I was caught in a trap that was closing in around me.

There was no escaping it now. I was here. I had to play my part.

Hopefully, it would only be the night I had to survive, and I could leave here with the answers I needed to save my skin, defend my people, and get back to my normal life at the Knoll.

All of that required the right armor, so I set about getting ready for the ball.

CHAPTER TWENTY-FOUR

I resisted the urge to tug my dress up higher over my breasts as I entered the ballroom several hours later. Despite the medieval sensibilities of this Court and the matronly manner of its Queen, it seemed that the current fashions in the Naboskova Court were anything but modest.

Each of the dresses available to me had been designed to display the bodies of those who wore them. Layers of sheer fabrics floated over the body, barely enough to conceal what lay underneath. Tight gowns of silk and charmeuse in peacock colors had strategic cutouts that threatened to reveal the entirety of my reproductive organs. One of the dresses was not so much an entire garment as it was a series of straps that after thirty minutes of rearranging, I still could not figure out how to fit on my body.

I'd finally settled on a soft and flowing gown in a light mauve that covered my entire body, aside from long slits that reached up well over my hip bones and a neckline scooped so low I worried a deep breath would expose my entire top half for the Court.

Whether it was the promise of an inadvertent burlesque show or the novelty of a former Summer Princess turned solitary Gate Keeper that commanded so much attention, I felt like every eye in the ballroom was on me.

I tried not to stare back, as I stood off to the side of the ballroom, but it was hard given the dazzling display they put on. Once again, I was astounded by the sheer variety of fae present. One woman's eyes glowed like the embers of a dying fire as her black skin sizzled in the cool night air. A male gorgon had his back to me, but every single one of the snakes that writhed on his head were watching every move I made, and I was pretty sure they were making lascivious suggestions.

I even locked eyes with a man whose face was mossy with spores and had sharp thorns that protruded along his cheek bones. He pursed his lips, and I immediately wondered if he could retract his thorns when he kissed someone, or if you accepted the sharp with the sweet of his affection.

The ballroom was filled with Court fae and roiling with their magic. I could only imagine the cornucopia of tastes that would have tempted me if I had access to my power. As it was, I could only feel the tingling buzz of it along my skin, mocking me.

I avoided looking at anyone directly. I knew I should attempt to engage them in conversation, try to learn what I could about Oriana or the other dead fae. With the wide berth they all gave me, though, I couldn't quite figure out how to approach anyone let alone ask why they thought someone would target and murder Winter royalty. Thankfully, Orion was nowhere to be seen, but the thought of him coming up behind me and stripping my lungs of air had me on edge.

When a server passed by with a tray of something bubbly and resembling purple champagne, I grabbed a glass and knocked it back.

"Careful with that," a voice said behind me. "It's stronger than it looks."

Wheeling around, I found myself face to face with Kiral, Lada's consort.

Surprised as I was to see him, I simply raised my eyebrows in annoyance. "Did you follow me all the way here from Atlanta just to warn me off the good booze?"

He clasped his hands behind him and stood looking down his nose at me. He was dressed in an outfit similar to Kellan's, a long-tailed coat with strong shoulders, slim pants, and ostentatious embellishments. While Kellan's was rendered in sophisticated blues and golds, Kiral's coat was a rich sunburnt salmon that set off his dark olive complexion. "I am an invited guest, half breed. Your presence is the one that needs defense."

"Were you invited?" I pressed. "Or was it the one who holds your leash?" I peered past him to find his mistress. "Ah, there she is. At the head table. With my date. Do you get jealous when she flirts with others? You seem like the jealous type."

He refused to take my bait, so he didn't see how Lada was laughing and hanging on to Kellan's arm as they spoke with the Queen. The Queen was lounging on a chaise like in her official portrait, right before the large hearth that took up half the wall of the ballroom. Lada and Kellan and a number of other handsome fae were enjoying each other's company while Kiral and I lurked off to the side, sniping at each other.

He noticed my discomfort. "Perhaps it is you who is jealous."

"Of what?" I scoffed.

"Of those who know where they belong," he said simply.

He turned then to gaze at his Queen, who fit beautifully into the tableau of powerful fae, as if she were painted into the moment. The artist would have used regal, saturated colors to signify each fae's importance, their individuality, yes, but also how they fit together. The Queen was dressed in deep emerald, Lada in rich purple, and Kellan in his navy blue. The hearth behind them gave a warm glow. They looked right together, pieces of the same whole.

Another waiter passed by with the purple champagne, and I snagged two fresh glasses, passing one to Kiral. "Don't you belong to that world? You're a Queen's consort. Her monogamous consort. I think that means you literally belong to her."

He accepted the drink and sipped. "Yes, I belong to Lada. And she to me. But that does not mean I am anything more than an interloper in her world." He didn't take his eyes off her as he spoke. "Do you know how I met Lada?"

"Of course," I said, lifting my voice high. "Lada and I share all of our deepest held secrets with each other. We're practically sisters."

He didn't so much as crack a smile.

"No, Kiral," I sighed. "How did you meet?"

"It was before she became Queen. I wasn't part of her Court at Eliades. I actually had sworn to Adrona, here, at Naboskova."

He had my attention now. If Kiral was originally from this Court, he might have some insight on why Oriana had been targeted. Why the killings were happening at the Whitewood Gate.

"As the heir to her throne, Lada had been encouraged by her mother to make nice with the neighboring Courts. Eliades has historically been one of the more isolated Winter Courts. Lada's mother Casimira recognized that no matter what the Winter Court believed about our role in the world, things had been changing in our realm. Our fertility was waning. Fewer and fewer children were being born. More young fae had begun breaking with the Courts, pulling away from our traditions and the Old Magic. They were moving to the Iron Realm, joining Summer, mating with humans more. Basically, chasing promises of things no one could guarantee.

"They weakened the Courts, robbing them of the collective power that makes them strong. More importantly, they left themselves vulnerable, separated from their heritage, their power. We were having fewer children, and our powers were growing weaker, even here in Fairy. More dangerous creatures were attacking travelers, and without strong numbers or protection from their Courts, they could not defend themselves.

"Casimira and Lada realized that only coordination between the Courts would keep the people safe. Though Queens have long been territorial with their people, the survival of our race was more important. So, our Queen sent her only child out to each of the closest Winter castles. Casimira ordered Lada to make friends with the young princesses, the heirs to each of the thrones, and create alliances between our regions. When she wants to, she can be quite charming."

I snorted, uncertain we were even talking about the same

person. "Charming? Like when she's threatening to kill me, or calling me 'half breed?' Bigotry is not exactly what I'd call charming."

"It's not just your blood purity that disgusts," he said. "It's you. A half human, first in line for her queendom's throne. And then you run away from the honor you never deserved, throwing away your responsibility the second it asked something of you." I opened my mouth to argue, but he raised a hand, imperiously looking at me like I was something he had just stepped in. "I do not care. Every coward thinks it wise to flee the battle. You have shown time and again exactly why blood matters. Thankfully, I pledged myself to someone of the strongest stuff."

I stood there, dumbstruck. My decision to abdicate had nothing to do with my blood or magic. Regardless, I didn't owe him any explanations about my decision to leave Summer and my duties as heir. I didn't have to defend myself.

I motioned for Kiral to continue his story. Best to get this over with.

After a long considering look at his laughing lover on display, he did so. "When Lada came to Naboskova, she was little more than a child. She'd spent three decades in her mother's Court learning how to serve as conduit and studying our people's history. We were the third region she'd visited, and the first to actually welcome her. She arrived as a guest, and Adrona threw a party in her honor. Not everyone was happy to see her. They thought she was here to steal power for herself or convince them to move to her region before she became Queen.

"The twins were especially cold to her. Orion and Oriana thought to scare her off as quickly as possible. They even sent some sot over to flirt with her and lure her out onto the terrace only to abandon her as a snack to the garden of living vines. But she saw the trap coming and offered the vine-wrapped would-be suitor back to the twins, all tied up with a bow.

"Orion and Oriana were embarrassed, but Liliana, their older sister and the heir to Naboskova was delighted. She carved the bait out of the vines and gifted him as to Lada as an apology. She and Lada have been best friends ever since."

I laughed despite myself. If I had encountered Lada only through this story, I might have developed a different opinion of her.

"Where do you come into this story?" I asked, finally.

He shook his head. "I was the poor sot wrapped in vines who thought he could outwit one of the smartest fae of any realm."

I should have seen that coming. "So that's how you became her consort?"

"No," he said, his voice an impatient sigh as he passed off his empty champagne glass to a passing server. "She didn't trust me for almost ten years after that. She was on a mission, and she didn't have time for dalliances. Besides, the twins had used me against her, and she knew better than to let someone loyal to another Court into her bed. She actually never took a lover in all of her travels across the Realm. But she kept me with her. I was at her side as she visited nearly every Queen in the Eternal Realm. I saw how passionately she spoke of our people, of her responsibilities to Winter and Fairy. I knew she was something special.

"When her mother succumbed to her madness and abdicated, I was the first subject to pledge to the new Queen of Eliades. It still took her another four years to learn to trust me and take me as her consort." He watched as Lada sat beside Adrona on the low couch.

The two queens were leaning in close and whispering to each other, darting glances out at people on the dance floor and sharing observations. One would think they were old friends, or at least a Queen and her most loyal subject. The idea that they were Queens of equal power in neighboring regions seemed impossible.

"That's not how things usually work with Queens," I said, speaking both to her diplomatic aims and her circumspect sexual tendencies. Queens had to produce heirs to keep a steady connection between their people and their region's gate. Adrona famously had six husbands, and while only two had produced offspring, she was happy to keep trying with all of them. By some reports with several of them at once.

The fact that Lada had spent almost half of her life improving connections between rival Courts and ignoring her more primal needs as a fairy queen was hard to reconcile.

"She is different." He faced me squarely. "Despite your opinion on Lada, she is doing what is best for her people. She will not turn her back on her region when they need her most, unlike some. She's a good Queen, and a good person."

"You really love her, don't you?" I said, touched.

He sneered. "What a profoundly stupid thing to say. Yes, Siobhan. I love my partner."

He didn't wait for a response but walked straight up to the queens at the front of the room.

Before he reached them, Lada sensed him and bestowed a smile wide and open and vulnerable. She stretched out a hand, and he swept toward her, kneeling and kissing her knuckles, gently and with reverence. Her brows softened from her amused welcome, and she lifted him slowly to his feet, even as she stood to meet him. They stood eye to eye for a moment, lost to each other.

Then someone said something I couldn't hear, and both Kiral and Lada turned to laugh. Kellan was right there at Adrona's shoulder, speaking earnest words to the lovely young woman who stood at his side. Liliana. The Heir of Naboskova.

While I stood on the edge of the ballroom, talking to no one and ostracized, I realized how little I would get out of this trip unless I did something.

As a waiter passed with another tray of the purple champagne, I ignored Kiral's warning, grabbed a third glass. The liquid bubbled and danced as it flowed down my throat, and I could feel my head already starting to buzz with its effects.

If I was going to achieve anything tonight, I needed to be present but obviously not myself. Hopefully this delicious liquid that tasted of raspberries and bees and green grass would help.

If not, at least I'd have a good time.

CHAPTER TWENTY-FIVE

Alone at the edge of Oriana's ball, I watched the throng of beautiful and horrifying fae dance and twirl around the dancefloor. Colors and shapes and configurations I had never considered were all on display as if this were a parade or a political production.

Gatherings in my home world were never like this.

The fae who took up residence in the Iron Realm were always careful to remember they were guests, interlopers in a place that wasn't always ready for them. As such, they tended to strive for as human a costume as they could manage.

At the Knoll, most fae used glamours to smooth over gills alongside their necks or hide branches in their hair as stiff gel-locked hair. Fur was disguised as clothing or completely hidden by glamour, while pointed ears were blunted, sharp teeth filed, and the hunger for the taste of blood and death was attributed to natural sexual lust.

Here, no one even attempted to layer disguises over their natures. They existed simply as they were. An iele approached a group near the door, and without seeming angry, they all raised their voices to shouts, so she could skim the top energy of their conversation without affecting their discussion.

A likho stood amongst a group of six perfectly, at ease. She was a slavic fae of misfortune, feasting on bad luck. While most in the Iron Realm avoided her kind, scared of attracting bad luck to themselves, several fae came up to her, happy to see her. One man asked her if they could have a private conversation, as he began speaking enthusiastically to her. She listened carefully, then gave him a kiss on the forehead and turned him loose to the room, ridded of the misfortune of his particular happenstance. He practically floated onto the dance floor, and she grinned like a Mother Theresa with three-inch incisors.

It was like that everywhere. Dew gathered in the folds of a glaistig's hair, letting us all know she would retire unless she could devour the spirit of a someone's energy soon. A sluagh and revenant accepted an offered plate of raw meat instead of the skewers of roasted lamb and vegetables. A young fyglia lifted her hands up to take the small bit of soul her father had sucked from his date, touched that he offered it to his daughter first.

All the while, I stood on the outer edges of this party where literally every type of fae existed as themselves, openly, without fear or judgment. Everyone except me.

I took my last swallow of liquid courage or whatever in Mab's cellar this purple stuff was and marched right over to the congregation of VIPs by the hearth.

They saw me coming, as the sea of fae on the dance floor literally parted to allow me passage. Kellan's artist-carved face lit up with a knowing smile, Adrona's thin lips pursed, and Lada scowled pretty as a kitten as I approached.

And the final part of the tableau, the princess Liliana stood with her arms spread wide. "At last. The Summer princess comes to warm our hearts with her presence."

I pulled up short. I wasn't sure whether she was trying to cut with her words or meant them sincerely. Her smile was wide, but the tightness around her eyes told me she meant something more. If she was anything like her mother, I should tread carefully.

Lada took a step toward me, but in an instant, both Kiral and

Kellan reached out a hand to stop her. She glared at them both but allowed herself to be held back and amazingly held her tongue.

"Indeed," Adrona agreed, not sitting up. "We hope you are enjoying yourself, Siobhan." She gestured to a passing server to bring more drinks for everyone.

My heart felt like it would beat out of my chest, evaluating just how much danger I was in. "You are a most gracious hostess," I said as I accepted a glass but didn't bring it to my lips. I had had enough. "Your castle is incredible, and this gathering is a worthy tribute to your loss." I realized then that Orion still had yet to make an appearance. He hadn't been here when I arrived, and I never saw him come in. I wondered briefly what could have kept him from this celebration of his sister's life.

Or maybe Adrona had heard of his attack on me in the hallway and warned him to keep his distance lest he ruin the genial atmosphere of the party.

Liliana didn't give me long to ponder his absence, sweeping forward to grab my arm. "Do excuse us, Mother," she called over her shoulder as she pulled me with her. "I wish for a chance to speak with our Summer friend alone."

"Lili, return her in once piece," Kellan said lightly. "Remember what we discussed. I still have plans for her."

My blood went cold at that. What sort of plans could he be talking about?

Liliana simply laughed and dragged me away before I could say anything.

She avoided passing through the crowd of strange fae and rounded the edge of the hearth to a set of glass doors that led to a small private garden area. It didn't extend as far as I imagined, closed in by the tall castle walls, but there were an assortment of chairs set amongst carefully maintained flowering shrubs and flowers. Despite it being late evening, everything was in full spring bloom as it had been around the Gate where we entered. A pleasant aroma filled the air that reminded me of night-blooming jasmine, honeysuckle, and rose.

A fountain in the middle of the space had a swan perched atop, her wings spread wide and neck stretched up in an elegant display that some would describe as joyful, but I knew to be a sign of aggression. If I wasn't already anxious about being alone with the Winter princess, I would have felt my hackles rise at the threat of that huge bird that looked almost too real.

Liliana selected one of the cushioned chairs on one side of a small table and sank into it with a sigh. "It is so much more peaceful out here, do you not agree?"

She indicated that I should take the seat beside her. As I sat down, a young man came out with a tray of cheeses, meats, crackers and pickled vegetables as well as two glasses of the purple champagne. He set them down between us and quickly retreated again.

Liliana picked up a cracker and spread some cheese on it. She offered it to me first, but when I shook my head, she shrugged and popped it in her mouth before taking a delicate sip of her drink.

I waited patiently, because Liliana clearly had a reason for bringing me out here. She simply stared back at me, waiting for me to make the first move.

We were at an impasse.

Finally, a smile broke out on her heart-shaped face. "You are not what I expected." She looked from my jeweled coronet down to my borrowed gown. "You are not the common boor I was led to believe."

"Let me guess," I said. "Given your friendship with Lada, I'm going to guess that she described me as a rabid raccoon with a tendency to bite innocent pureblood Fairy princesses completely unprovoked."

"Lada did describe you with more vitriol than virtue, that is true," Liliana laughed. "She is opinionated. And not a welcome ally to you."

"You could say that," I agreed, relaxing into my chair, despite myself. Liliana had an easy grace about her, an uncomplicated way of just existing that put me at ease. I took a piece of thinly sliced meat and layered it on a cracker. It was pleasingly salty and rich with a gamy flavor I didn't quite recognize. "Lada decided to hate me before she even met me."

"She is harmless," she said, grabbing an olive from the snack plate. "She does have reason for her dislike of you, though."

"Oh?" I said. Then I remembered some of what Kiral had told me. "Oh, yes. Like everyone else in both realms, she has opinions about my failure to live up to my responsibilities as an undeserving half-blood heir."

Liliana frowned a bit. "Not exactly." She stopped there and sat up from her recumbent position in her chair. She brought her legs forward and swung them toward me, leaning over to pin me with her eyes. "Your sister told Lada about your situation and arrangement with the Grey Meranti."

Before I knew what I was doing, I stood so quickly and violently that I sent my chair tumbling back behind me, ready to run. In an instant three fae appeared out of the shadows of the garden and two came out of the ballroom doors, all with weapons aimed at me.

For her part, Liliana didn't even flinch but waved her security away without taking her eyes off of me.

"So, it's true," she said as her guards dissolved back into the shadows, slightly more visible than they had been before. "You actually did it."

I stood there quivering, my chest pounding. My throat was thick with fear and pain. Few knew the full reason why I had left the Court and my position in it, and I had always intended to keep it that way. It wasn't anyone's business but my own.

But apparently my sister didn't share my desire to keep my reasons private if she was telling every antagonistic Winter royal who came to visit.

I knew that what I did was illegal in the Eternal Realm. That even though my choice was made in Atlanta over fifty years ago, Adrona could still charge me with crimes against the fae. But if she was going to do that, there was nothing I could do at this point.

"I did," I admitted.

Liliana gaped at me. "Why?" She crossed her arms around her middle, as if holding in grief and regret for something that had nothing to do with her. "Why would you do that?"

I began to pace around the small space. How did I explain this choice? Why should I explain my choice? It was mine. I didn't owe this random princess anything. I didn't have to justify myself to my people, or my mother, or my realm.

But if it would help her understand, if it would convince her to help me? Perhaps she would understand. After all, she was as I had been. She was the daughter of a Queen, the one required to take on the weight of her realm, to serve as conduit for her people and to suffer as the sacrifice her people made to access their power on the safe side of the Gate. She was born to the role as I had been and never had any choice in the matter.

And I had made a choice not to be a party to our particular curse.

Finally, I stopped pacing spoke. "I didn't want to pass on the burden that had been passed to me."

She gaped. "You killed your own child."

"No," I said firmly. "No, I ended a pregnancy that should have never happened. And I would do it again."

Her pretty cupid's mouth fell open, then shut, then open again, as if she were trying to process what to say to my admission. Then she thought better of it and stood, taking her drink with her. She stopped before the glass doors, watching the ballroom scene.

"It is no wonder then that she hates you."

"Lada?"

Liliana's shoulders rolled back, and she lifted her chin as she peered in the glass. "Do you know the average age of a fae that gets pregnant here in Fairy? If she ever gets pregnant that is."

I already did not like where this conversation was going, but I answered honestly. "No."

"From what we can surmise, over one hundred years. Most never conceive until they are closer to one hundred fifty. The Summer Courts claim better results by reproducing with humans and mixed fae. But do you know the average age of first pregnancy in the Iron Realm?"

My throat was dry and tight, but I forced a swallow. "No."

"Around eighty. Not much better." She swept back to her seat, lowered herself down and stared straight ahead. "My mother was over one hundred and five when she had me, and giving birth to the twins nearly killed her twenty years later. I have been trying to conceive a child for the better part of four decades, and Lada has tried for at least half that."

She then drew her gaze directly on me, and I could feel my blood cool. "Once our people were as fertile as humans and could deliver live children regularly every few years if we chose. Now, we struggle for a handful of children across the realms each generation. Our people are dying out, and our hopes for a future dwindle with each passing year."

"I know that," I said, quietly, as I picked up the chair I knocked over and sat down across from her.

"And you were given a blessing that most of our kind would literally kill to receive. The gift Lada and I and nearly every woman has been chasing for years with no results. You had the most perfect gift, and you threw it away."

"It wasn't a gift," I said, softer than before. She didn't understand. She thought only what everyone thought: that any chance at a child was worth sacrificing everything else.

But I never saw it that way. I never wanted to pass on the curse of my blood. Anyone I gave birth to would be another of Mab's line, and any daughter could be another potential conduit, a servant to her realm and her people, never free to love how and who she wants, and forced to make painful decisions about how to best protect her people.

But more importantly, I didn't want to be a mother. I wasn't prepared to be the caretaker of another creature, nor did I even know how to do that. I didn't know what a good mother looked like. My mother had been burdened by her role as Queen, by the curse that came with it, and by the madness that inevitably marked every interaction we had. I had been raised by nurses, teachers, random members of Court, and my sweet Magdalene.

If I wanted to have a child, I'm sure I could have made it work. I could have learned and grown into the role of a good and stable mother before I had to take over my designated role as Illythia's heir and the conduit of the Greenwood Gate.

But when I'd gotten pregnant as a thirty-year-old fae princess with no idea of which of my partners could have fathered the child? When I had absolutely no desire to give birth to a child that would become property of my palace and Court before I even had a chance to form a bond with it? I had made the only choice that made sense to me.

"It wasn't a gift," I repeated a little louder. "It was an accident. An unfortunate accident that could have turned into a disaster if I hadn't done something about it. And the fact that the Grey Meranti, the greatest sorceress I've ever met was banished from Court for helping me was one of the biggest crimes my mother ever committed against her people. And she's guilty of quite a lot."

I took a deep breath and tried to still my racing heart. This wasn't why I was here. I shouldn't be here constantly having to defend choices I had made decades ago. I shouldn't have to explain myself to yet another person who thought they knew my life better than I did.

Liliana smiled then. "Like cutting you off from your power, casting you out of Summer, and naming your sister heir instead?"

"Something like that," I mumbled, swallowing my grief and anger. Fifty years and the pain of that day was still fresh.

Liliana gestured to someone out of sight, and a servant placed two small glasses between us and filled them from the same flask. This new drink was amber colored in a smaller glass. "For protection," Liliana explained, lifting the glasses and passing me one.

"Protection from what?"

"From anyone learning what we are going to be discussing here in the next fifteen minutes. This potion confers honesty and secrecy. If you try to disclose what you learn from me, you will lose your power of speech for several months. Exceptions are if they already knew the information or if they learned it from an alternative source, though the nuances are tricky. The same goes for me, which is why it is worth your while to take this choice. You may be honest with me."

"And if I do not want to be honest with you?" I said, accepting the glass anyway.

"Then I will assume you are hiding my sister's killer or killed her yourself as my brother believes, and I will either have you executed before his curse is enacted or imprison you so that I may watch its effects in person."

"That's not much of a choice."

"No, I do not suppose it is," she agreed, lifting her glass to me. "A toast?" Then she waited for me to propose one.

"To honest choices," I answered, clinking my glass against hers and quickly downing the contents.

CHAPTER TWENTY-SIX

The liquid was thick, honeyed, and burned all the way down my throat. It had a slight spice profile with cinnamon, vanilla, and clove, but the way it coated the inside of my throat seemed to scald my esophagus despite its cold temperature.

I choked as it went down and noticed Liliana clearing her throat as it worked its way into her system as well. At least I knew it was working on her as well.

"All right, then," I said. "Fifteen minutes, you said?"

"It is not exact," she admitted, choking a bit and swallowing a bit of water to wash away the potion. Then she looked at me without hesitation or equivocation. "I too had an abortion. Two years ago. I say this not for your sympathy or to relate to you. I say it so you know you can trust me with what else I am going to say."

I blinked at her. "I'm sorr—"

"Don't. I said I do not want your sympathy." She took a moment and took a deep breath while staring at the flagstones between us. Then she pulled herself up straight, bringing herself to the edge of her chair to lean toward me. "I do not believe you killed my sister."

"I didn't," I emphasized, though I was still relieved to hear it.

"Nor do I believe it was the Fair Folk group."

"Oh," I said, more surprised at this. "But your brother—"

"If you will not allow me to talk unimpeded, this will take longer than we have."

She gave me a pause to allow me to interrupt again, but I wisely kept my tongue.

"It was your sister."

"Bryony? But—" I stopped myself and gestured for her to continue.

"Oriana's murder was a strategic political move, and though I cannot prove it yet, the evidence has been overwhelming." She lifted her chin and looked at me squarely. "All of the bodies were found near the Whitewood Gate. They were all members of Winter royalty and quite powerful magic users. And all three were pregnant, yet none had yet announced their pregnancies publicly. The first victim did not even know she was pregnant, according to her Court."

My blood went cold. Queens could detect pregnancies in fae from the moment of implantation. It was an evolutionary trait that allowed Queens to protect their people and ensure species survival. If the victims were all targeted for their pregnancies, then signs would point to a Queen's involvement.

There was only one problem with that.

"Bryony isn't a Queen yet. And she was the one who called me into this whole mess in the first place. She and Lada asked me to track down the killer before your brother decided I was really the one to blame. If she was the one who had Oriana killed, why would she ask for my help?"

"Do not be naive. It is beneath both of us." She crossed her arms and cocked her head at me. "Did your sister give you any resources? Any information? Did she even give you an idea of why Oriana was the one targeted?"

The garden was suddenly too hot. She was right. Bryony had given me reasons to investigate but had provided almost no clues. All I had to go on was the fact that she was dead, and the note presumably from the Fair Folk. "Not so much, no."

Liliana continued. "The greatest allure of joining the Summer Court and living in the Iron Realm is the possibility of children, the promise of fertility. It has been the number one reason many leave Fairy. For generations, it has seemed that it is impossible for fae to reproduce while spending all their time in our home. We Winter fae stagnate, we stand still. We do not age, we do not grow, and we do not often birth new life. It has been our rightful curse. We Winter fae embrace our magic and heritage. We do not grow stronger, but we endure."

"But…" I gave her the opening to continue the thought.

"But that has changed. We do not know why, but our fortunes changed. In Naboskova, particularly, but in Sapporo, and Oslo as well. Our people are finding themselves fruitful once again. Our magic is expanding, and the Summer Court has noticed. They have begun monitoring crossings between the realms more carefully, restricting Summer fae from leaving, and approaching my people to convince them to remain in the Iron Realm. But when my people realized they have full access to their powers and enjoy newfound fertility here, they have no reason to leave. And Summer fae have a reason to return home."

"And you will enjoy an influx of power as they pledge loyalty to you."

She smiled. "I am not Queen yet. But yes, eventually, I will be tasked with protecting and providing for them. And I will take my responsibility on with the honor and reverence it deserves."

"Sounds ideal for you," I pointed out. "And a raw deal for Summer. But that doesn't mean Bryony had your sister killed."

"If it allowed her to consolidate power and eliminate, or at least weaken, two threats at once, why wouldn't she?" She sighed and spoke to me as if I was a child. "If my sister, a Winter royal who never once passed through the Gate, announced her pregnancy and gave birth to a healthy child? It would undermine all the claims Summer has to their 'superior' way of life. She had to be stopped. By then blaming her death on the Fair Folk? Bryony also eliminates a threat on her side of the realms."

I thought carefully. It made sense, all tied up in a tidy package. It also sounded a lot like the theories Kellan floated to me about what was happening. I had to wonder how much of this was coming directly from Liliana and what had been poured into her ear from Kellan's silver tongue.

"You really believe all of that?"

To her credit, she shrugged and said in a low voice, "Well enough." She shook her head. "What I know to be true is Bryony is spiraling in her own self-doubt. She has been wielding power while your mother succumbs to her madness, but she has no faith in her security. She is anxious to seize control of Atlanta but is threatened both by the Fair Folk rising in her opposition and the specter of you still in town and looming over her shoulder."

"I don't want her power. I don't want the city."

"So you've said," Liliana said, a note of weary skepticism in her voice. "It doesn't matter. She sees you as a threat, and according to Lada and Thierry, she is acting increasingly erratic because of it." She sighed. "I want to be honest with you. You were brought here at my request."

I cursed inwardly. I knew Kellan had been lying to me. "Let me guess," I said. "Kellan set me up."

"Thierry has been here many times over the last few years, attempting to curry favor with my mother and myself. I respect his motives, but I do not trust him." She raised an eyebrow. "Nor, I suspect, do you. His Fair Folk group is a blatant attempt to seize power from the Summer Courts. Let him have it. I have no interest in ruling over a fetid swamp of mediocrity."

I had half a mind to throw my drink in her face. Whatever she wanted, whatever Kellan wanted, whatever my sister wanted, it didn't matter.

Atlanta deserved better than their machinations.

She ignored my glares. "Your friend has been attempting to play every side against each other. He is much like Lada. Willing to use any pawn to take the Queen of his choice."

"I have no interest in being a pawn in any of your power wars."

Her smile bared her teeth, and her soft, hearth-woman face transformed into something feral and dangerous. "If you would not be a pawn, then you must learn to be a Queen yourself." She softened her tone. "I am not asking you to lead a rebellion on your own. If Kellan is to be believed, that will come from his people. But your goals align with ours. We all want Summer weakened, especially in Atlanta. I want control of the Whitewood Gate here , and I believe we can help each other."

"What do you want me to do?"

"Not much. Thierry's group has the systems in place to absorb the dissolution of the Court, and he has done much to spread his propaganda. But he remains in the shadows. For whatever reason, he has been hesitant to come forward and admit his role in the Fair Folk, and it is to his detriment. Power comes to those who are unafraid to step into the light. Why not shine the brightest and let the moths flock to your flame?"

I scoffed. "You've got the wrong pitch for the wrong girl. Remember, I retreated. It was strategic."

Her lip curled in derision. "The more you say that, the less I believe you. You didn't retreat. You were forced to renounce your rightful place because you made a choice your sister would never have the strength to make."

Without waiting for a response, she raised a hand. The tips of her fingers curled and twitched, and I felt a tingle begin along my skin, seeping deeper and deeper, like a limb waking up. Then in a rush, I could feel it. My magic was back, as was my connection to the Gate.

Juniper and pine and green life filled my mouth. Then a taste of honey and lemon, cinnamon spice and wood smoke. Liliana's magic was a hot toddy, medicinal, restorative, grounding, but strong enough to knock you down if you weren't paying attention.

She noticed me licking my lips, tasting at her. "You have been incorporated into the wards of my castle. Your magic is your own to use as you please. Consider it a gesture of good faith and trust. And to remind you of the power you wield. I have been told exactly what you can do. You can steal magic from any fae you can taste. You can wield their power with more skill and force than they thought possible. And you can turn that magic back on them without mercy." She lifted her glass to me. "As you have already done against your sister's forces."

Tentatively, I pulled on her magic. I could instantly feel her connection to this home. As a berehynia like her mother, she had absolute power over everything within her home. For someone who lived in a medieval fortress, that meant she had immense influence over every single being within the walls. What's more is she could control the temperature of each room and body within the bounds of the walls, the growth of all living things, the state of all inanimate objects. She could even manipulate the very linens and dishware. And now I could, too. I could make them serenade me at dinner without batting an eye.

If she was right about my own powers, I could conceivably fight her and her mother for control of this castle and claim it as my own.

She gave that power to me in the hopes that I would use it against my own family.

"I didn't mean to kill those soldiers. It was an accident," I clarified. She had to know that I was not ruthless. That I wouldn't kill to further my own ends.

"I believe you. I also believe that you will do what it takes to serve your people. And when your sister proves her true aims and closes the Greenwood Gate entirely, as she has long wanted to do, you will do what it takes to oppose her."

I forgot to breathe for a second. "I'm sorry, what?"

"It is not common knowledge, but the means are already in place. Bryony has told Lada and Thierry alike that she will be restricting access to the Greenwood Gate and preventing its daily openings. The soldiers at the Gate were a first measure. Others will follow. She will be stopping all travel through the Gate, except at her discretion. Those who come from this side will be turned back or taken directly to the Atlanta palace for questioning with the heir. Those of mine on her side will not be able to return home without express permission from herself. Daily openings will cease, and Keepers will be restricted from accessing the Gate—in any way—to allow magic to pass through to the solitary of the region."

"She can't do that!" I nearly shouted.

Liliana did not react to my outburst. "Lada and Thierry both have confirmed her plans. She has declared that she will put permanent guards at the Gate and close it until her people can feel safe in their own city. Strong as you might be, my dear, you cannot oppose the entirety of Illythia's guard. Even if you turn them on each other."

I swallowed against the bile that rose at her words. She had to be wrong. Closing the Gate would undermine so much of what the Summer Court stood for. They believed that the fae have a right to live in the human world, that access to the Iron Realm was the key to our survival. But they also ensured that their people had access to as much magic as they needed from Fairy.

There was the rub, I supposed. With the Gate closed, those fae loyal to the Summer Court would still have magic, as much as they wanted, pulled right through their Queen. The only ones weakened would be the solitary fae who would be cut off from their birthright entirely. Unless they pledged loyalty and gave over their power and their autonomy to Summer. To Mother and Bryony.

It was a way to consolidate power. And it would force the very revolution Thierry was hoping for.

What was Bry thinking? She was going to lose her throne before she ever claimed it.

"I can talk to her," I began.

"The time for talk is over," Liliana declared, the patio freezing with her anger, the honey lemon taste of her magic cold on my tongue. "Talk has my sister dead, your sister showing her true despotic colors, and the people of both realms threatened. I don't care what you do with your human friends and your mongrel discontents. Keep them in the Iron Realm and rule over them yourself. Gift them to your slick friend who so desperately wants to be king. I care not. But help me stop Bryony and avenge Oriana."

I didn't want to go up against my sister, but I didn't know how I could stay out of this. If Bry was going to such lengths as closing the Gate, who's to say she hadn't had Oriana killed? If she was already doing this before she took the throne, how far would she go when she had real power?

Liliana was right. She had to be stopped.

"All right," I said. Instinctively I reached for my magic as I reached for the drink on the table. The taste of the Gate's power filled me before I washed it down with the purple champagne. "Let's overthrow my sister."

CHAPTER TWENTY-SEVEN

By the time I returned to my suite, I was exhausted from scheming and talking and nodding my head like I knew what Liliana was talking about. She was a shrewd political manipulator. Where I had been thinking she'd come out with a show of force, emotional appeals, and blunt power, she had a detailed plan for undermining Bryony's control more subtly.

"While Illythia lives, your sister's grip on the Court is tenuous as best. It is better for everyone, then, if we strip her of her power before she ever claims it."

Liliana gave me dossiers on every member of my own Court who had ever expressed displeasure with Bryony or Mother's rule. The words on the page swirled and blurred, thanks to the champagne, but it was clear that there were plenty of people dissatisfied with local rule. The reasons ranged from significant (a love match between a daoine sidhe and a half-human gremlin was rejected because it would produce inferior children and the daoine sidhe had been promised since birth to another royal sidhe) to trivial (Bryony had once said a dryad's overgrown grove was in need of a wax).

I was going to use my position at the Knoll to exploit these dissatisfactions and plant in their minds that it might be easier to defect to the Fair Folk, go full solitary, or go back to Fairy. Liliana banked on the idea that the majority of loyal Court fae would start requesting permission to go back through the Gate and defect to Winter. I would be there to open the Gate for them, guards notwithstanding, and she would welcome them back to a "proper Court."

I had my doubts of the plan, but I knew enough fae would start questioning Bryony's motives and legitimacy in closing the Gate in the first place. Such a drastic and unprecedented move would undermine their confidence in her ability to rule.

In addition, Liliana was certain that someone would soon be willing to betray the fact that Bryony was responsible for Oriana's death and those of the other royals. My sister would be blamed for a cross-Court murder. Her rule would be over before it began, Summer would be in disarray, and the Summer Court would scramble to respond to such a violation of the treaties between the realms. Liliana and Lada would be rewarded by the Courts, and Kellan and I could do what we wanted with Atlanta.

The plan was simple, straightforward, and likely to be effective, but the thought of putting it into action made me sick. Or maybe that was the residual effects of all the drinking and infusion of magic.

At the Knoll, I had always prided myself on being neutral, on being apart from this mess, but that was before I threw in with the Fair Folk, killed a couple of Summer Guards, and joined the schemes of a Winter Queen or two. To insist on neutrality at this point was just delusional. I might as well commit to my role, suck up my distaste, and do what needed to be done.

If I didn't want to be a pawn, I'd have to be a Queen.

So, when I wearily and unsteadily arrived in my suite, only to find grinning Kellan waiting for me in the sitting room, I squared my shoulders and greeted him as an angry and slightly drunk Queen would.

That is to say, I flexed my powers, borrowed magic from my hosts, and threw him across the room with a single glare.

He hit the far wall with a crunch, and the tapestry he dislodged fluttered down over his head.

He groaned and slowly pulled himself out from under the fabric that depicted a tarasque being ridden by an ancient Fairy Queen. Kellan's head emerged from under the six stubby bear legs of the creature.

"Was that entirely necessary?" he groaned.

"How much of this was your plan? How much of this did you orchestrate?" I glared, and I could feel my body vibrating with the barely contained power of the Naboskova castle. Liliana had opened her powers to me willingly, and whether it was the purple wine we had sipped throughout our negotiations, lowered inhibitions from exhaustion, or just the buzz of her magic, my head was swimming with possibility.

Mostly the possibility of ripping Kellan limb from limb for putting me in this situation to begin with. "You better start talking, or I start acting on my basest instincts."

He took my threat seriously as he pulled himself upright. "I'm not your enemy, Siobhan."

I blinked and a slash of power ripped across his cheek, drawing a line of bright blood that paralleled the perfect chiseled line of his jaw. Lada had once lashed out at me in the same way, and it was greatly satisfying to be able to turn that on someone else.

He winced, but he didn't raise a hand to wipe away the blood that trickled down his face. "We have the same goals."

I blinked and another lash across his other cheek.

He merely sighed. "Are you going to throw a fit, or are you actually interested in a conversation? Because I chose to work with you over Lada for a reason. You're better than this."

That brought me up short. He was right. I was reacting like Lada.

Perhaps I had overdone it tonight. My head was still spinning with champagne, with magic, with too many thoughts to control.

I took a breath and a step back and brought my attention to the cuts I caused along his face. Reaching out for his magic, I brushed against flavors of vanilla and bergamot, then smoke and tart gentian. It took a minute of concentration before I could I pull deeper to find the earth and stone fruit that I was beginning to recognize as his true taste. Leaning against that power, I directed it to heal the skin I had torn, and within a few seconds his cheeks were clear. Only the blood that dripped down onto his lapel remained.

Kellan looked down, disappointed as the blood soaked into the thick navy fabric of his fine jacket. He sighed again, and took the jacket off, leaving him in his high-necked black and gold brocade shirt. I noticed how the tight brocade stretched across his broad shoulders and highlighted his lean, muscular frame. He licked his lips as he noticed me watching him undress. "I don't suppose your magic extends to removing bloodstains?"

I glared in response. (It did, but I had not inclination to be nice.) He simply shrugged, laid the jacket down on the edge of the sofa and gestured for me to take one of the two cushioned chairs across from him. With a huff, I sank down into the cushion, thunking my head slightly on the wooden frame.

I realized belatedly I wasn't in any shape to have a civil conversation about anything. My current drunken state rendered me only suitable for bed or bad decisions. And I wasn't in bed.

When we were seated opposite each other, opponents, waiting for a challenge, he spoke. "I take it you and Liliana spoke. Since you're still here, you also reached an arrangement, which means you finally understand the very real threat your sister poses to our worlds."

My immediate instinct was to defend Bryony, but I bit my tongue. I had already admitted I needed to stop her, but I didn't need to defend myself to Kellan. He was the one who needed to explain. "Why bring me into this? You have the Fair Folk, you have all the connections. The Winter Queens love you. The Summer Queens welcome you. You could have taken care of whatever you need to do by yourself. Why involve me at all?"

I left unsaid the rest: *Why rip me from my comfortable life? Why pit me against my family? Why drag me into your mess?*

He didn't flinch from my words. "Because you have what it takes to rewrite this story."

"Explain."

"You're a Fairy Queen who isn't a Queen. You owe no allegiances to the Courts, you do not answer to either the Callieach or the Beira, neither Summer nor Winter. Yet you can open the Gate at will, channel powers, connect to other fae, and still remain independent. A solitary Queen. That's a symbol I can use to rally a force that will really make a difference."

"So, we're back to using me for your own goals."

"Not if you will finally step into your power yourself." He leaned forward, his eyes flashing with anger. "For Mab's sake, Siobhan, stop reacting to everything around you and fucking *act*. You have all this potential, all this possibility, and you're content to just sit back and let things happen to you."

"I am acting," I started to insist as my head spun around his words.

"You're responding! You could lead and liberate your people from the tyranny they've lived under their entire lives, but instead you are letting yourself be pushed and pulled by everything around you." He stood then and crossed the space between us in a heartbeat. He caged me back into my chair, his hands gripping the thick wooden back on either side of my head. He loomed over me, getting into my space and forcing me to look him in the eye.

His body was hot, nearly pressed along the length of mine. I was all too aware of the distance of inches between my dangerously low-cut silk dress and his broad brocade. Between the slits that had crept up over my hip bones as I sat, and his muscular thighs. A chasm of what if, a vacuum that threatened to swallow me whole. It made me dizzy.

"You are too powerful and too smart to be this passive. You're better than this. Figure out what you want, what moves you, or else stop wasting everyone's time."

"I don't know what I want. I—" I choked off my own words, licked my lips, and swallowed hard against the stormy swirl of doubt and desire in me. What did I want? What stirred me to action? I wanted to not be in this mess. I wanted to slap him. I wanted to tear his clothes off. I wanted to go home. I wanted to burn the Courts and this castle to the ground. I wanted to toss my sister in a cell in her own dungeon until she stopped trying to be the biggest and baddest Queen in the realm. I wanted—

"Stop it," he snarled as he leaned in even closer, his breath sweet like earthy red wine, his body vibrating with barely contained energy. "Stop overthinking. You hold so much power here. Bryony knows it. Liliana and Lada know it. I know it. Just do us all a favor and fucking do something."

I did.

I stopped my swirling thoughts and just acted.

Thirsting, I surged forward and crashed my lips into his, ready to devour him with a single gulp. He met me with the same intensity, his anger heating him through as his mouth opened to mine. His hands moved from the chair behind me to grasp me by the head, pulling me to my feet, and I clung to him as I rose to meet him, finally bringing our bodies together. His passion and my need collided, and it felt right.

What did I want? This. I wanted something real and immediate and grounding. He was right. I had been reacting and responding. So, for once I dove forward and took what I wanted. I wanted to take, and I wanted a taste.

But it was only a partial taste. His magic was stifled, chained inside him by the wards of the castle. Connected to Liliana's power, I released the wards with a thought and let his full flavor flood into me. Dark cherries and plums, spices like black pepper and tobacco, raspberry jam and leather and coffee and earth, he rolled through me.

I couldn't help the growl that rumbled through me at the delicious taste. It was all I wanted, all I *needed* in that moment. Despite the magic that pulsed through me, I was more present in my body and in that moment than I could ever remember being. I wasn't fighting against voices, against warring thoughts of every conflict surrounding me.

For the moment, there was only me and him. And he opened himself to me fully.

His hands were in my hair, loosening the jewels that draped over my forehead, then on my shoulders, loosening the gown that barely clung to me. My fingers moved on their own, freeing toggles of his brocade shirt, letting the silky fabric slide open on his chest, then sliding down his arms, exposing the firm, warm expanse of his chest.

I braced myself against him and pushed away to catch my breath for only a moment, gasping as I tried to wrap my thoughts around what was happening. I was stripped down to my bare skin and an ostentatious necklace, while he stood panting in nothing but his navy slacks. He watched me hungrily but wary.

"Are you sure about this?" His breath caught just for a hitch. He looked almost vulnerable as he waited for me to answer.

I shook my head. I wasn't sure about it. I wasn't entirely in my right head about anything, let alone something like this. I had Rhys. I hated Kellan. But I *wanted* him. I wanted his hands on me, to taste him, drink him down, have him fill me. I hated him.

I didn't know what I wanted.

"Then, we shouldn't." He took a shuddering breath and stepped back. "You're right. You've had a long day. And you have a partner." He started to look around for his clothing, anxious to cover up.

As he reached for his shirt, though, I grabbed his hand. "Stop."

"Siobhan," he said, avoiding my gaze. "It's okay. I pushed too hard."

"No," I said. It took me a moment to find my tongue, to stop the storm of thoughts and desires pulsing through me. I struggled to find a clear thought. "I don't know what I want about a lot. I'm still figuring that out." I stopped to clear my mouth, my tongue going dry. There was too much in my head. But this, in this moment, this. Him.

"Please," I finally said. "I know I'm not in the best state to ask for this. And you can say no. But I want this. I," I swallowed. I didn't realize it entirely until I said it. "I want you."

Kellan was silent for a beat. Then he dropped his shirt on the ground and surged toward me. A hand on either side of my face, he brought my lips to meet his. Softer this time, a meeting of understanding. He pulled back lightly, pressing his forehead to mine. "If you're sure," he whispered, his eyes closed.

"Yes," I whispered back, already moving back to bring our mouths together.

He answered with a growl of his own, pulling me to him, a hand on the back of my neck, another wrapping along my lower back, pressing me to him. The full length of him.

Coherent thought fled, as I gave in to my basest instincts, as I had threatened. But I wasn't reacting. This was my choice, and I would make the most of it.

CHAPTER TWENTY-EIGHT

I woke alone the next morning, my sheets scattered, but a blanket draped delicately over my naked form.

A set of new leather traveling clothes was laid out on a table along with my deerskin laundry, the dress I had worn, and the circlet of stones I had last seen discarded in the receiving rooms. My necklace was still around my neck. Despite last night's activities, I hadn't managed to strangle myself or break a clasp.

Chalk another one up to Fairy craftsmanship.

I put on the provided leathers, packed everything into a conveniently provided satchel, and cleaned myself up the best I could.

Mikka was waiting for me in the sitting room. She didn't say anything, but from the way her eyebrows raised, I knew she knew.

I avoided her gaze and went directly to the pot of coffee and pastries laid out on the table in the middle of the room. "I hope you at least came up with some good information, lurking in the bowels of the castle."

"Yeah, I found some fun people, but not good information. Turns out, Oriana was pregnant!"

I nodded, trying not to minimize the movement, lest it set my head spinning. "Yeah, I know."

"Oh," Mikka said, her excitement waning. "Damn, that was my big reveal. Pregnant princess murdered." She punctuated the words with a hand laying out headlines in the air.

I winced at her loud tone.

"Okay. Well. Other than that, she wasn't much loved, so there could be any number of suspects for her death. She was kind of awful to her staff, but Orion's worse. But it was mild stuff: royal privilege, and she was better than most of the visiting royals. No lovers to report, no major enemies. She was second for the throne, but chances were good that Liliana would produce an heir before that became relevant. Oh, and she was very vocal against the Summer Court."

None of that information was useful.

"Thank you for trying," I said, as I mixed in an obscene amount of sugar and cream to my coffee. Fairy might be great at magic and throwing parties, but they had the worst coffee. Bitter, watery, and under-flavored, I could use a shot of whiskey just to make it worth drinking.

And maybe to stave off this hangover.

Sipping at my drink, I gestured for Mikka to lead the way. Best to make our way back home.

We emerged from our rooms to find a full honor guard ready to accompany us to the Gate. "Her Majesty and Her Highness insist," Captain Dusan explained. There were seven Winter Knights as well as the good Captain to protect as us we passed through the Whitewood.

I didn't even try to protest. It's not like I was going to be able to keep quiet that I had been here or much of what had been agreed to when I passed through the Gate. Everyone would assume I had allied myself with Winter. I might as well announce the agreement with my full chest. I was a traitor to my mother. Here was my honor guard.

Thierry was waiting at the entrance hall with his own pair of guards. In his understated traveling clothes, he nodded discreetly and fell into step behind Mikka and me as we followed Captain Dusan out the castle gates.

I waited for a long while down the road for him to approach, to say something of what happened between us the night before. But he held his distance. I tried not to overthink what that might mean. Did he regret what happened? Were we going to pretend we hadn't done what we had?

I didn't regret it, nor did I feel guilty. Rhys and I had discussed me taking other lovers, so I hadn't cheated. But I never imagined it would be Kellan I turned to. Nor did I imagine it would happen so quickly and under those circumstances. Was it a one-time thing between us? Did I want it to happen again? Or was it just the result of too much champagne?

My questions fought against the headache that pressed against my temples. What I wouldn't give for a glass of water. For a lake of water. Why hadn't we brought water for a walk this long?

"How long will this take, Captain?" I asked, after some time had passed. It could have been only ten minutes, but my dry throat told me we'd been walking for hours.

"Our way to the Gate will be shorter than before, Your Highness," Dusan said. "Because we are leaving the castle with full support of the Queen, the path will bend to our destination. We should be there in less than an hour. And with an honor guard of this size, encounters with local fauna should be minimal."

"Thank you," I said, wondering if I should ask him for water.

Thankfully, the path was easier this time. The organic concrete seemed to be in better repair here, without the divots and random ankle-turning holes. Mikka practically skipped along beside me.

"You seem a lot happier than when we arrived," I remarked, pleased to see her in such spirits.

"I am," she said with a note of surprise in her voice. "I actually am."

"What changed?" I asked. "If it's okay to ask."

"It's always okay to ask," she said, looping her arm through mine. "I don't know exactly. I guess it started when you agreed to let me join you on this trip. I had something to look forward to. Some sort of adventure."

"Girl, if I had known that's all it would take, I would have planned a trip to Hawaii or something. Much safer and better beaches."

She laughed obligingly. "It's not just the trip. It's knowing that I would have a chance to do something, to be useful."

I squeezed her arm and pulled her in close to me. "Meeks. Your value is so much more than in your use. You are more my family than my blood relatives."

"I know that." She patted my hand. "But last summer, what Lada showed to me in the dueling ring. It shook me. And made it hard to reach out. To you, specifically."

"It wasn't real," I said.

"But it was," she said, slowing her pace. "She showed me you, after you had seen the Grey Meranti and Argus took you in. She showed me what you did with your situation. Your child. And then she showed me my own empty womb, shriveled and dead."

I stopped suddenly, dropping her arm. "She—what?"

She turned to face me. "I don't talk about it, but I'm nearly seventy this year, and I want to be a mother, Siobhan. I always have. I want to bear my own child and feel it growing inside of me. I want to be pregnant someday. But I have no desire for men. I never have. And while humans sometimes make things like that happen, no interventions have ever worked for our people." She looked off into the distance then. "Until now."

"I don't understand. What changed?"

She resumed walking toward the Gate. "Oriana took no male lovers."

Despite the clear road, I stumbled as I tried to catch up to her. "She what?"

"Oriana had no lovers, according to everyone at Naboskova. She had grooms and attendants and princes and any number of interested *potential* lovers, and she took none. Yet she found herself pregnant. She simply wished for a child, and one day she was pregnant."

"That is ridiculous," I said without thinking. "That's not physically possible."

Mikka frowned at me. "Siobhan, the magic of Fairy transcends physics every day. We cross through realms in the space of a thought, time passes at different rates, I call forth fire with no visible spark, just with a thought." To demonstrate, she snapped her fingers, and a ball of flame burst forth wildly enough that I flinched, and the guards behind us reached for their weapons.

I waved them down as I choked down the cedar smoke and pepper taste flooding my senses. My head cleared enough to hunger for her magic, and it was all I could do not to grasp at the rush of her power that filled my awareness. "Point taken."

"If Oriana can get pregnant just from enough desire next to the right Gate, who's to say it can't happen for me?"

I tried to swallow past the dry wad of cotton that felt wedged in my throat. Mikka was pinning hopes on a rumor she heard from a soldier in the barracks. I didn't want to point out the fact that it was much more plausible that Oriana had a hidden lover that no one knew about. Most royal fae weren't discreet about their sexual escapades, but that didn't mean it never happened that individuals didn't conceal their liaisons. My family never knew that Dariel had taken a lover in a Winter Court until he defected and left us for the highest Court.

I couldn't say that to Mikka, though. I had not seen such light in her for months. She had hope, something to live for. I wasn't going to be the one to snuff her flame. Not now.

"Maybe," I said. "Maybe it could happen. I hope it does. I want you to have everything you want." I reached for her hand and pulled her close, laying my head on her shoulder. "You're my sister. And you would make an incredible mother."

She wrapped her arm around my shoulder as we kept walking. "I always thought you would be an awesome mom, too. Maybe we could raise kids together. When the time is right, of course."

I stiffened but tried not to let her feel it. "Maybe." I didn't want to tell her that I didn't know if the time would ever be right for me for that. With the life I'd led, with the life I wanted to lead, kids did not fit into that. There was no guarantee I would ever be a good mother.

Especially if my magic took the course of my own mother's.

We would cross that flaming bridge of trauma when we came to it.

"You would make an incredible mom," I said sincerely. "And I will support everything I can to make that happen for you."

I hoped there was some way I could follow through on that promise.

CHAPTER TWENTY-NINE

As Dusan had said, we arrived at the Whitewood Gate within the hour and with no encounters with local wildlife. It was for the best, because after Mikka's revelation I wasn't sure I could handle the basilisk in this state.

Before I knew it, we stood before the Whitewood Gate.

It looked different on this side. The Greenwood Gate was a free-standing arch of river stones, stacked so precisely that they spanned a space wide enough that three people could walk easily side by side. It appeared handmade with stones that were of all different kinds, but the unique size and shape of every stone was slotted together with each other into a seamless whole.

The Whitewood Gate was different. These stones were not naturally worn by water and wind and time. They were carefully cut gemstones and quartz. Each one was a different color and make, some so dense and matte that they seemed to leech the color from the world around them, others prismatic and transparent, like rainbows captured in stone.

The whole arch dazzled in the shimmering purple light of Fairy, and I was glad we had a moment to appreciate it as the group assembled before our crossing.

Dusan gave us time but then spoke. "Her Majesty has prepared us for a number of things when we pass through. I would like you three," he gestured to Mikka, Kellan, and myself," to be aware of what we are going to do to protect you."

Kellan spoke first, his first words in my hearing since last night. "Thank you, Captain. We appreciate that."

"Given reports about increased presence of Summer Knights around the Gate, we anticipate a response unit of soldiers to take Her Royal Highness into custody and remand her to Her Majesty."

"Please just call me Siobhan," I said, already tired of the formalities. "I haven't been Her Royal Highness in almost fifty years."

"Yes, Your Hi—er, Siobhan," Dusan corrected. "We are under orders by Liliana and Her Majesty to protect Siobhan only until she retreats to the sanctuary of the Greenwood Knoll. We are not to engage once Her—Siobhan is protected by the wards of the Sanctuary. To further engage would be a declaration of war between our Queens and is more aggressive action than is wished by our Court at this time."

"Understood," Kellan said, still not even looking at me. "The Fair Folk will be able to defend her from the Knoll."

I was skeptical about what resistance Kellan's people could summon against the Summer Court's Knights at such short notice, especially given that he couldn't even talk to me after last night, but I held my tongue.

Dusan continued. "If we are too severely outnumbered, we are to retreat immediately and attempt a crossing through another Gate in the future. We cannot force you to retreat with us, but I would strongly advise you avoid attempting a crossing to the Iron Realm without our protection. We have heard that your magic is unpredictable and may not be contained easily."

"I can agree to that," I said, though a glance at Mikka cracking her knuckles told me that she at least was willing to test my abilities to fight through a full Summer regiment if it came to that.

"Very good." Dusan glanced over his Knights, checking their readiness. Only two of them had physical weapons, but I could see one woman extending long thorns out from her wrists while another rolled a ball of ice around in his hands. They were spoiling for a fight, and I was relieved to have their protection. "Forward, then."

Turning our group's attention to the Gate, we waited while Dusan took out a knife and drew a shallow cut across his forearm. As the first drops of blood welled to the surface, the Gate stirred, and I felt her magic flood through me.

The space between the stones of the arch shimmered as a waterfall of magic cascaded from the pinnacle of the arch and flowed down. I could taste as the way between worlds opened fully and the green floral and juniper flavors of the Gate's magic came alive. It hit me like a shot of gin and warmed me through.

There was an awareness to her, a recognition and a welcome. It felt like the Gate was opening her arms, eager to embrace me and pull me home. Belatedly, I realized I would finally be crossing through consciously. Instead of fear, though, I was eager and excited to pass through.

Dusan and five of his Knights passed through first, followed by Mikka and then Kellan. I took a fortifying breath and stepped through the shimmering surface of the Whitewood Gate.

I don't know what I expected exactly. Getting to Fairy, I'd been out of my head and had no recollection of passing through the Gate. But before that, my last experience with the Gate had found me trapped in a space between the worlds. There had been a vast and aware nothingness that overwhelmed and tore at my sense of self and place. It had been all encompassing and distant at once as it transformed me from the inside out.

I guess I expected something of equal significance this time. Something to mark that I had been changed from every other person who passed through the Gates every day.

Instead, I simply passed from one realm to the next as easily as walking from one room to another. The threshold of the Gate had no more significance in that moment than the threshold of any mundane building. I was simply in Fairy, and then I was home.

I was a little disappointed, to be honest.

But then I remembered Dusan's warnings and prepared myself for the inevitable onslaught of Bryony's anger at defying her orders.

There was nothing. No Summer Knights, no fighting, no stern faces telling me that I would have to answer for violating the Court's decrees, for killing those guards.

Instead, Dusan and his Knights stood by, scouting around the bright and cold empty clearing, trying to see if there was some threat on the perimeter. Mikka and Kellan stood awkwardly to the side, Kellan with a look of relief, and Mikka decidedly disappointed.

We were joined by the remaining six Winter Knights in a matter of moments, and we waited while the professionals swept the clearing around the Gate, searching for any signs of an ambush or a stern-faced official. With the lack of underbrush and thick foliage, they made quick work.

Nothing.

The captain came to report to us. "It seems we are fortunate. There are no forces here to confront us, and the way to the Sanctuary appears clear. I am not keen to test our good luck, though, and advise we move quickly to secure the three of you behind the wards of the Knoll."

We agreed and followed him and the knights up the path to the bar. The day was early still, cold frost clinging to the ground. I hope that meant it was still Monday, though it could easily be Tuesday with the way time passed differently between our realms.

I hugged my cloak around me tighter and watched my breath fogging the air. Monday meant I could get home to my own safe wards and figure out how to deal with Bryony tomorrow. Maybe I could still have Rhys over for our movie date. We could make dinner, discuss a plan of action, and I could explain what happened last night between me and Kellan. They'd understand, question my bad taste, we'd laugh, and then we could pretend to watch *The Mummy* before giving up and putting each other to bed.

I smiled. Rhys would put my mind at ease. They were always so reasonable and supportive. They'd tell me exactly what I needed to hear and then remind me that I didn't need some narcissistic, ambitious politician when I had someone loyal and reliable and good at home. I needed the comfort and safety and stability of Rhys, not someone I didn't know and didn't trust.

What I really needed was to get the taste of Kellan off my tongue.

Even now I could feel his magic rising. The taste of dark stone fruits and rich soil was distracting.

"Could you not?" I groaned at his back. "I just want to get to safety and home."

"I'm not doing anything." He stopped and turned to look at me, an eyebrow arched.

"I can taste your magic," I said. "You're doing something."

"I was just trying to sense if there's any threat we haven't found."

"Well, don't," I said. "We have an entire crew of knights to do that. And they don't taste like my favorite wine."

He took a step toward me and lowered his voice. "Is that why you couldn't get enough of it last night?" His words were teasing, but his gaze on me was intense and a little hungry, stirring another unbidden response as my core heated. I couldn't help the step I took closer, just to feel the heat of his nearness.

"It meant nothing," I whispered back at him. "I was just scratching an itch, and you were the easiest option at the moment."

He didn't respond. He didn't have to. He knew I was lying to myself. I had wanted him specifically. Multiple times. In multiple positions.

I took a step away and crossed my arms over my chest, trying to keep myself from reaching for him. He chuckled and didn't have to say anything further. It was like he knew what I was thinking.

He continued up the path toward the Knoll, and reluctantly, I followed, hugging myself against my discomfort.

We emerged from the bare trees to see the Knoll perched above us, silhouetted by the gray, featureless sky.

There was a single figure sitting on the back steps of the Knoll, a few steps down from the top deck. He wasn't looking at us, bent over his knees, but I recognized him immediately.

"Varon!" Mikka shouted and waved before breaking from our

guards and racing up the path. Dusan broke into a run after her, and the rest of us picked up our pace as we followed.

Something was wrong.

There were no guards waiting for us. Varon was hunched on the back steps on a Monday morning. The air was still and deathly quiet.

I watched as Mikka swept Varon into her arms, and he shook.

A ringing filled my ears as I found myself running toward them.

Before I reached them, Mikka turned a stricken face to me, her eyes huge with horror. It was the same expression she had worn in the dueling ring before she had taken Lada's knife to her own wrists. It was pure anguish and the look of someone that had lost everything.

No.

I stopped short of the steps. Out of reach.

Mikka said something, but the ringing in my ears prevented me hearing what she said.

The Knoll loomed over us. The back door was open, and Dusan had disappeared through it.

Where was he going? There couldn't be anything wrong in there. The Knoll was a sanctuary. The wards protected us.

Nothing could be wrong inside that building. It was safe.

My feet pulled me forward up the stairs.

I had to see. I had to know.

I felt a tug on my arm. Kellan had reached for me.

"Don't go up there," his voice cut through the muffle in my head. "What happened, you don't want to live with seeing it."

"Why do you care?" I said softly.

He stepped up beside me and put his hands on just below my shoulders, turning me to face him. "Believe it or not, I'm trying to protect you. I promised Argus I wouldn't let anything happen to you."

The earthen wine taste of him returned as he held me, grounding me in the moment.

I didn't want him to ground me. I needed to see what was inside my bar. Whatever it was. I needed to see it for myself.

"Siobhan, please." His eyes locked on mine, Kellan's magic quested for me, this time tasting of bergamot and vanilla.

I pulled on it and claimed it as my own, recognizing the flavor of magic and what it meant. "Let me go," I said gently, using the hint of his compulsion to make him obey.

He did so immediately, eyes widening with surprise.

"Take a step back," I said, the taste of him thick on my tongue.

With great effort, Kellan took a step away. "Siobhan, don't do this."

I turned away from him to see Captain Dusan and one of his Knights emerge from the large back door, their faces drawn and serious. Dusan began down the steps, intent on reaching us.

"Move back, Captain," I said, using more of Kellan's compulsive magic. Dusan instantly took several steps back up the stairs and away from me, as I continued toward the gaping maw of the Knoll's back door.

Crossing the threshold, I had to give my eyes a few seconds to adjust. Despite the gray, the morning was bright outside, while the inside of the Knoll was dark and full of shadows. I stood in the back hall for a moment, noting the spare coats that hung along the wall. I could taste the lingering magic of the fae who had last used them. One had notes of citrus tang and sweet bubbles, another cardamom, turmeric, and ginger. The scents of their power still hanging in the air, as if they had just been here and would return at any moment.

I could taste the magic of those who worked at the Knoll as well. Meara's saffron and rhubarb, Kaia's molasses rum and ginger, the hobs' hops and malt.

There was no wood smoke. No pipeweed. No brine.

I couldn't taste him.

I could always taste him in the bar.

He *was* the bar.

Mechanically, my legs pulled me forward.

The Knoll revealed itself as my eyes grew accustomed to the dark and the cavernous main room swallowed me up.

The lights were out. There was no fire in the hearth. There were no people scattered at the tables or spaced out at the bar. It was too early. Monday mornings we were mostly closed. Argus never locked the doors and would be willing to receive any who arrived from

Fairy, but generally our clientele wouldn't arrive until later this afternoon.

Still, there was a figure at the middle of the bar. A large man slumped over with a dark glass bottle toppled over beside his hand that rested limply on the counter. There was no liquid spilled, the contents of the glass apparently all drunk away.

The man faced the center of the room, showing me the dark salt and pepper of his hair, still thick and lustrous after almost three hundred and fifty years. I resisted the urge to run my fingers through it as I moved around him. On the other side was a note.

A note.

I couldn't look at his face as my stomach leapt into my throat. Turning away, I took deep breaths trying to still my heart and my roiling stomach. It didn't feel real. Nothing felt real. I floated.

Focusing on the empty bottle was safer. It was an older dark blue glass, something from the cellar or the private stash. It had a small wax seal on the front to mark the contents, but the writing was in a language I didn't know.

I picked it up and sniffed. Anise and regret. Deep grief and licorice and fig.

I had never touched it myself, but I knew this drink. Mettle. Distilled in Fairy from the tears of banshees, this drink made you feel your most intense emotions.

Argus had used it to help those who came into the bar unable to express or access deep feelings. It had only been brought out a few times. I'd seen a mother who lost her infant son brought to tears after three months of profound silence. She'd left healed and able to properly grieve and move on with her life. A young diwata who'd had his entire forest in the Philippines cut down for a new highway had been able to process the loss and return to the islands ready to plant a new home for his family.

The drink was powerful and only meant to be served in tiny amounts. More than an ounce, more than a shot, and the drinker risked being overcome by every emotion. It would destroy the mind and heart of even the strongest fae.

Argus was the strongest fae I'd ever known.

And the once nearly full bottle was now empty.

I set it back down carefully in the same spot it had rested beside Argus's open hand.

His lifeless hand.

Blinking furiously, I moved around his broad back once again. I didn't want to touch him, to disturb him. Whatever rest he found, he'd earned it.

And I wasn't ready to feel what waited for me on the other side of this dissociated numbness I'd discovered.

The note waited for me near his face.

I didn't look at him, just grabbed the sheet of paper and turned away. It was written on a strip of receipt paper.

It wasn't long.

"I wanted to protect you. I should have known better. You deserved better. I'm sorry. Freedom for all. Power to the least. I love you."

It was in his handwriting.

I fled out the back door and made it just to the edge of the Knoll's deck before throwing up.

CHAPTER THIRTY

The next few hours disappeared in a daze.

Refusing to go back inside, Varon told us that he had arrived first thing that morning –Tuesday, apparently. Not Monday. –to help Argus with an early delivery of mead and beer. They'd had a late night Monday when Mikka and I had failed to return on time and they had to cover being short-staffed. Varon had been worried, but Argus had assured him that the time slip was perfectly normal. He had every faith that we would make it home safely and to just suck it up and pour drinks.

"When I left around two a.m.," Varon said, "he was fine. There were only a few stragglers, and Meara was closing down the kitchen, and he told me to get some rest. That we'd get things unloaded early and go grab breakfast in the Square. But when I got here, he—"

Mikka held him as he wept on the stairs, and I went back inside with the Winter Knights. Captain Dusan, despite his orders to depart immediately when we were secured, took control of the situation. He dispatched a Knight to report to the Atlanta Court and another to seek resources from his own Queen.

A pillar of the solitary community was dead, and procedures needed to be followed.

By noon, the Grey Meranti had arrived with her preferred ankou, or fae grim reaper. Together they would prepare Argus's body for whatever came next.

He was a dragon. I assumed that meant a pyre of some sort, a cremation. But would he want a public funeral? Would he want just to be reduced to the ash from whence he'd come? Would we scatter them here or in Fairy?

My mind spun with such thoughts. There was no one else to answer these questions. His only family was here in the Knoll. The Knoll where he lived and served and made the world better.

And now he was gone.

I didn't know how to exist in this space without him.

Sipping nothing stronger than water, I sat at the far end of the bar from where I'd found him. I couldn't bring myself to go anywhere else.

Kellan left at some point, promising to return as soon as he could to help me with what followed. I barely heard him speak.

Mikka and Varon left together for their home a few miles up the road. They were twins, inseparable, and would comfort each other through this loss. Kaia arrived and told me she would get the word out and let our customers know we would be closed for the foreseeable future.

But we weren't just a pub. What if someone arrived from Fairy and needed sanctuary? Who would be here for them? Someone had to live at the Knoll. Someone had to be here.

So, I stayed.

Before she left, The Grey Meranti put a hand on my shoulder. Her ancient touch stilled all of the voices in me, bringing the first moment of clarity I'd felt since walking into the Knoll. "I understand. And it is right."

I didn't say anything as I reached up to hold her hand, her thin fingers strong and reassuring.

"It is yours to protect and preserve if you choose," she said. "He left this to you." She gestured around the Knoll. "We will talk more later.

But do not leave this place unless you wish. It is your home. And it is your safety. Seeking answers elsewhere will bring more grief."

She then swept from the room in a cloud of mist and left me alone with the remaining Winter Knights.

They avoided me for at least the next hour as they tried to patrol the perimeter, searched for further threats, for anything they could do. But with Argus removed, there was nothing left.

Nothing left at all.

So, I sat.

And they eventually gave up.

Dusan approached me. I could taste his simple taste of sweet and bitter in perfect balance, biting herbs and sweet comfort. He didn't have to say anything.

"Go home, Captain," I said wearily. "You have more than served your duty here."

"Thank you, Siobhan." For once, he didn't step on using my forsaken title. I guess the circumstances made us feel more equal. Death did that to people. Made us realize that titles and privilege and power only extended so far.

In the end, we were all going to be dust.

"Thank you, Dusan." I stood up from my barstool and faced him fully. His face of bark and moss had ceased to be strange to me, and I saw how much he struggled with leaving me here alone with my grief. I pulled him into a hug. The branches of his hair yielded as I pulled him close, whispering like willow against the sides of my face. "It will be okay. You tell Adrona that I will take care of her daughter's killer. Because our enemies are now one and the same."

He pulled back and considered me, realizing what I was saying. "You are sure?" He looked at the note that I had laid at my side, the short sheet of receipt paper that I had read over a hundred times already.

"I am."

I was more sure of that than anything. I wasn't sure who was responsible—and I truly doubted it was Bryony—but I knew that this murder connected to Oriana's death. The proximity of events, the circumstances were too close, too certain. Argus may have even figured out who had killed the Winter fae and was ready to expose them. The note alone told me it was connected.

The invocation of the Fair Folk motto: "Freedom for all. Power to the least."

They'd killed him to stop what he'd set in motion.

Whoever did this to Argus was going to pay with their life.

I hunched over my water.

The way they had done it hurt worse than anything.

No one could act with violence directly against a person inside the wards of the Greenwood Knoll. Someone had driven Argus to take the action himself.

Argus had lived through more than a few traumas in his centuries' long life. But nothing that had happened in the past few months would drive him to seek an end to things.

Someone had gotten in his head. Someone had convinced him to drink the Mettle, one of the most powerful potions in our bar, and then they had pushed him to his breaking point. They made him do it to himself. They had broken the strongest person I'd ever met, and had left him, alone, to be found by the people who loved him most.

They would pay.

"I wish you luck, then," Dusan said. "I hope we meet again under better circumstances." Then with a bow he gathered his knights and left to return home.

For a blessed few moments, the Knoll was quiet and empty.

Argus was gone. His ghost had yet to settle in if it ever would. There was no other staff. No guards. No soldiers.

Nothing but the white static that filled my head.

Then the Summer guards arrived. Several hours too late.

They'd apparently gotten the news.

Seven fully-armed Summer Knights arrived, activated and antagonistic.

That wasn't surprising. Who was among them, though, took me a moment to process.

Rhys was one of the first to walk through the door, their appearance utterly miserable. Their golden hair was slicked back with sweat, and deep bags hung under their eyes. I tried to catch their gaze, to communicate that I wasn't upset that they were part of the crew that was commissioned to bring me in. It was just their job.

They carefully avoided looking at me, standing at attention by the doorway and staring directly ahead.

More surprising was the fact that leading the group was Mother's personal Valkyrie warrior Captain Lyris. She was a tall Nordic woman with strong angular features and short blond hair that feathered away from her face. She looked like if Farrah Fawcett had taken up bodybuilding and could kill you with her big toe. Despite my despair, I almost laughed. The Court was pulling out the big guns for me, sending her on what should be a simple gopher job.

I guess Bryony finally realized she had underestimated me with only sending two guards for me at the Gate. She wouldn't make that mistake again.

"Siobhan Cambry Illythia, you are to come with us."

I stood. "Just so I know the terms, am I being charged with anything?"

Lyris pursed her lips. She knew me well enough to know this wouldn't be done cleanly. "Siobhan, don't make this difficult."

"I won't fight you," I assured, already standing up and moving toward the door. "I want to talk with Bry myself. I just want to know if she's going to make me cool my heels in the basement before she sees me."

"What difference does it make?" Lyris asked.

"Well, if I'm going to the dungeon, I'm making myself a batch of cocktails and bringing a snack and a book."

Though they still wouldn't meet my eyes, Rhys's lips quirked at my explanation.

"Her Royal Highness has requested you be brought directly to her," Lyris said.

"Can I still make a cocktail to go?" I asked.

"Siobhan." The tone in the good Captain's voice told me not to push it and the caraway and fennel taste of her magic made for a suit-able implicit threat.

"Fine," I said, following Lyris out the door without further nego-tiation.

There were three SUVs waiting for us in the parking lot. I was directed into the middle vehicle with Lyris and a driver up front and Rhys and me behind.

"I know it's Tuesday, and I obviously missed our movie, but can we have a makeup on our movie date?" I whispered as my partner slid into the seat beside me.

Their mouth fell open as they adjusted their sword to lay across their lap instead of stabbing either of us. "Are you serious, Siobhan? You can think about Brendan Fraser at a time like this?"

"I can always think about Brendan Fraser," I joked.

Rhys opened their mouth to say something else, but then they stopped. Maybe they saw the way my lip was trembling to hold a fake smile, or the twitch at the corner of my right eye. They instantly moved closer on the seat and wrapped their arms around me. "Oh, Shiv."

"Don't," I warned, my voice already wavering. I was barely holding on, and here was Rhys offering me a comfort that I knew wouldn't last. I couldn't afford to fall apart before I arrived at the palace. What-ever Bryony had planned for me, it wasn't a soft bed and a week to cry in my partner's arms like I needed.

I had to be strong. I had to keep it together.

And here was Rhys doing exactly what a partner should: giving me a shoulder to cry on and saying the empty words to someone who has experienced a loss.

"I'm so sorry. I know what he meant to you. I know how much you loved him. And he loved you."

"Stop," I whispered into their shoulder. "I can't do this."

"It's okay. We'll find some way to get you through."

The laugh I let loose into their arm was on the verge of completely unhinged. I pulled away enough to look up into their soft and concerned green eyes. "Get through which part? The part where I just lost the man who has cared for and protected me for fifty years? Who took me in when I had no one in the world and gave me a home? Or are you talking about the part where my sister is going to try to hold me responsible for that death and the others that have happened in her Queendom despite knowing for a fact that I had nothing to do with them? Or," I plunged forward as I shoved Rhys away to the other side of the SUV. "Or maybe you're talking about the part where all of this is just a smokescreen and my city is about to be torn apart by political players who all want to claim a piece of her because of the potential to control baby-making and the future of our race? Because that sounds like the most fun part."

Rhys rolled back their shoulders and took on a solid soldierly stillness as I raged against them. "I know it looks bleak right now—"

"Bleak?!" I couldn't stop myself from shrieking. "Mab's tongue, Rhys. We passed bleak almost a year ago."

"But," they continued as if I hadn't freaked out. "You don't have to go through this alone."

I laughed again. There was the last hinge of my sanity falling off. I leaned toward them menacingly, tasting at the cucumber and lime taste of them. "Are you going to go through it with me? Because I'm pretty sure you gave me the 'we should see other people' conversation earlier last week."

"That's not what I said, and you know it. I can't go through this for you. If I could, if I could take some part of this burden from you and make it easier, I would do that, Siobhan. But I can at most be here for you and support you as you do what you have to do. And if you get lost along the way, I will do my best to guide you back home." They reached over to lift my hand off the edge of the seat and used their thumb to stroke over the back of it, soothing. "And when you're ready to talk or accept comfort, I'll be here."

Before I could think or start crying, I snatched my hand back. I knew Rhys meant well, and I wanted nothing more than to throw myself into their arms and take exactly what they were offering. I didn't have time to feel anything but anger. Anger would protect me, keep me safe to face what was still ahead of me.

Rhys didn't protest any further, but they also left their hand on the seat between us, letting me know it was there when I was ready to take it.

It was a comfort. Even if I avoided touching them for the rest of the ride.

CHAPTER THIRTY-ONE

Mother and Bryony were waiting together in the receiving room when we arrived. They sat on twin thrones, dressed casually in coordinating shades of green, Mother in a dress, Bryony in a blouse and slacks. There were some forty courtiers in attendance with them, including Shiro, cousin Maylie, and several of Mother's lovers. Shiro and Maylie at least looked distressed to be standing in attendance, but most of the people appeared to be vaguely interested or even excited to witness this.

With every eye on us, the Knights escorted me in, Rhys at my side and Lyris leading the group. I was suddenly aware of how disheveled I was. I was still in my Fairy traveling clothes, my deerskin slacks, tunic, and even my jewels. I had completely forgotten I was still wearing them until the alexandrite on my forehead weighed heavily between my brows. I was travel-worn, sweaty, completely unprepared to be in view of the inner Court.

Ignoring my state, I held my head high, forcing my shoulders down and back, imagining a string held me aloft and pulled me toward the dais. I felt certain everyone could hear my heart pounding, and I tried desperately to avoid hyperventilating.

"As ordered, Siobhan Cambry Illythia is presented to this Court for judgment," Lyris announced. She bowed to her Queen and stepped aside to let me come forward.

Rhys likewise stepped back. No matter how much they supported me, they couldn't come with me for this.

I was alone.

I didn't look at my sister, who I knew was the architect of this farce. Instead, I looked at Mother.

She was beautiful as always. Her hair was not swept up into its usual artful curls but fell about her face in gentle honeyed waves. Her lips were a dusky rose, and her cheeks glowed with delight as she beamed at me.

"Siobhan," she said warmly. "What a delight to see you! It's been weeks."

I blinked slowly. That means she didn't remember our last visit, when she attacked me. "Did no one tell you why I'm here, Mother?"

"That's enough, Siobhan," Bryony said. "You are here because—"

"Because Argus is dead," I interrupted, unwilling to let her set the tone for this. "And someone in this Court killed him."

She sputtered. "My Court?"

"No," I corrected. "Mother's."

"Girls, girls," Mother said cheerfully, apparently unaware of the circumstances that had her daughters ready to draw each other's blood. "What is this? Siobhan, I thought you said Argus."

"Yes," I said.

"Dead?" she said, her tone unchanging.

"It's true," Bryony said. "We received word this morning, Mother. Remember?"

"Nonsense." Her smile did not dissipate, but I saw the light drain from her eyes as she processed the information. She turned inward for a moment, and I knew instantly what she was doing. I could taste her magic, the juniper and rosemary and sweet lemon as she reached out to her connections with her people.

I could almost feel the spiderweb of her power as it reached out in every direction, crossing into every being who had pledged loyalty to Summer, to the Oona above her, and to her minor Court specifically. Tiny sparks of connection lit her eyes and intensified the flavor of her power as she searched through the hundreds of loyalties that bound to her through the Gate.

She reached outward as far as she could, searching for the same thing I had sought so desperately in the Knoll. The same vacuum met her. That black hole of what should be with what was no longer.

Not that she would have found him in her web even if he was alive. He had never pledged loyalty to Summer or her as Queen. Not even when he was her lover almost two hundred years ago.

But she would have found traces of him. Whispers of his essence as he connected with her people, intimately, sexually, emotionally.

When she found no trace of him, she began to unravel.

I watched her hand reach out into the air in front of her, physically expressing what I was sure was going through her at the moment as her gaze went wide. She was questing through every single voice in her head, every power she could access, every corner of her expansive and overwhelming world, looking for any sign of her oldest friend.

She sifted through everything in her head, every connection she had reaching out through the city, and the longer she took and found nothing, the more her gaze drifted from us.

"I cannot find him," she said softly. She took a ragged breath. "Is it true?"

"I am so sorry, Mother," I said. "I found him myself. At the Knoll."

"The Sanctuary?" She laughed suddenly jubilant, instantly present again. "Then it's not possible. No harm can come to him there."

"Unless it is self-inflicted," I reminded her.

A murmur ran through the people gathered, but I ignored them. I knew it wasn't true. Argus would never.

"Argus would never," Mother echoed my thoughts. "Therefore, it must not be true! You are all simply mistaken."

"Dammit, Mother! Will you listen for once?" I shouted at her. "Argus is dead. Someone made him kill himself. The same someone who is killing royals in Winter and framing the Fair Folk for it. And the number one suspect is sitting on your throne and using all the confusion to grab power for herself." So much for Liliana's plan of subtlety. I barreled on. "I need you to hold Bryony responsible, or there is going to be war between you and Queen Adrona. Are you going to help me or not?"

"Enough!" Bryony said, trying again to seize control of the proceedings. "Mother, Siobhan killed two of your knights at the Gate, violated orders forbidding her from crossing into Fairy, has allied herself with a Winter Queen, and is planning to pit you against your own people." She shook her head at me. "I'm sorry for what happened to Argus, sister, but if anyone is to blame, it is you and your reckless and lawless behavior. You have been unpredictable and dangerous for far too long."

I couldn't believe what she was saying. "Are you seriously turning this back on me?" The cloying taste of vanilla filled my mouth as I angrily snatched at her magic.

"Ever since you came into your power, you've been a danger to yourself and others. You can't control what you do, you are willing to fall in with anyone who will nod and smile and let you run wild, hoping they can eventually use you to undermine this Court. Well, I'm over it."

"Bryony," Mother began.

"No," she said. "Kanha, Dulcea, please escort Mother back to her quarters. This is going to be upsetting to her, and we cannot risk an incident."

The dark-eyed man and blond woman closest at hand to Mother swept up to her. Kanha extended a hand, which Mother took willingly. He tucked it into his arm, as Dulcea swept around to twine an arm around Mother's midsection and kiss gently at her neck. Together the pair of consorts gently and lovingly walked her down and out of the room as Mother made half-hearted protests.

"I don't see why I shouldn't stay and help. My girls have never gotten along well, and I'm the one who can—" Her voice cut off as the doors closed behind her.

"Would that count as elder abuse?" I sneered at Bryony.

Immediately a spark of electricity jumped across the back of my right hand, causing me to jump and yelp.

"Bitch!" I screamed at my sister. I couldn't believe she would attack me in front of so many people.

"Oh, that wasn't me," Bryony smiled. She gestured to the back door where Mother had retreated, and there standing smug as can be were Lada and Kiral.

"We would not miss this," Lada said, striding past me to greet Bryony with a kiss on each cheek. She looked like an innocent child, tiny in a pristine white full-length dress with pale blue flowers embroidered along the hem. Her brown curls falling about her face with angelic softness. "After your tete-a-tete with my good friend Liliana, I had to let your sister know what was going on behind her back."

"Bry," I tried to reason with her. "You have to see what this white witch is trying to do. She's playing us all against each other."

"Says the sister who just tried to get me denounced by Mother." Bryony gestured for Lada to take the chair Mother had left, setting her up as equal beside her, once again. "This White Lady has been more forthcoming and honest with me in the short time I've known her than you have been with me in my entire life. And if anybody is playing anyone, it seems like it's you and your latest lover." I glanced over my shoulder at Rhys who stood impassively behind me.

"First Talisa, now Thierry Kellan?" Bryony continued. "Tell me, Siobhan, is this new kink you have for sleeping with murderous rebels a symptom of you coming into your power? Or is your magic acti-vated by your ambition and penchant for betraying everyone you know? I'm just trying to get a handle on where you stand."

I couldn't say anything that would make this better. "Whatever is between me and Kellan has nothing to do with any of this. I don't want to be a part of his group."

"So, you're defecting to Winter then?" Bryony sneered. "Did they promise you your own desolate queendom to rule in Fairy?"

"No! I don't want to rule anything!"

Lada giggled as she sank back into her chair and crossed her legs over the armrest, her long white floral skirt falling dramatically down the front of the throne. "Oh, of course. The eldest sister with no ambitions. Who is sleeping her way into power, striking secret deals with anyone who looks her way, and murdering the only decent man this side of the Gates. Shameful. I actually liked the old dragon."

"You don't get to say a thing about Argus," I snarled.

"Oh, no?" She glared down at me, and her dark eyes clouded with white. Her childlike face grew gaunt as the grave, and I felt her power touch me as I was filled with the fear and inevitability of my own death.

Then her power shifted and touched me deeper. It showed me Argus, his face on the bar, eyes open, frozen in a moment of grief and despair. He had been alone, drowning in pain. I hadn't been there.

My knees buckled under me, and I sank to the ground. I'd failed him. He'd died because I hadn't been there. He'd died with the taste of regret and cardamom and ginger on his tongue.

"Wait," I whispered to the ground. Mettle was a bitter drink. It tasted nothing like ginger or cardamom.

But I recognized the taste. I just didn't know where it came from.

Before I could chase the thought, a new wave of grief seized me as Lada focused her power further, filling my mouth with the taste of caramel and apples.

No, I thought. I seized the taste of her and let it fill me, chasing it back to her. Without standing, I pulled with all my concentration, grabbing her power like a lifeline and attempted to pull her down with me. I lifted my gaze from the ground to see her white eyes flicker to their normal black. She swung her feet down to the ground and stood.

The people around me took a step back as I pushed myself up to my feet to face her. My skin tingled as I noted the black pepper back-end bite of her magic and felt it fill me. "Oh, Lada, this didn't go well for you last time. Don't you remember?"

I turned the magic back on her and could feel a rush of energy as I overpowered her and my small world fragmented into a million pieces. Spinning into fractals, my mind reached outward, spiraling outward and touching every mind Lada touched. It was her Queen magic, and I was thrilled to learn I could seize even it as my own.

Lada and I were locked together for a moment as she battled me for control, but she quickly dropped away, and there was just the power.

Desperate needs and desires tugged at me and threatened to tear me apart. Every soul she touched, every magical creature she was connected to was now mine to command. It was too much. I wanted to give in to the multitude of thoughts and powers, let them rip away at me.

Instead, I reached deeper, past their fractured powers. I moved past the caramel apple taste of Lada, the storm of tastes, and found something deeper underneath it. There was something stable and real, lemony, sweet, and herbal that bubbled beneath it all.

It was me. My power. And I was stronger than all of this.

As I recognized that, I realized I could touch everyone in this room, take their power. Use it. I could taste them all. The cloying vanilla of Bryony, rich cognac of Shiro, Maylie a peach sparkling drink. Lada was caramel and apples, Kiral a mix of ginger and turmeric.

My power coursed through the room, affecting all. Bryony gasped as it struck her first and knocked her back into her throne, then it swept through, pushing everyone back and away.

Lada collapsed as my magic completely overwhelmed her. Her loyal consort was there to catch her, of course. Kiral immediately sought to ground her, to bring her back to herself. He touched her face, kissed her as she sank into her stolen throne.

Bryony looked at the guards. "Stop her! Siobhan is not to leave these grounds again. We can't let her out like this."

The guards recovered quickly and approached, but I still had Lada's magic. I pushed with her unique brand of compulsion and invaded their minds. As an Osenya, a White Lady, I could see exactly what terrified them, what would break them. I could steal from their own minds, break any of them, force them to revisit their worst memories or live through their worst fears. I could turn them on each other with hardly any effort.

Lyris feared losing her strength, her unwavering direction, and being trapped in a body too weak to move and a mind too feeble to do anything about it. Her second, a man named Antony, feared losing the love of his family, rejected by his wife and children and forced to live solitary. Rhys feared failure: failing to serve their Queen and Court, failing as a Knight, failing to save me from myself.

That got my attention, and the rest faded away. Still buzzing with power, I addressed Rhys. "Save me from what?"

Rhys licked their lips, their fear evident. "Siobhan, let it go. Whatever this is, it isn't you."

"What isn't me?" I pressed, moving forward to place a hand on their chest, their green knight's uniform slightly scratchy under my fingers. I was aware of everything, every fiber of the fabric, the thumping, elevated heartbeat of my lover as I terrified them. The sandalwood and cedar and cucumber taste of them was faint as they avoided their own magic. They knew it would call to me.

I slipped briefly and saw myself as they saw me. My black curls seemed to float around me on an unseen wind. My eyes were as black as Lada's, swirling with a green energy that crackled with menace. "What isn't me, Rhys?" I echoed.

"Acting like this. Like *them*." They reached up a hand to place over mine, pressing it into their heart. "You don't need to play their games, to fight like they do. You're better than that."

"You're right. I am better," I agreed as the energy of Greenwood pulsed through me. "I'm stronger. More powerful. I can do things they can only dream of." I pulled them closer. "I can put an end to all of this. I can make us all free."

"And do what? What is your plan, Siobhan? Will you lead the Fair Folk with Kellan? Will you be the new Queen?"

"Yes!" I said before I could think. Then it struck me what had come out of my mouth. No. That's not what I wanted. I didn't want to be Queen. I didn't want to overthrow my mother. Or even my sister. I wanted change, but that wasn't how I would get it.

"I mean, no." On the dais, Kiral had scooped up the unconscious Lada and was moving to another exit at the back of the room.

Bryony was watching me carefully, hesitant to move. I could hear her calculations. She hadn't killed anyone. She wasn't trying to destroy me or usurp our mother's throne. She was just trying to keep peace in a city that was unraveling around her.

And it looked like it was her big sister pulling at the threads that held this world together.

Still, she didn't want to act directly against me, to hurt me. She feared my powers, but she also feared the idea of going up against me and losing. She had to be strong to protect her city. She wasn't Queen yet and didn't have full access to the magic that brought with it. If she acted now, in front of her most immediate Court, they might not trust her when she took her throne.

I wanted to apologize but was distracted as hectic thoughts of the others in the room filled my head.

Only half fae and still more powerful than her sister.

Someone subdue this crazed pixie.

Siobhan should have been Queen. Halfbreed or no.

Freedom? I'm already free.

Will there be refreshments if she doesn't kill us all?

Crazy bitch. Will someone stab her already?

"Siobhan," Rhys said, bringing my attention back to them.

I struggled to release the thoughts flooding my head. "I'd like to see you get close enough to try."

"What?"

"The stabbing." And squinted, trying to pinpoint who had thought that. "And I don't appreciate the slurs."

A complex and resinous bitter taste wafted by.

"Cynar!" I recognized the taste. "Who tastes like cynar here?" My head whipped around, trying to figure it out.

"Siobhan," Rhys reached a hand to my chin, pulling my focus again.

"It's an amaro, uniquely made from artichokes," I explained, still trying to find who could taste like the apéritif.

The edges of the room grew fuzzy. Sleep beckoned.

I wasn't tired.

But dreams coaxed at me. Verdant fields of sweet grass to munch on.

Wait, not mine. Another dream.

Safe place.

The Knoll. With Argus and Mikka and Varon and Meara.

Argus was dead.

He didn't have to be. Maybe I could bring him back. I had only begun to explore the extent of my magic.

I could be even stronger if I used the Gate.

I reached out for Greenwood, and it responded, eager to join the swirl of my power. My skin crackled with its energy, with the energy of those around me.

With this much magic, perhaps I could do the impossible.

"Can I bring him back?" I whispered to Rhys who struggled to keep eye contact with me. "Spear through the chest will solve most problems!" The words flew from my mouth borrowed from someone else in the room.

"Rude!" I shouted back to the gathered courtiers. "There's better amaros anyway!" I knew the moment Bryony finally resolved to do something. "Don't!" I threw up a hand to stop her, and with a rush of vanilla, a blast of her own favored electricity shot from my hand. It came to a stop just in front of her, ricocheting off a shield that I threw up at the same time. The shock on her face was evident. She hadn't expected it. Hadn't prepared for it. Hadn't defended from it. My own instinct saved her from being blasted with her own magic.

"I'm sorry," I said. "I didn't—"

She didn't hesitate but immediately fired back with her own bolt of lightning. It never reached me. I merely blinked as it blipped away.

She started yelling, but suddenly I couldn't hear her. I couldn't hear anything outside my head.

Inside was different.

End this. The voice was vast inside my head. *You are above them. You were meant for more.*

The voice was not mine. Then it was mine. I echoed the words, the sound of it sonorous and deeper than anything that should have ever left my mouth.

I wheeled. Whose. Who whispered to me? Who made me speak their words with my mouth?

I'd kill them.

"I've got her."

"You don't. Let me help."

The voices were on either side of me. Arguing.

"Siobhan." That was a familiar voice. "Easy. It's okay."

A new taste arrived. Earthy with a spice to it. A garden in the first rain after a long drought. Hints of cedar and cherries.

"Not you."

He chuckled. The taste of Kellan was always powerful. Stronger than I remembered from last time.

Not strong enough.

You waste time. Your enemy escapes. The vast voice was as big as my head and stretched from here to the Gate and back.

"Where?" I demanded. "When? Were they here?"

You had him. He weakens you as he weakens the other. His goals are his own.

Rhys reached a hand to cup my chin. "Hey, I'm right here. Come back to us."

Your friend died because you weren't ready. You need to be ready.

Pipeweed and brine over my tongue, tinged now forever with regret and anise. "He died alone."

"I know. I know, I'm so sorry." Rhys again. They had pulled me into an embrace. There was stubble along their chin that scratched at my temple as they kissed me gently. "But you're not alone. We're right here. I'm right here."

Sweet kisses. Familiar and safe. Rhys's kisses felt like home. They had offered comfort when I was ready to accept it.

I felt the vast voice slipping away. Rhys's mouth met mine, and as their basilisk tongue searched along my lips, looking for some way to break through, I felt myself crawling back to reality. The feel of their hands along my body, the taste of their magic, all guided me back to my body.

Then hands that tasted like dry malt and hay and toffee seized me from behind, and I reacted. The green I had pushed away flooded back into me, and I had only one thought as the world disappeared.

Finally.

CHAPTER THIRTY-TWO

I don't know how long the Green had me. All I knew was sensation, flooding awareness of nothing. It was like I floated in a roiling sea. Waves of power pulled me under, tumbled me about, tossed me as driftwood in a hurricane.

In the tumult, there was no passage of time, no knowledge of how long I was tempest tossed. I simply drowned and drowned until I could finally come up for air.

The first thing I noticed when I did was that lovely taste of earth and cherries and deep red spice that quenched my thirst but left my tongue dry and wanting more. I recognized the taste of him, and I didn't push him away.

Kellan's magic swept through my consciousness in a way that was strange and exciting. There was none of the comfort and stability of the grounding that Rhys's magic brought me. No, this was exhilarating and elusive as it spun through me, inviting me to dance with it.

The press of his lips and the thrill of his tongue stirred something in me that brought me back to awareness. One hand held my face, as his thumb brushed along my cheek, while the other held me close about the waist, pulling me tight to him.

My body and mind responded, pressing in closer, anxious to feel alive and present. The nearness of him, the reality of him made me real, and I was able to fight my way back from the Green every-ness of my magic.

I clung to him, desperate to drink down his spiced red taste. Never mind that it was Kellan. Arrogant and duplicitous, protective and passionate, enigma that he was. He was real and *here*, and he forced me to be as well. I wanted to be here. With him. Even if for just the moment.

Giving into the desire that seized me, I grabbed the back of his head, while my other hand reached for his pants. I didn't know where I was or who was with us. All I knew was that I needed him in me, right then and there.

A hand encircled the wrist that attempted to undress him, and the kisses under mine melted away into husky chuckles. "While I appreciate the enthusiasm of a repeat, no. You would hate me in the morning," he said, his voice as thick as my lust.

"I don't care," I growled back, trying to twist my hand back to its task.

"I do," he replied, refusing to let go and pulling away.

I opened my eyes and found him with his hand around my eager arm, the other still cupping the side of my face. His pupils were blown with desire, and his perfect chestnut hair was tousled from my ardor.

"Welcome back," Kellan said, his voice breathless.

I licked my lips, relishing the taste of him still. More than grounding me, I felt myself responding to him more and more. It felt like waking up from the deepest dream. Like a gulp of cold water on a hot day. Like a lungful of air after holding my breath too long.

There was a growing want in my core that warmed me and had me aching. His touch, his strength, the way he pulled me away from the edge and back into myself had my body thrumming with arousal. He made me feel alive, and I wanted to hold onto that feeling forever.

It was time to stop denying that I did want him. Desperately.

"More," I said, hungry to chase this desire further.

"Siobhan," he said, a note of regret in his voice, even as he cupped a hand at the base of my neck, his fingers threading through my hair. "Not here."

I looked around and realized we were still in the middle of the ballroom. The assembled Court had mostly fled, Shiro nowhere to be found. But there were several dozen guards standing around us, ready to move in an instant. Rhys stood amongst them, arms at their side, no hint of emotion on their face as they watched me clinging to Kellan tighter than kudzu on an oak.

"Release her," Bryony's voice broke into our stolen moment.

Kellan flinched. "I'm sorry." And he released me.

The moment he stepped away, the huge swell of my magic fell away like an avalanche, crashing around me, leaving me empty and bare. Nothing further to sustain me, I collapsed. The guards rushed forward to grab me, pulling me up, and the room spun.

"Seize him as well, Lyris, Rhys," Bryony said much too calmly.

"What?" Kellan said, as Rhys and the captain grabbed him by the arms and held him at swordpoint. "Bry, you can't be serious. I just did you a favor."

"Thank you for stopping her, Kellan," Bryony said as she walked right up to him. "But as the confirmed leader of the Fair Folk, you are hereby under arrest. You will be charged for crimes against the Court of Atlanta and her people, including treason, fomenting a rebellion, and the murders of Argus Ladones and Oriana Adrona, possibly among others."

"This is ludicrous, Bryony. You know I didn't kill anybody." He struggled as my lover and Lyris pulled him from the room. "Listen to me. Your Highness. You know I didn't do it."

I could do nothing but watch as my head swam with the aftereffects of my magic surge. Bryony came to stand before me and looked down with pity as I hung boneless between two guards I didn't know. "What am I going to do with you, Shiv?"

"Good question," I said breathily as I blinked weakly and tried to focus on her. "I did ask you for help. You kicked me out."

"A mistake," she admitted. She leaned over and tenderly pushed one of my black curls out of my face. "I have been listening to entirely too many people who lie to me for too long. You, Kellan, even Lada and Kiral." She stood up straight and clasped her hands in front of her. "Orion and Kiral came here just before midnight spinning a tale that you had killed Argus before you went to Fairy because he tried to stop you from turning your back on your people. I laughed them out of here, because if there's anyone you've ever been loyal to it's that giant dragon."

She shook her head sadly. "Then this morning, I get actual Winter Knights here, in my palace, to tell me and Mother that Argus is indeed dead. I don't know who did it. I don't know if it was Kellan trying to manipulate you for his own goals. Or if Orion did it to get even for his sister. By Diana's grace, maybe it really was you!" She laughed, an unsteady edge in her voice showed how near she was to breaking. "I don't even know who you are anymore, Siobhan. What you did here today? I don't know what you're capable of."

My throat constricted and my eyes filled with tears. I couldn't even argue that it wouldn't happen again. Not only had I lost control and reacted emotionally with magic I couldn't control, but I had done it time and again. Even when I knew it was a problem, I hadn't stopped myself. I hadn't been able to talk myself down or even stop myself from reaching for the magic in the first place.

I liked the way it felt, having power. I liked feeling like I mattered and that I was someone to be considered. I felt like a Queen when I touched that power. And just like a Queen, I was losing control of myself.

Maybe she was right. If I couldn't find some way to harness it, maybe I shouldn't even have this power.

"I didn't mean to hurt anyone," I said, weakly.

Bryony reached for me again, like she would reassure me, hug me, make me feel better. But then she stopped herself and pulled away. "I don't know if I believe you," she said, steel returning to her spine and her voice. "And it doesn't matter. There's too much happening that I don't understand, and I can't risk you going around as unstable as you are. I will be holding you here until we can get to the root of your magic or until you can prove you have mastered it. You'll be attended by the Yaksha twins who will keep you from accessing your powers except under strict supervision. I wish there was a kinder way, but you have not left me with a lot of choices."

I paled. The Yaksha twins were Mother's not-so-secret weapons. They fed and sustained themselves on not just Fairy magic, but on fae powers. When they were present, they could nullify the most powerful fae's magic. Rumor held that they could even drain a Queen, but they were so loyal to Mother, I'm not sure it had ever been tested.

"Bryony, please," I began, my breath still shallow. I was already so drained, I wasn't sure there was anything for the Yakshas to feed on, but I didn't want to try it.

"Save it," she said. "I'm going to get to the bottom of this, but I can't have you complicating things for me anymore. I'll give Kellan to Orion to resolve your curse, and then I'll clean up the rest of your mess. But this whole thing is over. If you want to master your magic, you will be doing so under my supervision. If you want to help with whatever is happening with the Gate and all these knocked-up fae, you can offer your theories from the palace. Enjoy your old rooms. You'll be spending a lot of time there."

The guards didn't even give me a chance to get my feet under me, as with a wave from my sister, they hauled me away. Down the hall, up the back stairs, and straight to my former suite. I was dropped unceremoniously on a deep-set couch in the receiving room and barely pulled myself up before the doors slammed, leaving me alone.

Alone. Thankfully, the Yakshas were not there waiting on me. I wondered how long it would be before they came to feed. Bryony knew I was still drained from my display earlier and wouldn't need to be subdued immediately.

I groaned. What had I been thinking? How could I have attacked Lada? Rhys had tried to talk me down, to speak reason to me, and what had I done? I'd lost complete control. I'd sampled from everyone in the room and lost control. Their voices and fears had overwhelmed me, and I'd been high on the feeling of their power to let them go.

What had I done in those moments before Kellan brought me back? Had I hurt Rhys? Attacked Bryony again?

She was right. I was a danger to myself and others. I couldn't stop reaching for this power, the thrill it gave me. When I was in my magic, I was something more, something stronger than I was by myself. I had power, and it felt good.

But I wasn't in control.

Shame flooded me. At least the choice was out of my hands now. I couldn't use my magic even if I wanted. I was locked away.

As was Kellan. I wondered where Rhys and Lyris had taken him. Had they stashed him in the basement holding cells? We called it the dungeon, but the rooms down there were actually quite comfortable. He'd have a proper bed and his own bathroom facilities before they turned him over to Orion.

Maybe they had taken him directly to the Winter prince. Bryony had said Orion and Kiral had come to her last night, so chances were he was still nearby. Those bastards had tried to frame me for Argus's murder, while Liliana tried to convince me it was all Bryony's doing. I was sure Orion would gladly displace the blame again onto Kellan and let him pay the price for the loss.

Never mind that we'd been together in Fairy, with witnesses from Orion's own Knights. The grieving prince just wanted to rage, to have someone to pay for the wrongs committed against him. As if that would bring his sister back.

It wouldn't. It wouldn't bring Argus back. It wouldn't bring back Baerd or Gair or Talisa or any of the rest of them. It was just pain on top of pain.

It didn't make sense.

Wait.

It really *didn't* make sense.

Varon had said that he was with Argus at the Knoll until at least 2 a.m., and Meara had still been there when he left. But Bryony had said Kiral and Orion had been at the palace before midnight. Time might pass in unexpected ways in Fairy, but here it still passed linearly. There was no way they knew about Argus unless they were the ones who killed him.

And Kiral was on his way back to the Gate right now.

I had to stop them.

I pushed myself up from the sofa and took a staggering step toward the door. My head throbbed and spun, and if I didn't pull myself together, I knew I wouldn't be able to leave this room under my own power, let alone go after Orion and Lada's lackey. But I had to try.

Closing my eyes and taking a deep breath, I tried to find a steady center as the ground seemed to rock beneath me. Nothing felt real, as I felt outside of my body, floating above myself, watching as I stood in the opulently decorated rooms, alone, powerless. What I wouldn't give to have Rhys, or even Kellan there to ground me.

A rush of air buffeted me, and when I opened my eyes, Lyris, Rhys, and Kellan stood before me. I swayed. Was I now hallucinating visions as well as voices?

My knees buckled, and Rhys was there to catch me.

"Are you real?" I asked, despite feeling the very solid muscles of their arms around my waist and under my shoulder.

"She's not in great shape," Rhys said over their shoulder.

"She'll be in worse shape if we don't get her out of here," Lyris replied, her brow creased with worry as she checked the door and made sure it was locked. "Are you sure you can handle it?"

The skin under Kellan's eyes was bruised with exhaustion, and his shoulder hunched slightly.

"I don't know," he admitted, straightening. "I'll take you first." He held out a hand, which Lyris accepted, and they disappeared into thin air.

"Oh," I said, nodding to myself and sagging back into Rhys's imaginary arms. "Definitely not real." After all, everyone knew magic didn't work like that. People couldn't just teleport like they did in the movies.

I must be passed out on the sofa. Or maybe the Yakshas had arrived after all. Did they inflict visions when they drained you?

"Come on, Siobhan," Rhys said, pulling me up to my feet. "Pull it together. We're going to need you."

"For what?" I said, willing to indulge my dream. I could at least see where my subconscious led me.

"We're getting you out of here. Back to the Knoll. We can keep you safe there."

I shook my head. "It didn't keep Argus safe. Orion and Kiral got him there anyway. They killed him."

"What?" Rhys turned me around to face them. "How do you know?"

"Bryony," I said as another wave of dizziness seized me. I leaned forward, and Rhys let me rest on their shoulder, holding me close. I breathed in the cucumber taste of them. "She said they came to tell her Argus was dead before he was even killed. Doing Lada's bidding, no doubt."

Rhys held me closer. "I'm so sorry. We won't let them get away with it. But they're probably already safe in Fairy."

I shook my head, reaching for my connection to the Gate. She hadn't been opened since Kellan had released me, hadn't stirred. She felt almost as depleted as I felt, like her magic had been as tied to mine as mine had been to hers. "She's closed."

"Lada?" Rhys questioned.

"No, the Gate. She won't open for them." I didn't realize it was true until I said it, but I knew the Gate would not respond to their blood. Not if I didn't want her to. She was mine to command. If I willed her to remain shut, she would do so.

"Then we can stop them," Rhys said.

With a pop of displaced air, Kellan suddenly reappeared in the room. He was gasping for breath, and the bruises under his eyes were more pronounced. However, he did what he did, it took a lot out of him. He was burning himself out. "We have to go, now," he said. "Lyris is with the Queen, but they'll realize I'm not in my cell soon, and they'll come here next. I can't get us to the Knoll itself, because of the wards, but I can get us to the Gate." He reached out a hand, waiting for me to accept it.

"How do you do it?" I asked. Instant travel or teleportation wasn't supposed to be possible, even for Queens. It was why we had to rely on the Gates to travel between the realms.

"How do you borrow the powers of others? How does your partner here turn their enemies to stone with nothing more than a constipated look in their eyes? It's fucking magic, Siobhan. Now take my hand and let me get us out of here before I don't have the energy to do it anymore."

I reached out and accepted his offered hand, while Rhys took the other. An overwhelming taste of cherries and earth filled my mouth, stirring something inside of me, and the palace disappeared.

There was no sense of movement, of displacement. In a moment, we were simply at the Gate, where Lada stood leaning on Kiral with Orion on her other side. Two Summer guards lay dead to the side, their blood seeping into the ground in front of the still-dormant Gate. I could feel her energy, aware of us, but she was stubbornly holding the doorway closed.

The trio of Winter fae turned as we arrived, and before we could get our bearings, Orion swept an arm, sending a burst of wind at us. Kellan flew away, but Rhys held tight to me, as we were thrown back. They took the brunt of the fall as we landed together, but my head still hit the ground hard, sending stars across my vision.

I was still blinking them away as Orion stepped over me.

"I've had enough of you," he said, as he raised a hand, ice spreading across his palm and arranging into a long dagger aimed directly at my heart. "The curse takes too long. It is time I ended this."

Out of energy, out of magic, and out of options, I closed my eyes and waited for the blow to land.

CHAPTER THIRTY-THREE

The cold blow of the ice dagger never landed, so I cautiously opened my eyes to see Orion still poised above me, frozen in place. The irony of that made me chuckle, but the expression of fear on his face pulled me short.

Kiral stalked up behind him, still supporting Lada, who looked as rough as I felt. "The Gate," he sneered, his free arm dripping blood where he'd tried to activate the Gate. "What did you do to it? Why won't it open?"

Rhys groaned, and I rolled off their arm, pushing myself up slightly. The ground seemed to lurch, so I couldn't offer the mocking grin I had hoped. "Having trouble?" I said to the ground instead, as I reached for my magic. This close to the Greenwood Gate, I should have been able to stabilize myself, to find some reserve of power to get me to my feet.

The Gate, though, resisted me as well. I found the edges of her green taste, but it didn't flood me with power as I had hoped. It almost felt like she was waiting for something.

I expanded my senses, reaching deeper, but all I could taste were the fae surrounding me. The caramel and apple taste of Lada was faint, her magic still weak. Orion was cranberry and ginger spiced but also muted. Rhys and Kellan were not actively calling on their powers, so the overwhelming taste was Kiral. Cardamom and turmeric, ginger, lemon, and star anise, with a hint of vanilla.

"Why won't the Gate open with sacrifice?" he demanded shaking with anger even as he braced his Queen against him. "Two deaths, my own blood freely given? Every sacrifice has opened the Gate longer and longer, but now, suddenly, nothing is working. Why is the Gate closed?"

I lifted my head then, rocked back on my heels, and shrugged petulantly. "My sister did say she was going to shut it down. Maybe take it up with her?"

Lada lifted her head from Kiral's shoulder, a skeptical squint marring her wide-eyed porcelain doll face.

"No. There is more here," she said haltingly, as if she was trying to figure something out. Her eyes struggled to focus. With her in a weakened state, I didn't have to worry about her attacking me.

Granted, she didn't have to worry about me either.

It was the least high stakes confrontation of our entire enmity.

Lada's head lolled on her lover's chest, as her long fingers clutched at his arms. "We must pass through, my love."

Kiral pulled her close and laid a gentle kiss on her forehead. "Wait here." He made sure she was steady on her feet, before he released her, bent down, and hauled me up. I nearly blacked out as stars danced across my vision, and I struggled to keep my feet under me. He dragged me, kicking and unsteady from the edge of the clearing over to the Gate, where he slammed me, smacking my forehead on the stones.

If this kept up, I was sure to have a concussion by the end of the day.

"Open the Gate, half breed," he snarled, "or I will unleash your greatest regrets until you beg for your own end."

"Is that how you did it?" I said, bracing myself against the edge of the stone Gate, and staring him down. I wanted to look into the eyes of the one who had killed Argus. The one who had driven him to his depths and left him to succumb to his own worst inclinations. "Is that how you killed him? What did you show him to drive him to suicide? Or do you even know?"

He lifted an arm, as if he would reach out to me, and either wring me by the throat or do exactly as he threatened and drive me to my own end. But Lada reached out suddenly, grabbing him by the wrist.

"Kiral?"

The temperature of the Knoll's clearing dropped several degrees. Lada's voice sounded as young and vulnerable as a child forgotten down a well, but there was a foundation of steel behind it. He turned to her, because there was no way to ignore the command.

"Did you kill Argus Ladones?"

The question hung in the air, and I didn't realize until that moment that Lada didn't know what her lover had been up to on his trips to our realm.

I traced back through my memories, wondering when I had tasted their magical signatures. Kiral's chai cocktail was all over the palace, the Gate, and the Knoll. But the only place I could recall Lada's magic was in the palaces, with Bryony, with Adrona. She was playing a political game, while her lover was all over the map, tending to needs deeper and more nefarious.

I had assumed he was doing her bidding. He was her loyal, monogamous lover, after all. She was his Queen.

The way she was looking at him now, though, I realized that he was his own agent, and she might not have been aware of all he did on her behalf.

Briefly, he flushed but quickly recovered. "I did what I had to do for you," he said forcefully, before holding her tighter. "Reserve your strength, love. I will get you home and safe, soon."

She pushed against him. "Stop," she said, her voice still in that innocent octave, but the steel had passed into a molten stage, her strength returning. "I must know. In all we have worked for, in all we have sacrificed, did you compromise it to go after a personal grudge?"

I suppressed a snort. Lada herself had reacted emotionally nearly every time I was in the same room as her. And yet, given the power I knew she was capable of, and the instability that her power subjected her to, I had to begrudgingly respect that she hadn't tried to kill me more frequently. If I'd been in full thrall of these powers every time I encountered her, I'm not sure either of us would have survived this long.

"No," Kiral insisted, as he grasped her hand. "My love, we have found our path. There is life, possibility. Here and at Whitewood. The more sacrifices to the Gate, the more our people have thrived. Life for life, we are making our people stronger. If we can unite them all under your rule, we can restore our former glory. More importantly, we can start our family, build a future for our children."

"But why kill the Keeper?"

"He was an obstacle," Kiral said, angrily. "He had convinced Oriana to flee Winter with her baby. She was going to seek sanctuary in this realm, so Liliana couldn't use her. He was offering to help her defect. It would have undermined everything you've worked for."

Lada took a step away from her lover, toward the edge of the clearing where Orion still stood frozen in place over Rhys's unconscious form. She spoke to Kiral but kept close watch at Orion as her words filled the clearing. "Is that why you killed Oriana and the others?"

We all saw as the knowledge hit Orion and fulfilled the bonds of the curse. The pain of the realization pulled his eyes into pinpricks, and the electric copper taste of the curse snapped through the clearing at once. If I hadn't already been knocked prone, I had no doubt I would have staggered to the ground as the tight strictures of the curse released me. As it was, Orion seemed to sag, even as he remained frozen, the vitality drained out of him.

The curse was satisfied, the magic gone. And the loss of it looked like it might break poor Orion.

Lada cocked her head and considered him with a close approximation of pity on her face. I hadn't thought her capable of it, but there it was. Empathy. A bit of sorrow and concern.

Then, as though she'd downed a shot of hard whiskey, she twitched her jaw back and straightened, turning toward her lover.

"I had thought it was to motivate Orion to our crusade, but it was just because you thought your friends were going to defect. To leave the Winter Court. To leave you. It was out of jealousy."

"You knew?" Kiral's anger disappeared, as he approached and reached a hand to cup her cheek.

She nodded and leaned into his touch. "I suspected from the beginning. You hoped the Winter Court would join us against a common threat. That we might finally unite and pull back from the Eternal Realm for good." She shrugged out of his reach and stepped around him to stand in front of Orion. "He will never forgive it. He hears us, and when I release him, he will try to kill you."

Kiral sighed deeply. "I know." He reached for the knife he had on his belt, unsheathed it. "Another sacrifice to the Gate."

"No," I said. I didn't harbor any lost love for the Winter prince, but I didn't want to see Orion murdered either. I clung to the edge of the Gate, and though I tried pushing myself up, my spinning head filled with stars and blacked around the edges. There was no way I would be able to stop Kiral. I fell back again, resigned.

"Wait," Lada said softly. She reached for her lover's arm. "I can't let you kill him."

Kiral frowned, confused. "You said yourself he will kill me."

"I know," she agreed. "But I need to know something."

Kiral held the knife loosely at his side, but I could see his grip twitch tighter around the hilt. "Anything, my love."

"How did you convince him to take his life?"

"The dragon?" Kiral's disgust was clear. "I made him see his little princess here attack her mother and then get strung up by her neck at the palace. She almost made it come true herself today, so it wasn't hard to plant the idea when helped with the Mettle drink."

"You made him see." Lada shook her head sadly. "You used my abilities."

"Well, of course," he said. "You have been sharing blood with me for years. I've gotten quite skilled at casting visions."

She locked eyes with me. A moment of understanding passed between us. She looked so sad, so disappointed. "But I never gave you consent to use my magic in that way."

He had just a moment of confusion before, with lightning quickness, she snatched the knife out of his hands and a flick of her wrist slashed the tip across the bare neck he presented her. A spray of blood splashed against the bodice of her white gown.

Time seemed to slow down as I saw his heart break and his life leak away from him at the same time. He collapsed down to his knees and looked up at me in terror. I almost wanted to reach out to him, to find some way to staunch the river of red that came from his open throat, but without my magic, without my strength, there was nothing I could do for him. My fingers bit into the stones of the Gate, as he bled out in seconds and crumpled into a heap at his Queen's feet.

Though Lada stood over him impassively, I could see the tears welling in her eyes. "I never gave you consent."

His hot blood stained the ground, pooling around his body and soaking into the near-frozen moss, warming it as it spread across the ground. The hem of Lada's white dress dragged through it, and I watched as it crept up to the edge to her embroidered flowers.

"He was your partner," I said, my throat tight with fear. She had killed him so effortlessly, I wondered how quickly she would dispatch me, now that I was defenseless before her.

"He betrayed me," she said simply, though I could see how her lower lip trembled. She had made her choice, even though it hurt her. "He betrayed what we worked for, and he killed his own. He violated our laws, and he violated my trust." And she smiled ruefully. "And I liked Argus Ladones. If he had to die for his role with the Fair Folk, his death should rightly have fallen to me."

She turned her head then with a smile, and the moment Kellan popped into existence directly behind her, she froze him as she had done to Orion. "It is a lovely trick you wield," she said dispassionately. "But if you hope to surprise me, you will have to have more than tricks."

Her eyes then clouded over with white, and she cocked her head at him. She was going to do to him what she'd done to Mikka, what Kiral had done to Argus. To make him see death and loss that would break him from the inside.

And in my state, I could do nothing to stop her.

I clawed at the stones of the Gate, willing it to wake up, to give me some way to intervene and save Kellan, to stop this. My nails gave way, ripping and tearing my skin as Kiral's blood began to seep through the toes of my boots.

The Gate stirred, lapping at the death and blood that was offered. Kiral, the dead Summer Knights, my own bloody fingers.

It wasn't enough.

Lada stood with her back to me, focused on Kellan. And my bar knife still hung at my waist.

I didn't stop to consider whether it was a good idea. I pulled out my knife and stumbled forward. Before she could realize what I was doing, I stabbed Lada just inside her right shoulder. She staggered, but before she could react, the world blew apart.

The Gate was awake.

CHAPTER THIRTY-FOUR

The glade around the Greenwood Gate disappeared as the Gate swallowed me whole. I wasn't sure if the effect was just in my head or if I had once again passed through the arch into the liminal space between the realms. All I knew was the vast nothingness that engulfed me.

The floral and verdant green gin taste filled my awareness, and the pain of my headache and exhaustion of my magic drain disappeared. I was whole and hale, surrounded by an all-encompassing vastness that tore my mind in all directions. More potential power and more pathways to eternity than I ever imagined overwhelmed me.

Nothing and everything, awareness of all and understanding of none, and it would rip me to shreds if I didn't ground myself, if I didn't tether myself to something real.

And then it ended.

There was a touchstone. Something real emerged.

Some*one* real.

At first she was just a figure. Something substantial in the ephemeral. Familiar, but strange as she took shape.

Then she stepped into my awareness.

"Hello, Siobhan," she said.

That voice. It was the one that spoke to me in those deepest moments of madness. The one that rooted deep into me. That spoke substance, when most voices were smoke.

It was the Gate.

"Hi," I said, uncertain how someone addresses something abstract.

I waited for her to take a form I could concentrate on, but she shimmered in and out of reality. One moment taking shape, where I could make out a slender feminine form with fair skin and dark hair. The next, a ghost.

She was still something to anchor me to a point in reality, and I clung to the feeling of her, the rosemary and juniper taste.

"You're real," I said, understating what I felt to be true. She was more real than almost anything I knew, anything I had experienced. She was all-encompassing. She *was* reality. She was the voice inside my head, speaking to my soul.

"As are you," she said, and though I couldn't make out a smile on her face, I could hear it in her voice. "I'm glad to finally meet you."

The fact that she was real threatened to throw me from the secure place I'd found. It felt too big, too important. Why was she here, why did she choose to talk with me?

Why now?

The sacrifices that had been made, several fae deaths, my blood, the blood of a queen twice given. They were all things we were told would open the Gate. But was that what brought her here? In this personified form?

"It helped," the figure admitted.

"You can—"

"Yes, darling. You have been speaking to me through your mind for months. I have been listening. I have accepted your offerings. And I am willing to help you reach your potential."

"What does that mean?" I said, even as I felt something within me expand.

The last time I had passed into this space, I had found a magic I didn't know existed. I had been able to taste, to touch, to borrow other fae's magic without taking their blood.

My awareness grew, and it felt as though the world would overwhelm me. I could feel the Eternal Realm, the Iron Realm, and so many beings within them. A million voices, a million powers, a million different flavors colliding into my mind, crashing inside of me until I felt certain I would shatter and fracture into nothing.

"Stop!" I screamed. "It's too much!"

At once, the magic receded and the voices hushed.

"It will get easier," she said. "You will learn. You will grow into it. Again." The power rushed at me, and I felt like my mind was breaking. The force of it pressed in from all sides until I thought it would be better if I were simply crushed to death. There was nothing but the searing magic, absolute in its scope.

A dam was breaking somewhere in my mind. If the power did not sweep me away entirely, I don't know what would be left standing in its wake. I couldn't control this magic. It would control me.

"Please. No. I don't want it!"

Again, the tide receded, and I was empty and wrung out.

"Why would you not want it?" The Gate woman asked. "It is your birthright. It was what you were born to."

I gasped. "I gave up my birthright years ago. I didn't want it then, and I don't want it now."

A tension filled the air as the figure before me ghosted in and out of reality. I could tell she was angry, as reality seemed to pull tight as a garrote around me. "You will learn," she repeated. "Again."

"No!" I reacted instinctively, using every bit of the magic I could touch and feel to wrap around myself. I felt like I had just encased myself in a protective cocoon, and I concentrated on it pressing outward, repelling anything further that might come.

"No?" she said, fury in her voice. "You are my beacon. My light in the dark. You guide me back. You will accept my gift, and you will tether me to your world."

I didn't understand what she was meant. It was almost like she was describing me as her consort, grounding her to reality. "I can't do that," I said, holding tight to my protection. "I can't be that for you. I won't."

"You do not get to choose," she said. "The magic holds us together. Anytime you reach for it, I am on the other side."

She was right, I realized. Every time I had reached for the Gate to touch my power, the rush of that power had come with her taste: juniper and rosemary and lemon. She was connected to that magic as inextricably as I was. She was a part of it, as *it* was a part of me.

If I continued to use the power she offered, I would eventually lose myself, just like every Queen that came before.

"Then I relinquish it," I said.

I couldn't harness the power, so I released the reins. I started with the protective barrier I had erected, and taking a deep breath, I let it go. Something within me unfurled, like relaxing a muscle that had been flexed or unclenching my jaw. A weight shifted, and the part of me that had clung to that magic was suddenly empty and free.

The Gate woman's figure flickered and faded, but a fire seemed to catch in the air around me. The vast nothingness seethed and roiled, tossing in a rage that burned like whiskey going down.

A wordless scream exploded all around me, and I was thrown out of the liminal space, back into the Iron Realm beyond it.

Blackness seized me as the air rushed from my lungs, and it took several seconds to gather my wits. I was back on the cold moss in the center of the clearing, just beyond the stone arch of the Gate.

Or rather where the arch should be. As someone with strong arms helped me to a seated position, I gaped at the ruin before me.

The Gate had blown apart. The rough river stones that made up its strong crown were scattered in all directions. Only a few rocks still stood piled on either side of a hole where the Gate should be and a doorway between the worlds now pulsed with power, unconstrained by its stone frame.

The shimmering purple and green of Fairy bled into this realm, leaking into the sky above and pooling in a swirling maelstrom of clouded magic in the clouds.

"Siobhan," a strained voice said in my ear. Rhys was holding me, propping me up around the shoulders as we both stared in horror at the wrongness of all that magic filling the air. "What is it?"

Energy crackled as the vastness of the liminal space polluted the air around us. It sparked and rumbled with a malevolence that was terrifying and vast. Alive and hungry and wrong in this world, it seeped and crept wider across the sky. At every point it touched this realm, it hissed and sputtered, devouring and consuming every atom. It didn't belong here, but it was more powerful than the substance of this realm. Without something to contain it, it would overcome the natural fabric of the human world, and it would destroy it.

"It's Fairy," Kellan said, rushing to us and kneeling by my side. His eyes flashed with thunderclouds and lightning as the magic affected him. "And it's going to keep flowing here if we don't stop it. We need to close the Gate."

"The Gate is gone," Rhys said, pointing to the gaping maw where the arch had once stood. "How do you propose we do that?"

Around us, the ground trembled, the whole world reacting to this intrusion. The sky rippled and cracked, roiling with the copper and ozone of blood and lightning. The grass taste of Fairy bubbled around me with an acidic aftertaste of earth and a new woodiness. Life and energy, death and threat fought each other as the world struggled for balance, cleansing, this realm trying to expel the magic, the wrongness that erupted through.

Movement attracted my attention as Orion rushed to Lada who still lay bleeding near where I had stabbed her. Her blood soaked the ground and fed the bottom of the rip in the world. So long as her life force, a Queen's magic held the portal open, the contamination would continue. The power of Fairy would pour into this realm until it destabilized everything.

And though I had just realized what using my magic might cost me, I knew I didn't have a choice if I wanted to stop what would happen next. No one else could staunch her blood, but doing so might open me to the Gate's influence.

I accepted Rhys's help and got to my feet. "I have to heal Lada." I grasped Rhys's hand and made them look at me. "But I have to let go of my magic immediately after. I need you to help ground me. Or I'm not sure I'll find my way back again."

They squeezed my hand back. "I understand."

Then I turned to Kellan. "I might need you, too." As we locked eyes, I could feel the stirrings of that stifled desire to have him touch me again, to have his hands threaded in my hair and holding me to this world.

His jaw grew tight as he grit his teeth, but he nodded. "I'm here. Whatever you need."

With that reassurance, I rushed to Lada's side. Orion reacted immediately, his hand thrown up and ice already swirling in a wind of his power. I ignored him and knelt by Lada, who lay sprawled on her side in her friend's lap. Eyes closed and breath ragged, her ivory skin was paler than I'd ever seen it. In stark contrast, her white dress nearly shone red with blood as it oozed from the knife still in her back.

"Sorry," I said, as I fell to my knees in her blood, braced one hand against her arm, grabbed the hilt with my other hand, and yanked it out of her. She screamed, and the blood flowed more freely.

Before I could second guess and remind myself what this might cost me, I reached deep inside and beyond me for the crackling magic of the Gate in the air. I opened myself as wide as I could and felt the waiting storm of Fairy surge into me. The moment it hit the reserve of magic that was wholly mine, my resolve melted like cotton candy in the rain.

Just as I knew it would.

I crumpled beneath the weight of the power. The magic that felt like a contamination in the world around me rushed in like I was the only storm drain on a flooded city street. Immediately, I felt myself crumpling under the weight of it.

Then there was the whisper of her voice, the tang of her gin and rosemary taste. I reached out blindly, for anything, anyone that would tether me back to myself, pull me away from her grasp.

Something solid latched onto me tasting of cucumber and cedar. Rhys. I held tight to their hand and felt them at my back. Their voice was in my ear, and I could feel their fingers as they brushed aside my hair, their lips light against my neck. "Hold tight. I've got you." Their strength bolstered me, and I reached deeper to heal Lada.

Her caramel apple taste was still strong, despite her wound, her power sustained by her own permanent connection to Fairy. Even this grievous wound wouldn't kill her if she was given medical attention. Or magical attention. I concentrated on her wound, on the wrongness I had inflicted when I split her skin and spilled her blood.

Repairing the cut was easy for me. I made a connection with her body and let it tell me what it needed to heal. The answer was simple: a matter of telling the muscle, the veins, the skin to go back to where they belonged. It was its natural state. I only had to nudge it in the right direction, provide it a scaffold, a framework to grasp onto as it healed itself. Once I reminded her flesh of the way it should be, provided it with a ladder to climb to health, her body did what it needed to do. The cells of her stitched together, seeking restoration, its natural state. The blood loss would take time to recover, and she'd be weak for a while yet, but she would suffer no lasting ill effects.

Then I felt it. Something else was off. Something beyond her injury was not as I expected. I followed the feel of that strangeness and found something in her body that wasn't there before. Two somethings.

Lada was pregnant. With twins.

Their heartbeats were faint, and I worried for a moment that I had harmed them when I stabbed their mother. But no. They were young yet strong. If I had to guess, I'd put them at three months gestation. Maybe a little less.

Which means Lada was well aware of their existence. And had been when she killed their father.

I rocked back on my heels. Even without Rhys's presence, this information would have been enough to ground me in reality.

Lada's breathing had steadied, as had her heartbeat and those of her children. Orion was watching me warily, uncertain what I was doing, but unwilling to stop me given I had just saved Lada's life after I had tried to take it.

"Go," I said, pointing to the portal where the Gate had once stood.

"You will be able to pass through, but I'm closing the Gate. Maybe for good."

Orion didn't ask how I knew or attempt to argue with me. He scooped up Lada and dashed for the ripple that shimmered and leaked. The pair of them were gone in a blink, but their passage woke the Gate further. The spread of the Fairy light grew, pooling above us and beginning to spin. A roar filled the air as the edges of the magic warred with the static air of this world.

"Siobhan," Rhys said, clutching at my hand as Kellan hovered nearby.

"I see it." I had stemmed the flow of Lada's blood. That should have been enough to close the Gate, but clearly something else was needed.

There was no arch, no Gate to speak of. The portal was expanding, the magic leaking everywhere. The ground shivered again, and I could feel the instability in my veins. The world around me was struggling to hold equilibrium as another world bled into it. If it came down to it, though, I had no doubt. Fairy would win. The power of that realm would shatter this one.

And then what?

I had to stop it. I had to close the rift. The worlds were not meant to overlap in this way.

Kellan put a hand on my shoulder. "Blood isn't enough. I've tried to touch it, but there's no hold for me. I can't do what you can do. You have to do this. You need to repair the wound."

"What does that even mean?" I growled.

He shot me with his familiar look of disdain, and it was almost comforting. "What you just did with Lada, you need to do with the rip in the world."

Abstractly, it made sense. A hole had been torn in the fabric of the world. Sacrifice pulled the skin of the realm open, and Fairy seeped through, like blood through an open wound. To heal Lada, I had pulled on my connection to her and her magic and told the cut to repair itself.

If Kellan was right and the situation was comparable, it should be easy to reach for the muscle and flesh of this world and tell it to heal around the injury I'd inflicted on it. But nothing about this felt comparable. It felt beyond me, too vast and powerful and dangerous.

And yet…

I tried to recreate what I had done with Lada. The first step was finding her magic, finding her essence. I reached for the rosemary juniper taste, and it seemed to bite back at me. It rushed at me, antagonistic and hungry, but wrong.

That was not where the injury lie.

The woman who rested in the liminal space of the Gate was not the source of this injury. This rip wasn't to her.

Which meant she wasn't the Gate as I had assumed.

I filed that information away for later.

Reaching deeper, I encountered the other taste: the verdant Green that lay beneath the herbal gin. It was like a shot of wheat grass, natural and clean and alive. I had almost forgotten it, as the more stringent taste of the rosemary overcame it. *This* Green. This was Fairy. This was the magic that sustained my people.

And twined with it was something else that I recognized and connected to. Something spicy and alive and almost pungent. It was complex, like soil and tobacco and leather, familiar as the wood grain of the bar under my fingers or the feel of sand in my toes. I wanted to dive into it, to wrap it around me like a wool blanket and breathe in its rich layered taste.

It reminded me of Kellan, and I chased after that feeling of coming home.

I twined together the taste I found, the green and the red, the growing and the alive, the potential and the reality of all that could be. Heedless of the consequences, I dove into it, reaching for all that these two sides of my world could offer.

The vastness of both crashed into each other, bruising and tearing at each other at every point they met. Their union was at odds as they fought each other, clashing together and ripping only at themselves.

Then I felt it. The wound.

It wasn't the Gate. Blowing apart the Gate didn't create the rip; it only removed the bandage.

This went deeper. I'd uncovered a deep hurt and let it bleed through unfettered into Greenwood. I didn't have to close the Gate or rebuild the stones. The arch had only ever been a bandaid.

I had to repair what was injured beneath it.

And from the look of the spreading magic storm above us, I had to do it fast.

I had already found the root of the magic. I had tasted it and knew it. The same magic pulsed through me. I just had to focus on the rip formed between them. The realm knew what it took to heal, the world felt it without my help. I didn't have to do anything but encourage a return to its natural state. Like flesh, I could stitch it back together. I just needed the right scaffolding.

But flesh was easy. I knew how my body felt, how skin held blood in and muscle and bone, how they all bound together and created a body.

The scaffolding was beyond me, beyond my knowledge. What made a solid barrier between the realms anyway?

These realms though were both a part of me. I was half human, half fae. I was a part of these worlds. They were a part of me. And I didn't need to understand them to hold their truths within me. I simply needed to open up my own scaffolding and let it read the substance of what it should be in my blood.

In my hand was the knife I had used to stab Lada. I had opened up her back with a wound I had easily healed with only a fraction of my power. I wondered if I could do the same to myself.

"Hold tight," I said as I stopped thinking. I knew as soon as I unleashed the full potential of my magic, my control would be gone. I would either repair the rip, or I would make it worse.

Rhys grabbed my shoulder, and a moment later, Kellan took hold of my other one. Then I took the knife, plunged it into the spot just below my ribcage, and screamed as the magic of both realms flooded into me.

CHAPTER THIRTY-FIVE

I wasn't entirely sure how what I did worked. One minute I was stabbing myself in the gut for the greater good, the next I was waking up in a world that was still whole and full of the taste of Kellan and Rhys.

Rhys told me watching me stab myself in the gut had been one of the most terrifying moments they had ever experienced. Then not being able to reach me as the magic took over, had been a close second. But Kellan had managed to keep them from panicking as I healed myself and the rift together. They told me that it was all they could do to hold on to me as the power surged around and through them. The swirling maelstrom collapsed over us, retreating into where the Gate had stood even as my blood ceased flowing. The rift stitched together as cleanly as my stomach, and the world went back to the way it was.

But the magic that was in me would not let go so easily. Rhys had worried that I would turn that power on them, but Kellan had acted swiftly. His had pulled my face to his and laid such a kiss on me that Rhys said even they blushed.

The madness ceased, and I had whispered thank you before

collapsing in their arms. I woke up in the Knoll's office hours later, fully healed and with the worst hangover of my life.

Several glasses of water and handfuls of ibuprofen later, I was able to rest safe in the knowledge that Fairy had not torn this realm to shreds. I was still here with all of my faculties more or less in place, and the body count was minimal.

We reopened the Knoll two days later.

"Shiv, can I get a round of whiskey shots?"

Leland stood on the other side of the bar, a shy smile on his face as leaned against the edge. His chestnut hair hung lightly in his eyes, and I had a tender urge to reach out to wipe it away.

Instead, I clenched my hands into fists at my side. "Do you want the whole bottle?" I asked. There were six of the clurichaun at a central table, and if they were doing a full round of shots and expected to do another, it would make more sense for the table just to split the cost of the bottle.

"Nah," he said, looking pointedly at me. I knew they were mourning Baerd and Argus, and there was a ritual element to how things were done with the clurichaun. "Just the shots."

I nodded, understanding.

"One for you, as well," he added, as I grabbed the bottle from the shelf behind the bar.

"Oh," I said, cringing. "Thank you. I'm not drinking at the moment, but I appreciate it."

He accepted the six fingers of whiskey I passed him on a tray, as he considered me. "Good for you," he said finally, and he walked away.

I realized belatedly that I should have offered to bring the drinks to the table myself, but Leland was already halfway across the Knoll.

I poured soda water into a glass and hit it with a dose of sweetened lime juice. Then I threw in a splash of cranberry juice. I shot the drink back and appreciated the tart and sweet in balance with the bubbles. It would be improved with an ounce of gin, but I didn't think I could stomach the taste of alcohol for a while.

No magic. No drinking.

No problem.

I wondered what Argus would think of that.

I looked up to the ceiling, as if I could see through the wooden boards to his rooms. I had already moved a full three suitcases of my clothes and select keepsakes into the apartments that existed above the bar. I hadn't unpacked yet, but I was slowly moving in to take on my responsibilities.

Before I fully moved in, I would have to remove Argus's things. And I wasn't ready for that.

I wasn't ready to accept control of this space.

It was too big, too much responsibility. If the past few weeks had shown me anything, it's that I wasn't ready for it. I wasn't worthy.

But someone had to be the Keeper of the Knoll. The bar had no down hours. If anyone walked in needing sanctuary, if they crossed between the realms, if they arrived at our doorstep, someone would be here to accept and welcome them.

Not that I figured we would be having lots of new visitors with the Gate gone.

At the very least, someone had to hold this family together.

I looked around at the somber crowd gathered. The regulars were all here. The clurichaun had their group in the center of the room, but there was a small group of maenads, a few elementals, and the local dryads.

Mikka and Varon were together by the door. They'd been inseparable since finding Argus. I worried about the resurgence of Mikka's depression, but I knew her brother would be there for her no matter what. They would protect and comfort each other.

Meara was holed up in the kitchen, throwing herself into developing new recipes. She'd barely emerged except to demand new ingredients. She insisted that busy hands helped, and if the Knoll was going to survive the death of its Keeper and the Gate, we'd have to offer enough to keep the solitary fae coming around.

Which also explained the sudden busyness of Milo and Tobin. They'd decided that the future of the bar was a hub for the coming revolution, and they'd announced plans to help work with Kellan to organize the Fair Folk into a proper fighting force. With the Gate shattered, Summer believed that the solitary fae and the Fair Folk were crippled, cut off from their power. After all, the Summer fae could still access their magic through their conduit. So long as the Queen remained connected to Fairy, they didn't need the Gate per se.

But we weren't powerless. I could still feel my connection to Fairy. I knew that when I needed to, I could open the ways myself, with or without a Gate. If it became necessary, I could act as conduit for my own people, empowering them to protect themselves, take a stand, do what they needed to do to overcome whatever was coming next.

If I agreed to accept the cost.

I feared the next time I dropped my shields and opened myself to that magic again. Would I be able to come back? Would I expose myself to the Gate Woman's influence? Would I lose myself entirely?

Or would Rhys or Kellan be there to help me find my way back?

One of them was always at hand. Rhys had nowhere to go now that they'd compromised their duties in breaking me out of Bryony's captivity. They were content to hang around the Knoll and keep an eye on me.

Kellan had been around a fair amount as well. I guess as my de facto consort, he felt a responsibility to be there in case I needed him. The billionaire lurked in a back booth and had whispered conversations with various members of the Fair Folk who came in but otherwise kept to himself. I wondered how long he'd be content to sit around and wait for me to slip up.

He'd have to wait a long while. I wasn't planning to taste magic any time soon, even if the Fair Folk needed it. With all that group had cost me, had cost this community, I wasn't sure any of their goals were worth the sacrifice. I planned to stay sober as long as possible.

With that thought, I poured myself a soda water and pulled out a bottle of Argus's best scotch.

"I would like to propose a toast," I announced to the bar.

"A toast," they echoed. I passed a glass to Rhys at the end of the bar, Mikka and Varon came up to accept the scotch I poured for them, and even Meara poked her head out to take a measure of the drink.

I waited until everyone was situated and began to speak.

"We've suffered a lot of loss. Family, friends, and people we loved and relied on are gone, leaving gaping holes in our lives. The Knoll feels a little emptier, the world feels a little bleaker, and the days all feel a little harder to get through. I know I'm not the only one struggling to remember why I get up each morning. This all feels so hard. It's too much. I can't do this."

I had to take a breath and wipe away the tears that filled my eyes. Argus had been so much better at this. From the back booth, Kellan lifted his glass of bourbon in support.

Somehow that fortified me.

"But the truth of the matter is, we can do this. We can keep moving forward. I'm not going anywhere, and neither is the Greenwood Knoll. I'd love to say that the worst is behind us, but we all know that's not true. Things may have to change a little around here as we figure out a city without a Gate. There are likely going to be consequences for what's happened, and though I don't know what those are yet, I do know we're not going to like all of them. But we can face them together. We may have to fight against some of them—"

Milo and Tobin whooped from the kitchen, and the clurichaun chuckled in agreement.

I smiled. "Some of you apparently like that idea better than others. Either way, I want to assure you, I'm not going anywhere. This is my home. You're my family. And family sticks together."

I lifted my glass to Mikka and Varon, who raised their glasses back toward me.

"We're going to have to rely on each other a lot more than we're used to." I looked to Rhys and then to Kellan who both nodded to me in agreement. "But I have never known a stronger, more resilient group of people than those who also call this place home. So, I would like to propose a toast."

"A toast!" The echo was shouted this time with a renewed sense of life, of home.

"To the Greenwood Knoll. To the people who have given their all to keep her standing, to make her safe, and to make her a home."

"To the Knoll!" Their voices carried up to the rafters. Though tears again filled my eyes, I lifted my glass to the room and knocked back my soda. The bubbles tickled my nose and filled my throat with longing. I wished Argus was here to know his people would continue to stand together.

Whatever came our way, we would face it. And we would survive.

That was worth celebrating.

COCKTAILS FOR WINTER'S STING

Winter's Sting – HOT BUTTERED RUM

For my book's title cocktail, I wanted a good cold-weather drink that is rich and comforting, but also captures the diverse array of spices and flavors that enter the Greenwood Knoll with every story. A hot buttered rum is the ultimate comfort drink. The butter adds a richness that is unique and unusual in cocktails, while the cinnamon, vanilla, and nutmeg evoke holidays, special breakfast spreads, and the feel of cozying up to a hot fire on a cold night.

- 2 oz dark rum
- 4 oz hot water
- 2 tsp brown sugar
- 1 tbsp softened butter
- Vanilla extract
- Cinnamon, nutmeg, allspice

In bottom of heat proof mug or glass muddle sugar, vanilla, spices and butter. Add rum and hot water. Mix well and garnish with a cinnamon stick and fresh grated nutmeg.

~

Maenad's Kiss – SPARKLING HONEY RYE

Fire drake Mikka has a thing for the maenads at the Greenwood Knoll. She might not stay with them for a long time, but she's always up for a good time. When her distinctive smoky fire and their bubbly citrus mingle, it creates a sweet kiss of a cocktail.

- 2 oz whiskey
- 2 tbsp honey
- 2 tbsp lemon
- 8 oz prosecco

Mix whiskey, honey, and lemon into a cocktail shaker with ice. Shake until cold. Strain into two champagne glasses. Top with prosecco.

~

Kiral – INDIAN WINTER

Kiral is the afterthought in his own life. He plays second fiddle or supporting character to royals, the assistant, the consort. He lifts up others, but never gets a chance to shine. So I wanted to give his drink a bit of something special. The star of this cocktail is the simple syrup. Infusing cardamom with honey gives an aromatic, slightly minty and nutty taste you won't find in your typical American cocktail. It's both earthy and elevated, kind of like Kiral's opinion of himself.

- 1 ½ oz vodka
- ½ oz honey cardamom simple syrup
- ½ oz lemon
- Egg white
- Angostura bitters

- Star anise

Make the simple syrup ahead of time. Mix ½ cup water, ½ cup honey or sugar and 4 lightly crushed cardamom pods. Heat mixture until honey or sugar is completely dissolved. Strain and set aside to cool. For cocktail, mix vodka, syrup, lemon and egg white in a cocktail shaker with ice. Shake until egg white is completely emulsified, approximately 60-90 seconds (yes, it's a long time). Strain into a coupe glass. Garnish with star anise.

~

Orion – CRANBERRY SPICED MOSCOW MULE

Orion is Winter fae royalty, born to a Queen and taught that he matters more than most. By using a complicated cranberry-infused syrup in a otherwise basic cocktail, I think this drink evokes the spirit of Orion. It has no chill, no matter how cold the cocktail is served.

- 2 oz vodka
- 1-2 oz Cranberry simple syrup
- ½ oz lime juice
- ¼ oz cranberry juice
- 4 oz Ginger beer

To make the cranberry simple syrup, mix 1 cup honey or sugar, 1 ½ cup water, 2 cups cranberries, 2 sprigs thyme, 1 peeled thumb of ginger, 2-3 crushed cardamom pods. Heat and bring to a low simmer for 15 minutes, stirring until sugar or honey is dissolved and cranberries have softened. Cool before use. To make the cocktail, mix vodka, simple, lime juice and cranberry juice in a cocktail shaker over ice. Mix well, strain into a copper mule mug, and top with ginger beer. Garnish with sprig of thyme

~

Lada – CARAMEL APPLE MARTINI

Lada is someone who comes across as complex, but at her heart is very straightforward. She doesn't pretend to be anything other than who she is. That, in my mind, makes her a martini. She and Semele share an apple flavor profile because they are two sides of a changing world. Apples are primarily a sign of harvest, of the fall and changing seasons. For Lada's cocktail, that mixed with burnt sage and a hint of winter.

- 2 oz apple cider
- 2 oz vodka
- 1 oz butterscotch schnapps
- Garnish: caramel apple sauce, brown sugar, and cinnamon stick

Prep martini glass by rubbing rim on a plate of caramel apple sauce, then dipping into a plate of brown sugar. Swirl to coat. Then in a cocktail shaker, mix apple cider, vodka and schnapps over ice. Shake until mixed, then strain into prepped martini glass. Garnish with a cinnamon stick.

Liliana – HOT TODDY

Liliana is the personification of the old world of the Fairy kingdom. She is the rightful heir of a long line of Queens and her job is to hold that line no matter what. If she has other ideas, other wants, she hides them or kills them altogether, just to preserve the world she knows and loves. That makes her cocktail the ultimate cure-all drink for what ails you. Combining whiskey, honey, and lemon plus any medicinal herbs you want to add, Liliana's hot toddy will make things better.

- ¾ cup hot water
- 1 ½ oz whiskey
- ¼ oz honey
- ¼ oz lemon
- Garnish: lemon round, cinnamon stick

In heat proof glass mix whiskey, honey and lemon. Add hot water and stir until honey dissolves. Garnish with lemon round and cinnamon stick. Can substitute rum or brandy for the whiskey.

ACKNOWLEDGMENTS

I always heard it was harder to write a sequel than the first book in a series. They're right. Thank you to everyone who made this book possible.

I can't give enough thanks to my editor and publisher. John Hartness, I'd call you my fairy godmother, but Sarah Sover has the trademark on that at Falstaff. I'll dub you my redneck knight in dented armor. With your loud voice, you silence the room, and then hand the mic to others so they can be heard. You are a reminder of what the publishing industry could be. Erin Penn, you have been an amazing editor and champion of my work. Thank you for everything.

Thank you to my incredible family for always giving and making space for me to make art. I know sometimes that just means respecting a closed office door, while others it means letting me disappear at bedtime for several days in a row so I can take advantage of my most creative time of day.

To my incredible village: Shannon, Isadora, Sarah, Liz, y'all keep me sane, even when it feels like I'm losing my grip. Thank you for always being there when I need grounding, an extra hand, or an escape. I love you so much.

To my Con families: y'all remind me why we do this crazy thing. Telling stories, connecting with readers, waxing rhapsodic about geek lore, fantasy tropes, and romance. Like Zorro! You inspire me and keep me writing. I would continue writing just to keep attending events with y'all and protecting the spaces that we call home.

To Jordan and Tessa, you spoil me rotten. I don't deserve either of you, but I am forever thankful that you love me as much as I love you both. More than anyone, the two of you have kept me writing. If I think of giving up, I just think of Jordan's glare, or Tessa's pout, and then I get back to it. Thank you for loving me and my art that much.

To the Megatherium Club: you don't just provide the best cocktail inspirations; you give me reasons to keep toasting the future. I know I don't get to see you nearly as much as I would like. I promise, my life won't always be quite so crazy. (My kids will eventually grow up.) A toast! To twenty-year friendships worth celebrating.

And finally, to my readers, thank you for joining me through this story. It started as a fun lark to get me through the early days of the Covid pandemic. While stuck inside with two young kids and remote work, I was playing with cocktails and dreaming of fun times out with friends. The idea of a place where people could be themselves, enjoy some karaoke, and maybe engage in some radical mutual aid. That I could turn this lark into a full urban fantasy series never occurred to me. I hope you enjoyed Siobhan's latest evolution as she comes into her power.

ABOUT THE AUTHOR

Sara T. Bond is a science fiction and fantasy author. She uses spaceships, fairies, and ghosts to hide the fact that she has big thoughts and wants to share them with the world. With a background in academics, political research, campaign management, and even a short, lucrative career in high-end fashion retail, those opinions are wide and far-reaching. You're as likely to find her at karaoke night with a good cocktail as you are to find her fighting the good fight at her local political rally or her kids' PTA.

Born and raised in Atlanta, Sara now resides in Seattle with her husband and two feral but fantastic children. Find her at www.sarat-bond.com and on various social media platforms.

FRIENDS OF FALSTAFF

Thank You to All our Falstaff Books Patrons, who get extra digital content each month! To be featured here and see what other great rewards we offer, go to www.patreon.com/falstaffbooks.

PATRONS

Dino Hicks
John Hooks
John Kilgallon
Larissa Lichty
Travis & Casey Schilling
Staci-Leigh Santore
Sheryl R. Hayes
Scott Norris
Samuel Montgomery-Blinn
Junkle

Thank You for Supporting Independent Publishing!

We believe that you should be able
to read your books, your way.
That's why this Falstaff Books
print edition includes a digital copy
at no additional cost!

Just scan the QR code with your device,
follow the directions on Prolific Works,
and enjoy!
You can also join our newsletter when prompted,
and never miss an awesome Falstaff Release!